"It would be a serious mistake to dismiss *Hide Me Among the Graves* as something less than art. It's literary fiction in two senses of the word. First, it's a fascinating fictionalized look at some of England's most interesting authors—not just Polidori and the Rossettis, but also the long-underappreciated Trelawny. Second, it's written impeccably. Powers is a master of suspenseful plotting, and his descriptions of the gaslighted streets and underground tunnels of 19th-century London are awesomely creepy.... Above all, though, *Hide Me Among the Graves* is just pure fun. Powers knows how to temper terror with humor, and he knows something that a lot of adventure writers never learn: Without well-rounded, fully realized characters, it doesn't matter how good your concept is. It's a smart, exciting and perfectly constructed novel, and it's hard as hell to put down. Let the kids have their overwrought, sullen romances— *Hide Me Among the Graves* is a vampire novel for readers who still believe in the power, and the joy, of great literature."　　　—NPR

"A fine example of the work of a much-beloved author, and a spooky ride through Victorian London to boot.... Powers's work engages with something prerational that is buried deep, deep in our brains, and that won't be bullied into submission by mere reason."
　　　—boingboing.net on *Hide Me Among the Graves*

"[*Three Days to Never*] contains so many genuine pleasures...plenty of action, humor and unexpectedly touching human drama.... [A] welcoming entry point to [Powers's] singular fictional universe."
　　　—*San Francisco Chronicle*

MEDUSA'S WEB

MEDUSA'S WEB

Tim Powers

WILLIAM MORROW
An Imprint of HarperCollins*Publishers*

P.S.™ is a trademark of HarperCollins Publishers.

MEDUSA'S WEB. Copyright © 2015 by Tim Powers. Excerpt from *Three Days to Never* © 2006 by Tim Powers. All rights reserved. Printed in the United States of America. No part of this book may be used or reproduced in any manner whatsoever without written permission except in the case of brief quotations embodied in critical articles and reviews. For information address HarperCollins Publishers, 195 Broadway, New York, NY 10007.

HarperCollins books may be purchased for educational, business, or sales promotional use. For information please e-mail the Special Markets Department at SPsales@harpercollins .com.

A hardcover edition of this book was published in 2015 by William Morrow, an imprint of HarperCollins Publishers.

FIRST WILLIAM MORROW PAPERBACK EDITION PUBLISHED 2016.

Designed by Lisa Stokes

Library of Congress Cataloging-in-Publication Data has been applied for.

ISBN 978-0-06-226246-2

16 17 18 19 20   OV/RRD   10 9 8 7 6 5 4 3 2 1

To Steve and Tammie Malk

With thanks to:
Manny Aguirre, Chris Arena, Fr. Hugh Barbour, Amelia Beamer,
John Berlyne, Jim Blaylock, Jennifer Brehl, Fr. John Chrysostom,
Russell Galen, Steve Hickman, Ron and Val Lindahn, Fr. Jerome
Molokie, Kelly O'Connor, Faust Pierfederici, Joni Labaqui,
Laurie McGee, Jim Pepper, Chris Powers, Serena Powers, Ellen
Sandoval, William Schafer, Joe Stefko, Rodger Turner, Michael
and Laura Yanovich

"When you are in the fingers of this unwisely summoned beast, you find yourself in a hundred conflicting motions all in the same moment. You grieve, you dance, you vomit, you shake, you weep, you faint, and suffer enormously, and you die . . . the sovereign and sole remedy is Music."

—*Francesco Cancellieri, Letters of Francesco Cancellieri to the ch. Signore Dottore Koreff, Professor of Medicine of the University of Berlin, about Tarantism, the airs of Rome, and of its countryside, and the Papal palaces inside, and outside, Rome, 1817*

THE FRAXINUS-BEO TRANSLATION

"The past isn't dead. It isn't even past."
—*William Faulkner*

PART I

The Monkeys Can't Let Go of It

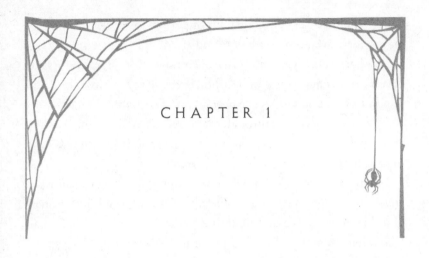

CHAPTER 1

"THAT'S A SINGLE HEADLIGHT, turning into the parking lot."

The woman stood at one of the tall French windows, peering through the rain-streaked glass down the slope outside. The day had not ever been very bright, and the light in the overcast sky was now fading. "And I can hear the engine—it's a motorcycle, isn't it? Probably the same terrible old Honda he had when he moved out."

Her cousin sighed and rolled his wheelchair across the worn carpet to pause beside her. "It's a motorcycle," he agreed. "Now it's behind the trees."

"And the engine has stopped. It's him."

Her cousin nodded, still peering at the corner of the parking lot visible below. "And that car now is probably his sister."

"Oh, Claimayne, I *don't* like them coming back here to Caveat." She reached out and unlatched the window and pushed it open; a gust of cold air twitched at her short brown hair and rolled the chilly scent of wet clay through the musty air of the dining room.

Claimayne Madden hiked his wheelchair back. "Relax, Ariel, I heard he's a drunk these days. Probably all pouchy and fat."

Ariel Madden turned and scowled at her cousin. "*Shut up.*"

Claimayne grinned and held up his hands.

Ariel pulled her cell phone out of her blouse pocket. "And give me a spider. I want to do a before and after."

"What?" His eyes were fully open now. "No—for God's sake, have a drink; chug a glass of bourbon if you have to. Close the damn window and sit down. You've been four years clean!"

Peering again down through the wet terraces of waving bamboo and pampas grass, Ariel snapped her fingers and stretched one hand toward him.

Claimayne went on, "A before and after? You won't be able to *do* anything; you used up your *volition,* years ago! You'll just sit here blinking at them like an idiot. And your after will just be an hallucination, not any real view of the future—they nearly always are."

"I haven't done one in four years," she said impatiently. "I'm probably a virgin again."

"Listen to yourself. If you try to force your later self to *do* anything, you'll probably get an embolism."

Her hand stayed extended toward him.

Claimayne shrugged and let his hands fall into his lap, and he stared at the carpet for several seconds. Then he dug into the pocket of his silk dressing gown and laid a folded slip of paper in her palm.

Ariel touched the screen of her phone a couple of times, then, without looking, unfolded the piece of paper and held the phone a foot above it and touched the corner of the screen. The phone clicked faintly, and she gave the paper back to Claimayne.

"I'm e-mailing it to myself," she said, tapping at the on-screen keyboard now. "It better not be just one of your poems."

"You're a big girl," he said, pocketing the paper. "You want to take it up again, that's your choice."

"Your disapproval is . . . hypocritical."

Claimayne sighed. "I suppose, I suppose. Do what thou wilt, child."

Her voice was mocking: "Thank you, *Tetrarch.*"

She hurried out of the dining room, the knock of her boots echoing in the high arches of the ceiling as she stepped into the tiled hall.

Claimayne rolled forward again and leaned out of the wheelchair to get hold of the wet window latch, but his fingers slid ineffectually off the cold metal, and he gave up and sat back, panting.

When Ariel strode back into the dining room she was folding up a sheet of paper obviously fresh from the printer in the library at the other end of the house. "I *may* not look at it at *all*," she said defensively as she tucked it into her blouse pocket beside her phone, "much less *twice*. Can you see them yet?"

"I haven't looked. Do you want to go down and tell them that we're lodging them in the old apartments by the parking lot? Even with the cones across the garage road, they may imagine they're staying up here in the main house."

"If they drag their luggage up here, they can just drag it down again. I'm not going out in that rain."

SCOTT MADDEN LEANED HIS motorcycle on the kickstand and unhooked the bungee cords that had held a bulky black-plastic bag and a folded tarpaulin against the sissy bar. Setting the bag on the puddled pavement, he unfolded the tarpaulin and draped it over the motorcycle, careful not to let it touch the hot exhaust pipes, and he picked up the bag and was pulling off his helmet as he trudged across the gleaming asphalt to his sister's twenty-year-old Datsun. He paused beside it for several seconds, as the rain thumped on his head, then leaned down and opened the door.

"They'll give us rooms, Madeline," he said.

"I know." She swung her legs out and stood up. She was wearing jeans and an old Members Only jacket over a sweater, and she bent back into the car to get a baseball cap and pull it down over her curly dark hair. She seemed thinner than the last time Scott had seen her. "I bet they hate us, though," she added, straightening up. "They blocked the road up to the house."

"Maybe the garage road's washed out. Claimayne doesn't hate

anybody, and Ariel's hated me for years. God knows why." He smiled sourly. "And they shouldn't worry; the will won't stand up anyway—she signed it an hour before she killed herself. Grotesquely. Hardly of sound mind."

"At least it's free food for a week. Assuming they feed us. If not, there's apples and avocados and pears growing all over the property." Madeline nodded solemnly. "Can you carry some of my stuff too? I brought work along."

Madeline Madden had been a professional astrologer since moving out of Caveat seven years ago, having learned the craft from an old woman who had been a tenant there back in the days when their aunt still rented out apartments. Scott, in turn, had become a graphic artist under the informal tutelage of a painter who had rented another of the apartments.

"Sure. I may want to stop on the stairs and rest once or twice."

As Madeline walked around to open the trunk, Scott stared over the roof of the car at the now vacant apartment building beyond a row of shaggy eucalyptus trees on the east end of the Caveat estate. The long gray two-story box was the newest structure on the property, having been built in the 1970s. The buildings up the hill had accumulated one by one since the 1920s, most of them incorporating bits salvaged from various torn-down hotels and movie sets. Their aunt Amity, affluent from the sales of her series of popular novels, had added to the architectural clutter after she bought the estate in 1965.

He looked up the hill, and he could just see the rooftop gables of the sprawling main house, which was three stories tall in most places. As children, he and his sister had sometimes stood outside and picked out a window and then gone inside to try to find the room behind it, often without success.

Our childhood home, Scott thought with a shiver as he took a canvas bag from Madeline.

The long stairway up to the main house was a curving track

through a jungle of trees and vines, and the old granite steps were slippery with drifts of soggy dead leaves. Above the panting and scuffing of their progress, the only sounds were raindrops tapping on shiny leaves and the soft clatter of a stream somewhere nearby tumbling over stones—Hollywood Boulevard was only four long blocks south, and the 101 Freeway even closer, but no whisper of traffic or horns found its way over the intervening trees and rooftops to this slope.

Stopping to rest in the rainy breeze wasn't tempting, and the two of them trudged up one uneven step after another without pause, and within a few minutes they stood panting on the rain-flattened grass in front of the main house. The hooded porch light was on, islanding the porch and the narrow yard in an amber glow.

It was the only sign that the place was inhabited. One of the dining room's row of French windows was open, though Scott couldn't make out anyone in the dimness within, and the deep-set windows on the second and third floors and in the three rooftop gables all just mirrored the darkening gray sky, with no lights behind them. There might have been smoke trailing from one or both of the square chimneys at the east and west ends of the house, but not enough to be visible. Angular lumps in the grass near the house proved on closer inspection to be fallen roof tiles, the baked red clay mostly covered with green moss.

Scott stepped up onto the marble-railed porch and set his bundle and Madeline's bag on a cement bench. She came puffing up beside him and set a suitcase and a valise beside the bag.

Her brother was facing south, away from the light over the front door, and Madeline turned that way too. The 101 Freeway was a string of red and white lights across the middle distance, and the stacked-disk tower of the Capitol Records building beyond it was a spottily lit silhouette dimly visible through the veils of rain.

Just as Scott took a deep breath and turned around to knock, the lock clunked and the door was pulled open; for a moment there was nothing to see but the dark entry hall, and then Claimayne's slippered feet, and a moment later the entirety of him in his wheelchair jerked into view from behind the door.

Scott barely recognized him; Claimayne seemed at once older and younger than he remembered. The man's face was smooth and unlined, but it had the tight, glossy look of excessive cosmetic surgery, and he was gleamingly bald. Under a dressing gown, he wore a green velour shirt with what appeared to be a two-inch gold spring on a fine chain around his neck.

"Cousins!" said Claimayne jovially. "I'm afraid you've been put to some unnecessary exertion—"

A tall woman in a long black skirt and short denim jacket stepped up from behind him, holding a folded sheet of white paper—and though she was slimmer now and her dark hair was a good deal shorter than it had been when he had last seen her thirteen years ago, Scott recognized Ariel. And he realized that he was reflexively smiling, for Ariel had been a bright and welcome companion in the days before he had moved out of Caveat in 2002.

She's three years younger than me, Scott thought, two years older than Madeline—she's thirty-three now.

To his surprise, she was smiling too, with evident wry humor. Her eyes were the pale brown of dry sherry wine.

"Claimayne means you're *going* to be put to some exertions," she said, and her voice was the same husky contralto that he remembered vividly. She tucked the paper carefully into her blouse pocket. "You're to stay in your old suite upstairs here at the main house, but nobody's dusted in there yet and there's only bare mattresses on the beds."

Claimayne's eyebrows were halfway up his pale forehead; clearly this was a surprise to him. I'll bet a couple of the apartments down the hill have got freshly made beds, Scott thought. And if that's so, we'd really be better off staying in them.

Beside him, Madeline shifted her sneakers in the splashing puddles; Scott guessed that she too would be happier staying down the hill.

But for more than a decade he had had no contact with his cousin Ariel—for the first few years after he had moved out of Caveat he had sent cards and letters only to have them returned unopened, and he had called only to have her hang up the telephone at the sound of his voice—and he realized that he couldn't refuse this not-entirely-convenient offer.

"*Just,*" drawled Claimayne, "for the week my mother specified in her *will,* of course."

"Of course," Scott said to him; then, looking back up at Ariel, he added, "And thank you. We'll be happy to fix up the rooms ourselves."

Ariel stepped behind Claimayne's wheelchair and pulled it out of the way. "For God's sake, come in out of the rain."

Before turning to the luggage on the bench, Scott glanced at the word engraved in the stone lintel over the door—the word *CAVEAT* survived on the left side, but whatever had followed it on the right had long ago fallen away.

As in *caveat emptor,* he thought. Let the buyer beware. But the noun here, whatever it had been, was long gone.

"Will you come *in,* Scott?" said Ariel.

"Right, right."

When the newcomers stood dripping on the tiles of the entry hall with their bags in a pile beside them, Ariel gripped one of the handles at the back of Claimayne's wheelchair and then leaned against the wall. "Sheets and pillows where they always were," she said quickly. "I'm afraid I won't have time to help. Dinner's at six, and in the meantime there's cookies in the kitchen—if you don't knock the plate on the floor." She added the last with a faint smile, making Scott wonder if he had once done that. "Dinner was ench— ench—" She stopped speaking and looked down at the floor.

"Enchiladas is my guess," said Claimayne. "I think Ariel will be wanting a lie-down about now." He waved one hand toward the stairs. "You two remember the way, I'm sure. There's a spare electric heater in the laundry room—I think you'll want to have it running in the doorway between your rooms. This place gets cold at night." To Ariel he added, "Hold on to the handles and shuffle along, my dear. I'll steer you to a chair."

IN THE DINING ROOM Ariel let go of the wheelchair and sagged into a chair by the window.

For nearly a minute she just stared blindly ahead, gripping the arms of the chair. At last she lifted her hands and stared at them as she alternately stretched her fingers and clenched them into fists.

"They're your hands," said Claimayne softly, "whatever shapes they may assume."

"I remember."

"Take your time. It's been four years."

Finally she took a deep breath, let it out, and was able to frown directly at Claimayne. "I saw them in the flash-ahead; they were still here. Will still be here, when I look at your damned spider again and do the after."

"If it wasn't just your subconscious serving up an hallucination," said Claimayne. "It nearly always is that, you know. It's not a reliable method of precognition."

"I know, I know. But this looked real. They told me it was Friday, three days from now, where they were; we were upstairs here, at night, the lights were on. They better not have been lying, it better not have been any further in the future than that. I told them they're ghouls and grave-worms, and then I was back here and now, hanging on to your wheelchair." She rubbed her eyes. "How long was I gone?"

"Maybe half a minute," said Claimayne.

She scowled at him. "I looked at the spider just before you opened the door, so I only saw them in the flash-ahead, but he looks fine then, not pouchy and fat. Is that right?"

Claimayne rocked his head judiciously. " 'Fine' might be over-stating it, but . . . yes, he looked presentable enough."

"So it probably *wasn't* a hallucination. His litter mate is a scrawny little thing, though, isn't she? Always was." She swiveled her head toward the window with some effort. "Did they go back down the hill?"

"No, my dear, you told them they could stay up here, in their old family suite. They're upstairs now."

"I did not. Did I? Why would I say that? Was I smiling?"

"Yes. So was he." Claimayne raised one eyebrow. "I see a *rap-prochement*."

"I don't. And there was never anything to rapproche! He would have married that pie-wagon Louise if she . . . hadn't had at least the minimal sense to cancel the engagement."

"It's unlikely to have been a real view of this upcoming Friday. Maybe your subconscious this evening decided, purely from prag-matism, to try to marry one of the imminent owners of Caveat." He gave her a heavy-lidded look and smiled. "You're not blood related, you recall."

"Then my subconscious is a masochist. I'd marry . . . *you,* first, and I don't like you at all. Owners! That will is a joke."

"I do think a judge will agree with you about the will. Oh, and you told them to join us in here for dinner. Apparently Rita is going to make enchiladas. Will you feel up to it?"

Ariel sat up straight with some evident effort and rolled her shoulders and flexed her fingers. "Just three days ahead, and into my own body," she muttered, "and it feels like I dug ten ditches."

Her cousin spread his hands. "You've evidently forgotten what it's like."

Ariel stood up unsteadily and moved her feet around till she was facing the hallway door. "Yes, I'll be here for dinner. I want to see him get pig drunk." She began walking carefully out of the room.

"That might help," called Claimayne.

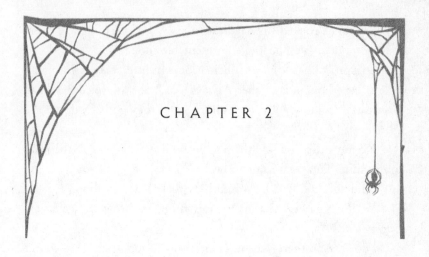

CHAPTER 2

"ARE YOU COMING?" ASKED Madeline. Scott had set down his bundle and one of her canvas bags halfway along the dim hallway that led to the three connecting bedrooms their family had once occupied.

One wall of the corridor was paneled with a row of mismatched old doors; they had been salvaged from a number of long-demolished hotels and apartment buildings, and though there was only plaster behind them, he knocked at the one that was supposed to have come from the Garden of Allah bungalows on Sunset Boulevard, torn down in 1959.

In the shadows he saw Madeline's reluctant smile. "Aunt Amity always knocked on that one whenever she went by," she said. "I remember."

He picked up the bags and walked up to where she stood. "And she always said, 'When is a door not a door? When it's a wainscot.' That's paneling. Which all these doors are, now that they've just got a wall behind them."

"It was from that woman's home, wasn't it? That silent-movie actress."

"Nazimova," Scott agreed. "After she went broke and made her estate into bungalows so she could live in one of 'em."

He dropped the bags again to open the door of their parents' old room. They shuffled in slowly.

Madeline clicked the wall switch up, and the bare overhead bulb cast a harsh yellow glow over the bare floor and the cobwebbed shelves.

The ceiling above the bed was mottled brown, and a foot-wide section of plaster had at some time fallen onto the mattress, which appeared to have been soaked by at least one winter's leaked rains. Two short wires stuck out of the wall above the baseboard where the telephone had been connected.

Scott wrestled open the north window to air out the mildew smell, though the breeze was cold.

"God," whispered Madeline with a visible shiver, "they're *really* gone now, aren't they?"

He knew what his sister meant; in the days when their parents' room had still been regularly dusted and swept, it had been possible to imagine that their mother and father might one day return, with reassurances and unimaginable explanations. But Arthur and Irina Madden had disappeared in 1991, when Scott had been twelve and Madeline had been seven, and redundant evidence at this late date shouldn't have been needed to confirm that they were gone for good.

"When I had money," he said quietly, "I hired a private investigator to look for them. Social Security numbers, dates of birth—nothing."

Madeline sniffed and nodded. "That's good, anyway, that you did that."

"Let's look at our rooms," he said, stepping past her and pulling open the door that led to Madeline's old room. He leaned in to switch on the overhead light. "Look, yours isn't bad at all!"

Scott took Madeline by the elbow and led her across the bare hardwood floor into her old room, where a poster of the Woody character from the movie *Toy Story* was somehow still tacked up on the wall, and then he walked on into his old room and turned on the light there.

Fortunately the roof had not leaked over their rooms, and the ceilings were hammocked with cobwebs but unstained. As Claimayne had said, though, the rooms were chilly.

"I'll fetch that heater," Scott said.

Madeline crossed her arms and leaned into the connecting doorway. "She doesn't seem to hate you anymore. These rooms could use some air too." She walked across to his window, twisted the latch, and tugged, but it didn't move.

"I'll get it in a sec," he said. "You're right, she seemed downright friendly. I'm glad." He brushed some dust off an empty shelf. "Claimayne looks pretty weird these days, doesn't he? I wonder how long he's been in a wheelchair."

"Since a couple of years before I moved out in '08."

"What's wrong with him?"

"I'm—not sure."

"Oh." After a pause, Scott went on, "What's that gold thing he wears around his neck?"

"It's supposed to be the DNA coil. Double helix. He likes to look at it."

"Well, he's a poet, right? It's probably a metaphor for something."

Scott had dumped the contents of the plastic bag he used for luggage onto his bare dusty mattress, and he flipped through the pile of damp shirts and socks till he found a pack of Camels. Blobs of water were visible under the cellophane, shifting as he handled the pack. "My trashbag leaked," he observed glumly. He began pulling out the damp cigarettes and laying them in a line on a dusty shelf.

When he turned back to the bed, he noticed the corner of an envelope under a crumpled shirt, and he pulled it free and held it up.

"Have you opened yours yet?" he asked.

"The lawyer said her instructions were to wait till we were here. 'In residence.'"

"Well, we're here. Maybe there's a five in it." Their aunt Amity had always put a five-dollar bill inside their birthday cards.

"I hope so," said Madeline. "It's probably all we'll get."

"She meant well, with that last will."

The envelope had stayed dry, and Scott tore it open. All it contained was a folded slip of paper about six inches square, and he unfolded it and looked at it—

—And he tried to fling it away, but he couldn't move. Inked on the paper was a jaggedly eight-limbed abstract figure, and he could feel a strong alien reciprocity between it and its reversed image on his retinas; the figure seemed to rotate, or to be about to, and the corners of the limbs were suddenly bristly with finer lines, and now it appeared to consist of a dozen fissipating legs, curling and spinning.

He was breathless and his heart was suddenly pounding, and for a long, long moment he was not even conscious of his own identity.

Eventually he was aware of shifting shapes with vertical sides and no comprehensible scale, and he knew that their apparently infinite height was an optical illusion.

The shapes moved aside and he fell through them, and he found himself sitting up in a bed with sunlit curtains flickering to one side. The colors were muted and the things in front of him were hard to focus on. He saw a banner, with letters on it, and he tried to make unfamiliar eyes read the words. At last he pieced it out—*WELCOME HOME SCOTT*. He swung his field of vision to the side and recognized a four-cornered shape as a blue bedside table. Among a cluster of small orange cylinders was an oval object with a handle on it—probably a mirror, and he pushed a spotted old hand toward it, clutched it, and brought it to a point in front of him. It was indeed a mirror, and he was able to recognize the face it showed him.

It was his aunt Amity's face, expressing his own alarm in wide eyes and bared dentures.

The shapes lost their distinction, and again he was aware of the endlessly-vertical-seeming shapes—but they parted once more, and he seemed this time to be *pulled* between them, and then he was staring at a brown rectangle with a stylized Medusa head imprinted in gold on it. The hand he moved toward *it* was slim and smooth, with long, tapering fingers and long nails—evidently a woman's hand—and around its wrist was a silver bracelet made of links in a chain. The hand was clutching what he could peripherally see was a slip of paper with another eight-limbed pattern on it, so he quickly focused instead on the brown rectangle, which he now saw to be a folder of coarse-textured deckle-edged paper, with a ribbon and a red wax seal holding it closed.

He remembered having seen that folder before, long ago.

He voluntarily reached out and touched it—and the air quivered around it, and a profound rolling vibration made a blur of his consciousness—

—And then he was sprawled awkwardly facedown across the springy surface of a dusty mattress, panting against crumpled damp flannel.

Scott rolled over and sat up, gasping at sharp new aches in his shoulders and jaw, and he clawed at the mattress and his tumbled shirts and socks to fix himself into the real world. He could feel that the square of paper was still in his hand, damp with sweat now, and he tore it to pieces without looking anywhere near it.

He was aware that he could see, but the shapes of what he knew must be wall and shelf and window all seemed to be just patches of varied color at no contrasting distances.

His heart was thudding rapidly in his chest, and he was panting through clenched teeth. "Don't," he managed to say, "look in your envelope." I'm back, he told himself; I'm here, I'm myself in my own body, and I won't go there again.

"I won't," Madeline squeaked. More levelly, she went on, "You told me to, a second ago, but I won't. Scott, you're scaring me. Are you all right?"

He peered up at the tall, narrow angularity that he knew was his sister and forced himself to comprehend that her shape and the number of her eyes didn't actually change when she turned her head from side to side, profile to full face to profile.

"Sorry," he said. "I—think I'm okay now, or I will be." He slid his shoes back and forth on the floor, glad to feel the texture of the wood through the soles. He looked in her direction and forced his voice to be steady as he asked, "Do I look all right? My face? Am I slurring my words?"

"You look fine," she said anxiously. "What, do you think you had a stroke? You're talking fine."

"Not a stroke." *I hope to God,* he thought. He waved his hand, with shreds of the paper still clinging to it. "It was the same thing that happened that time when we were kids."

Her head shifted, evidently nodding. "I saw it was a spider," she whispered, "on the paper, just glimpsed it."

"A . . . spider? I didn't see any spider. No, it was the symbol, like that other time. It must have triggered a flashback of that old shock . . ."

"That kind of symbol is called a spider. I guess Aunt Amity left one for each of us."

Scott shifted on the mattress to stand up but sank back, wincing. His face was cold with sweat. "I—damn," he said, "I feel like I need a wheelchair myself. I told you to look at yours? While I was out?"

"Yes. Your voice was all wobbly. Are you normal again?"

He shook his head. "Getting there. Why the hell would Aunt Amity give us those?"

"She was crazy, at the end. She killed herself."

Scott's gaze flickered around the bare room, and he was at least able to note the darkness in the horizontally divided window rectangle. "How long was I out? Miss dinner?"

"No, not even a full minute." Madeline leaned against the connecting doorway. "What happened?"

He sighed deeply. "I—I had a hallucination. A couple of them. Aunt Amity herself, with a 'Welcome Home Scott' banner, was one of them." He wiped his hand on the mattress and then rubbed his face hard. "*Don't* open your envelope. You might not have the same reaction, but we both had the same shock back in '92." He leaned back and stared at the corner where the ceiling met the walls, and he was very relieved to see the relative depths of the junction in perspective. "You remember what it was like?"

And now he could clearly see that Madeline was only nodding her head, not changing the shape of it. "That was twenty-three years ago," she whispered. "You didn't—see Usabo again?"

"Usabo." Scott managed a weak laugh. "That's right, we called it that. Yes, I think I did, actually, though he . . . I didn't *see* him this time. In the hallucination he was inside that brown cardboard folder, like before, but this time it stayed sealed, it didn't get opened."

Madeline was hugging herself, gripping her elbows, and she cast a quick glance over her shoulder toward their parents' room. "If the folder didn't get opened, how did you know it was him?"

"Oh, Maddy, you remember how it felt—like magnetism, shaking air—" He was shivering.

She nodded. "The roaring that's just outside your hearing. Him *aware of* you."

"That sensation, anyway." Scott exhaled as if ridding himself of the visions, then inhaled deeply. "Our subconsciouses have monsters in them. How old were we?"

"It was the summer after mom and dad went away. 1992. I was eight, in second grade; you were thirteen, in seventh."

Scott nodded. "That's right."

SEARCHING THEIR PARENTS' ABANDONED room in the lonely summer of 1992, they had found a section of upright wooden molding on the closet doorway that had swung aside when pressed on the door-side edge, revealing an opening in the wall. Scott found it ironic now that when he had reached into the gap, little Madeline had warned him about spiders. What he had found propped on a two-by-four a foot below the opening was a manila envelope.

It had proved to contain a dozen small white envelopes; each bore an obscure handwritten label, eleven in black ink and one in red. The carefully printed label on that one was *Oneida Inc,* and the envelope wasn't sealed. In it was a piece of folded paper much like the one he had looked at here, moments ago.

And young Madeline and Scott together had unfolded it and looked at the eight-limbed symbol inked on it. And together they had fallen through the moment of breathless loss of identity into the perception of the featureless vertical things that Madeline later called the Skyscraper People, because the things were infinitely tall but seemed alive . . . and then—as they had always recalled it afterward, in any case—they had found themselves sharing the experience of sitting in a leather-covered chair in a rocking room with a porthole in one paneled wall. The body they had seemed to occupy moved and spoke, but—unlike Scott's recent ability to move "his" hand in a hallucination—the two children were passive viewers of the moment. The pair of tanned hands in front of them was holding the stiff brown paper folder with the Medusa head printed on it in gold, and the hands broke the seal and shucked off the ribbon—while, somewhere off to the side, a voice was raised in sudden protest or warning—and flipped the folder open.

And, experiencing it at one remove through the view of the man in the chair, Scott and Madeline had looked at what Madeline later referred to, in fearful whispers, as Usabo.

It had been another of the eight-limbed symbols. This one was more minimal and uniform, at first; then its eight arms had quickly bloomed with a spinning infinity of filaments and spilled the young siblings again through the world of vertical surfaces into, not one vision, but thousands of them.

Later, Scott would try to diminish the experience by comparing it to riffling through a million snapshots at once—with brief but animate glimpses of cars, faces, bodies clothed and naked, cityscapes viewed far too briefly for any hope of recognition, guns firing—or comparing it to spinning inside an enormous sphere made of active television screens; but he could never manage to forget the vast, unseen, inaudibly roaring creature around or within whom all these visions whirled like fragments of houses in a tornado.

When the visions subsided, they had found themselves still in their parents' room; Scott was gripping the telephone receiver and pressing it to his ear.

In a few minutes they had been able to walk and see clearly, and they tore the paper into dozens of tiny pieces; then, fearful at having destroyed something that grown-ups had evidently considered important, Scott had cut out a similar-sized piece of typing paper and hastily drawn a random eight-limbed figure on it, then folded it and put it into the *Oneida Inc* envelope and tucked that back into the big manila envelope with the others. When they pushed the redial button on the phone, they found that the number Scott had apparently tapped out while in the vision had only four digits.

Their aunt Amity had noticed their lack of appetite and their clumsiness and evident exhaustion, and they had been too enervated to lie about what they'd done—Scott gave their aunt the big envelope and admitted that he and his little sister had looked at the "squiggle" in one of the envelopes inside it. And Aunt Amity hadn't been angry—instead she had shuffled through the dozen little envelopes, then wordlessly clasped the package to her chest before hurrying out of the room, and when she returned without it, she had taken Scott and Madeline out to the Snow White Café for as much ice cream as they wanted to eat.

SCOTT STOOD UP NOW from the mattress and his scattered clothes, and though he held his hands out to the sides, his balance seemed mostly restored; but he found that he'd taken an involuntary step toward the hallway door.

"It was that way," he said, pointing at the wall to the right of the door. "West of here, and a bit south. The folder. A woman was holding it." Slowly he lowered his hand, though he was staring at the wall as if trying to see through it and out over the clustered lights of Los Angeles. "I almost feel like I could find the place. It feels like I'm partly still there."

Madeline nodded. "That wears off. It's supposed to be sort of a hangover the spider visions give you."

Scott turned to face her. "The spider visions?" He shivered. "What, does this happen a *lot*? To other people?" He recalled something she had told him earlier. "You said symbols like that are called spiders. Who calls them that?"

"Claimayne and Ariel. You moved out of Caveat thirteen years ago, before they started doing them."

"Doing them? *Looking* at them, you mean?"

She nodded.

"Good God. But it can't be like this," he asked, waving a still-shaky hand at himself and the mattress, "for them?"

"I think it is. I never saw them do any, but a lot of times they seemed like they'd been beat up. And Claimayne was in that wheelchair before I moved out."

"But—" Scott's chest felt hollow and cold. If the spider symbols had the same effects on his cousins as this one had just had on him, then his experience couldn't be dismissed as the unique triggering of an old personal trauma.

How can eight lines on a piece of paper do that? he thought. Some kind of static, impersonal hypnosis? Maybe it's something like those stereogram pictures, clusters of dots that some people can see images in; suppose there are some that just invite your subconscious to provide the images.

"They look at these, these *spider* things, deliberately?" He shook his head. "*Ariel* does it?"

Madeline nodded unhappily. "Claimayne says it hurts but it keeps you young, and you saw he does look sort of younger, or something. And I think he and Ariel were using them for fortune-telling—when I was in high school, they were making money for a while, like with the stock market. Then not."

"Do a lot of people do this? I've never heard of it."

"People who do it don't talk about it, I think," Madeline said. "Apparently there's pretty bad predators."

"So how did Claimayne and Ariel learn about them? They're both recluses!"

Madeline made a face. "He learned about them from spying on his mother."

"Aunt Amity did that—" he began incredulously, then reminded himself that his aunt had left one of the things for him, and presumably one for Madeline too; and he remembered how happy she had been when he and Madeline had given her the manila envelope they'd found in the wall. "Did *you* ever do it?"

"After Usabo? No."

"You're not missing anything." Except for that timeless moment of nonself, he thought. He went on quickly, "Just a bunch of goofy hallucinations, and sore muscles afterward. If they made money consulting the things, it was just luck, like—" He stopped, for he had been about to say, *like doing what your horoscope advises.* Instead he finished with, "And Claimayne had some plastic surgery."

"You don't think the visions are real?" Madeline asked. "Views of real events?"

Scott squinted at the wall again, then shivered and shook his head. "No, how could they be real? I saw Aunt Amity just now, and she's dead." I even seemed to *be* Aunt Amity for a moment, he thought uneasily.

Madeline shrugged. "Usabo seemed pretty real, when we were kids. And we both saw the same thing then, that folder with the Medusa head on it, and the Usabo spider inside it. Can two people have the same hallucination?"

"They can believe they did," he said firmly, "if they're kids, and they talk it over afterward. We saw the spider symbol that was in the envelope, so we imagined a scarier one and came to believe we'd actually seen *it*. These *visions* are no more real than the Wizard of Oz. And the Medusa folder was obviously just one of us thinking of the Medusa mosaic on that wall in the garden, and putting it into our story. Our shared story." He nodded, reflecting that what he was saying made sense. He went on, "It's bad enough to—"

He stopped talking, for a loud grinding and clanking had started up in the walls. "What the hell!"

Madeline smiled and bit her lip. "That's Claimayne's elevator. They installed it after you moved out—it wasn't quite as noisy as this at first. I guess it's time for dinner."

"Oh!" Scott made himself relax. "Okay. So let's—forget about all this morbid old stuff, and don't look in your envelope, right?"

"Right."

"We should get into dry clothes. Drier, anyway. I should have brought a tie—Claimayne won't say anything, but he'll be disappointed."

Madeline nodded and stood away from the door frame. "He's not much of a Martian."

Scott blinked at her, wondering if he'd missed a sentence. "I, uh, suppose not."

"I mean, Mars is the ruler of Scorpio, and he's a Scorpio. But Mars must not have been in Scorpio when he was born, or he'd be more assertive." She turned to her own room and took hold of the doorknob, but paused. "Why did we call it Usabo? I forget."

Scott laughed shortly, still very shaky and wishing she would let the subject go. "Right afterward, we saw a storage yard, and the letters on the sign had been messed up by the wind. It was supposed to say, SEE US ABOUT OUR SPECIAL, but—"

"I remember now. It said SEE USABO U TOUR SPECIAL. And we pretended it was talking about what we saw. What we thought we saw." She gripped the doorknob tightly. "I don't ever want to see him and tour special again."

Scott looked down at the shreds of the paper on the mattress, and he wiped his hand on his damp jeans. "I don't either," he said. But he remembered that initial moment of being outside of time and his own identity, and he had to repeat, more to himself this time, "I don't either."

Madeline was peering at him and opened her mouth to say something, but he waved at her and said, "I'll see if I can fetch that heater up here without falling down the stairs."

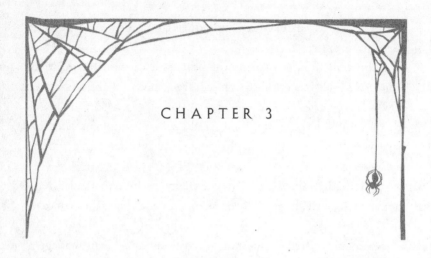

CHAPTER 3

THE DINING ROOM TOOK up most of the southern side of the ground floor, with a narrow kitchen tucked up against the west chimney behind a pair of swinging doors. Lights in frosted-glass wall sconces cast a lemony glow over the long room and threw shadows against the plaster ceiling from the open-work beams high overhead, and two of the French windows were opened now onto a view of the rainy night and the freeway lights in the distance. The air in the dining room shifted with the smells of wet vegetation and hot enchilada sauce.

The walls were cluttered with framed pictures and mirrors and shelves crowded with tiny figurines, and a pair of glass-fronted bookcases flanked the door to the entry hall. Four places had been set at the long table, two on each side, and two bottles of wine stood in the center; the place at the head of the table, where their aunt Amity had always sat, was bare.

Claimayne, wearing an embroidered dressing gown and a blue silk scarf, had already maneuvered his wheelchair to the place that would have been on his mother's right, with his back to the windows, and Ariel was just sitting down beside him when Scott and Madeline stepped in from the hall.

"Ah," called Claimayne, "our future landlords!" Ariel scowled fiercely at him.

Scott pulled out a chair on the other side of the table for Madeline. "We'll let you both stay on rent free," he said lightly as she sat down.

"*We* might let *you* stay," said Ariel, "as the handyman. Isn't that what you do these days, now that you're always too drunk to be an *artist* anymore?"

Scott had begun to pull out a chair for himself, and after a momentary pause, he continued the motion and then sat down carefully.

Madeline shifted beside him. "Scott's an apartment manager," she said, "at a complex off Sunset. Not a handyman."

"We all have a whole week together," said Claimayne to Ariel, carefully pushing one of the bottles of wine toward her. "Would you pour? According to my mother's will. It would be more effective theater if you began amicably, so that your venom later will have some prominence."

"Her *will*?" said Ariel, almost spitting. Claimayne pushed the bottle again, and she picked it up with both hands, a bit shakily. "She killed herself before the ink was dry on it! Didn't just kill herself—got out of bed and climbed up onto the roof, with a *grenade*!—and blew herself to pieces! Sound mind, my ass!" She rubbed her jaw, as if it hurt to speak, and glowered at Claimayne. "And you were no help—in your room with the door locked, crying and cussing while she did it, and then sick in bed for four days while *I* arranged her funeral, which you didn't even *attend*."

"And pour," Claimayne prompted. As Ariel splashed wine into his glass and hers, he smiled. "Hamlet said 'The Everlasting hath fix'd his canon 'gainst self-slaughter'—she opposed the canon with a grenade!" He shook his head and added thoughtfully, "I'm afraid that for a long time she had entertained thoughts of suicide."

For a moment no one had anything to say, and the hiss and clatter of the rain outside the open French windows was the only sound; then, evidently to break the silence, Madeline said, "Entertained? I can see . . . harboring thoughts of suicide, indulging them . . . but not *entertaining* them."

Scott simply held still, waiting for the tingling in his face to subside. Wow, he thought shakily. Ariel's cheerful welcome an hour ago was clearly faked, a calculated setup for this attack.

He leaned back and opened his mouth, and instantly Ariel was staring at him; he shut his mouth and looked away.

What she had said was true. He had resented computer-generated art and the alleged necessity of using social media like Facebook, and when he had neglected or skimped several commissions because of being drunk, he had soon found himself effectively blackballed as a commercial graphic artist. After that, he had tried to sell his paintings—at juried shows, then at nonjuried shows, and finally at any sidewalk arts-and-crafts fair, often alongside booths selling food dehydrators and innovative mops—and finally he had thrown out all his paints and brushes and lights and air brushes and compressors, and bitterly vowed that he would never again even sketch a sleeping cat.

White light flared silently outside the French windows, and a moment later Scott twitched as thunder cracked and rolled its echoes over the dark hills. Ariel half stood up, apparently meaning to close the windows, then just shook her head wearily and sat back down. Scott noticed that she was now wearing a little silver gyroscope on a chain around her neck.

"She was in very poor health, these last few years," Claimayne went on imperturbably. "Colon cancer, chemotherapy, several operations—during the last year she had no rectum to speak of."

"For God's sake," Ariel burst out, "who'd *want* to speak of it? We're indifferent to your mother's rectum." She winced and closed her eyes, then gingerly rubbed the corners of her jaw.

Scott's own jaw was aching, and he had just reached up to massage it, and he was wincing too, when she opened her eyes and stared at him; both of them lowered their hands, and after a few seconds they looked away from each other.

Madeline said, he thought, that Ariel does spiders.

The swinging doors to the kitchen opened then, and white-haired Rita, who had been the housekeeper at Caveat for as long as Scott could remember, sidled in carrying a wide tray.

"Rita!" exclaimed Madeline. "We're back!"

The elderly Mexican woman smiled warmly at her. "Not to stay long in this terrible place, I hope, Madeline sweetie!"

Claimayne ignored her and waved toward the far side of the table. "Do have some wine," he said. "Ravenswood zinfandel, 2009."

Madeline picked up the bottle Ariel had poured from and filled the glass in front of her.

When Rita had shifted four steaming plates from the tray, Scott said, "Rita, is there maybe a Coke in the refrigerator?"

"I think maybe there is, Scotty," she said and carried the tray back into the kitchen.

"On the wagon for all to see and admire," observed Ariel, "with a bottle upstairs for dessert."

"Scott hasn't had a drink in more than a year," said Madeline, cutting into one of her enchiladas with a fork. "He told me so."

"*Oh*," said Ariel, "*well* then." She turned to Claimayne. "And we've got a bunch of high-hat strangers coming over here on Saturday. Do you have any *other* intruders lined up?"

"That man is coming over here on Thursday," said Claimayne, "at one thirty, to talk about my mother's unpublished books."

Ariel nodded. "That Ferdalisi guy. Your mother refused to see him."

"She was paranoid in her old age. Thought the gas man was an agent from the Vatican." Claimayne tried to lift his wineglass, but only managed to make the base of it rattle against the table. " 'Dip into the wine thy little red lips,' " he said to Ariel, " 'that I may drain the cup!' "

Ariel scowled at him, then sighed and rolled her eyes. " 'I am not thirsty, Tetrarch.' "

In spite of his aching muscles and his embarrassment at Ariel's unexpected scornful remarks, Scott couldn't repress a reminiscent smile, for Claimayne and Ariel used to do this Salomé-and-the-tetrarch routine when all four of them were living at Caveat. It was lines from the dialogue frames of a silent black-and-white movie called *Salomé* that their aunt Amity had watched frequently.

Claimayne had been a teenager in those days, older than the rest of them and too resolutely sophisticated and ironic to see any value in the strange, slow old movie his mother was so fond of, and his cousin Ariel, eight years younger, had happily cooperated in his mockery of the stilted sentences on the dialogue frames.

Ariel, as Claimayne had frequently observed, was a genuine Madden. She had been orphaned at the age of seven, but her father, Sam Madden, had been the brother of Edward Madden, Claimayne's father, and the fifteen-year-old Claimayne had had no objections when his mother took the girl in to live at Caveat. Scott and Madeline's father, Arthur Madden, had merely been adopted by their grandfather, and though they had grown up with Claimayne and Ariel, Claimayne had never regarded them as real family. Young Scott and Madeline had laughed at Claimayne's jokes but had seldom made any of their own.

Scott recalled that Aunt Amity had stopped watching the movie when he had been in the sixth grade.

Claimayne was still holding his wineglass and blinking at Ariel, who impatiently took his glass and drank off half the wine in it. When she clanked it back down on the table, it was light enough for Claimayne to lift it in his trembling hand.

"Aunt Amity's unpublished books?" ventured Scott. "Thank you," he added when Rita brought him a glass of Coca-Cola and ice.

"It's good you quit the drinking," old Rita said to him quietly. "You be careful here." Scott nodded and mouthed *Thanks*.

Claimayne gulped some wine and then began cutting up his enchiladas, gripping the knife and fork tightly. "*The Shores of Hollywood,* in 1992, was my mother's last published novel. She kept writing them after that—a good two dozen of them—but even in '92 her vogue had passed."

"The ones after '92 were no good," spoke up Ariel.

Claimayne pursed his lips as he tried to work his fork under a bit of cheese and tortilla. "No worse than the previous ones, I think, or not much worse. The only real difference was that the novels she wrote after *Shores of Hollywood* were all written in the third person—that one was the last of her first-person novels."

"Are they all," asked Scott, "the unpublished ones, still about Cyclone Severiss?"

Cyclone Severiss was the protagonist of all Aunt Amity's published novels; the Severiss character had been a female private investigator in the Los Angeles of the 1920s. Scott had read most of the published ones and had always privately thought that Aunt Amity had tried so hard for period accuracy that the pace of the books dragged.

"The ones I've looked at," answered Claimayne. The food dropped off his fork, and he patiently set about recapturing it. "In any case, this fellow Ferdalisi wants to look at them, and any notes she might have kept."

"He's a publisher?"

"Or an agent, or something. We're hosting a memorial party here on Saturday, as Ariel mentioned, with some literary and film folk, so maybe he believes there could be a resurgence of interest in my mother's work."

"And some money," put in Ariel. Looking across the table, she added, "You two will still be in residence, to act out the charade of her insane so-called 'last will'—but you don't need to mingle at the party."

Scott kept his attention on the food in front of him and just nodded, but Madeline looked at her cousin across the table. "There was a cannon too?"

Ariel stared at her in incomprehension, faintly shaking her head.

"Claimayne said there was a cannon," Madeline went on, "as well as a grenade."

"Canon law," said Claimayne, smiling at her over the mess he'd made of his plate. "God's law. Canon with only one 'n' in it. My mother went against it, you see, with her grenade. I'm sorry I wasn't clear about that."

Madeline nodded magnanimously. "Well, it's hard to be clear about grenades," she allowed.

Claimayne nodded vaguely, then turned to Ariel. "Salomé!" he said. "Bite but a little of this enchilada, that I may eat what is left!"

Ariel glanced at his plate. "No," she said. Then she gave Scott a narrowed look. "On her last day she made these stupid banners for you two, with a felt marker and an old box of accordion tractor-feed paper—'Welcome home, Scott,' and 'Welcome home, Madeline.'"

Scott's expression didn't change, but he felt his scalp contract and he carefully laid down his fork. He didn't look at Madeline.

"Oh?" he said in a neutral tone.

Ariel gave him a thin smile. "You won't see them. I threw them in the trash."

"Oh," said Scott.

"Oh," echoed Madeline weakly.

Claimayne smiled. "Our Ariel just is *not* sentimental, is she?"

BEFORE GOING DOWNSTAIRS TO dinner, Madeline had found sheets, blankets, pillows, and pillowcases in the same linen closet they'd always been in, and she and Scott had made their beds and got the windows open. Madeline had found a broom to sweep the worst of the dust and cobwebs away, and Scott had carried up the electric heater and plugged it in and stood it in the connecting doorway between their rooms.

Now, the awkward dinner having finally come to an end, they

had trudged back up the stairs, and Scott had absently knocked at the Garden of Allah door, and they were in Madeline's room. The air was now comfortably warm. Madeline was leaning back on her elbows on the bedspread and Scott was sitting cross-legged on the wooden floor.

After several seconds of silence, Madeline sat up and exclaimed, "No more real than the wizard of Oz!"

After a pause, "Maybe Ariel was listening, outside the door," Scott began, "when I was talking about the Welcome Home banner . . ." But he shook his head unhappily. "Maddy, damn it, how *can* they be real visions? What *is* this, some kind of—"

"It could have been like a psychic Instagram," interrupted Madeline. "Like Aunt Amity recorded a message, a video, on that spider you looked at."

Scott grimaced. "So what are you saying . . . when we were kids, we really did see an actual guy on a boat open that folder and look at the Usabo spider?"

Madeline had drawn up her knees, and all Scott could see were her wide eyes as she said, "We didn't *see* him, we *were* him, remember?"

Scott got stiffly to his feet. "I think Ariel was listening at the door."

Madeline straightened her legs and sighed. "Maybe."

For several seconds neither of them spoke.

Then Madeline said, "She is awful mean, Ariel. Do you want to stay here for a week?"

Scott was glad to abandon the disquieting spider topic. "Do you?"

"I don't know. We *might* inherit the place," Madeline said, and continued even as her brother was shaking his head, "if we stay the week, like Aunt Amity put in her will. And it's free food for a week, and a quarter off the month's utilities at my apartment. That's not nothing."

And I'll have to at least split my week's pay with Ellis for filling in for me at the Ravenna Apartments office, thought Scott. Better eat a lot of the free food.

But, "True," he said.

"Ariel liked you, when we first got here. Then she didn't. What's up with that?"

Scott felt his face heating up again. "She was pretending, at first."

"You think so? I don't think so."

Madeline got up and crossed to the open window and knelt on the floor to look out at the rainy night. Scott knew that the view was of the long garden that sloped up to a row of garages at the top of the hill.

The breeze blew Madeline's curly dark hair away from her face, and the house creaked like an old ship at sea.

"We could look at all our old places, while we're here," she said. "The garden looks the same, as much as I can see. I can just make out the wall that's got the Medusa mosaic on it, unless all the stones have fallen out by now." She pursed her lips, perhaps finding that an uncomfortable subject, and went on quickly, "And we could check out the basements. I wonder if our scare-bat is still down there."

Scott smiled reluctantly and shook his head. In their childhood explorations of Caveat, they had not neglected the extensive cellars that stretched under all the buildings on the hill, and even under gardens and lawns. In a brick alcove under the main house their flashlights had found a gold-painted four-armed lug wrench stuck upright in a yard-wide square of lumpy concrete; Madeline had eventually stapled together scraps of cloth to make a coat and hat to hang on it, and Scott had painted a clown face on a plastic egg that some-body's stockings had come in, and hung it under the hat. Madeline had decided that since no crows were ever likely to venture into the cellars, they should call the little figure a scare-bat. She had taken to dressing it for the seasons—red-and-white felt and a conical red hat in December, a witch's hat and black dress in October . . .

"If we can still fit through all those passages," he said.

"Sure, we weren't little kids anymore by the time we found the basements."

Then she stiffened. "Scott," she said sharply, "that cat is walking in midair."

Scott got up and crouched beside her.

She pointed out the window. "There!"

Off to the left, a white cat fifty feet away in the darkness was picking its way along in a straight line. It didn't seem to mind the rain.

"It's on that wall with all the seashells stuck in it," Scott said. "The old croquet court is on the other side."

"*No,*" said Madeline, "I remember that wall, but it's gone now, look!"

Scott peered through the rain, and in fact it did seem that the old wall was gone—the darkness below the walking cat seemed to be farther away than the cat.

"A metal rod," he said, almost angrily, "a two-by-four . . . hell, a telephone line—"

"It's Bridget!" exclaimed Madeline. "*Bridget!*" she called out the window.

Bridget was a cat they had had in the '90s. She had died of some cat malaise in young Madeline's arms.

The cat out in the darkness turned its head toward the window, and for a moment paused there.

"*Bridget, Bridget!*" called Madeline again, and Scott saw tears on her cheeks. "*Come here, girl!*"

After a long pause, the cat resumed its walk, and in a few moments disappeared around the block of deeper darkness that was the northwest shoulder of the building.

Scott braced himself to stop his sister from climbing right out the window, but Madeline only sat back on her heels, knuckling her eyes.

"Madeline," said Scott cautiously, "Bridget—"

"Oh, I know she died! I was holding her, and she was stiff when we buried her out there!" She waved a hand vaguely at the window. "But—it was her. And that wall is gone."

All Scott could think of to say was, "Don't yell anymore. Claimayne and Ariel—"

"Their rooms are at the other end, on the front side."

"Right, well . . ." He realized that he was shivering. The cat had *obviously* not been Bridget. The cat had *obviously* been walking on *something*. A clothesline, probably. He gripped the wet windowsill and got his feet under himself and managed to stand up without eliciting any strong pains from his knees. "It's—it's only for a week." He leaned against the wall beside the window for a moment, then pushed off and crossed to the doorway to his room, stepping around the buzzing heater. "I'll leave the connecting door open."

SCOTT WAS AWAKENED IN the night by the sound of muffled sobbing, and when he sat up in bed, the room was dimly illuminated by moonlight, and he was startled by the bare shelves and the absence of furniture in the familiar room. Did that have something to do with why Madeline was crying?

He had flipped the blankets aside and stood up before he remembered that he was an adult, and that this hadn't been his room for many years.

He hurried to the connecting door, and his bare foot collided with the heater, knocking it over.

As he leaned in the doorway and rubbed his toes, smothering curses, Madeline sniffed and said, "Watch out for the heater." He heard her shift in her bed, and she added, "I'm sorry I woke you up. I'll be quiet."

"Well—what's wrong?"

"Oh. Being here again—I just miss everybody that's gone."

"So do I." As opposed to the ones that are still here, he thought. A line from Coleridge occurred to him, and he sleepily recited it: "'And a thousand thousand slimy things lived on, and so did I.'" Then he added, "Sorry, that's from a poem."

"Not a helpful poem. Scott, are we gonna be okay? I mean, ten or twenty years from now—are we going to be—with—people? We're not now."

Scott shrugged in the darkness, but said, "Of course. And they'll be glad of it, too."

She laughed softly. "I'm sorry. Let's go back to sleep. Set the heater up again, it turns off if it's lying down."

"Right." Scott set the device upright again and turned back toward his own room.

"It's got a ball bearing in it," said Madeline.

Scott nodded, though she was unlikely to see it, and returned to his bed.

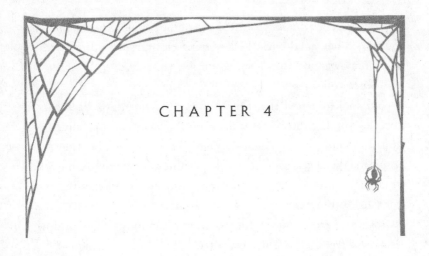

CHAPTER 4

BY MORNING THE SKY had cleared, and the sun was casting the shadow of the house across the western lawn all the way to the shaggy palm trees lining the driveway that curled up to the garages and down the hill on the other side to Gower Street. The breeze was chilly and smelled of mesquite and the distant ocean. Claimayne had already angled his wheelchair out onto the west balcony, and he was sipping coffee and setting pebbles on folded slips of paper laid out on a little wrought-iron table when Ariel stepped through the doorway and lowered herself into the chair opposite. She shivered, frowning behind very dark sunglasses, and pulled her bathrobe more snugly up to her chin. Her silver gyroscope pendant lay across her shoulder.

Claimayne glanced at her, his round bald head reminding her of the gilded Buddha statues he kept in his room. He gestured at the slips of paper. "Hair of the dog? They're all clean, freshly copied, never looked at. I don't like dirty ones for breakfast."

Ariel shuddered and turned away. "No, thank you."

"You sure? You could burn it right afterward—no possibility of an after, that way, no flash-ahead vision—just the not-me rush."

The breeze paused, and for a moment the eternal creaking of the old house was the only sound.

Ariel reached out and touched one of the pebbles, then made a fist and pulled her hand back. "I'm staying clean," she said unsteadily. "Yesterday was the exception that proves the rule."

"Since you say so."

She looked across the table at him. "In yesterday's flash-ahead, three days in the future—two days, now!—Scott and Madeline were patient, friendly. They obviously knew I'd arrive mad, but they were calm. And then I was back here, sick, pushing you into the dining room while they marched away up the stairs. So you saw the exchanged *me* from that future point—and I was *welcoming* to them?"

Claimayne took a mouthful of coffee and carefully set the cup down. "If it *was* a real flash-ahead, a real after, and not a hallucination—"

"It was real."

"—which I apologetically but profoundly doubt—then apparently when you look at the spider again, two days from now, you won't have any quarrel with Scott and Madeline anymore." He leaned back and smiled. "Maybe you charm them into signing a preemptive quitclaim in the meantime, who knows? They seem passive enough. Maybe we offer them a solid buyout to forestall even the remote risk of a judge validating my mother's crazy last will. You—"

"Buyout. I could go a couple of hundred dollars, I think. I wish we'd invested better."

Claimayne shrugged. "We did what we could, when we could, with what we had—and we're secure for a few years yet." He eyed the slips of paper on the table wistfully. "And sometimes the cumulative clogging effect *does* relent—phases of the moon, variations in air pressure, blood pressure, tire pressure?—and volition *is* still possible in the befores and afters, for such as we."

"It relented for me last night. I called them ghouls and graveworms—which is to say I will call them that, two days from now. That's volition. And . . . and the exchanged 'me' from up there had volition: I was hospitable! What did I say?"

"If it *was* real, my dear, you have only yourself to blame for our dwindling fortunes. Instead of cussing at them, you should have found a newspaper and noted some stock prices or horserace winners."

"Damn it, what did I *say*?—to them, last night?"

"Oh—I had started to tell them that they had gone to needless extra trouble in dragging their luggage up the steps, as they were to stay in the street-side apartments, and you interrupted and said no, they *were to be* put to some extra trouble, namely making up the beds in their old rooms here. You were entirely cordial, smiling—'Scott, come in out of the rain.'" He slid a paper out from under one of the pebbles. "You don't mind if I—?"

She waved the back of her hand at him. "I've been four years off them. Yesterday was a—"

"Fluke," suggested Claimayne. "An aftershock, a late postcoital shiver."

"You're a filthy old pig."

"And you've got another . . . fluke, coming, day after tomorrow—right?—so you can come back to yesterday and be their *chum*."

"Go to hell."

Claimayne smiled. "Salomé, unfold this spider for me, that I may look at it in your hand!"

"Fuck you, Tetrarch."

Claimayne laughed softly and opened the paper and stared at it.

Ariel watched his bland face lose all expression as he closed his eyes; he inhaled sharply and his hands gripped the edges of the table as if he were afraid his wheelchair were tipping over; for a full minute neither of them spoke, and finally he sighed and opened his eyes. He focused them on his hands and the table and Ariel in slow succession, and then out across the lawn, and finally he nodded.

The crumpled paper was still in his hand, and he rolled it between his fingers. "Do you"—he paused to clear his throat—"have a lighter?"

"No. I quit smoking too, you recall."

"Wise, wise." He dipped the rolled paper into his coffee, held it there a moment, then lifted it out, squeezed it into a ball, and tossed it into his mouth. "No possible future point for that one, you see," he said after he'd swallowed it and shuddered a bit.

"I should have burned the one I looked at yesterday, as soon as I came down from it. I still could burn it, without looking at it again, never let *it* have a future point."

Claimayne's shoulders twitched in the beginning of a shrug, then slumped. "You'd still have said what you said, somehow."

Ariel eyed the remaining slips of paper under the pebbles on the table, then resolutely looked away. Softly she asked, "Why do we do it?"

"You remember."

"Not in words."

"It's a gap in continuity, time stops, and we're not—we don't have any identity." His smile now seemed forced, and there was a misting of sweat on his smooth forehead.

She shook her head. "For no more than a couple of minutes, at most! And then we're—right the hell back where we were before."

"As our clocks reckon it, sure. As a bystander would reckon it. But that gap—ah, Ariel, that gap is infinite! Our departure and return are two points very close together in time, but remember that there's an infinity between any two points."

The creaking of the house stopped, and the balcony shifted under their chairs; then the faint squeaks and prolonged groans began again.

Ariel was on her feet and stepping into the doorway. She grabbed the handles of Claimayne's wheelchair, but he slapped at the hand he could reach.

"The house isn't going to collapse, my dear. Stop shaking me and sit down."

"Maybe not, but the balcony's going to fall off!"

Claimayne grinned at her. "Impossible! If it did, we'd be killed, and then who would look at your spider from yesterday, and retroactively welcome Arthur's children? As long as you don't consummate that exchange, don't do the after, you're immortal, right?"

Ariel edged cautiously out onto the balcony again and slowly resumed her seat. "No," she said, "you were right, I'd still have said what I said." She touched the balcony rail. "This place *is* collapsing. Little by little."

"Well—you may be right, at that." Claimayne tugged all the papers out from under the pebbles and put them in the pocket of his dressing gown. "How long since that fellow tightened all the screw jacks under the joists in the basements? It would never do to have the floors collapse during the party on Saturday."

"Joey the surfer? He quit when your mom blew herself up on the roof. I'm going to get Scott to take over the job, while he's here."

"Scott? I don't like the idea of him clowning about with those things. Hire another fellow."

"No, I want to order Scott to crawl around in the mud down there."

Claimayne shook his head, then winced and closed his eyes. "I suppose he can't do much harm. I think I'm going to be . . . sitting in a hot bath now, for an hour or so."

Ariel nodded dubiously. "I remember it always hurts."

ARIEL WAS IN THE narrow kitchen spooning ground coffee into the percolator when Madeline stepped in from the slantingly sunlit dining room in yesterday's jeans and sweater.

Ariel gave her an unfriendly look, set the tin lid on the percolator and then reached into a jar of sugar cubes; and when she tried to pull a handful of them out, her fist was too wide for the mouth of the jar. Madeline recalled stories of monkeys being trapped that way.

"You look like a monkey trying to pull his hand out," she said.

"You look like a monkey trying to pull his head out," Ariel

retorted instantly, releasing the sugar cubes and yanking her hand free.

Madeline thought about that. "His head? His head wouldn't be wider. A squirrel's might be, if its cheeks were full of nuts."

"What are you *talking* about? I meant trying to pull his head out of his *ass*."

"Oh." Madeline decided to let it go. "I came down to get coffee."

"I just put it on, it'll be ready soon. I've got some jobs for you and your brother. The heater on the roof—"

"I'm an astrologer," said Madeline.

Ariel paused, her mouth still open. "Astrology won't fix the heater."

"It's hard to imagine," agreed Madeline. "Make a list of the things that need doing, and I'll take it upstairs to Scott. I'm sure he can do work here; he's got somebody filling in for him at the apartments where he usually works. Right now he wants coffee—he's not feeling very well."

"Oh, he killed the bottle upstairs after dinner?"

The window over the sink was open, and the white curtains flapped in the breeze from over the shadowed lawn.

"No," said Madeline, "I think he has what you and Claimayne had."

Ariel reddened and turned away and pulled open a drawer on the far side of the sink. She lifted out a pad and pencil and began hastily scribbling.

"It's winter," she said over her shoulder, "and the rooftop heater doesn't work. Cups are in the cabinet by your head, sugar's still in that jar, though I was going to put some in a bowl, and the coffee should be ready in a minute. The kid we had working here said the heater's pilot light won't stay lit. The kid kept the ladder leaned up against the house, since he was up on the roof a lot, but after Claimayne's mad mother used it to climb up there, we threw it behind the poolhouse. You think Scott remembers where that is?"

"The *Hispaniola,* sure." When they'd been children, the long-abandoned poolhouse had been their make-believe pirate ship, named after the vessel in *Treasure Island.*

Ariel looked around at her. "That's right." She turned away again and resumed writing. "And there's apparently a lot of things called screw jacks under the floor joists of the house—under all the buildings—and they need to be tightened up or this whole place will collapse. I think I can find a map for him of where all the screw jacks are."

"I'll tell him to fix the heater first." The coffee bubbling up in the glass knob at the top of the percolator was brown, and Madeline turned down the heat and fetched two cups from the cabinet.

"There's," said Ariel hesitantly, "trays up there too."

Madeline smiled. "Thanks." She levered a wooden tray free of the pans around it and set it on the counter, set the cups on it, then poured coffee into them. Lifting the tray, she added, "I'm sorry about the monkey thing. It's just that I read—"

"Just shut up and take the poor boy his coffee."

As Madeline sidled out of the narrow kitchen into the dining room, Ariel called after her, "I've read that too—the monkeys can't let go of it, the peanuts or whatever, and they get trapped."

With no hand free, Madeline nodded in acknowledgment.

Her shoes knocked and scuffed on the uncarpeted stairs and then on the worn planks of the second-floor hallway, but she paused for a moment beside the door to what had been Aunt Amity's bedroom, on the other side of the hall from the row of salvaged doors with nothing but wall behind them; and when she walked farther and kicked the door of Scott's room and he pulled it open, she said, "There's some kind of noise in *her* room."

Scott took the tray from Madeline and set it on the recessed shelf in the plaster wall, beside the row of cigarettes he had laid out last night. "We have to get furniture up here." He picked up one of the steaming cups, then hastily set it down again. "What sort of noise?"

"Very soft, like—a lot of mice running for their lives." She touched the other cup and left it where it was. "I don't want to go sit in my stupid office today. Astrology's too sad."

"You've got an office now?"

"Well, it's still the living room in my apartment. The landlady thinks I run kind of a *botanica*." Scott knew that meant a Hispanic witchcraft shop. Madeline sat down on his bed. "I'm not going."

"Do you have an appointment?" She nodded. "Is the person going to pay you?" She nodded again. "Then I'd say you better go."

"We're going to inherit this house in a week."

"You know we're not. Why is astrology sad?"

Madeline made a face. "Because you can't get there, to where it's describing! The sun and the planets aren't circling the earth anymore—I mean, nobody thinks that anymore, except maybe my clients—but astrology is based on that old business. And the calendar has moved on since our charts were written; the sun comes into the Taurus constellation in May now, for instance, but we do the calculations as if it still comes in in April, like it did a thousand years ago. We're always describing the past, but we can't *get* to the past!" She waved a hand. "But there I am anyway, calculating what the exact sidereal time of a native's birth was, figuring what the ascendant was at that moment, then looking up where all the planets were—"

"Native? What, you get work from a reservation or something?"

"That's what we call clients." She waved a hand impatiently. "You know—natal, birth date."

"I thought you just went by what month they were born in, like they have in the newspapers."

"No, that's no good—that would be like deciding what one guy's blood alcohol level was by measuring everybody in the bar and figuring the average. And doing it a month late anyway!" She shook her head. "Ariel says you have to fix the heater on the roof. The pilot light won't stay lit." She laid the list on his bed.

"I can probably do that." Scott picked up one of the cigarettes;

it was mottled brown, but apparently dry, and he lit it and blew a plume of smoke toward the opened window. "So all that horoscope fish-and-bull-and-scorpion stuff doesn't really apply?"

"I don't think it ever did, much. The actual plain star charts don't look at all like the constellations, the pictures you're supposed to see in them." She shivered and looked out the window at the green slope of the garden. "But—" She shook her head and stood up. "We should tell somebody—well, you're the handyman here, now. For a week. You should do something about the mice. If it is mice."

"But what?" said Scott. When she gave him a blank look, he went on, "You said they don't look like the pictures, but—"

"I don't like to talk about it."

Scott shrugged. "Okay."

"Well," she began, then went on in a rush: "See, I don't think it was ever about the stars—not originally, anyway. It was about a big, moving two-dimensional black surface with a lot of little white dots on it. I think the old astrologers connected some of the dots in those goofy ways, insisted on their made-up pictures of bulls and lions and crabs from mythology, to hide the way *earlier* guys had connected them. Bulls and fishes aren't naturally two-dimensional, but . . . I think some things are." She pushed her dark hair back with both hands. "One time I looked at a star chart and tried to connect the dots in different ways, to maybe get more believable pictures."

"So what did you—" he began, but stopped when he saw her woebegone expression. "Not . . . more spiders?"

"It was in my head! It's been in my head for twenty-three years. I burned the star chart after I saw I had traced a bunch of eight-legged patterns across the stars. None of them were . . . you know, *hot,* but I think if I'd kept trying, one of them would have been."

"Shit." Scott drew deeply on his cigarette, and the end glowed. "It hasn't been in *my* head, not till I got back to this damned old house, anyway. You think old Babylonians or somebody used star charts to trace your filthy spiders on? How old *are* these things?"

Madeline blinked rapidly. "They're not *my* filthy spiders, Scott! Who was it looked at one just last night?"

He took a deep breath and made himself relax. "Well, Ariel, for one," he said mildly, "if I had to guess, since she looked as racked up as I felt, at dinner."

Madeline shrugged. "Anyway, I don't know how old the things are. Claimayne used to say the Vatican has been trying to suppress them ever since at least the Borgia popes."

"It's weird nobody ever heard of them."

"Well, obviously a few people have. But they don't want to call attention to themselves. It's too likely to be bad attention." She kicked her valise. "I should go into some other line of work. I saw an ad in the paper for a job that included lighthouse work. I think that would be nice, like in *Captain January*."

Scott thought about that for a moment, then said, "Uh, are you sure it wasn't light . . . housework?"

Her face was blank. "Oh. Damn. I bet you're right." She sighed. "I wonder if they even have lighthouses anymore. Captain January had to move out of his, and they took Shirley Temple to an orphanage."

Scott jumped then at a loud snap, and when he looked at the window, he saw a web of cracks across the glass of the raised frame.

"Somebody threw a rock at our window!" Madeline exclaimed.

"And broke the inner pane but not the outer one?" Then Scott stepped between her and the window. "Don't look at it," he said sharply.

He was wearing a long-sleeved flannel shirt, and he gently knocked out the glass with his elbow, averting his eyes and being careful not to break the glass in the outside frame. Several of the broken pieces slid out from between the frames and whispered away in the thick shrubbery below.

"Nobody threw a rock," he said.

Madeline was staring at the floor. "Can I look now?" She glanced at him, and her eyes widened when she saw the expression on his face.

"What, don't tell me it was another of the damn *patterns*? Showing up in cracks in *glass*?"

Scott now looked at the shards still stuck in the raised wooden window frame. "Well—I don't know. I just glanced at it out of the corner of my eye, but—no, you've just got me spooked. This house *is* crooked, and settling. All kinds of stresses." He knew he was talking to himself as much as to her. "Not surprising that windows would break."

"You're supposed to tighten some screws in the basements too, Ariel said."

"I bet. I'm glad we're *not* going to inherit this place—it should have been·condemned years ago."

"We might." She picked up her cup and took a sip of coffee. "Inherit it. Could I have ten dollars for gas? What about those mice?"

Scott flicked his cigarette out the window and stepped away from it. "Let's look."

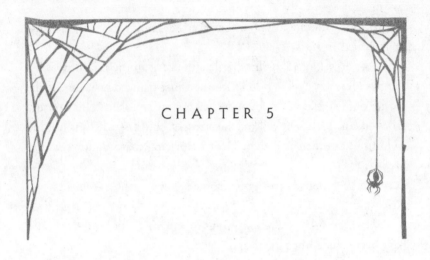

CHAPTER 5

THEY WALKED OUT OF Scott's room and down the hall to the right, to the door of their aunt's old room. The hall was in shadow except for daylight from a window at the far end, and reflected light up from the stairs ahead of them; Scott resisted the temptation to step to the other side of the hall and knock on the Garden of Allah door. *When is a door not a door?*

Madeline cocked her head beside their aunt's door. "Hear it?"

Scott listened, and now he could hear a faint, irregular rippling. "I don't think it's mice." He turned the knob and pushed the door open.

Their aunt's bedroom was a sickroom. A big hospital bed with a bare, segmented mattress and high aluminum side rails occupied a good deal more of the floor space than her old bed had, and an IV pole with bare hooks stood on the far side of it. The window was closed, and the room smelled of Lysol and laundry soap.

The walls, at least, were as Scott and Madeline remembered them—photos of various silent-movie stars, half a dozen ornately framed mirrors, and varnished pine bookcases with all the Cyclone Severiss novels in their bright dust jackets. The byline on all the books was Amity Speas, their aunt's maiden name, since the first one had been published in 1965, three years before she had married Edward Madden.

On the top of a blue bedside table was ranked a collection of orange plastic pill bottles beside a mirror with a handle, and on a lower shelf was a black computer keyboard, its cord trailing on the bare wooden floor.

The soft, irregular clicking noise was coming from the keyboard— Scott could see keys rapidly dipping and springing back up like the keys of a player piano.

Below it, the USB plug lay on the floor, clearly not plugged in to anything.

"She's still writing!" whispered Madeline.

Scott's face tingled, and he said, "Stop it!" more harshly than he had meant to. He found that he had grabbed Madeline's arm and backed into the hallway even as his eyes were tightly focused on the impossibly working keyboard, and he could no longer hear the faint clicking over the ringing in his ears.

The keys kept rising and falling, one at a time but rapidly.

Scott tore his gaze from the keyboard and made himself step into the doorway again and look around the room. The bookshelves, the yellow lace curtains, and the trees outside the window gradually reasserted themselves as parts of the normal world, isolating the abnormality on the bedside table shelf.

He made himself relax, at least to the extent of releasing his sister's arm, though he was as aware of the keyboard as he would have been of a luminous snake in the room.

"Okay now," he said, carefully keeping his voice level, "*that's* just too damn weird. And the cat last night? Let's get *out* of here, Maddy, pack our stuff and go right now, this minute."

Madeline was wide-eyed and chewing her knuckle, but she said, "We need to know what she's saying! Scott, it's *Aunt Amity*!"

Who greeted me with one of these damned spiders *yesterday,* Scott thought, *posthumously.* He was so anxious to get out of the house that the whole structure seemed to be tilting him toward the stairs.

"She loved us," insisted Madeline. "*Can* we just walk away from it? From her?"

"I—yeah, I think *so*, Maddy, sure. This *isn't* the Aunt Amity we knew! This is the crazy old lady who climbed up on the roof with a grenade last week. And she's *dead*!"

"It must have hurt her terribly, climbing all the way up that ladder with her bad foot. We've got to see what she has to say." Madeline stepped into the room and set her coffee cup down beside the pill bottles. She crouched to lift the keyboard off the shelf, then stood up and stared at the dipping keys. After a few seconds, she turned it toward him. "Can you read it?"

Scott reluctantly watched the black keys popping up and down. They were all among the shiny ones in the middle and left side of the keyboard; the function keys along the top and the number keys to the right were dusty. "Uh, '*me get in* . . .' No, she's too fast for me. You need to plug it into a computer. You've got a computer at your apartment. I'll come with you. Let's go right now."

Madeline rolled her eyes at him. "I'm *certain* this typing won't happen away from this house, Scott! She's *here*, she's all over the roof! And if it stopped because we took it away, it might never start again!"

"Madeline, this place is *haunted*. You know? *Actually*." He had lowered his voice, as if afraid the keyboard might overhear him. "Paranormal stuff, like on TV. We'd be crazy to stay here, for anything."

"That stuff can't *hurt* you. And she loved us, and she's trying to . . . communicate."

"And she's dead! And who says it can't hurt you?"

Madeline just shook her head.

"Maddy, can you listen to reason for just a minute?"

"Not right now, I'm sorry. I'm not leaving."

"Do you intend to *sleep* here again? At *night*?"

"Scott—yes. If she's still talking. If she says anything that makes me think I have to stay."

Scott bared his teeth in agonized frustration. "I—won't leave while you're still here, I won't—"

"I'm sorry, Scott!"

He shivered and allowed himself a whispered shout, then took a deep breath and said, "Let's go find a goddamn computer."

"I'll stash this in my room till we find one," said Madeline. "I think she'd be more comfortable away from the hospital bed."

WHEN MADELINE ASKED ARIEL if there was a computer they could use—citing the necessity of getting their e-mail—their cousin curtly directed them to the library and told them that the password was *adelaida*. Madeline ran back upstairs and shortly reappeared with the vibrating keyboard wrapped in a sweater, closing the library door after she'd handed the bundle to Scott.

The room was almost as small as the kitchen on the opposite side of the house, though an ornate marble-fronted fireplace dominated the east-side wall. A relatively new black Hewlett-Packard computer stood on the crowded desk, with a flat-screen monitor beside it, and a printer sat on a low filing cabinet next to the desk. The keyboard sitting in front of the computer was white plastic, apparently a replacement for this black one that Aunt Amity had taken with her into her sickroom.

Stacked below the south-facing window were several of Aunt Amity's old computers and a tractor-feed daisy-wheel printer. The floor-to-ceiling shelves on the remaining two walls didn't seem to have changed since Scott had last seen them—they were still jammed, vertically and horizontally, with his aunt's research books on the history of Los Angeles, and he could also see the narrow spines of Claimayne's two collections of poetry. Scott thought he could even still catch the faint aroma of the unfiltered Pall Mall cigarettes their aunt had smoked incessantly.

He carried the sweater-wrapped keyboard, which he had to remind himself was not a living thing, across the carpet to the far side of the desk. The cable swung loosely like a tail.

"Get Word running," he told Madeline.

"Don't you want to plug in her keyboard first?"

"No, you'd never get anywhere with her keystrokes interrupting everything."

"Oh, right." Madeline pushed the power button at the top of the computer and sat down in the padded office chair. The computer rang four notes and the printer beeped, and Madeline typed in the password and then clicked the mouse.

She clicked it a few more times and then said, "Okay, Word's up."

Scott pulled the white keyboard's plug out of its USB port in the back of the computer and replaced it with the plug dangling from the keyboard he was carrying.

"Wow, it's going," said Madeline, staring at the monitor. Scott hastily unwrapped the black keyboard and set it down behind the computer, then hurried around the desk to crouch beside his sister.

Words were appearing rapidly across the screen:

climb down in their eyes her eyes i know i know charlene
hes a man no good it needs to be her i know i know if it was
then i remember all in one room cowboys fighting richelieus
swordsmen fencing lovers holding hands and all the shouting
at once the tablecloths and even the walls fluttering in the
wind charlene listen to me get in her eyes and climb down to
it I know i know cyclone i already know

"It's just gibberish," said Scott quickly. "She doesn't have anything to say, she's just talking in her sleep." He reached across for the mouse, but Madeline caught his hand.

"It's not total gibberish," she said. "It's her Cyclone Severiss character talking to someone, someone named Charlene."

"Incoherently! Let's just go. There's nothing here that's—"

Madeline startled him by abruptly giggling, though she immediately caught herself and stopped. "Claimayne said *Shores of Hollywood* was the last of her first-person novels," she said. "I think this is the first of her last-person novels."

Scott shook his head tensely, half lifting his hand toward the mouse again. "I don't think this one is going to be a hit."

The text they'd read was repeated several times, and even Madeline seemed ready to unplug the keyboard, when new lines appeared:

behind my eyes vast forms that move fantastically evil things
in robes of sorrow no the way out of the tomb is through
madeline branded in her eyes not roderick

Madeline gasped. "Me!" she exclaimed. "She's talking about me!"

Scott glanced toward the closed door and put a hand on his sister's shoulder. "Quiet, she's not talking about you. It's from—"

Madeline had not stopped staring at the monitor screen. "She is so! Right there—"

"It's from 'The Fall of the House of Usher,' a Poe story, look at me! Look at *me*! There's characters named Madeline and Roderick—and that 'vast forms' business is from a poem in the same story. There's no thought there, no consciousness! She's just regurgitating bits of old stories, including her own." He looked at the screen. "It's just repeating again anyway, see?—cycling the same stuff over and over." He stood up and walked around to the back of the desk again. "I'm unplugging her. Ariel or Claimayne might walk in here any second."

"You're sure?" Madeline looked over the monitor at her brother. "About this Poe thing?"

Scott unplugged the black keyboard's cord and plugged the white one's back in. "Yes, I can show you the story—the book was in this house at one time, probably still is, somewhere." Stepping around to the front of the desk, he highlighted the lines on the monitor, but before he could hit the backspace key Madeline caught his hand.

"Save," she said.

"Those two," he said, nodding toward the door, "are likely to check the recently opened files and notice it, even if you tuck it at the bottom of an already existing file." He rolled his eyes, then went on, "Oh, cut and paste it into an e-mail form, and mail it to yourself, then close this file without saving. You can open the e-mail at your apartment and read it over all you like."

"Or here. But that's a good idea."

"Here?" Scott decided to try one more time. "There's no reason now to stay here. You've got her text, it just repeats—"

She turned the chair to face him. "Scott, do you honestly think these two bits are all that's going to show up? Coherent or not?"

He took a deep breath, paused, and then just let it out in a defeated sigh. " . . . Well, I guess that is . . . unlikely."

The black keyboard behind the computer was still softly clicking away.

"I'm going to keep it in my room," Madeline said, "And at night when everyone's gone to bed, I'll plug it in again."

Scott shivered at the idea of reading the ghost's text down here at night, but he folded the sweater around the keyboard. "You think it'll still be typing, by then?"

"I think it's been typing away ever since she died."

"No," said Scott unhappily. "They must have gone into her room since then, they'd have noticed." He shook his head. "I bet it's just been going since you and I arrived here last night."

Madeline frowned, then nodded. "Since you looked at your spider. It's us she wants to communicate with."

She took the bundled keyboard from her brother and hugged it to herself, then pulled the library door open and hurried away down the hall toward the stairs.

Scott glumly opened AOL and checked his e-mail—there was nothing but subject lines announcing percentages of discount on the prices of things he wasn't interested in—and when he had shut down the computer and stood up and turned toward the door he saw that Ariel was standing there.

"You can earn your keep," she said. "The heater—"

"Madeline told me. On the roof. I think I can fix it."

Claimayne's silk-slippered feet on the wheelchair footrest appeared in the hall behind her, and his voice said, "Where was *she* off to in such a hurry?"

"Work," said Scott. "She's got deadlines with clients."

"I suppose that was a chicken," said Ariel.

Scott glanced at her in puzzlement.

"Wrapped up in her sweater," Ariel went on. "Doesn't she read chicken entrails?"

"Oh! No. Astrology."

"Same sort of thing."

Scott shrugged, and he heard Claimayne chuckle in the hall.

"And," Ariel went on, "in addition to unclogging toilets, do you do the paperwork, at that apartment building you manage? Pay bills and invoices?"

Scott kept his voice level. "Yes. I leave the checks for the owner to sign."

"Good. It's almost the end of the month, and you get the job of sorting through the bills and writing checks, at least for the utilities and taxes. Nobody's attended to that lately. I was doing it for a while, but—"

"It was a mess," put in Claimayne. "I had to call all the creditors and apologize."

Loudly speaking over his last few words, Ariel said, "*Bring the checks* back here. Claimayne and I are on the account, either of us can sign them."

"And I'll probably have to apologize to everybody again," said Claimayne.

"Back here?" said Scott.

"Aunt Amity has an office behind the Chase bank on Sunset," said Ariel, "till the end of the year, anyway. Next door to a tax accountant. Claimayne, give Scott the key."

Claimayne rolled his wheelchair forward, and his pale face was strained in a frown. "One of us should be with him; we can bring the key then."

"Oh, for—give him the key while you're here, and not . . . you know, off distracted somewhere. He's going to be busy all day on the roof and in the basements anyway."

After a pause, Claimayne smiled at Scott and hitched around in the wheelchair to reach into a pocket of his dressing gown, shaking his head. "She's so *alpha*," he said. He pulled out a bracelet-sized ring with a lot of keys on it, and he selected one and worked it off the coil. "Don't lose it," he said. "I'm only fairly sure we have a spare."

"Right." Scott took out his own key ring and threaded the new key onto it.

"I'd take gloves," said Claimayne thoughtfully, "up on the roof. It wasn't far from the heater that my mother set off her grenade." He smiled. "There might be bits of her still around."

"I wouldn't be surprised," said Scott quietly.

Ariel gave him a sharp look, but only said, "So go get the ladder out."

"Okay," said Scott, "what does the heater do, exactly, that's wrong? And have you got some tools? A socket set, a voltage meter . . ."

THERE WERE TWO BATHROOMS on the second floor, and Madeline had chosen the one with a shower rather than a bathtub. Now, in fresh jeans and a brown corduroy shirt, she sat down on the bed in her room and unsnapped her leather valise.

In among her account book and dozens of blank astrological

charts was the envelope the lawyer had given her, and she slowly tugged it free of the other papers.

Her aunt Amity *had* asked that it be passed on to her.

"I think you did mean me," she whispered, "at least partly, when you typed my name." She held the envelope up to the light from the window and was able dimly to see crisscrossed lines inside. "Am I your way out of the tomb? Your guide?"

Scott and I were the children of your deceased husband's adopted brother, Madeline thought, but after our parents disappeared, you raised us, an eight-year-old girl and a thirteen-year-old boy, as if we were your own children.

Madeline stroked the edge of the envelope.

When Scott set one of the uphill garages on fire with a makeshift rocket launcher, and when I was playing in your car and got it into neutral and helplessly rolled backward onto Vista Del Mar Avenue and collided with a UPS truck, you quickly forgave us. And when Scott and I found the envelope full of spiders and confessed to having looked at one, you didn't yell at us at all. After you put them away, you took us out for ice cream so we'd feel better—though it pained you to walk on your bad foot, even with a cane—and you assured us that we'd feel better soon, and that any nightmares we might have would pass, which they mostly did. Now I wish we had admitted that we tore up the Oneida Inc one and replaced it with one that Scott drew. I'm sorry we kept that from you, when you were so forgiving.

Simply, you loved us.

Madeline stood up and looked down through the open window at the garden in morning sunlight. The sage and rosemary bushes had spread beyond the boundaries that Madeline remembered, obscuring many of the gravel paths, and dandelions and wild anise filled the squares that were once mowed grass. Tall flowering weeds furred the wide top of the Medusa mosaic wall, and the little pool below it had either been filled in or was completely obscured by long crabgrass.

At the crest of the slope, only the red tile roofs of a couple of the garages were visible over the treetops against the blue sky.

Madeline had moved out of Caveat seven years ago, leaving her aunt with Ariel and Claimayne and the solitary writing of her endless unpublishable novels. Scott had left six years before that, to get married, though when that Louise woman left him he hadn't moved back in.

We never came back, Madeline thought. Ariel hated Scott, so he stayed away, and I . . . somehow the whole house, the whole compound of added-on wings and garages and odd little bungalows and endless cellars, seemed like a convalescent home to me—Ariel and Claimayne were both suffering from their spider addictions, and Claimayne was soon confined to his wheelchair because of it . . . and old lame Aunt Amity was generally shut up in her little office, typing, typing . . .

Madeline turned back to the room and looked at the envelope she was still holding.

Scott looked at the spider in *his* envelope, she thought. Aunt Amity made Welcome Home banners for each of us. Ariel threw them away and said, You won't see them, but Scott saw his.

And Scott did not see the Usabo spider again. He said he knew it was there, but it stayed safely inside the folder that had the Medusa head printed on it. He apparently sensed it, powerfully—but no hands opened the folder this time. That was good.

Madeline tucked her finger into the flap of the envelope—Are you there, Aunt Amity? she thought, waiting for me, with your little Welcome Home Madeline banner?—and when she exerted force, the flap simply came open.

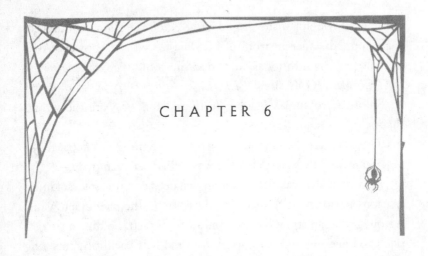

CHAPTER 6

QUICKLY SHE PINCHED OUT the slip of paper and let the envelope fall, and she looked at the ceiling as she unfolded the paper.

Madeline realized that she had passed the point of being able to keep from looking at it, and so she lowered her head and stared at the eight inked lines radiating crookedly out from the hub.

She couldn't move. She could feel the reciprocal reversed images on her retinas because they completed the figure on the paper, quickened it, and the ink pattern and the images inside her eyes were spinning, and curling and bristling with an infinity of ever-finer lines.

As if she were tilting outward on the roof edge of a tall building, Madeline's breath caught in her throat, and her skin seemed to contain only rushing cold air, and she had no name or memories and nothing changed, forever.

Eventually she dimly realized that there was motion, that she was perceiving what as a child she had called the Skyscraper People, the vertical-sided things with no perceptible bases or tops, which seemed somehow to be alive, and she was aware that their apparent height, any height at all here, was just a compensatory trick of her brain. They parted before her—

And she found herself sitting up in the bed with the high side rails, and through a distorting blur she could see a long white rectangle some distance in front of her. She forced a pair of eyes that were not her own to focus, and soon she could recognize letters— WELCOME HOME MADELINE.

She tried to speak, but her teeth and tongue were the wrong shapes.

Then she was among the infinitely tall-seeming geometrical figures again, and they parted as she was pulled between them—

And now she was sitting on an ornately embroidered sofa in a spacious parlor with framed tinted prints on the pale green walls. A young woman stood by the window to her left, holding a curtain aside and peering out, her narrow face and hair backlit by morning sunlight.

Madeline felt the remembered subsonic roar—it rippled her view of the room, and she shivered with a current that almost made her feel that she could leap right out of this unfamiliar house. *Usabo is nearby,* she thought. *Why did I do this?*

"Natacha," the woman said without looking away from the street, "he won't let you leave him."

Madeline choked, for she had tried to inhale just as her mouth began to speak. "He doesn't need me, Fridi," she found herself saying. "He's got you. Hell, he's got lots of girls." She realized that the odd thumping sensation in her palms was her fingers snapping. "Do you see my taxi?"

The woman turned to look at her. "I don't see it. He might let *you* go, but he won't let you take *that* away." She nodded toward the knees of the body Madeline was occupying, and Madeline found herself looking down.

In her lap was the brown folder with the Medusa head imprinted in gold on the cover; the remembered red wax seal over the ribbon held it closed. Her hands were unfamiliar, with long tapering fingers and painted nails, and a silver chain bracelet was draped around her right wrist.

"It's mine," came the voice out of her mouth. "And I'll be gone, where he can't find me, or it—long before he gets home from his hunting trip with DeMille."

"Oh, Jesus!" exclaimed the woman, stepping quickly back from the window—and a moment later Madeline heard boots thumping on a porch beyond the front door, and then the door was kicked inward.

Madeline found her viewpoint rising as she faced the man who stood silhouetted in the doorway. She could see that he was curly haired and broad shouldered, and the object in his right hand was a long shotgun.

"You leave me, Fridi?" he shouted at the woman by the window, his voice seeming to shake the walls of the parlor. Madeline could see suitcases out there on the porch by his feet.

And then her voice was saying, "*I'm* leaving you, Kosloff." Beyond the man, she saw an antique checkered taxi slow to a stop at the curb. "Get out of my way."

"Damn," the man shouted, pointing at her hand, "you not leave with the Beardsley!" Madeline could feel the rough texture of the Medusa folder against her fingers. Outside, the taxi's horn honked.

"I will," she said, and moved to step past him toward the door and the sunlight outside—

—and the shotgun barrel came up and fired, and the deafening explosion knocked her off her feet. Her ears were ringing and all she could see was the afterimage of the muzzle flash, but she rolled into a crouch on the carpet and ran away from him, toward a hallway.

Another stunning boom sounded behind her, and a fist-sized patch of the wall ahead of her burst into dust and stinging fragments. She gripped a door frame and swung around it into a bedroom— the window ahead of her was open, and as two more blasts shook the house, she crossed the room in three awkward strides and dove through the window without touching the frame.

She tumbled through the green leaves and pink flowers of an oleander bush. As she rolled over in the grass, she saw that her skirt was dark and gleaming with blood, and a pain like hot coals pressing into her thigh finally caught her attention. The first blast of shot had not entirely missed her.

Limping now and sobbing through clenched teeth, she flailed across the lawn to the old taxi and wrenched open the rear door.

"Go," she said shrilly as she threw herself in across the seat, and the driver stepped on the accelerator.

"Damn, lady," he said, exhaling, "that guy shoot you?"

"Get me to a hospital," she said, clutching her thigh with both hands above the tangle of bloody shredded linen. The headwind blew the door closed. Her face was sweaty and cold. Madeline was aware that the just-inaudible roar and vibration were gone, and the woman seemed to notice the absence too—she glanced back, and whispered, "He's got it now, damn him."

"Okay," said the driver, nodding rapidly, "okay. Blood on my cushions, you can't help it, okay."

He drove fast past boxy black cars parked under tall palm trees, then steered right, onto a bigger street. Madeline wondered frantically when this hallucination, or vision, would end, and she listened to the woman whispering, "Damn spider didn't work, here I am still, damn spider didn't work . . ."

Tears were mingling with the sweat on her face. Her mouth said, "Where—are we going?"

"Hollywood-Leland Hospital," the driver said tensely, staring out through the windshield as he swerved around cars that looked to Madeline like Victorian cabinets, "Sunset and Vine."

Madeline's view shifted to the cab's sagging fabric headliner as a low moan shook her throat—was the woman dying?—and Madeline managed to impose her will on the relaxed vocal cords, and speak. "It partly worked," she said. "I'm with you."

The body shivered. "Are you me?" came the woman's voice.

Madeline waited until the woman's throat relaxed again, and she was able to exhale and form the words, "No, I'm Madeline."

A choked laugh preempted anything further she might have said. "Madeline," said the woman's voice, "hold my hand, would you?" The view swept down to the woman's hands gripping her thigh. "Well, we can't let go. Hold my thumb."

The blood-gleaming thumb of the right hand lifted away from the soggy linen, and Madeline found that she could move the left one; she curled it around the other, and then both thumbs were clamped down again.

"Stay with me," said the woman breathlessly.

The woman's throat was too tense now for Madeline to reply through it, but she managed to nod the head slightly.

The eyes closed, and Madeline was aware only of the shaking and jogging of the taxi and the hot throbbing in her leg until someone was lifting her out and laying her on a moving surface, and soon a pinprick in her arm brought welcome oblivion.

WHEN MADELINE BECAME AWARE of herself again, she was lying facedown on a hard surface. She tried to get up, but her arms wouldn't support her, and she lay panting in dimness, drooling onto what she could feel was a wood floor. In front of her was an array of different shades of dark brown, divided into rectangles narrower at one end; she crawled forward, and one of the rectangles expanded. She reached a hand toward it and realized that the shifting pale shape that intruded into her view was her own hand, and when it stopped moving, it was because her fingertips felt unyielding polished wood.

Her perspective largely came back then, and she saw that she was in the upstairs hall at Caveat, touching the door that had been salvaged from the Garden of Allah. *When is a door not a door?*

Her tongue and the hinges of her jaw ached, and it occurred to her that it was because two other bodies had just briefly overlapped with hers—Aunt Amity's and then the Natacha woman's.

Madeline drew her legs up and winced; her left thigh throbbed with an ache that seemed to go all the way down to the bone. She prodded her jeans, but the fabric was dry and the flesh of her leg felt springy and intact, and she exhaled in relief.

Carefully she turned her head to look up and down the row of unopenable doors. South was more or less in front of her, and what she had seen in the spider vision had been somewhere a bit west of that, and not far away; close enough that a hospital on Sunset and Vine was apparently the nearest one. She was sure that she could find the house where Natacha had been shot . . . if it was still there. The cars had looked like models from the 1920s.

She was panting, and she made herself relax and take deep, slow breaths. I'm back in 2015, she told herself. I'm Madeline Alice Madden, and I'm at Caveat.

With the doorknob to brace herself on, she managed to get to her feet, and she limped back to her room to call her client and cancel their astrological appointment for today.

THE ONLY PATCH OF pavement Scott trusted to foot the aluminum ladder on was around back, west of his and Madeline's rooms.

He slung the leather tool bag over his shoulder and started climbing carefully; when fully extended, the ladder had a tendency to flex, momentarily lifting its top rails from the roof edge above, and so he moved slowly. Aunt Amity is lucky she didn't fall off this damn thing and break her neck, he thought. Well—she did make it alive onto the roof, anyway.

The breeze from over the top of the hill was cold on his back, but he was sweating and promising himself that he would find a better way down from the roof—several rooms and a garage had been added onto the building over on the east side, and he hoped to be able to find a low roof he could simply drop from, onto soft dirt.

Suddenly the breeze at his back was warm, even hot, and he inadvertently shook the ladder as he whipped his head around—

—and then he just clung to the ladder and stared.

The view out across the garden was divided on a wobbly diagonal, and the upper section showed bright sunlight on trees and bushes greener and more luxuriant than they had been when he had carried the ladder over here, while in the lower section, which was higher on the left side, he saw flickering puddles and leaves shaking with rain in dim light.

The two views were separated by a slanted, blurry gray line, and as he watched, it thickened like a peculiarly undispersing fog erupting from a crack across the landscape; he gripped the ladder rails tightly as the gray expanded to fill his vision.

A loud crack twitched the air and shook the building, and then in an instant the gray was gone, and the garden lay spread out in its ordinary winter disorder under the chilly blue sky.

His head still turned to look over his shoulder, Scott stared out across the slope and for nearly a full minute didn't let himself blink, for fear the normal landscape might fracture away again.

At last he relaxed, and after a few deep breaths even resumed climbing the ladder. It was an aftershock, he told himself, a residual flash of anachronism from the spider I looked at yesterday. Maybe spider users experience this sort of thing all the time. He managed a frail smile. I should ask Claimayne.

There had been some sort of sharp explosion at the end of the hallucination—had that been close thunder echoing out of the rainy-garden half of the vision?—or had it been the heater on the roof blowing up because Claimayne was adjusting the thermostat downstairs?

Up at the roof edge at last, Scott crawled out across the flat tar-paper, walking on the palms of his hands, until the tool bag bumped over the low coping and his feet lifted from the next-to-last ladder rung, and then he got up no higher than a crouch.

The weathered four-foot-square aluminum box that must be the heater stood on flat two-by-four sections several yards in front of him, just this side of the slanted shingle roof that covered the front half of the building. Evidently this northern half of the structure had been added on at some point and been provided only with a flat tarpaper roof. No wonder the ceilings below it leaked. Fresh black tarpaper sheets held down by cinder blocks were spread out a few yards to his left, presumably where Aunt Amity had detonated her grenade.

He looked away from it and stood up cautiously, and before stepping toward the box he turned to glance back down over the roof edge at the garden. Off to the right, past the Medusa mosaic wall and out in the east yard where a couple of abandoned bungalows sat in sagging disrepair, he saw the lengthening shadow of a cellar door being lifted. He remembered it—it didn't sit flat on the ground, but was uptilted about ten degrees, like the storm-cellar door in *The Wizard of Oz*.

Two children climbed up out of the cellar; from this distance he could see only that they were a girl and a taller boy, both in jeans and T-shirts. He thought of calling out to them, but their shadows didn't seem to fall in exactly the same direction as the shadows of trees that were closer, and instead he just watched as they scampered away south, toward the poolhouse and out of his sight.

He frowned and turned away, and now his attention was on avoiding any pieces of his aunt that might still be scattered across the roof. He saw only a couple of scraps of lacy yellow cloth, but those might have been from anything, and he walked across to the aluminum box.

One side of it was deeply dented, and the service panel lay a few feet away, bent and twisted; but it still had a little puddle of rainwater on it—at least there hadn't been an explosion up here lately.

Scott pulled the tool bag off over his head and knelt by the now-open side of the furnace housing. Inside, a few inches above the dusty aluminum floor, four iron mixing tubes hung behind the manifold pipe, and their air shutters were not only open but appeared to be rusted that way. The furnace was obviously old—a sooty thermocouple wire was bent over the nozzle of a pilot light; at the apartment building he managed, all the furnaces had flame sensors and ignition coils instead.

Claimayne had said the fan came on, but no heat issued from the vents.

The gas shutoff valve was on the outside of the housing, but Scott left it in the on position and pulled a yellow Bic lighter out of his pocket. He turned the pilot light knob, then waved a flame over the nozzle while he pushed the reset button, and a thumb-sized blue flame sprang up, enveloping the end of the thermocouple wire. Scott held the reset button down for fifteen seconds, then let it up. The pilot light wavered and went out. Apparently the thermocouple was no longer producing voltage to hold the interior gas valve open, whether because Aunt Amity's grenade had fractured it or because of plain age.

It would be easy enough to buy a new thermocouple. He reached around the outside of the housing and twisted the handle of the gas valve to the crosswise off position; but it was rattling loose in its housing, probably a result of the grenade concussion. Really, Scott thought, they should replace the whole unit.

He straightened up and looked north. From up here on the roof he could see over the row of garages on the ridge to the tree-tops above the houses that were farther up in the hills, and above them, clear in the morning air despite the distance, the white letters of the Hollywood sign. He took a step toward the roof edge and looked down, and he saw someone now standing in the garden by the Medusa mosaic wall. Squinting against the sun and the rooftop breeze, he saw that it was Madeline.

He opened his mouth to shout to her and ask her to help him find a better way down from the roof, but he glanced warily up at the sky first; when he looked down at the garden again, she was no longer visible—evidently she had walked around to the far side of the wall. He crouched, bracing himself with one hand on the roof coping, and waited for her to reappear.

When a full minute had gone by without her stepping out from behind the wall, he sighed, fetched the tool bag, and got up to go look around for another way down from the roof.

HAVING CALLED HER CLIENT and canceled their appointment, Madeline had gone downstairs and stepped out through the back kitchen door and begun walking at a slow pace along one of the gravel paths, sometimes having to duck under a thorny mesquite branch or step wide around shaggy Jerusalem sage.

The aches in her joints and face had seemed to be loosened by the crisp morning sunlight, and she had moved steadily east along the overgrown paths toward the sun until she was in the shadow of the Medusa wall.

The bathtub-sized pool below the wall had indeed been filled in, or removed altogether—if she hadn't remembered splashing in it as a child, she wouldn't have known a pool had ever been there. She looked up at the surface of the wall above the pool—a new crack, fuzzy with green weeds, ran down one side of it, and rain and sun had popped many of the mosaic stones out, but the Medusa face was still intact at the center.

The face was no more than six inches across and made of only twelve flat stones, black and white—two black rectangles for the eyes, a smaller one for the mouth, white triangles for the cheeks and a fan of them for the forehead—but the tendrils of the snaky hair spiraled out in all directions across the rest of the wall, in a variety of shades of purple against a gold background. Madeline remembered how they seemed to glow, even to pulse, in the coppery light of late October afternoons.

And in fact their colors were faintly rippling now, as if the stones of them were dark opals; and Madeline's shadow dimmed the glow of a patch of them in front of her.

She turned around, and it wasn't morning anymore—the sun

hung in remote wings of gold and topaz clouds in the west, just above the seashell-studded wall that divided the garden from the croquet court. The sunlight was horizontal—what Aunt Amity had called "Griffith's magic hour," because the director D. W. Griffith had believed faces were best photographed in that fleeting evening light.

At her left, the house was farther away than it had been only a few moments ago, and she didn't recognize the windows and doors. One of the upstairs windows glowed, and Madeline could hear someone playing a slow passage from *Scheherazade* on a violin— and she realized that no other sounds intruded on it. She was belatedly aware that there had always been a faint background hum, even here, a very weak infusion of the mingled noises of automobiles and sirens and helicopters and probably even distant voices, and that it was now absent. And no faintest hint of exhaust fumes tainted the jasmine-scented breeze.

The Medusa mosaic had no crack across it, and none of the stones were missing.

Madeline looked away from the Medusa's face—and moved around the north end of the mosaic wall, toward the shadowed path by the east side of the house—for she could feel an almost unbearable happiness welling up inside her, and she didn't want to put that stark little black-and-white face into this experience, whatever it was.

There were none of the remembered structures added on to the east side of the house now, and so she strode quickly across the neatly mowed grass—all her aches and weariness were gone—and soon rounded the corner to the front of the house, and then she paused, breathing deeply. The marble-railed porch was the same one she remembered, but the slope below her was visibly terraced now, not a jungle, and ranks of red and white roses waved in the shadows.

And below, beyond the slope, was Hollywood, lit only by the twilight glow in the sky. No, yellow lights shone here and there in the scattered shapes of houses, but there were no lights on the freeway. In fact of course the freeway was gone, or rather not built yet, and there was only a view of distant muted lights in the space where the Capitol Records building would one day stand.

The steps that led down to the parking lot were swept, and no branches or vines hung over them. The apartment building no longer stood down there to the left, and the parking lot was half the size she remembered, and unpaved.

Two girls in dresses were hurrying up Vista Del Mar, and Madeline could clearly hear their voices. One was worried that they had left the water running in Uncle Cecil's swimming pool, and the other hoped it hadn't overflowed and flooded the tennis court.

Madeline began stepping down the cement stairs, and so quiet was the evening that the girls heard her and stopped to look up the slope. Madeline smiled and waved . . .

But the light brightened abruptly, and a sound like distant surf drowned the faint rustling of the leaves. The black parking lot gleamed in bright sunlight below, and the apartment building reared its unlovely stuccoed walls down there to her left.

She yelled "Wait!" in the hope that the connection to the past might not quite have ceased; and then she sat down on the steps, hidden from the street and the house by the overhanging trees, and cried.

A FIRE ESCAPE CLUNG like scaffolding to the east side of the house, and Scott had at last decided it was the best way down from the roof. He held the tool bag out over the edge and let it drop to the roof of the garage two stories below.

He was able to hang from the roof edge and drop three feet to the iron-grille platform outside the third-floor windows, and he exhaled in relief when the grille under his shoes didn't give way. He started down the rusty ladder to the next platform, carefully placing his feet squarely on the rungs and gripping the cold rails.

The next ladder ended on the flat roof of the long-unused garage that had been added on to this end of the house. The leafy branches of a tall mesquite tree shaded the north side of the roof, and he considered climbing down it to the ground; but the mesquite had thorns, and he recalled that a trapdoor on the roof gave access to a wooden ladder that was bolted to the interior garage wall.

When he was able to step away from the ladder and stand up on the sagging garage roof, he noticed a narrow metal rod and a tangle of wires a few yards away on the tarpaper. He carefully shuffled out across the roof to it, and he knew it was the remains of an umbrella only because he recognized the wooden handle—the beak was broken off now, but the rest of the carved duck's head was familiar from his childhood. This had been his aunt's favorite umbrella, cherished because it had allegedly once belonged to the silent-movie star Clara Bow. A few scraps of the purple cloth he remembered still clung to the bent ribs, as yet unfaded.

He stepped back and gingerly craned his neck to look back up at the top edge of the third story, a stained and flaking ridge against the bright blue sky. Had she carried her precious umbrella up there, along with the grenade? He tried to remember if it had rained last Wednesday; had she sat up there for a while, looking out across the garden from under the umbrella?

His aunt had always said that Madeline was to get the Clara Bow umbrella one day, and Scott considered bringing it down; but he couldn't imagine Madeline being glad to have it now.

He picked his way back to the house side of the garage roof, retrieving the tool bag, and crouched to pry up the old tarpaper-covered trapdoor. When it came creaking up, he pushed it over the other way and lowered it to the roof, and then he peered down into the square hole.

The garage below wasn't completely dark, and he remembered that there were three windows in the broad door at the far end. He sighed and sat down on the edge and found the rungs with his feet.

The wooden ladder held up under his weight, and when he was

standing in the shadows on the cement floor, he looked up at the square of blue sky in the garage roof and thought he should some-how have shut the trapdoor. But from the brown-streaked walls and the sour mildewy smell he concluded that the roof leaked anyway, and to hell with it.

Against one wall leaned a tinfoil-paneled plywood spaceship as big as an SUV, constructed for some 1950s science fiction movie, and in the dimness Scott could see the three foam-rubber space-alien manikins leaning against it, their big bald heads a bit saggier than they used to be. Madeline had never wanted to explore in here, and even teenaged Claimayne had found the aliens obscurely troubling. "They always look to me like they want to get a life," he had told Scott once, "by force if necessary."

Shoved up against the opposite wall was a twenty-foot-long model of the Los Angeles skyline with metal disks still suspended on cobweb-draped wires above it to represent flying saucers.

The cement floor in between was littered with leaves and sagging cardboard boxes, and Scott kept his hands out in front of him in the dimness as he made his way between old stoves and stacks of chil-dren's bicycles toward the three windows at the east end.

The big garage door would certainly not swing up anymore, and the ordinary door set into it was locked; but when he kicked it, the bolt tore out of the frame and the door swung outward, letting in fresh air and a dazzling glare of daylight on weedy pavement, and then the hinges pulled free and the door toppled over onto the drive-way with a clatter that echoed back from the cypresses at the east end of the estate.

Scott stepped hesitantly out onto the cracked old driveway. It ran north to connect with the garage road, and in the other direction sloped down past the vacant apartment building to a vine-hung and long unused gate that faced directly onto Vista Del Mar. He shoved his hands in his pockets and began trudging around the north side of the house, toward the garden and the door to the main house cellars.

ARIEL PUSHED OPEN THE front door under the broken Caveat lintel and glared up the hall and into the dining room.

"Claimayne!" she called. There was no answer, so she quickly tapped up the wooden stairs to the second floor and hurried down the hall, away from Scott's and Madeline's rooms to Claimayne's door, and knocked on it.

"Oh, go away," came her cousin's weak voice.

Ariel tried the knob—the door was unlocked, and she opened it and stepped into the room. In the sudden dimness she peered around at the faintly gleaming glazed ceramic pigs and rats and the gilded Buddhas to be sure where the walls and low tables were, and then she focused on the recumbent form of her cousin sprawled across the four-poster bed. His wheelchair stood in front of the bedside table.

The smell of incense imperfectly covered the aggressive menthol-and-eucalyptus tang of Bengay. One streak of daylight slanted in between the heavy velvet curtains, and for a moment she saw her own taut face reflected in one of the dozen mirrors on the walls.

"Later, later," whispered Claimayne.

"Now," she said, crossing the carpet to stand beside the foot of the bed. She could feel the floor sagging under her feet and hoped it wasn't about to give way. "I just walked outside."

"Good. Do it again."

"Claimayne, what's *happening* around here? Is it Scott and Madeline? I was going out to get in my car, and then all at once it was evening, and the car was gone and there was some kind of old Laurel and Hardy car there instead! And I had *not* looked at a spider! And—"

She was interrupted by a deep boom that shook the house and momentarily made the floor springy. The shellacked mahogany pillars of Claimayne's bed were carved coiled dragons, and they seemed to sway.

Ariel tried to sustain her anger, but her heart was thumping and she couldn't take a deep breath. "And what is *that*? That's the second time in ten minutes." She paused, but no further explosions followed, and the floor held steady.

Claimayne sighed and rolled over to sit up against a big embroidered cushion, his gold DNA pendant under his chin now. He yawned and pulled the pendant down onto his chest and reached weakly for a glass on the bedside table. "Dip into the wine thy little red lips, Salomé, that I may drain the cup!"

Ariel leaned across the wheelchair and picked up the glass and put it into his shaking hand. "It's already near empty; finish it yourself."

He did, though he spilled some drops onto his dressing gown lapel, and then handed the glass back to her.

"That explosion," he said, "you've heard it before. It's my mother, blowing herself up on the roof."

Ariel momentarily hoped Scott had climbed down from the roof; but, "What do you mean?" she asked. "Come on, please—that was a week ago."

"And how long ago do you suppose that 'Laurel and Hardy car' was parked on the side road? All of this is your fault as well as my own. And my mother's. Though I'm the most guilty, I suppose." He tried to hike himself farther up, then just slumped back with a gasp of pain. "Damn. We should host a youth camp, you know? They could put up tents in the garden and out by the bungalows."

"You really are a vicious pig," said Ariel, setting down his wineglass. "You can't get out and leave spiders you've looked at in playgrounds anymore, so you want to . . . get your filthy rejuvenation *here*? I wouldn't let you."

Claimayne waved a pale hand dismissively. "It was just a thought. But I might leave a couple around for our guests. They're appreciably younger than I am."

"I don't think you'd want to soak up any of Scott's vitality. You'd probably get the DTs. But you could probably use a dose of anorexia from Madeline." Ariel looked nervously at the dim ceiling. "*Do you* know what that explosion was? It can't have been . . . what you said."

"You just saw a car from nearly a hundred years ago, and you don't believe you can hear a noise from only a week ago? It was my mother."

Ariel was horrified to realize that she believed him. "Claimayne," she whispered shakily, "this has got to *stop*."

"Actually," drawled Claimayne, "your first guess may have been right—it may be the fault of our guests most of all."

"What, that old car I saw is their fault? Or the grenade going off again on the roof?"

"Both, and more. The dishes and windows—and my vinyl records!—that are breaking in spider-pattern cracks." He opened his eyes wide for a moment. "Do you remember 1992?"

"Some. I was ten years old." She touched her own silver gyroscope pendant.

"I was eighteen. Arthur and Irina had disappeared on New Year's Eve of '91. My mother had apparently lost a collection of spiders in '91, and I think Arthur and Irina stole them from her; then the summer after those two disappeared, my mother got the collection back again. I think she took them from Scott and Madeline, who must have found their parents' hiding place."

Ariel was aware of, and instantly suppressed, an eagerness to know what had become of the collection. You don't do that anymore, she told herself—you don't want to lose yourself, your self, anymore—and these would probably have been dirty ones, ones that somebody else had looked at. I only did freshly printed ones that had no possible flash-aheads or flashbacks connected to them . . . after I knew how they worked, anyway.

"I was a sneaky boy," Claimayne went on with a reminiscent smile. "I snooped and found them . . . but there was one she hid away where even I couldn't find it. They were labeled, and she kept a list— the one I never could find was labeled *Oneida Inc.* In a penciled note she called it her retirement check. I think my mother never looked at it; I think she was saving it for an extremity, but"—he gave a circular wave that took in the whole troubled house, the whole anachronistic compound—"I think Scott and Madeline may very well have looked at it. I remember that they were both very sick, with characteristic symptoms, on the day my mother got the collection back."

In a small voice Ariel asked, "So is it . . . special, that one?"

Claimayne's laugh seemed forced. "One spider to rule them all, one spider to bind them," he said lightly. "And I believe this may be a *detoxified* version of it, of the Medusa, who ordinarily turns her viewers to stone." He had found a handkerchief among the bed-clothes and now dabbed ineffectually at the wine stains on the lapel of his dressing gown. "Not literal stone, you understand—just something like a total nervous-system seizure and death, from helplessly performing a million actions at once."

Ariel frowned and shook her head. "And all this Medusa spider business makes an old car show up in the driveway?"

"Oh, Ariel. What happens—sometimes!—when you look at a spider on Monday and then somebody else looks at it on Friday?" She rolled her eyes impatiently, but he persisted, "Go on, what happens?"

"You overlap with each other for a minute or so. You're in his body on Friday, and he's in yours on Monday. If you're lucky, you can *act,* do stuff, in his body."

"Do you know why?" When Ariel shrugged, he went on, "It's because the spider you both looked at, or which you yourself looked at both times, doesn't see those two times as *two* times. Nor as two places. To the spider, it's one event."

Ariel shuddered, remembering that she had looked at one just yesterday, and in fact had yet to do the "after" by looking at it again two days from now.

"You make it sound as if they're *alive,*" she said.

Claimayne was staring at her. "Amateur!" he said with a smile. "Dilettante! How long were you a steady user? You must have *sometimes* sensed that they're . . . something like alive."

She shook her head, frowning, and whispered, "I don't know."

"We're three-dimensional creatures—four, really, since we extend in the fourth dimension, too, which is time. The spiders exist in a different sort of universe. They're two-dimensional, appearing motionless to us but perpetually spinning in their own frame of reference, and probably entirely unaware of us, even when we spike one into our universe by providing it with a reciprocal image of itself, inverted and reversed, on our retinas."

"And so I see old cars."

"All right," he said gently. "All right. Somebody—was it Woody Allen?—said that time is nature's way of keeping everything from happening at once. Well, you and me, and my mother, and Art and Irina, probably, and even their two bungling *curiosi* children, all of us have so often used the spiders to make separate moments combine, in this house—made an hour of one day also be an hour of a later day—that time is breaking down, here, everything *is* beginning to happen at once. And so 1920 or '50 or '70 leaks into 2015 sometimes, even if no spider is being quickened in either time at that moment."

Ariel nodded dubiously. "Like a cabinet door that's been opened and slammed too many times, and now it swings open all by itself, even when nobody touches the knob."

"If you like. That old car you saw was visible for a minute or so here—I expect it was brand-new when you saw it—and I imagine some residents of this house in the old days were sometimes startled to see a Honda or a Prius parked out there, or to hear a Beatles song echoing out of the house. We've bored so many holes through the timeline of this house and grounds that it's like a load-bearing wall riddled by termites." He smiled. "And I think our foster cousins may be the biggest termites of all."

"Because they looked at that one of your mother's?"

"Exactly. That's the big one, and I think that's the one that's really crumbling our local chronology. That's neat, I must say," he added, and paused to rummage in the bedside table drawer for a minute. "Damn. Do you have a pen? No? Well, remind me of 'crumbling our local chronology,' will you?"

"It's not iambic."

"It'll do as anapest. And I think our cousins, or one of them, will look at the big spider *again*, soon, and that is—has been, will be—the stress that's really fragmented everything here. Everywhen."

"Let's make them leave. I never wanted them here again in the first place. Can't we make them leave?"

"No. Can't violate the terms of my mother's provisional will until it's disallowed. And what would that change? It doesn't have to be one of them that looks at the Medusa spider next time. If it happens in this house, then all this . . . chronological erosion will have been caused no matter who it happens to be that looks at it. And I don't think we'd be *having* these incidents unless *somebody* is going to look at it here."

Claimayne shrugged, and it occurred to Ariel that her cousin's airy detachment was a pose.

"*You* want it," she said. "You want to be the one. Why? Why did your mother save it without looking at it? Retirement check? What the hell *is* it?"

Another boom from the roof rattled the window behind the velvet curtains. Ariel stepped sideways to keep her balance.

Claimayne had winced at the sound, and his pale fists clenched on the bedspread. "There she goes again," he said quietly. "Does it occur to any of you that my mother died last week? And it was only four days ago that we buried her? That was my *mother;* are you sure you're all quite clear on that?"

Ariel bit her lip but made herself go on: "Will it—I'm sorry—will the Medusa spider bring her back?" For a moment she thought of her own parents, bohemian amateur mycologists who had died from eating misidentified *Amanita phalloides* mushrooms in a salad; seven-year-old Ariel and fifteen-year-old Claimayne had been present, but neither one had liked mushrooms.

"Can it," she said, "do that?"

Claimayne laughed now, but not pleasantly. "Bring her *back*. Yes. Me too, ideally. As opposed to intolerable *forward*." He slumped against the cushion and closed his eyes. "I don't think I'm destined to outlive her by very long. So—backward it is, as richly as possible."

"What do you mean? Are you sick?"

He gestured toward his unnaturally smooth face and said, "I'm still full of youth, obviously—ill gotten though it may arguably be. But there have been—chest pains, angina! Shortness of breath, pains in my jaw and arm. Trifles of that nature." He coughed. "And I don't get overlaps from my future anymore. I look at spiders, intending to look at them again when I'm fifty, sixty, seventy—and I get no after-visions at all, not even hallucinations. I've never had a flashback from myself much older than I am right now. You'd think I'd have got through *once*."

Ariel nodded, and then was a little surprised to find that she felt no sorrow or alarm at all at the prospect of Claimayne's death. I should, she told herself. I should be at least as nostalgically saddened as I'd be if . . . oh, if the Medusa mosaic wall were to fall down in the next rain. I grew up with these things, after all, ugly though they may be.

Why don't I mind? she asked herself.

She summoned up a frown and a tone of concern. "But the clogging effect—after a while, and you've definitely been at it for a while, you stop being able to really sense the future body—you get hallucinations instead—"

"Not *always*. You're convinced you really did talk to Scott and Madeline on the day after tomorrow."

"Well, maybe you're going to *quit* soon! I did; no reason you can't. That would explain you not getting any overlaps from yourself in the future."

"Quit. Oh yes, *quit*. And . . . join a monastery, become a vegan, take up philately?" He waved the idea away. "And Ariel, I—I have bad dreams about this house—all jumbled up, so there's no door that leads outside anymore, and my mother's explosion on the roof is constant, like a drumbeat, and, in every room I enter, those old rubber space aliens from the east garage are there again, but in the dream they're . . . people I've overlapped with. Emptied."

"I'm . . . sorry," was all Ariel could think of to say, and she tried to mean it.

He rolled over on his side, facing the picture-decked wall. "Leave me alone," he said hoarsely, "can't you?"

Ariel stood for a moment, staring helplessly around at the indistinct Chinatown clutter on the shelves and walls, then turned and hurried across the carpet to the door.

Squinting in the relative brightness of the hall, she hurried to her own room, entered and closed the door behind her, then pulled out the bottom drawer of her dresser, pushing aside a stack of sweaters as she lifted out a rubber-banded bundle of twenty-dollar bills. She tucked it into the left pocket of her jeans and tapped the right pocket to make sure she had her keys.

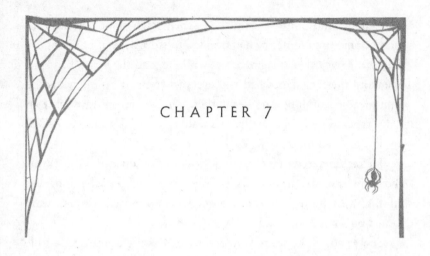

CHAPTER 7

SCOTT REMEMBERED HAPPY CHILDHOOD explorations in the darkness among the towers of mismatched bricks and cinder blocks and sections of vertical four-by-four lumber in the basement under the main house, but as his flashlight illuminated them one by one now, he was chilled by the realization that these makeshift supports under the floor joists were all that were keeping the rooms above from falling into the cellar. His flashlight beam picked out the steel cylinders of at least a couple of industrial screw jacks in the receding dark gallery, but even these were footed on crumbling bricks or stacks of wood or, in one case, a truck wheel-rim. Attempting to give their levers even a slight tightening twist might just burst the junk they were standing on.

A new thermocouple for the roof, he thought nervously, and a truckload of heavy-duty screw jacks and sturdy footings. The bathrooms in the northeast corner of the building on each of the three floors were tile over cement and must weigh several tons altogether.

The house creaked steadily over him, like, he thought, a gallows with a big body hung from it swinging in the wind on a moonless night.

He kept the flashlight beam on the dirt floor as he stepped away from the patch of sunlight by the opened cellar door behind him, for since his time someone had decided to store a lot of boxes of old *National Geographic* magazines down here, and the boxes had split open and the magazines had slid everywhere; and by the walls the light gleamed on long puddles, either from the recent rain or from leaky pipes. The cool draft from ahead was spiced with the reek of mildew and old mud.

He remembered that the dirt floor sloped down after a few yards, and so he was careful not to slip. When it leveled out, the floor was mud, and he hoped the screw jacks—or improvised towers—were footed on something solid.

Scott paused, hopelessly swinging the flashlight beam from side to side as he peered into the remote dark expanse. He recalled areas where one had to crawl through low brick arches, and he didn't see any use in threading his way through them today, just to verify that the joist supports were no good.

Just as he was about to retrace his steps, he heard a scuffling from the darkness ahead, and a scared voice that he recognized as Madeline's cried, "I'm here, I'm here!"

He pointed the flashlight in the direction her voice had seemed to come from and soon picked out her sneakers poking out from behind a brick column.

"Maddy, it's me, Scott." He shuffled forward through the mud. "How did you get—"

"Scott!" Now he could see her pale, wide-eyed face above the shoes. She moved her head as if to look past him.

Scott made his way to the column she was crouching behind, and when he shined the light around, he recognized this corner of this basement. The crayon drawings of bats and moons that little Madeline had taped to the brick wall here had long since fallen down and moldered away, but the gold-painted four-armed lug wrench still stood upright in a square of lumpy cement near the brick wall. He tried to remember the words someone had incised into the cement.

"Who were you thinking it would be?" he asked. "Ariel? Claimayne?"

Madeline turned her head away from the light and touched the lug wrench. "Oh," she said, "somebody else—somebody I sort of met in this house once. Anything seems to be possible." She went on quickly, "But another person was dragging something, this way, and I didn't want to meet whoever *that* was."

Scott nervously turned around to sweep the darkness with the flashlight beam, but he saw only wet brick and upright four-by-fours and mud. He couldn't hear anything except Madeline's breathing and his own.

He sighed and turned the light back into the alcove. Madeline gave him a blinking, twitchy smile and stood up carefully, bracing herself against the wall. "I'm glad you're here."

Even though I'm not who you were expecting, thought Scott— the person you sort of met in this house once.

"Maddy," he said, "who do you mean—"

"It was just a dream I had once, never mind."

Scott nodded doubtfully. "How did you get down here?" Before he'd been able to open the cellar door, he'd had to brush a lot of dirt and leaves off it.

"I crawled in through a basement window beside the porch. I was afraid the freeway was getting closer. Fast. Can you *bear* it?"

He gathered that she meant, *Can you believe it?* "Actually I wouldn't be surprised, today." He turned the flashlight's beam onto the lug wrench.

"And I always did feel safe beside the scare-bat," she added, brushing her trembling fingers across the top socket of the thing. Scott could read the words pressed into the cement at the foot of it: *Hic iacent curiosi.*

He turned the flashlight beam onto the floor behind him, and his sister limped forward onto the illuminated patch of mud. He swung the light ahead of her, and she painstakingly made her way along the path it traced out while he followed. On the ascending dirt slope he supported her with his arm, though when they reached the level floor above she was able to walk more steadily to the daylight below the open cellar door at the east end. She made hard, gasping work of climbing the ladder.

At last they stood up on the grass in the sunlight. Madeline was panting, and her hands and the knees of her jeans were black with mud.

"You don't seem to be in the best shape for scrambling around in cellars," Scott said.

Madeline frowned at him. "I'm in fine shape," she said defensively. "I'm just sick. If I didn't stay fit, I wouldn't be able to climb Mount McKinley."

"You climbed Mount McKinley?"

She shook her head.

"You're planning to?"

"No, but I'm able to." She waved the topic aside. "Thanks for getting me out of there. I don't think I ever could have got out on my own. Ever."

"Madeline," he said, haltingly, "this morning when I was climbing onto the roof—"

She raised a hand. "Don't tell me, yet, okay? And don't ask me about what happened to me today, or why I'm sick. We can talk about it later, when it's less . . . recent."

"Like after the sun goes down? You're . . . still sure you want to stay here? You know I think it's a mistake."

"I think I am sure, in spite of everything. Else. So far." She gave him a haunted smile. "You really *don't* have to stay, on my account."

"I really *do*, you know," he said sharply.

She nodded seriously. "I guess big brothers have to do that sort of thing."

ARIEL PEERED OUT PAST the half-opened kitchen door, but her black Kia Optima sedan just stood unremarkably in the driveway a dozen feet away, its windshield gleaming in the noon sun. The shadow under it didn't waver, and no anachronistic shapes seemed imminent. Beyond the car the western lawn stretched a hundred yards to the palm trees by the garage road, and above them she could see the white line of a jet trail in the cobalt blue sky. The sounds were just the usual whisper of wind in the palm fronds and the creaking of the house.

It looks like solid 2015, she thought, and she stepped cautiously out of the shadows and pulled a pair of sunglasses out of her purse and put them on.

She walked around to the driver's side, still limping a little, and when she had climbed in and pulled the door closed she threw her purse onto the passenger seat, then tugged an iPad out from under the seat and turned it on. Tapping into a deep-web server, she entered a web address with a .dark suffix. The familiar picture came up—a movie poster for the Ingmar Bergman movie *Through a Glass Darkly*—and in two blanks at the top of the screen she entered a password and her zip code, then tapped the sign-on icon.

A map of the Hollywood area came up, with a pulsing red dot on Santa Monica Boulevard just a block or two east of Las Palmas. She had no particular recollection of that neighborhood but started the car and backed down the driveway till it joined the branch driveway that led up the hill to the ridge garages and Gower Street beyond; from long practice she was able to back and fill until the car was aimed downhill, and she coasted between the tall, shaggy palm trees down to Vista Del Mar.

One spider to rule them all? she thought, remembering Claimayne's words. What could that mean—*containing* them all? Like a master key that opens all the doors? The car's windows were rolled up and the confined air was hot and smelled faintly of the anchovy pizza Claimayne had demanded two days ago, but Ariel was shivering. And the rest of Aunt Amity's stash of spiders, she thought—those would probably be very dirty, lots of people would have looked at them already, you'd be linking with all those reciprocating retinas, overlapping all those physical lives, and they'd be merging with you, even sharing your bloodstream—young losers, sick old folks, drunks—it exhausted you last night even to merge with your own healthy three-day-future self!

You don't want it.

She turned right on Franklin and then south on Argyle in the momentary shade under the 101 Freeway overpass, and then she was out in the sun again, driving past the high windowless back wall of the Pantages Theatre and through the wide Hollywood Boulevard intersection. On her left now was a big parking lot and on her right the stark white Stalinist-looking east face of the new W Hotel, all of it throwing needles of noon glare into her eyes even through the polarized lenses of the sunglasses.

Why did he have to come back? Why did Aunt Amity *want* him to? He left us all.

Ariel felt her face redden now as she remembered the note she had written to Scott thirteen years ago, when she had been twenty and he had been twenty-three. After he had moved out, intending to marry that Louise woman, she had found the note in the bag of trash he had left in his room, with *idiot teenager!* scrawled across her signature. I was *twenty,* she thought now, not a teenager!

And I'm thirty-three now and stuck living in declining circumstances at Caveat with my demented wheelchair-bound cousin—what's the way out of that?

What's the way out for Scott? Or even Madeline? Back to their shabby south-of-Sunset lives?

According to Claimayne, Scott and Madeline saw this big spider when they were kids. And look at them now. I wonder if it was worth it.

You can't know whether it was or not. Not yet, anyway.

Argyle ended at Sunset in front of the blue pillars of the Nickel-odeon On Sunset studio, and she turned right.

You don't want it, she told herself again.

She peered ahead through the glittering windshield. If she turned right instead of left at Las Palmas, she'd pass Miceli's, the Italian restaurant Scott had several times taken her to, long ago. Seeing the brick wall and the green awning of the place would bring back memories. You don't want that either, she thought. Damn it, you don't.

What she most wanted, she conceded to herself dejectedly, was a clean, fresh-printed spider, and just that infinite moment of separation from everything, especially from consciousness, from her self.

But she turned left on Las Palmas, and then left again at Santa Monica Boulevard, and she rolled down the window and took deep breaths of the hot pavement-scented breeze.

The sidewalks along this stretch of Santa Monica were empty except for a half-dozen men lined up at a white taco truck down the street; the north side appeared to be builders' supply lots and the south side was little anonymous office buildings . . . but she saw a pale green light in the dusty window of a shop on her right, and she swerved in to the curb. The sign above the shop said BOTANICA, which was plausible cover; the Hispanic botanicas all dealt in semimagical herbs and oils and candles, and in any case this one probably hadn't been in business more than a week or so and might not be here tomorrow. The spiderbit shops had to move around a lot. Spiderbits was the slang term for people who had quit or were trying to.

Ariel got out of the car and dropped two quarters into the parking meter, then stepped across the sidewalk and pushed open the shop's door. Bells attached to the frame jingled.

The air was cool inside and smelled of camphor and mint; Ariel took off her sunglasses and blinked around at the plastic bottles and aerosol spray cans and shrink-wrapped coyote skulls that crowded the shelves and tables, and she jumped when a plastic angel by her knee began bobbing and squeaking.

"Proximity," said a man behind a long counter at the far side of the shop. "You got near it."

"Magic?" asked Ariel dryly.

"Motion sensor. Rechargeable battery." He took off a pair of glasses, then relaxed and laid them on the counter. "Oh, hi—haven't seen you in a while."

She peered at the bald young man and nodded. "You were running a video arcade by the chicken and waffles place on Gower." She walked forward, careful not to jostle any of the bottles of money-attracting or spell-repelling oils; the man's name, she recalled, was Harry, or at least that's what one called him, and he was always dressed in a gray sweat-shirt, possibly always the same one. The droopy mustache was new.

"Car stereo shop next, I think," he said.

She nodded, sure that whatever his next green-light shop would be, it would not be a car stereo shop. Spiderbit outlets drew nasty sorts of predators, and locations of the green-light shops were always secret and temporary.

"I need some more stuff," she said.

"I've got it all—distorting veils, stick-on windshield ridges, high-octane tarantella CDs . . . Mundane stuff too, while you're here—plexiglass to replace your glass windows, tapestries in case of wall cracks, Bakelite dishes, plaster for rounding off multi-angle corners—"

"No MP3?"

He shook his head. "Try downloading one of the 18/8-time tar-antella numbers and the bad guys track your credit card, no matter how good the site's security encryption is. And it always turns out to be an ordinary three-quarter time tarantella anyway."

Ariel shook her head. "The tarantella music would upset my cousin. He still uses."

The bells on the street-side door jingled then, and Ariel looked around quickly; a short man in horn-rimmed glasses had come into the shop, but, seeing another customer already there, he turned around and walked out, pulling the door closed behind him.

Harry had stepped back from the counter and quickly put the glasses back on. His eyes appeared to be just swirls now behind the bull's-eye lenses.

He didn't take them off when he looked back at Ariel. "I may close early. You said your cousin still uses?"

"Yes, but I've been clean—"

"You live with him? Does he know you came here today? Does he know where this *is*?"

"No—I didn't know it myself till I got in the car and got on the website. And he's in a wheelchair and never leaves the house and he never has contact with anybody. He just lives for his *Medusa*, using the same old ones over and over."

"Huh." Harry relaxed and slowly took off the glasses. "He calls it Medusa? That's a very old term for it."

Ariel shrugged. "He learned about it from his mother, I think." She shivered and gripped her purse more tightly. "And then I learned about it from him."

Harry stepped around from behind the counter and walked up to where she stood. "The term is a lot older than his mother, kid. Have you heard of *La Mano Negra*?"

"Black Hand. Sure. Italian extortionists in Chicago, wasn't it?"

"That was a different crowd." Harry's breath smelled of Altoid mints. "*La Mano Negra* was a secret society in Andalucia, in Spain— the police called them anarchists, but all the legitimate anarchist groups—"

Ariel gave him a faint, quizzical smile. "I like the idea of legitimate anarchist groups." She reached to the side and touched a can of High John the Conqueror good luck spray.

Harry shook his head, dismissing the interruption. "Well, they all said they had nothing to do with any *Mano Negra*, and in fact the group that the police rounded up in 1884 and executed— and burned all their papers, unread—were more like a religious order."

"Uh . . . Christian?" She picked up the can and pretended to read the directions.

"Hardly. Their secret symbol was a black hand . . . with eight fingers. Their public symbol was a stylized Medusa head."

"With eight snakes growing out of her head," guessed Ariel, thinking of the Medusa wall in the garden. Harry nodded. "Eighteen eighty-four," she went on. "I got the idea the spider patterns were invented in the 1920s."

"Hell, *La Mano Negra* was centuries old by the time the Spanish police wiped them out; and they weren't the oldest branch, though they were the biggest." He waved as if to indicate how old some of them were, and his hand brushed Ariel's shoulder. "Yeah, and spiders were a sort of secret fad with rich movie folks in the '20s, but those designs seemed to be more from India."

Ariel was impatient to get out of the shop and this neighborhood, and she popped the plastic cap off the spray can, wondering if she might have to give old Harry a squirt in the face. "I bet there've been these shops forever, too, huh?" she said brightly. "Always charging too much for the merchandise."

Harry looked down at the can in her hand and shrugged, and after a moment he stepped back behind the counter.

"So what did you want?" he said gruffly.

"Bull's-eye glasses," she said, nodding at the pair he was holding, "both sunglasses and clear ones like that—one, no, three sets of each, damn it." Why, she asked herself angrily, am I taking care of Scott and Madeline too?—when Claimayne says they're probably to blame for everything? I really am like the monkey that gets trapped because she can't let go. She shook her head and went on, "And a reversing single-mirror periscope." I won't get them reversing periscopes, she thought. They can find their own. "How much for all that?"

"A hundred and fifty bucks."

She knew the glasses and the periscope barrel would be cheap plastic, but she had complained about the prices once, a couple of years ago—when Harry was running an apparent comic book store with the pale green light in the window, in Bellflower—and he had told her she was free to shop around openly for such things if she liked, and why not pay with a credit card while she was at it and really risk drawing attention to her peculiar purchases.

She pulled the roll of twenty-dollar bills out of her purse and flipped through eight of them and pulled them free. "I know you don't give receipts," she said, "but I would like the ten bucks change."

"What, did you always pay with the exact amount before? I don't give change. There's folks who can track it back to me." He opened a drawer below the counter and, after rummaging around in it, found a Snickers candy bar. "This was going to be my lunch, but you can have it," he said.

He tossed it across the counter and tucked the twenties into his pocket, then began filling a T. J. Maxx shopping bag with unmarked boxes from shelves behind the counter. Ariel put the candy bar in her purse.

"Flash bangs?" asked Harry.

"I beg your pardon?"

"Stun grenades, military reloads. They don't hurt anybody, just blind them with the flash and deafen them with the bang. Disorientation. Just drop it between you and somebody trying to show you a spider, and you're both out of action for a while."

"Sounds like fun. And how much are they?"

Harry nodded at her bundle of twenties. "You don't have enough there."

"That's good. Just give me what I asked for, thanks."

He slid the filled bag over the counter to her, and Ariel nodded and turned toward the door.

"I won't be here next time," Harry called after her.

"See you at the car stereo store."

"Is that what I said?"

She pulled open the street door, and she was squinting in the sudden hot sunlight as she crossed the sidewalk and fumbled out her car keys. When she had opened the passenger-side door and dropped the bag onto the seat, she put on her sunglasses, and she saw that the short man in glasses who had briefly come into the store was now leaning against the wall of the windowless and possibly abandoned one-story stucco building on the far side of the botanica.

Ariel watched him as she closed the car door. He was wearing rumpled dark wool trousers and a sport coat over a red T-shirt.

He nodded at her and slowly took off his glasses and tucked them into his jacket pocket, then pulled out another pair and put those on; even from several yards away, Ariel could see the circular ripples in the lenses.

He opened his mouth and said, "I've known spiderbits to blind themselves, so as to avoid maybe seeing one in a broken plate."

Ariel didn't say anything.

"And then," the little man went on, "they're afraid to sleep, because they might see one of the patterns in a dream. Sometimes they kill themselves."

"It can't happen from a dream," spoke up Ariel. "There's no physical original, and so no reciprocal image on the person's retina."

The man nodded. "I know that. Too late to tell them, though." He took a step toward her, and she tensed and darted a hand into her purse, where, down among the lipsticks and wallet and hairbrush, she kept an old Seecamp .32 semiautomatic pistol that had belonged to her mother. High John the Conqueror spray would have been enough for Harry, but this guy was an unknown.

"Could you spare a couple of bucks?" he said. "For a fellow spiderbit."

"No," she said. She hadn't found the pistol, but she impulsively pulled out the Snickers bar. "You can have this—it cost me ten bucks."

He nodded again, so she held it out at arm's length, ready to run.

But he just took it and began tearing off the wrapper. "When the spiders go," he said, then paused to take a big bite. Chewing the mouthful was a stressful job that didn't seem likely to end soon, and Ariel had started to turn toward her car when he went on, "Do you think all the spiderbits will die?"

Ariel was startled. "Where would they go?" she asked. "The spiders, I mean."

"Back to their own universe. And we've all got extra life from them, haven't we? Through them, anyway." He took another bite.

"Well," said Ariel dismissively, "I don't think they're going anytime soon. Uh—" She tried without success to remember the spiderbit phrase for good-bye and made do with, "Have a nice day."

She had walked around the front of the car when he swallowed audibly and said, "Nobody gets flashbacks from the future anymore. Now is as far up as they go."

Oh really, thought Ariel bitterly. Only yesterday I got a flashback from the future. The idiot future.

She opened the driver's-side door and abruptly remembered the phrase. "Look away!" she called.

"You too," he said.

Ariel got in and started the car and drove forward, intending to take Vine north to Franklin. And as she shifted to the left lane it occurred to her that the overlap from her future self which she had experienced yesterday had only been from a couple of days ahead. That was pretty close to "now." Claimayne may have misinterpreted the absence of any flashbacks from his future; instead of being an indication that he wouldn't be around for much longer, it might mean that the spiders would all shortly stop working.

Her face was tingling in the confined air inside the car. What then? she thought. The ink can't disappear from the pieces of paper— will the eight-legged patterns lose their psychic potency, become just inert marks? It would be as if the alcohol in all the liquor bottles in the world suddenly disappeared, leaving just flavored colored water.

She had to restrain herself from pulling over to the curb and downloading to her phone the app that would give her a ten-second view of a spider, even though such apps were notoriously insecure. You d*on't* want that anymore, she told herself desperately—even if— even *if* the opportunity is about to disappear forever.

And in any case I know that the spiders still work for at least two more days, and I get to look at one at least once more.

She gripped the steering wheel more firmly and sped on toward Vine Street.

THE MAN IN GLASSES watched the pretty woman's car recede, and he pulled a phone from his jacket pocket and tapped a speed-dial number.

"I got one," he said a few moments later. "I don't know the name, but she's in a black Kia Optima." He recited the memorized license-plate number and then described Ariel. "She gave me a ten-dollar candy bar," he added. "Huh? Don't kid around. Full payment."

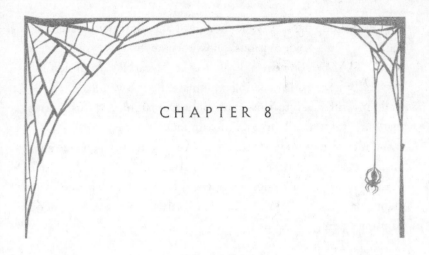

CHAPTER 8

IN SPITE OF THE breeze, the early evening seemed to have paused, like a dancer halted on tiptoe. Dark clouds filled the northern sky, but the low sun bathed the back garden slope in a diffuse yellow light that cast no shadows; the gravel paths and bare tree branches were all in sepia tones, but the leaves of the lemon and bay trees glowed a vivid emerald green. The trees and untrimmed shrubbery looked closer than they really were, and the whole scene had the appearance of an "outdoors" movie set on a soundstage.

Scott had scuffed to a halt after walking past the Medusa wall to look around at the landscape, and for the first time in more than a year he felt the impulse to paint what he saw. The breeze faintly carried the smoke from some neighboring chimney, but he could almost smell acrylic paints and Crystal Clear spray fixative, and his fingers were unconsciously curled as if holding a brush.

He was reassured to glance to the west and see that the sun was perceptibly lower than it had been when he had last looked, and that the remembered seashell-studded wall had not appeared—he didn't want another anachronistic vision like his bisected view of the garden from up on the ladder this morning . . . or those two children, whose shadows had fallen a few degrees wrong for this time of year.

Let this cup pass away, he thought. I am not thirsty, Tetrarch. I can't stay here—spider visions, ghost cats, keyboards typing a dead woman's last-person novels! Back here at Caveat! It's my childhood, perversely served up as a living nightmare. I don't want to—I can't—walk any further into this impossibly animate decay. Vast forms, that move fantastically to a discordant melody . . .

Madeline will understand, when I repack my bag and ride away on my bike back to the Ravenna Apartments. Ariel will be glad. Claimayne won't care one way or the other. And back at the apartments, back in my 2015 life, I'm not likely to start thinking about painting again.

Right. I'm gone.

The resolution put a spring in his step as he turned back toward the house, and he seemed able to breathe more deeply. This is a sick place, he thought—

And abruptly he remembered Madeline saying, a few hours ago, *I'm just sick. If I didn't stay fit, I wouldn't be able to climb Mount McKinley.* And he remembered finding her terrified in the darkness beside the scare-bat in the cellar, expecting to be rescued by somebody she . . . how had it gone? Somebody she had sort of met in this house once.

He stopped walking, his mouth open as if to say something.

What will happen to her, here, he thought, if I leave? She'll keep reading her covert printouts . . . Aunt Amity's ghost-fingers curling up toward her through the keyboard . . .

Will she wind up huddled by the scare-bat in the dark again, for its negligible comfort? She used to make little paper costumes for it.

The light on the neglected garden was more golden now. We used to play back here, he thought, and all over the compound; those two children I saw from the roof—were they Madeline and me, glimpsed across the fractured years?

The evening still seemed stopped.

No, he thought at last, unhappily, I can't do that, I can't leave her here. She *would* understand, and that would make it monstrously worse.

He exhaled, and for a moment allowed himself to reconsider—get on the bike, kick it to roaring life, gun it down Vista Del Mar and then speed away west on Franklin, never looking in the rearview mirrors—but already those actions had an imaginary tone, like his occasional thoughts of reuniting with Louise.

The breeze flicked his hair and he resumed walking, more slowly now, down the path toward the big old house he'd grown up in. I should shower and change before dinner, he thought emptily.

ALL THE FRENCH WINDOWS in the dining room were open during dinner, and the jacaranda trees outside, their highest branches still lit by the westering sun, waved in the cold breeze that fluttered the napkins and made Claimayne draw up the collar of his dressing gown—though he wouldn't permit the windows to be closed, weakly citing fresh air as a necessity for a person in his condition. Ariel was subdued and kept glancing uneasily over her shoulder as if trying to see past the trees, and she managed to swallow about a third of the spaghetti on her plate before it evidently got too cold. There were no satiric quotes from the old movie about Salomé and the tetrarch tonight, and Madeline kept glancing at the empty chair at the head of the table.

Scott mentioned the repairs needed for the roof and the basement, and noted that he had ridden his motorcycle to the Home Depot on Sunset and bought a new thermocouple, but none of the others found these topics diverting.

Claimayne grumbled about cleaners and caterers who were due to arrive on Saturday morning. "And a plumber," he said, waving toward the hall.

"How are we paying for this big party of yours?" Ariel asked him.

Claimayne tossed his fork across the table. "Credit cards! It's an investment. And this Ferdalisi fellow may give us some money for my mother's unpublished papers. You can't win if you don't . . . *play*."

Dessert was still due, but Scott caught Madeline's eye and rocked his head toward the stairs, and she nodded slightly and rolled her eyes. They both stood up and asked to be excused, which was met with dismissive nods from Claimayne and Ariel.

Scott and Madeline hurried out of the dining room and tiptoed up the uncarpeted stairs, and they didn't speak until they had stepped into their parents' room and closed the door.

"House of Usher is right," said Scott, sitting down on the wrecked old mattress. He had bought a fresh pack of Camels while he was out, and now lit one with shaking fingers. He glanced at the gathering darkness outside the window. "Hard to believe we're only a few blocks north of Hollywood Boulevard here," he added, exhaling smoke.

"Or in 2015," said Madeline. "I'll be back," she added; she hurried through the connecting door into her room, and a moment later she returned carrying the sweater-bundled keyboard. "I'll sneak down, get Word open, and plug this in," she said, "and I'll hide it behind the monitor and turn the monitor off, so nobody'll know it's working."

Scott nodded bleakly, and she stole away down the hall.

He lay back across the plaster fragments on the mattress and blew smoke up at the exposed and discolored laths in the gap in the ceiling. The house creaked in the wind, and he imagined he could feel it shifting on the makeshift supports in the basement.

He was thirty-six years old, but all at once his memory of the parents who had lived in this room until he was twelve overwhelmed him. Through eyes suddenly blurred with tears he could almost see his mother's desk against the far wall, piled with shoeboxes and paperback books, and he thought he could nearly catch a whiff of his father's Dominican cigars. The air seemed to twang with the after-echoes of their voices.

I believe I needed you, he thought—I believe Madeline and I both needed you. Neither of us is quite okay, since you two disappeared. What was it that you preferred to us? How could you not ever call us, not ever write? How could you hear the words *Hollywood* or *Los Angeles* without thinking of us alone here?

When Madeline returned, Scott had his elbows braced on the windowsill and his head out in the wind, and he was blinking down at the darkening garden, where he had so recently considered escaping to from all this.

"Are you sick?" came her voice from behind him.

"No," he said. He wiped his eyes before he straightened and turned around, but Madeline clearly noticed that he'd been crying and sucked in her lips in sympathy.

"You were remembering them, weren't you?" she asked quietly.

"Hard not to, here. I'm sure you remember them better than I do."

He waved the subject away. "So," he said hoarsely, "why are you sick?" His hair was sweaty, and he pushed it clumsily back from his forehead.

She frowned at him in evident puzzlement. "Am I sick?"

He sat down on the mattress again and lit another cigarette. "This afternoon you said not to ask you about what happened today or why you're sick. So—here we are—what happened today? And why are you, or were you, sick?"

"Oh! That." She leaned against the wall. "I guess I pulled a boner."

He closed his eyes and shook his head. "What?"

"You know, made a dumb mistake? I looked at the spider in the envelope from the lawyer, this morning. The one Aunt Amity left for me." She peered down at him as he shook his head. "You didn't mention that I would *become* Aunt Amity, and see the 'Welcome Home' banner *through her eyes.*"

"You said you weren't going to look at it!"

"I know, I know. But I got to missing her, the way things used to be here, the past. The past," she repeated. "It's always out there, isn't it? I hate *now*. I hate that whenever you look at a clock, it shows a different time. What's the use of knowing what time it is, if it's always changing? And it's always *later*!"

Scott nodded, momentarily again picturing the room as it had been when his parents slept here. "Did you," he asked, "happen to see anything . . . else, in the spider hallucination, besides the banner in the sickroom?"

She nodded vigorously, standing by the dark window. "*Did* I? *Anything?* Yesterday you said you saw the folder that had the Usabo spider in it. I did too, in a whole scene—I was in a house, holding that folder and waiting for a taxi, hoping to get away before some guy got back; but he kicked in the door and he had a shotgun and he shot me!" She patted the thigh of her jeans. "In the leg. Oh, Scott, it was so . . . *real*! It hurt a *lot*! And I jumped out a window and the taxi was there, and it was a 1920s flivver. The driver took me to a hospital, but I didn't have the folder anymore by then. I think Kosloff got it. That was the name of the guy who shot me, and my name was Natacha. And when I came down here, in the hall, I had a big bruise on my leg!"

Scott shook his head unhappily. "Did you by any chance have a bracelet on, made out of a chain?"

"Yes! What the hell, Scott!"

"When I saw the folder yesterday, I was in a woman's body, I think. And I saw a chain bracelet on her—my—wrist."

"But listen! After I came down from it, I went for a walk in the garden," Madeline went on, nodding toward the window. "And I looked at the Medusa mosaic, and it's kind of busted up these days, and then—" There were tears in her eyes. "Then all at once it was twilight, Scott, and the mosaic was whole, and I didn't hurt anymore, and I walked around to the front of the house and—and Hollywood was like a village, beautiful—!"

She was crying softly now, and he stood up, but she waved him back. "No freeway," she said, her voice hitching, "hardly any lights—there was a cool breeze that smelled like roses and fresh-cut grass. And I started down the steps like I was walking into Narnia, and then it all went fluey, and horrible 2015 came crashing back. It was all too loud, and I swear the damn freeway seemed to be sliding toward me, so I crawled under the house." She sniffed. "I wish I could go back there, and stay."

"I'd be happy just to go back to about 1990," said Scott quietly. "The way we all were then." Long before my talent for drawing was important to me, he thought.

Madeline nodded, looking at the molding around the closet door. "I wonder why we both saw the Usabo spider, yesterday and today—or not *it*, but the folder we knew it was in."

"Maybe we'd always see scenes that include it, since we saw it . . . face-to-face, that one time." He was looking at the door frame too. "Maybe it marked us—imprinted itself in us."

"Yuck." Madeline rubbed her arms vigorously, as if to get rid of clinging spiderwebs. "Back then, when we looked at it, right in this room—what do you remember?"

"Well," said Scott reluctantly, "this room was empty. Mom and Dad were gone by then, and Aunt Amity had already put all their stuff in storage one day while we were in school. To spare our feelings. And we were poking around, looking for any kind of note they might have left, like under the floorboards, and we pushed on that section of the closet-door molding."

"But what do you remember about . . . what we *saw*? When we found the envelope full of spider papers and looked at that one?"

"Oh. Yeah. We were in a room, a cabin, on a boat," he said, "in a man's body, and we watched his hands—our hands, for a moment—break the seal and open the folder."

"When I saw it today," said Madeline with a shiver, "the wax seal was still whole."

"It was when I saw it yesterday, too. But when we were kids and saw it, we saw the seal get broken—and then we were looking right at Usabo, and we fell into a million . . . flashbacks?"

"Memories?" said Madeline with a visible shiver. "Experiences? It felt like they were dissolving me like a Bromo fizz in a glass of water. But a young man was there, too, outside of the boat cabin and the hard waterfall of experiences—"

Scott frowned. "I don't remember a young man. You never mentioned any young man."

"When I knew you didn't see him, I was too embarrassed to tell you. He, I still remember it like it just happened, it seemed like he took my hand, and he said, 'My dear, my dear, it is not so dreadful here.' That's from an Edna St. Vincent Millay poem, and you could have knocked me over with a feather when I read it in a book, years later. He led me into a garden—music in the night, when stars are bright; he was handsome—gorgeous—and he was so kind to me! I was eight years old, and he was just a cheese dream—I fell in love with him." She smiled. "How could I have told you something like that?"

"Was he," asked Scott gently, "the one you thought had come to rescue you in the cellar this afternoon?"

After a pause, she said, "I suppose. Yes. I hoped."

"Ah." Scott recalled that Madeline had never had any kind of boyfriend, though she was thirty-one now—a couple of years ago there had seemed to be a suitor, but she had dismissed Scott's speculations with the statement that "It's just a Plutonian relationship," leaving him unsure whether she had meant to say platonic or had cited some astrological principle—and he now wondered if it could be possible that she had always been pining for this young man she had seen in the vision.

My poor crazy sister, he thought, with her lonely apartment office and her month-in-the-past astrological readings and her imaginary Sir Galahad. Mom and Dad, where were you?

He stood up and crossed to the closet door; and the foot-long section of molding swung open when he pressed on the inside edge, just as it had twenty-three years ago.

Madeline followed him and clutched his arm. "Do you think

there's anything else in there? You took whatever you could reach, that time."

Scott unbuttoned the cuff of his shirt and rolled it back. "I can reach farther now." He slid his hand down into the dark gap, hoping there weren't any literal spiders in there.

"But your arm's fatter."

"More muscular." He felt the two-by-four on which the manila envelope had stood, and now he crouched to reach farther down; and just when he thought he couldn't force any more of his forearm through the narrow gap, his fingertips brushed a folded edge of paper. "Something," he said in a strained whisper.

He pinched the fold of paper tightly between two fingers and carefully began pulling his arm back. "If I drop it," he whispered between clenched teeth, "we'd have to break open the wall to get it."

Madeline nodded. "Don't drop it," she advised.

At last Scott had tugged it up far enough so that he could reach in with his other hand and take a firm hold of it; and he dragged out of the gap another manila envelope and slapped dust off it against his thigh. It felt empty.

"More spiders, do you think?" asked Madeline breathlessly. "Another copy of the *Oneida Inc* one?"

Scott wondered if she hoped to see her young man again. "Does the hallway door lock?" When she stepped to it and twisted the deadbolt knob, she nodded. "It's high time we locked it," he said.

As she snapped the bolt home, he unwound from around the pair of attached cardboard disks the string that held the envelope closed, lifted the flap, and pulled out six sheets of black-and-white photocopy.

The top sheet was a copy of a page of closely written notes—Scott's face went cold when he recognized his mother's handwriting, and he saw Madeline flinch. He slid it behind the other five sheets without reading it.

The next sheet had two birth certificates copied on it—

apparently someone had laid them both on the glass of a photocopy machine; or, judging by the spotty lines, laid a previous photocopy of them on the glass. The certificate at the top of the page had been issued by the State of New York, and formal slanted handwriting filled in all the blanks—he had to turn the page sideways to read the name and the date of the report: *Charlene Claimayne Cooper* and *March 15, 1899*. Someone had scrawled across the document in gray lines, possibly pencil on the original, *Mother*. The second birth certificate reproduced on the page was titled "Certified Copy of Birth Record," and the entries in the blanks were typewritten: Amity Imogene Speas had been born to Charlene Claimayne Speas in Los Angeles on August 20, 1944.

"Aunt Amity's mom was forty-five when she had her," observed Madeline. " 'Charlene' is who Cyclone Severiss is talking to, in that ghost writing Aunt Amity is doing through her keyboard. Could she be talking about her mother?"

Scott shrugged and slid the page to the back.

The third sheet was a copy of a California marriage license, authorizing various sorts of justices, judges, priests, or ministers of the gospel to solemnize the marriage of Paul David Speas and Charlene Claimayne Cooper; it was dated February 28, 1921.

On the fourth sheet was just a still-familiar gray rectangle with *Oneida Inc* hand-printed on it. Scott vividly recalled that the original printing on the envelope had been in red ink.

Scott looked up, remembering that he and Madeline had destroyed the spider that had been in that envelope. "Oops," he said.

Madeline giggled nervously.

The last two sheets were copies of photographs, held together with a paper clip.

Scott raised his eyebrows.

The top photograph was of a slim young woman facing the camera nude, both arms raised to push the long dark hair back from her face. She stood on a Turkish-looking carpet beside a long, crumpled silk bolster, and behind her was a theatrically ornate settee with embroidered pillows scattered on it.

And he recognized her. Aunt Amity had been older when he and his sister had known her, but he had seen the dust-jacket author photos on her novels from the late 1960s, and this was clearly her, right down to the mole on her throat.

Madeline looked away, blushing, and said, "Put it down, Scott!"

"I will." But he looked at the second paper-clipped photocopy. It was of a photograph with the same setting, the couch and carpet and long bolster, but in this one the young Amity Speas was passionately embracing and kissing another naked young woman. A Post-it note on the second photograph read "IS following 244."

"How old do you think she was, then?" asked Madeline, still looking away.

"What would you say, mid-twenties? She was born in '44, so this would be like 1970?"

"She was married to Uncle Edward then, and he didn't die till I was in kindergarten, 1990!"

"I guess Aunt Amity was a wild girl, back in the free-love days of the '60s."

Finally he turned to the sheet that had been on top, the copy of handwritten notes their mother had made. She had written:

Single-spaced, business-style, letter-quality printer. Look
serious! 100k from AM, poss. double? Yes. For return
+ "protection" from big wheelbugs. 10% finder's fee to
"Ostriker"? If he sqawks. & point out he shd be grateful no
expose of him, i.e. wheelbugs.
& WDT murder?

Madeline, standing beside him, read it too.

"Even little wheelbugs would probably be pretty bad," she said solemnly.

"What are they?"

"I don't know. Some kind of bugs, I guess."

"Those photos," mused Scott, "especially the second one, would have been a big scandal in 1970, and Uncle Edward might have divorced her over them. Wheelbugs might be old slang for, you know, tabloid reporters."

"It sounds like they traveled on unicycles."

"*AM* must be Amity Madden. A hundred thousand dollars, or twice that—were our parents *blackmailing* her?"

Madeline sat down on the mattress. "Don't hate me—but—I could believe it."

Scott remembered their father's constant talk about big pending movie deals, and how each of the big deals eventually just stopped being a topic of conversation, and he remembered his mother and father both hanging up the phone if the caller took more than three seconds to reply to "Hello?" because there was always a four-second delay before bill collectors came on the line, and he remembered his father's chronic defensiveness at having been adopted into the Madden family. And as a child Scott had picked up the impression that Uncle Edward had sometimes loaned money to his adopted brother, but that after Edward's death, Aunt Amity had refused to lend him any more.

"I could believe it too, Maddy."

"Mom and Dad never liked her, did they? Remember how upset Dad got about that board she gave him for Christmas?"

Scott nodded. Aunt Amity had hired somebody to rip the carpeting off the stairs, and a week or so later, on Christmas of 1991, she had given their father a two-by-four with a section of the old carpet glued around one end. Scott recalled that their father had turned pale and left the room.

Madeline shook her head. "I guess Mom and Dad got the big blackmail payoff and decided to leave us with Aunt Amity, while they ran off to the Riviera or somewhere."

Scott wondered how far that amount of money went in 1991. Further than it would in 2015, certainly. "Claimayne gave me the key to Aunt Amity's office, on Sunset," he said. "I'll snoop around in there tomorrow, see if there's any correspondence with them. Child-support payments, at least, you'd think."

"I wonder who Ostriker was, and why he killed this WDT person."

Scott didn't mention his suspicion that the murder of "WDT" looked like something else with which his parents had considered blackmailing Aunt Amity.

Madeline stood up and unbolted the door. "Do you think Ariel and Claimayne are still downstairs? I should go see what Aunt Amity is typing now."

"I heard Claimayne's elevator coming up awhile ago. Sounded like somebody was bulldozing the house."

"That's right. Ariel's probably upstairs too." She stepped into the hall and closed the door behind her.

Scott brushed some more dust off the manila envelope and saw that his mother had written on it, in ink, *Backup copies.*

He peered inside and saw that the envelope contained still one more item—a little folded slip of white paper. He pulled it out carefully, and when he peered into the fold, he glimpsed the expected limbs of another spider pattern. He closed it quickly. On the outside of the paper their mother had written, *Before* and *After. Before* was crossed out, and *After* therefore seemed more prominent.

He walked back through Madeline's room to his own.

He had brought a Michael Connelly paperback along in his bundle two days ago, and it was now a bit warped but no longer damp, and he tucked the little *Before* and *After* paper into the book and set it on the shelf beside the row of mottled cigarettes.

Then he tucked the papers back into the manila envelope and shoved it under his mattress.

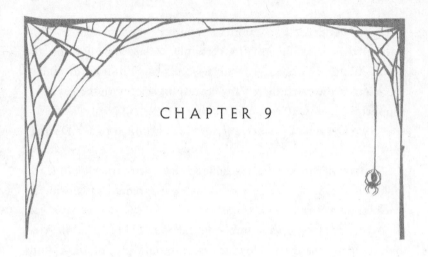

CHAPTER 9

CAVEAT WAS SILENT THE next morning as Scott descended the stairs to the hall by the dining room and pulled open the front door. Madeline was in the shower upstairs, preparing to visit her apartment office; he hadn't seen Ariel and didn't hear her in the kitchen, and he had not heard the grinding and clanking of Claimayne's elevator.

Scott crossed the porch and the unmowed patch of grass and started down the long flight of cement steps on the slope, putting on his goggles and helmet and cinching the strap as he watched the view of the Hollywood skyline disappear behind closer apartment-building walls.

His old Honda started up the third time he tromped on the kick-starter—the electric starter motor had died long ago—and his foot was clicking the bike into gear as his fingers released the clutch; the bike surged forward and he leaned it out of the Caveat parking lot and south onto the narrow lanes of Vista Del Mar Avenue. Rooftops and overhanging eucalyptus trees threw blue shadows across the damp asphalt ahead of him, and the cool air whipping at his collar was fragrant with spicy clay and thyme.

He was in the left lane when he recalled that Vista Del Mar would dead-end at the 101 Freeway wall by the elegant old Hollywood Tower apartment building, so he slanted the bike left through traffic onto Franklin and then turned right on Gower. Sunset Boulevard would be the next big street after Hollywood Boulevard, and he would follow Sunset all the way west to Aunt Amity's office.

Traffic on Sunset was light on this Thursday morning, and he seemed to catch nothing but green lights, gunning the bike through the cool headwind past the white Cinerama dome and the ringed glass tower of Amoeba Music. The Ravenna Apartments building, where he was the manager, was on Hayworth Avenue, arguably on the way to the west end of Sunset, so when he saw the big Rite Aid pharmacy on Fairfax he made a left turn. He might as well see how things were going in his absence.

The apartment building was eleven upstairs units over garages, arranged in an open square facing Hayworth, and the office was on the ground floor under apartment eleven, on the right side of the central breezeway. Scott parked his bike on the cement apron out front, relieved to see that the office door was open and the lights were on inside.

Behind the desk, shaved and in a clean white shirt and altogether looking reliable, Sam Ellis was tapping at the computer keyboard but looked up when Scott walked in.

"No crises?" asked Scott with careful cheer, not putting his helmet down. Reassuringly, the office had only its usual smell of orange-oil furniture polish. "Yet?"

Ellis, a retired engineer, was the longest-residing tenant, and in his sober periods had sometimes assisted Scott in the maintenance work around the place.

Ellis shrugged. "A couple of people this morning complained that one of the washing machines wasn't working, but they didn't think to check if the thing was plugged in. What it was, Laroux in six had his electricity turned off 'cause he doesn't pay bills, and he unplugged the washer so he could plug in his phone charger and run an extension upstairs to his place."

"And he's late on the rent," Scott said, "because he had to bail his girlfriend out of jail, he says."

"You got a loser there."

"Well, you have my e-mail and the phone number up at the Vista Del Mar place—hit me with anything you can't settle." Scott sighed. "I'm going to be up there for four more days—"

"Oh, and half an hour ago a woman came by looking for you." Ellis peered at a note on the desk and said, "Louise Odell. She didn't leave a number."

Scott's breath stopped in his throat, and a full second later the backs of his hands tingled.

"What did she—say?"

"Just were you here, tell you she came by."

" . . . Ah."

Scott nodded and walked back outside into the morning air, mechanically putting on his goggles and helmet again and straddling the bike to jump on the kick-starter.

It's been eleven years, he thought as he worked the throttle grip.

Her last name is still Odell.

Don't think about it now, not right now. Maybe you even need to be . . . *properly braced,* before you think about it.

He rode over to Fairfax and up to Sunset, and directly across the boulevard from the white, vaguely aerodynamic-looking Chase Bank building stood a bright red sign that read THE LIQUOR LOCKER. It stood out vividly against the whites and grays and greenery of the rest of the view.

Oh . . . *okay,* he thought. Just to be on the safe side.

He swerved the bike into the shop's narrow parking lot, switched off the engine, flipped the kickstand down, and hurried inside; five minutes later, with a pint bottle of 101-proof Wild Turkey bourbon tucked securely in his jacket pocket, he was riding up the driveway into the parking lot behind the Chase Bank.

There was a two-story strip mall at the south end of the parking lot, and Scott saw the tax accountant's sign above the top row of windows. An elevator was visible behind glass doors on the ground floor, and Scott parked his bike and went inside.

A WHITE CHEVY BLAZER circled the back parking lot and pulled into a space at the back of the bank. The driver's face was lean and tanned, and his close-cropped hair was gray. He lifted a 7-Eleven Big Gulp cup from the console and took a sip, then put it back and lit a cigarette. He squinted through the smoke for a moment in the direction of the strip mall, then sighed and picked up from the passenger seat a notepad with a Bic pen clipped to it.

Under the previous note on the top page—*Ravenna Apartments, where he works*—he now wrote—*Liquor Locker—then his aunt's office, already checked.*

He tossed the pad down and turned on the radio.

THERE WAS A SHORT corridor on the second floor, with blue carpeting and two bright red doors, and one of the doors was the tax accountant's and the other was not. Scott knocked on the second door, and there was no answer, so he pulled out his keys.

As soon as Scott held up to the keyhole the key Claimayne had given him, he could see that it wouldn't fit. He pushed it at the keyhole anyway a couple of times, then sighed and put his keys back in his pocket and pulled out his wallet.

I hope this is the right door, he thought.

From one of the wallet's flap pockets he pulled a paper clip and a blade broken off a spark-plug feeler gauge, and he gave the feeler gauge blade a slight flex to flatten out the curve it always picked up in his wallet. Tenants at the Ravenna Apartments sometimes took it on themselves to change their door locks, and several times he'd had to pick a lock. The paper clip was already straightened, and the last quarter inch was bent at a ninety-degree angle.

He fitted the blade into the keyhole and rotated it lightly back and forth; clockwise was the direction with perceptible give, so he kept slight pressure in that direction as with his other hand he fitted the paper clip into the top end of the keyhole. He raked the lock, dragging the paper clip out to loosen the pins, then set about levering up the five pins one by one with the bent end, starting at the back of the lock. Within thirty seconds he was able to twist the feeler gauge blade all the way to the right, and the door was unlocked.

He turned the knob and pushed the door open against a pile of advertisements and business envelopes; the room was dark but he didn't see anyone, so he stepped inside and closed the door behind him. He put his makeshift tools back in his wallet and tucked it into his pocket.

The air was stale with a hint of old cigarette smoke. Wooden Venetian blinds blocked the view to the south, and in the dim glow of daylight around the edges of the blinds he could see a desk by the window and what appeared to be an old enameled iron bathtub against the hallway-side wall.

He crouched to gather up the scattered mail from the carpet, then straightened and flicked a switch on the wall, and fluorescent lights behind pebbled panels in the ceiling glowed stark white. He was relieved to see that the envelopes were addressed to Amity Madden—this was the right office.

The big white object against the near wall was indeed an old claw-footed bathtub, its white enamel chipping away in many places to show rust underneath. The holes for faucets gaped empty, and the drain had no pipe attached to it.

He shrugged and walked around the desk and sat down in the wooden chair behind it.

The room, he reflected, would be more appropriately lit by

incandescent bulbs behind nicotine-yellowed shades. A black Olympic manual typewriter sat on the desk beside a black Bakelite dial telephone, and the pens in the leather cup on the other side of the fuzzy green blotter were thick, probably fountain pens. A ceramic ashtray next to it had *Chasen's* printed on it in script, and the half-dozen cigarette butts in it had no filters. The pictures on the wall all seemed to be photographs of Aunt Amity, young and vivacious, with various evident celebrities of the 1960s, of whom in a cursory glance Scott was able to identify only Johnny Carson and maybe onetime L.A. mayor Sam Yorty.

His gaze drifted to the bars of sunlight between the slats of the Venetian blinds, and he forgot about the envelopes he was holding. He could feel the flat bulk of the pint bottle against his side. What could Louise have wanted to say? *Can you find it in your heart to take me back, Scott, I . . .* But the unlikelihood, no, the sheer impossibility of that, made him exhale so sharply that he nearly spat on the desk.

Probably she figures it's been so long that we're amiable acquaintances now, he thought, and she wants some artwork done—or more likely some plumbing or electrical work.

He shook his head. Right now, concentrate on the task at hand. It's family history and Madeline's weird entanglement that need your attention. The bottle is just a precaution against . . . *eventualities*. Forget about it for now. For now.

He dropped the mail onto the desk. The desk drawers were locked, but with just the paper clip he was able to open every one of them. He pulled all of them except for the big file drawer right out of the desk and laid them on the carpet.

HALF AN HOUR LATER, having added a couple of filtered cigarette butts to the ashtray, Scott had set a number of things from the desk drawers onto the blotter. There was a hardcover book inexplicably sealed in a plastic Bank of America CoinSafe bag—through the unprinted sections of the clear plastic he could see that it was something called *Valentino,* by Irving Schulman. On top of it he had set a battered leatherbound address book. Next to them were two stacks of papers and a locked cloisonné box that he had found inexplicably duct-taped to the back side of the truncated middle drawer. The keyhole of the cloisonné box was too small for the paper clip.

The first stack of papers he had assembled was of the currently outstanding bills, going back two months. On top of that stack he had laid Aunt Amity's checkbook, and he intended to write checks for the bills and take them to Claimayne or Ariel.

The next, bigger stack consisted of canceled checks. Most of these were to local businesses like Gelson's market, or to the gas company and the Los Angeles Department of Water and Power, but in a White Owl cigar box in the big file drawer he had found some more. Every month for at least the last ten years, which was apparently as far back as she had kept old checks, Aunt Amity had written a thousand-dollar check to one Genod Speas—and Speas was Aunt Amity's maiden name. Could this Genod be a brother of hers?

The current bills were all he arguably had any business with here. Everything else was his aunt's private stuff, and it all rightfully belonged to Claimayne now. Scott knew he had had no right even to look through it, much less take some of it away with him—as he meant to do—but Aunt Amity, or Caveat itself, had a hold on his sister, and he felt nervously justified in investigating anything that might have a bearing on that.

He turned to the address book. Entries in pencil and fountain pen ink filled the age-yellowed pages, and he saw the names Genod Speas and Adrian Ostriker, but his parents' names didn't appear in it, and most of the telephone numbers were only four digits long. He tossed it on top of Aunt Amity's checkbook.

The file drawer was mainly packed with green cardboard hanging files, and each file was tabbed with a year—they extended back to 1965, and he now began hoisting them out one at a time and leafing through their contents, which all appeared to have to do with her novels. There were contracts and royalty statements and letters from agents and editors, and proofs of cover pictures, but no personal items. He skipped ahead to 1991, the year his parents had disappeared, but it held only correspondence between Amity and her editor at Putnam's—they were offering her less money for her then-newest book, *The Shores of Hollywood,* than they had paid for the previous one. Scott recalled that they would simply reject her next one, and every one thereafter, and the 1992 folder provided only early indications of that eventual ongoing misfortune. The following folders were even sparser.

He had hoped to find some correspondence with his parents, but as far as the contents of this desk were concerned, they might never have existed.

Scott fitted the latest folder back onto the rails and slid the big drawer shut, and then he sat back and stared at the cloisonné box that had been hidden on the back side of the shortened top drawer. At last he pulled out his wallet and retrieved the spark-plug feeler gauge, and he worked the blade into the seam between the box and the lid, but when he tried twisting it, the box came apart in his hands.

"Shit," he whispered, automatically looking around the empty office.

He lifted the lid away, and lying on top of the separated panels of the box were four folded pieces of paper—and he knew what they must be. He was aware that his heartbeat seemed to be . . . not so much faster as harder.

"Were these special, Auntie?" he whispered.

He noticed now that each of them had faint writing in pencil on the bottom edge of the folded flap: *Il Dottore, Innamorati, Scaramuccia,* and *Il Capitano,* which he recognized as the names of characters from the Italian *Commedia dell'arte.*

Why had Aunt Amity hidden them behind the drawer?

When Scott noticed that one of his fingers was lightly flipping an edge of the *Il Dottore* paper, he hastily put them all down and got to his feet. A dusty raincoat hung in an alcove next to the bathtub, and he folded it carefully around all the papers and the books and the broken cloisonné box and its contents, tying the belt securely around the bundle so that it wouldn't come open while it was strapped to the sissy bar on his motorcycle.

He remembered to fit the drawers back into the desk before he left the office.

CLAIMAYNE HAD WHEELED HIMSELF out through the kitchen door into the sunlight, and then had Ariel hold a cushion-layered wheelbarrow steady while he got up and shifted himself into it; then Ariel, with a picnic lunch in a blue nylon backpack, had trundled the heavy wheelbarrow out along the gravel path to a cleared spot in front of the Medusa mosaic wall. She was sweating and cross when she finally lowered the back end of the wheelbarrow and flexed her hands off the handles. Her new bull's-eye lens sunglasses had slipped down on her nose, and she impatiently pushed them back into place, though it meant that she couldn't clearly see whatever she was looking at directly.

The wind at noon was still cold enough to make her zip up her yellow nylon windbreaker before she shrugged out of the backpack. She unbuckled it and took out a towel and spread it over the weeds below the wall and sat down.

"You're sitting in Alla Nazimova's bathtub," remarked her cousin. His dressing gown was buttoned up to his neck, and a conical bamboo hat sat on his bald head.

"Where it was," said Ariel.

"It's still there, somewhere along the time-thread."

"Said the termite tetrarch. That Ferdalisi fellow is due when?"

"One thirty. We've got more than an hour. Don't wear your novelty glasses when he's here."

"What does he want, exactly?"

"I don't know, *exactly*," said Claimayne with a shrug, lifting his eyebrows; and it occurred to Ariel that he was probably lying. "He's interested in my mother's novels and notes, at any rate. New critical editions, a movie option?" He shrugged again. "Money, with luck."

Ariel considered telling him what the stranger had said to her out in front of the spiderbit shop yesterday—but she wasn't sure he'd consider it good news that he might live many more years without spiders. And in any case, that weird little man had hardly been a reliable source of information.

From the backpack she pulled a wrapped sandwich and a carton of macaroni salad with a plastic fork and a paper napkin rubber-banded to it, and she reached up to hand the carton to Claimayne. "It's too late in the year for these picnics. I think the ground's still damp from the rain." Next she lifted out a half bottle of Storybook Mountain zinfandel with the cork already pulled and loosely replaced, and she passed that too to Claimayne; and finally she pulled free a thermos for herself.

As she unscrewed it and carefully poured hot coffee into the plastic cap, Claimayne tugged the cork out of the bottle and flicked a splash of wine toward the mosaic wall.

"I think she took the tub away so she could sit in it in the privacy of her office," he said. He splashed some more wine toward the wall.

"I should have opened a full-size bottle for you," said Ariel, "if you're going to give half of it to your beheaded Medusa." She recalled Harry's story about the nineteenth-century spider worshippers in Andalucia, and their Medusa symbol, and she looked away from the wall.

"Not beheaded," Claimayne corrected her. "You can see in the earliest mosaics that the old Greeks knew she was never anything *but* a little bitty head—with eight long, lovely, snaky tresses. It's too bad this mosaic is only the artist's imagining of her!"

Ariel gripped her plastic cup more tightly but said with careful flippancy, "Sure, and if it was a real portrait, everybody who looked at it would turn to stone, right? We could go into the statuary business. I'm glad Perseus killed her."

"I told you it doesn't literally change a person to stone. The Greek noun is really something more like 'rigidity.' And Perseus didn't kill her, he just brought her to Sephiros, though he was careful only to look at her in a mirror." Claimayne lifted the bottle to his lips and took a sip. "I wonder if poor young Madeline knows that the oldest Sumerian astrologers knew her too. And according to an old Hebrew midrash, when David was being pursued by King Saul, David hung a spider tapestry over the cave he was hiding in, and Saul's soldiers were too disoriented to find him." A gust of wind blew a dry leaf into his macaroni salad, and he picked it out with trembling fingers.

"Greeks, Babylonians, Hebrews!" Ariel shivered. "Are the things really *that* old?"

"At least."

After a pause, Ariel said, "I think poor young Madeline is brain damaged."

"Actually, I think she *is*. No, not damaged, precisely— permanently concussed, say. Permanently distracted, at least. I told you I think she and her brother both looked at the one my mother was saving for *special*."

"Scott seems all right."

"On the surface," agreed Claimayne, "but I'll wager dementia sets in at an unusually young age."

Ariel frowned and opened her mouth to say something, but through the open kitchen and dining room came the rattling growl of an inadequately muffled motorcycle engine, which stopped after a few seconds.

"Speak of the bedeviled," said Claimayne. "And he parks his velocipede up here by the house now! Cheeky."

Faintly they heard thumping on the interior stairs, and Ariel lowered her glasses to look up toward the open window of Scott's room.

"Scott?"

Scott's face appeared in the window, his dark hair tossing in the wind as he glanced around at the paths and shrubbery of the untended garden. Ariel waved, and he waved back and then ducked back inside.

Claimayne raised an eyebrow. "You called to him why?"

"I—don't want him thinking nobody's home, and snooping around." She pushed the glasses back up on her nose.

"I'm always home these days." After a pause, Claimayne went on, "I've got microphones in their rooms. Your Scott has hired some people, on spec, to forge letters from my mother stating that it's her intention to leave everything to him and Madeline. Back-dated a couple of years, to make it look as though it was her intention for an extended period, not just something she dreamed up on the day she killed herself."

Ariel stared in his direction, though she could see only shifting rings through the lenses. "You're such a liar. Not that I don't think he'd do it, if it occurred to him, but—when would you have put in these microphones? You didn't know they'd be staying up here in the main house till I said they could, and they've been underfoot ever since."

Claimayne laughed and had another swig of wine. "It's a good idea, though." He smiled across the weeds at the little black-and-white Medusa head. "*You* know what those two are up to, don't you, darling?" he said to it.

Over the wind in the trees they could again hear shoes knocking on the interior stairs, and a moment later Scott stepped out through the kitchen door. Ariel hesitated, then took off the glasses and tucked them into her blouse pocket.

Scott trudged up the gravel path and paused a few yards short of where Ariel sat on her towel and Claimayne in his wheelbarrow.

"I'm, uh, home," he said diffidently. "Back, I mean."

"We'd ask you to join us," said Ariel coldly, "but I don't want any more towels getting muddy."

"And I don't think there's another wheelbarrow," put in Claimayne.

Scott waved it off. "I've got stuff to do. Claimayne, I picked up your mother's mail and checkbook, and I hope there's a lot of money in the account, since you're a couple of months in arrears on everything." Claimayne was frowning and opening his mouth as Scott turned to go back toward the house, but before he could say anything, Scott stopped and looked back and added, "Who is Genod Speas? A brother of your mother's?"

Claimayne's mouth snapped shut, then opened again as he exclaimed, "Fuck me!" He took a deep breath, then said loudly, "I told you not to go into my mother's office unless Ariel or I were with you! What did you—"

"You gave me the key," said Scott.

"I did not! Did you break in? I'll see that you—"

"You did give him the key," interrupted Ariel.

"I gave him the *wrong* key! He broke in!"

"That was the wrong key?" Scott shook his head. "Actually I never even tried it. The door wasn't locked."

"Bullshit it wasn't locked! She never—"

Ariel burst out, "Oh, who cares? I told Scott to deal with the bills, and he's doing it. Probably your mother did forget to lock the door."

Claimayne visibly forced himself to calm down. "How do you know about Genod Speas?"

"She was writing checks to him," said Scott. "They were in the same drawer as the rest of the old checks." He cocked his head and stared at Claimayne. "Why? Who is he?"

"Yes, her brother, her older brother. You went through her desk? Did you find a little cloisonné box?"

"The only drawer that was unlocked was the one with the old checks and the checkbook in it. There wasn't any cloisonné box in that one."

Claimayne gave him a truly venomous stare. "Do not go back there. Ever."

"Jeez, Tetrarch," said Ariel, a bit awed by her cousin's uncharacteristic anger.

Scott shrugged. "I've got no reason to go back. I brought all the bills here, and the checkbook." He took his key ring out of his pocket. "I should give you that key back. It probably goes to something." He worked the key off the ring.

Claimayne held out his palm, and Scott dropped the key onto it. "Oh, and while I've got you," Scott said, "do you know what became of our parents' stuff? Furniture, books, junk? I'm sure your mother didn't just throw it all out."

Claimayne gave him a blank stare. "You miss the orange couch? The heraldic wet bar?"

Ariel snorted and giggled.

Claimayne closed his eyes. "I have no idea."

Scott frowned and started to say something, but then he jumped and spun to face the house, for a very loud, close boom had shaken the air.

Ariel looked past him at the roof, but there was nothing to see.

"It's just Claimayne's mother blowing herself up," she explained. "We get reruns."

"I heard it yesterday too," said Scott, still staring at the house.

"Like I said, reruns."

Scott nodded slowly, and half turned as if again about to say something, then just walked away toward the house, still nodding.

Ariel turned to Claimayne, and she forced a breezy smile. "Will that *stop*, before the party on Saturday, do you suppose?"

Claimayne seemed distracted. "What? Oh—well, that's rather up to her, isn't it?"

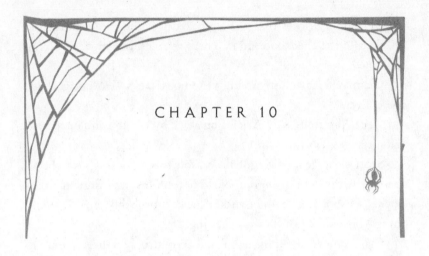

CHAPTER 10

BACK UPSTAIRS IN HIS room, Scott locked the door and leaned against it, staring at the bundled raincoat on his bed and trying to think of the other things in it, not just the spiders. At last he took a deep breath and let it out, pushing away from the door and crossing to the bed.

Reruns! Like Madeline's brief walk to old Hollywood yesterday?

He unbuckled the raincoat and flipped it open. To start with, he picked up the book in the plastic bank bag and tugged at the plastic until it tore and he was able to pull the book free and get a good look at it. The picture on the dust jacket was of the old silent-movie star Rudolph Valentino in some sort of Eastern headdress, carrying a young woman in his arms. Opening the book, Scott saw that it had been published in 1967, with deckle-edged pages and a section of black-and-white photographs, all of which seemed at a first hasty glance to be of Valentino in elaborate costumes. He saw no underlining or laid-in papers, but there was writing in ballpoint ink on the front flyleaf—and it was in his mother's well-remembered handwriting: *Keep it, I've got more copies.* The ink had spread and faded a little, over the years. His breath caught in his throat, and he put the book aside for now.

Why are we back here? he thought. She's gone, they're both gone.

He could feel the hard angularity of the bottle in his pocket, but when he sat down on the bed, his attention was on the four pieces of folded paper that had been in the cloisonné box. A moment later the *Il Capitano* one was in his hand, and he was tapping a tooth with it.

He told himself that he shouldn't, he shouldn't give in to this and throw away all of . . . all of what, precisely? His relationships, his accomplishments?

He wished he had arrived at the Ravenna Apartments earlier this morning, when Louise had been there. What *could* she have wanted to see him about? She had left him eleven years ago because he had seemed to have no prospects, and now, having found and lost a moderately successful career, he was back in that same position again.

He remembered her as she had been in 2002—a sophomore at USC majoring in education, tall and young and clear-eyed, her blond hair generally pulled back in a ponytail, athletic shoulders and legs fairly radiating health—idealistic—and he wondered what she was like now. Successful at something, certainly. She'd be thirty-three now, the same age as Ariel.

What could she see in . . . the man who had been hunching about on the roof and in the cellars of Caveat yesterday, hungover from having looked at a spider; who was in fact holding a spider in his hand right now . . .

"Fuck it," he said and flipped open the piece of paper and stared at the eight-limbed pattern on it.

And for an indefinite period the world stopped, and he was bodiless in a space so different from reality that familiar things like personal identity couldn't follow. Later, when his consciousness had coalesced enough to be aware again, he was among the featureless vertical entities that seemed to extend away to infinity above and below him, and his abandoned body in the bare Caveat bedroom clenched its teeth against whatever might be coming next.

And then he was standing in a small lamplit dining room that was separated by an arch from a living room; under his too-tight shoes was a carpet that covered the middle of the polished hardwood floor, and a crown molding soffit overhead ran around three sides of the room, with decorative mugs and mismatched ceramic figures arranged in rows. He could hear music, turned down low, piano and orchestra.

Through the arch he could see a gray-haired man sitting at a desk facing away from him, and the lace curtains on the far side of the desk showed only darkness beyond . . . and then Scott realized that another man was standing right beside him here in the dining room.

Scott would have jumped in surprise, but the body he was occupying didn't shift at all. After a few seconds, his head turned to look at his companion, and Scott found himself looking at a young man's lean, tanned face. The man's eyes were wide and his lips were pressed tightly together. He met the eyes Scott was looking out of and nodded toward the living room.

As Scott stepped forward, he felt a sharp pain in his toe that would have made him gasp if he had been able to. And he could feel that he was once again in a woman's body; but he lacked the volition to look down and see if the remembered chain bracelet was on the wrist, and though he was aware of that hand holding something, he couldn't know if it was again, or still, the Medusa folder.

Stepping between a chair and a couch, Scott was distracted by the pain in this body's toe—did the woman have a piece of glass in her shoe?—but he found that he was speaking. "Mr. Taylor," came a woman's voice from his throat.

The man at the desk looked around, then pushed back his chair and stood up. He reached to the side and switched off a radio on a nearby table, and in the moment the music ceased, Scott recognized it as some Debussy piece. "The Sunken Cathedral"?

In the glow from a standing lamp beside the couch, Scott could see that the man wore a three-piece suit and a tie, and the expression on his long patrician face was only quizzical, with one eyebrow raised. "You should have called," said the man addressed as Taylor. "I was just editing a scene before going to bed. But tell me, why do you sneak in through the kitchen, and with a gun?" He spoke with a detectable British accent.

Scott still wasn't able to make this body look down, but he realized that the textured pressure in his right palm was the grip of a handgun.

He found himself speaking. "Editing a scene? I thought you were between pictures." His lungs filled, and the woman's voice went on, "I want the Medusa spider."

Scott was able to see, peripherally, a machine on the man's desk; two big open-sided reels flanked a console with a light glowing in it, and a round, flat metal can as big as the reels leaned against it. A foot-wide mirror on a swivel stand stood on the other side of the machine, tilted forward.

"I think I know what you mean," said the older man slowly. "But I was under the impression that *you* had it—bought it from a not entirely reputable rare-book dealer in London."

Scott found himself speaking again: the woman's voice said, "You haven't been under that impression lately. You know very well that Theodore Kosloff stole it from me two years ago, *shot me in the leg to get it,* and he'd let me shoot *him* before he'd give it back to me."

"As you say. But, child, why come to me?"

"Because I know you bribed one of his girls, Fridi, to photograph it for you—she was too scared to *steal* it like I tried to do. Fridi's an old friend of mine, and she told me about it, even told me about the warpy glasses you insisted that she wear while she took the picture."

She wiggled her foot, and the pain in her toe seemed to lance up through her shin to her knee; Scott felt the skin around her eyes tighten in a wince.

The young man standing beside Scott muttered something, and the woman's voice said, "Wait outside, see that we're not interrupted." Then Scott was aware of her forehead kinking in a frown that felt like puzzlement, and her voice started to say, "I'm not sure I'm—"

And before she could finish the sentence, Scott felt another personality strongly exert itself in the woman's body. "Wait outside," her voice repeated, and it seemed more musical now.

The young man nodded and stepped past Taylor to the front door, and without looking at anyone he pulled the door open and disappeared outside. The curtains above the desk fluttered in the moment before the door was closed, and Scott had caught a brief glimpse of a moonlit gazebo out there.

Taylor gave her a frosty smile. "Very well—yes, Fridi is right. And, as the thing was yours originally, I'll have the developer send you a copy. You didn't need a gun to compel me."

"You appear to be editing a film there," came the woman's newer voice. "What sort of film is it that has to be edited in a mirror?"

Before Taylor could summon an answer, the woman went on, "Never mind. You let Fridi guess your purpose—you're using images of the Medusa spider to make some sort of exorcism film! Setting repetitions of the image in the fast tarantella frequencies to nullify it. You probably use the Medusa's image a dozen times, a hundred, in that film!" The gun, a blued-steel revolver, appeared for a moment in Scott's vision as the body pointed at the desk with it, and the remembered chain bracelet was indeed visible on the wrist of the slim hand holding it. "All I want is one frame of the film, one that's got the image on it."

Frowning now, Taylor raised a steady hand. "You must know I've tried to stop the havoc this sickness has caused in our community, Natacha! You can't really want—"

Scott felt a smile tighten his face, and then his mouth opened: "I think Natacha did really want it. Not as badly as I do."

Taylor lowered his hand, and his face lost all expression. "Who are you? Do I know you?"

"I won't even be born for a long time."

Taylor shook his head slowly. "My God, Natacha came here in a before? And then lost her spider before she could do the after?"

"She did the after, but I did an after-after, and I'm stronger than she was. Now, just as a formality—will you give me one of the frames with the Medusa spider image on it?"

Taylor shrugged. "Very well. One frame." He turned toward the desk, but the woman stepped swiftly to the side, apparently unmindful of the pain in her foot, and her eyes saw that Taylor had flicked open a cigarette lighter and had his thumb on the flint wheel.

The gun muzzle flared and rocked upward as the short, hard explosion shook the air and numbed Scott's eardrums, and Taylor was thrown forward across the desk; after one ringing moment, he straightened and took a step toward the door, but he sagged and fell backward, and then he was lying on his back on the rug, staring sightlessly at the ceiling.

The woman's shoulder jiggled. "We've got somebody else aboard too, haven't we?" said her voice. "And when are *you* born, stranger?"

The young man had hurried back inside, and he stared in evident horror at the body on the carpet. He waved a hand toward it, and a chain bracelet was visible on his wrist too. "Natacha!" he whispered. "You had to *kill* him?"

Scott's perspective moved forward to the desk, and then he was peering without comprehension at the machine. He saw the woman's hand twist a knob on the console and then spin one of the reels, and a glistening length of film snaked from one reel through the machine to the other, while the lighted panel flickered.

She spun the reel on the right over and over again until the left-side reel spun free and the end of the film was slapping against her hand. She flipped up a little lever on the spindle and pulled the right-side reel off the machine, fitting it into the film can and spinning the wide lid on tight.

Her arms clasped the can to her chest, and a subsonic roar made the room seem almost to vibrate out of focus, and for a moment Scott was convinced that gravity itself had briefly wavered.

Scott felt the woman inhale and exhale deeply, and then she was crouching and pulling off a high-heeled shoe. The flat head of a thumbtack was pressed against the underside of her big toe, and she got her fingernails under it and tugged the point free; a drop of blood showed on the skin in the moment before she thrust her foot back into the shoe. Then she straightened up, and her head jerked back toward the dining room. "Out the way we came in."

Now Scott was hurrying back across the dining room and through a small dark kitchen to a back door; the young man pulled it open and they stepped down to a sidewalk on a narrow street. Scott caught a whiff of jasmine on the night breeze. Moonlight frosted the tops of waving palm trees and the tile roof of the apartment building across the street, but the woman and her companion were in deep shadow as they hurried left down the sidewalk to a wider street. On the far side of the intersection another apartment building was visible, and Scott was able to read *Roxy* over the doorway arch. Headlights illuminated a neatly kept hedge along that far curb, and a car swept past the intersection, then another; they were both angular upright black cars of the 1920s.

And then his vision lost depth, and the moving patches changed from the black and white of a moonlit street to points and curls of gold against blackness.

He was lying on his back, and his hands told him he was on a rug; and after a minute of breathing deeply and blinking, his vision recovered depth perception and he could see that he was in a dim room with lots of hanging brass vessels and gold statues on shelves. And then, turning his head stiffly, he could make out a bed with spiral-carved pillars, and a curtained window.

The aches that racked him were particularly strong in his hips and back and jaw, but he got up in a crouch and looked around, and behind him was a closed door. The knob turned when he had hobbled across to it, and when he pulled the door open, he exhaled with relief to see the familiar second-floor hallway of Caveat; as if to confirm it, the old structure creaked and shifted perceptibly. He stumbled a few steps forward, and he realized from the position of the stairs and the far window that he had just come out of Claimayne's room.

That's all I need, Scott thought desperately—to be caught coming out of his room! Why the hell would my briefly abandoned body have made its way *there*? He pulled the door closed behind him and limped down the hall to his own room.

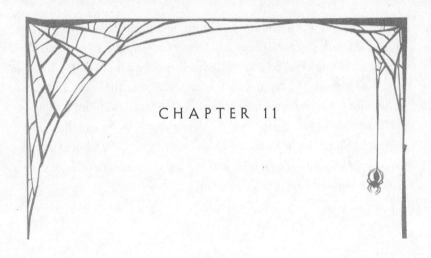

CHAPTER 11

THE RINGING OF A telephone was echoing in his parents' empty room, but the telephone itself was gone.

Scott had taken a couple of Madeline's Advils and lain down on his bed, waiting for the postspider aches in his joints and jaw to abate, and he had managed to drift off into a restless sleep and a dream in which he shuffled endlessly through his aunt's canceled checks, but the ringing phone brought him upright and swinging his feet to the floor.

He followed the ringing noise through Madeline's room and into his parents' empty sunlit room, and then he stared blankly at the two wires sticking out of the wall where the telephone had once been connected. The pulsing metallic clangor was coming clear and unmuffled from that corner of the room.

Somewhere there's the actual phone, he thought, and it's silent, but if I could find it and pick up the receiver I could talk to . . . whoever's calling.

His hands flexed uselessly. *Claimayne, where did your mother put our parents' stuff?*

At the seventh ring Scott automatically began waiting for an answering machine to pick up, but the ringing kept on. Wherever the phone is, he thought, the answering machine isn't hooked up to it anymore.

Feeling foolish even though he was alone, but reasoning that sounds here, now, were fragmented in space and time, he knelt by the wires and ventured to say, "Hello?"

The ringing stopped. The following silence seemed to fill the room, crowding him. He wished he had brought the Valentino book with him from his room, so that he could look at his mother's handwriting on the flyleaf.

"Mom?" His forehead was chilly with a sudden dew of sweat. "Is that you?"

But his heartbeat was all he heard, and after a full minute of kneeling on the floor, he wearily got to his feet, feeling the various aches undiminished.

He shambled to the window, but Claimayne and Ariel had apparently finished their lunch and gone inside. The wheelbarrow no longer stood in front of the Medusa wall.

He straightened and turned to face the far corner of the room. The apartment where Natacha had shot Mr. Taylor had been in that direction, southeast, and not far away.

Back in his own room, his scuffed leather jacket was on the floor, and he bent and picked it up, feeling the swinging weight of the bottle in the pocket as he wearily thrust his arms into the sleeves. The three remaining folded spider papers were still scattered on the bedspread, and he gathered them up and shoved them into the same pocket as the bottle.

He looked toward the door—the direction was still clear. He picked up his helmet and opened the door and stepped into the hall.

SCOTT RODE UP THE ramp from Argyle onto the southbound 101 Freeway, and since he wasn't sure when its course might diverge from the destination he sensed, he stayed in the slow lane, passing pastel-colored apartment buildings beyond the high freeway walls and the more distant turrets and roof peaks of the Scientology Celebrity Centre to the north. At about Beverly the freeway began to swerve to the left of his psychically insistent course, and he downshifted off the freeway at the Rampart exit and, after a moment of indecision at the traffic light, turned south. When he got down to West Sixth Street he felt that he had passed it, and he made a left turn and sped along past the clustered trees of MacArthur Park.

At Alvarado Street he intuitively swerved north, and he knew that he had passed his goal in the same moment that he recognized the Roxy Apartment building on his left. In full daylight he could see the cornices and decorative friezes above the arched windows of the first floor, and its masonry was visibly tan now; it had appeared gray in the moonlight when he had seen it in the spider vision a little more than an hour ago.

He leaned the bike into a hasty U-turn, and a moment later made a left onto a very narrow street called Maryland, and he swerved past a startled fruit-seller's cart into the parking lot of a Ross Dress for Less clothing store. He braked to a halt, reached down to switch off the engine, then slowly levered down the kickstand with his foot, swung his leg over the gas tank, and stood up on the parking lot asphalt.

He took a few tentative steps as he pulled off his helmet and goggles, and then stopped. The breeze was chilly in his sweaty hair.

He knew he was standing precisely where the woman Natacha had stood when she had shot Taylor. And the apartment it had happened in was long gone. From the moment when he had started his motorcycle, he had felt that he was following a line toward an end point, but in fact the end point was in a time he couldn't get to.

THE DRIVER OF THE white Chevy Blazer was caught by surprise when Scott looped back, and he had to continue on up to Third Street and then turn right, and then down a long alley of the back ends of apartment buildings, all graffiti and fire escapes and abandoned mattresses propped against low, bumper-scarred walls; and when he finally rocked across Maryland Street into the Ross parking lot, he drove well past where Scott was standing and braked crookedly in a parking space closer to the store. His 7-Eleven Big Gulp cup had fallen onto the passenger-side floor and spilled open.

His cell phone was already in his hand, and he was talking before the SUV had entirely stopped shifting on its shocks.

"This is Polydectes. That Madden guy on the motorcycle is at the place where Taylor was killed! Right, Alvarado and Maryland—yeah, the Scott one, he came right here from the Madden house on Vista Del Mar . . . no, he's off the bike, and I think he's standing, listen to me, I think he's standing exactly where Taylor's bungalow was, in '22." He lit a cigarette with trembling fingers as he listened, and then he interrupted, "Sure, sure—but I'd say it's a good bet that he's got a hypertemporal line on the big spider."

He listened for several seconds, sitting hiked around on the seat to keep an eye on Scott Madden and the motorcycle, then said, "I haven't seen any of the Montreal crowd, but that doesn't mean they're not here. If they are, they probably saw me come in here fast—but it was from a different direction, yeah, they'd figure I just need to buy a pair of pants . . . *pants*, this is Ross, they sell clothes . . . okay, right, action only if there's interference."

SCOTT WALKED SLOWLY BACK to his motorcycle, and when he had put on his goggles and helmet again and got the bike's engine started, he rode north on Alvarado, not hurrying—and not aware of the white Blazer behind him, much less of the white Saturn a few car lengths behind it.

As he reflexively worked the throttle and clutch and gearshift and the gathering headwind fluttered his shirt collar, Scott was trying to fit evident facts into a chronological order.

The Natacha woman had told Taylor that a man named Kosloff

had stolen the Medusa spider from her and shot her while doing it, and in fact Madeline had experienced that in a vision yesterday.

Later Natacha and a companion had gone to the apartment of this Taylor, and then somebody—somebody from a more recent time period—had overridden Natacha's control of her own body, and had shot Taylor, probably fatally.

Scott's right hand was gripping the throttle, but he vividly remembered the recoil of the gun in his palm; and then Taylor had taken a step toward the door—reflexively, hopelessly, trying to walk away?—and Scott had seen the little hole punched in the back of the man's jacket. Taylor had fallen over backward to the floor, and Scott remembered the empty look in the blankly staring eyes.

Scott was shivering and afraid he might vomit.

Abruptly his vision changed. The shapes of cars and buildings and pavement in front of him didn't shift or disappear, but his view had lost all depth, and he seemed to be riding straight at a flat surface with projected shapes at the edges moving away from the center.

By sheer sense of balance he kept the motorcycle upright as he squeezed the front brake and trod on the back one, and, guessing that the diagonal tapering line at his right was the curb, he slanted in toward it and brought the bike to a skidding stop. Cars audibly roared past him on his left, presumably corresponding to shapes that appeared and diminished on that side. He swung his right foot off the footrest and sagged in relief when the toe of his shoe bumped the gritty corner of the cement curb.

He clicked the gearshift pedal into neutral and then let the engine idle as he stared down at the shapes that were his hands, moving one in front of the other, and after a few seconds he was able to see that they moved in cubic space, and he could see that the gas tank was below them, and his shoe on the curb was below that. He looked up, along Alvarado Street, and the building and cars clearly receded from near to far.

The view kept on appearing to have depth, so after several deep breaths, Scott squeezed the clutch, stepped on the gearshift, and carefully angled his way back into the northbound traffic.

Focus, he told himself uneasily as he clicked up through the gears and the headwind chilled his damp face.

And Natacha claimed that Taylor got hold of a photograph of the Medusa spider, he thought, and incorporated multiple copies of the image into a film: *an exorcism film, setting the image in tarantella frequencies to nullify it.*

And Natacha had walked out with the film.

An exorcism, to nullify the Medusa spider. And—wasn't tarantella the name of a dance?

Just past Temple Street he leaned the bike to the left onto the oak-lined on-ramp for the northbound 101 Freeway, heading back toward Caveat. A white Chevy Blazer and a white Saturn steered into the on-ramp close behind him.

ARIEL FOUND TO HER surprise that she was relieved to hear Scott's old Honda roaring up the garage road. She and Claimayne had been talking to Jules Ferdalisi for ten minutes in the dining room, and she still wasn't sure what the man really wanted.

Claimayne now gestured toward the stack of notebooks and papers Ariel had laid on the table. She had set a corkscrew on top of them to keep the pages from blowing to the floor in the breeze through the open windows. "But that's all the . . . *peripheral writing* that she left," Claimayne said, a note of impatience beginning to flatten his voice. "What sort of thing are you after?" He seemed to have a specific answer in mind, coaxing Ferdalisi to give it. "Do say."

"I'm envisioning multimedia," said Ferdalisi. His ear-to-ear beard with no accompanying mustache, and his bald head, made his face appear to Ariel to be upside-down. "Music, and film, and reading. Dance. I want to convey the whole woman." He frowned and pouted his lips. "I don't mean to be offensively personal."

Claimayne blinked. "Uh . . . oh?"

"But," Ferdalisi went on, "her suicide—I know only the fact of it, not the means or place, from the newspaper accounts. But—was the moment captured by some security camera?"

"No," said Claimayne, clearly surprised at the question.

Ferdalisi frowned and pursed his lips. "Did she—I beg your pardon—herself make a video recording of the event? So many people do think to make such a record of significant . . . *milestones,* these days. The end of a, a noteworthy life—"

Ariel clenched her throat against a reflexive giggle and managed to cough instead.

Claimayne leaned back in his wheelchair and stared at the high ceiling beams, and Ariel thought he looked baffled and disappointed. "No," he drawled, "but an animated sequence might suffice. The old Warner Brothers cartoons—"

"Or Itchy and Scratchy," ventured Ariel in a choked voice.

"What do you mean?" Ferdalisi snapped at her, and she was sure he knew what she had referred to and was trying to make her feel frivolous.

"In the TV show *The Simpsons,*" she said slowly, "Bart and Lisa—those are two characters, it's a cartoon—they often watch a cartoon show called *Itchy and Scratchy.*" She smiled at him. "A cartoon within a cartoon, you see? And it's very violent—"

"I think they've even used grenades on each other," offered Claimayne. "I know someone who knows Matt Groening."

"That's the writer of the show," said Ariel. "You might approach him."

The kitchen door squeaked, and then Scott's shoes were clumping on the linoleum floor in there, and a moment later he pushed through the swinging door and walked into the dining room.

"Oh," he said, halting when he saw the three sitting at the table. "Excuse me."

"No, sit down," said Ariel. "We were talking with this gentleman about making an animated cartoon of Claimayne's mother blowing herself up on the roof."

Scott nodded. "You know," he said, "I used to live in the normal world. I still remember it."

"I apologize if I—" began Ferdalisi.

Ariel stared at the man curiously. "You came here to produce a *snuff* film?"

"No." Ferdalisi was blinking rapidly at Ariel. "I came here in good faith—"

"I knew somebody would," said Claimayne, "if we waited long enough."

"*You* didn't come in good faith," said Ariel to Scott. "You and your sister. Will you sit down?"

"My purpose is scholarly!" Ferdalisi burst out. His face was red. "I am in a position," he went on, and Ariel forced herself not to interrupt with a joke about his position, "for one thing, to pay you a great deal of money." Ariel had been trying to place his accent, and now that he was speaking angrily it was recognizably Spanish.

Scott pulled out a chair in front of the windows and sat down, setting his helmet on the floor.

Ferdalisi peered at him and then quickly looked back at Claimayne—but Ariel was sure she had seen a twitch of recognition in the man's eyebrows.

Claimayne reached out and patted the cuff of Ferdalisi's tweed jacket. "I do apologize. This *is* my mother we're discussing. It's a touchy subject, right?" He sat back. "Do *please* tell me what sort of material you are thinking of."

Ferdalisi scowled for several seconds as if to show that he was not easily mollified, then said earnestly, "Her involvement with old Los Angeles—she did extensive research—did she have no files?"

Claimayne nodded at the papers on the table. Ariel thought he was almost teasing when he said, "I've printed out her computer files—"

"No no, I mean paper, old paper." Ferdalisi took a deep breath. "Did she have any . . . notes to herself, drawings, little doodles . . . symbols? I believe I read that she kept a lot of such things, folded up. I asked about a *video* because in that final moment she might have been holding—" He stopped short and looked at the ceiling. "Her suicide happened on the *roof*?"

Ariel involuntarily glanced at Scott, and his eyes met hers for a moment before they both looked away. *Little doodles, symbols . . . folded up*, she thought, and she guessed that Scott was thinking of the same thing.

"To be closer to God," Claimayne told Ferdalisi. Ariel thought there was a note of satisfaction in his tone now, as if he'd finally got an answer he'd wanted. Still without looking at Ariel, he went on, "I'm the representative of the family in these legal affairs—why don't you and I conduct this discussion in the music room, away from"—he nodded toward Scott—"the poor relations."

Ariel started to stand up, but Claimayne waved her back. "I can wheel myself," he said. "You can stay here and play checkers or something with the boy."

WHEN THEY HEARD THE music room door down the hall squeak and snap closed, Ariel stared across the table at Scott.

"Your old woman came by here this afternoon," she said. "I went upstairs to fetch you, but you were asleep on your bed, so I told her you weren't home."

Scott's face was throbbing, but at the same time felt very cold; he was sure Ariel must mean Louise. He raised one spread hand.

"That Louise character," Ariel went on. "Do you remember her? I may have said you were passed out drunk."

Scott was somehow sure Ariel had not said that, but he thought of the bottle in his pocket and cleared his throat. "What did she, uh, want?"

"I didn't ask. She drove away."

Ellis must have told Louise this morning, Scott thought, that I'm staying at the old family estate this week.

"Did she—" he began, then just shook his head.

"What, leave a number? No. Say she'd try again, or call? No."

Scott nodded. "Okay."

"Why did she break off the engagement, however many years ago it was?"

Scott met Ariel's gaze. He was suddenly very tired, and here in the old dining room again it was easy to see her as the smart, cheerful companion she had been in the old days.

He smiled faintly. "She thought my ambitions were unrealistic." He waved a hand. "Unsustainable."

"Drawing, painting, all that?"

Scott nodded.

"Well, ultimately she proved to be correct there, didn't she?"

Scott's face was still cold. He took a deep breath. "Shrewd girl," he agreed, exhaling.

"I bet she heard you're supposed to inherit this place, and that's why she's surfaced again."

"That's likely."

Ariel was frowning. "You don't hit back."

Scott reached down and picked up his helmet, then pushed his chair back and got to his feet. "I've always liked you, Ariel," he said. "I'm sorry we somehow—"

"Liked me?" she interrupted. "Not *always*. Maybe you—"

A door banged open down the hall, and Scott caught the whir of Claimayne's approaching wheelchair. There were no accompanying footsteps.

"What?" asked Scott quickly. "Why not always, maybe I what?"

She waved it away and stood up.

Claimayne's wheelchair wobbled as he rolled into the dining room, and he gripped a wheel with his left hand to stop.

For a moment he didn't speak. Then, "There's a . . . *dip*, in the floor here," he said. He looked up at Scott and smiled. "A low spot, a concavity. It's always been there. Do you remember, we all played with Hot Wheels cars here—we'd send them racing past this spot and they'd . . . curve."

Scott nodded.

"It's deeper now," said Claimayne.

" . . . Okay."

"So I'd like you to," and suddenly Claimayne's face was red and he was roaring, "*crawl down there in the goddamn basement and fix it!*" He fumbled in the pocket of his dressing gown and pulled out a heavy-looking stainless-steel revolver.

Scott gasped and stepped away from Ariel in case Claimayne actually meant to shoot at him. "Claimayne—"

"*If,*" yelled Claimayne, and then he went on in a calmer voice, "you can't find it while you're down there, look for a spot of light." And he pointed the gun at the floor and pulled the trigger.

The resounding pop of the gunshot set Scott's ears ringing; splinters spun away from the new ragged hole in the hardwood floor.

Ariel stepped forward to take the gun from Claimayne's hand. His pale fingers released it with no struggle.

She looked around at the walls and up at the ceiling. "We're lucky that didn't bring the whole house down," she said, speaking more loudly than usual. She looked past Claimayne down the hall. "Is Mr. Fricassee using the dubious facilities?"

"Ferdalisi." Claimayne laughed shortly. "I wish he *would* try to use the toilet on this floor. No, he left by the back." He coughed in the gunpowder smoke. "It seems we don't have anything *concrete* enough to merit his . . . assistance in various matters."

"Hence your rage at the floor," said Ariel. "I didn't like him anyway."

"Quite right," said Claimayne, dabbing at his eyes now with a handkerchief. "Shouldn't like people."

Ariel shook her head and walked around the wheelchair toward the hall.

"Salomé," called Claimayne, "hand me back my gun, so that I might shoot our houseguest!"

Over her shoulder she said, "Who'd fix your damn floor, Tetrarch?," as she pulled open the front door.

Scott started after her. "Ariel, wait—"

Standing on the threshold with the breeze tossing her dark hair, she turned to face him. Her fingers held the gun loosely at her side. "Could you just not speak?" she said. "Could you please do me that one favor?" And then she had spun away and was hurrying down the path that led along the front of the house to the driveway.

Scott hesitated, then stepped back inside and closed the door.

"She doesn't like you," remarked Claimayne from the dining room.

Scott sighed. "Quite right," he said, then turned to the stairs.

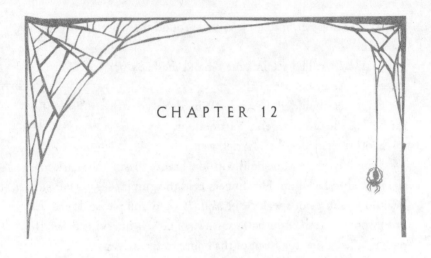

CHAPTER 12

SHORTLY AFTER RETURNING TO his room, Scott heard Claimayne's elevator knocking and banging in the walls; a minute later Madeline came trudging up the stairs, and Scott turned around when she appeared in the connecting doorway between their rooms. Her hands were shoved so deeply in the pockets of her old Members Only jacket that the thin green fabric was taut and her arms were almost straight.

"Maddy," Scott said, "did you take a paperback book out of my room?"

"Yes," she said, "it's on the windowsill by my bed. I was reading it. Listen, I—"

"Thank God." Scott hurried past her and picked up the Michael Connelly book and flipped through it, but there was no folded slip of paper tucked into the pages now. He looked back at Madeline. "*Tell* me you took a piece of paper out of this."

"I dog-eared your place. A dog-ear's better than a bookmark; it can't fall out, unless the whole pages does. But—"

"Damn it, where's the, the bookmark?" She stared at him blankly, and he went on, "Maddy, it was a spider of Mom's. She wrote *Before* and *After* on it, and she crossed out *Before* but not *After*. You see? It's still unconsummated. And I had it in this book—"

"It's on the floor. Now will you—"

Scott peered quickly around at the floor of her room. "Where?"

"I don't know, but it must be. Or maybe I threw it out. Did you *want* it? A spider?"

"No, but I don't want somebody finding it."

"You should have torn it up. But if it's not on the floor, then I threw it out, obviously. And a good thing, too. Will you listen?"

Scott moved around the bed, looking at the old floorboards, and finally got down on his hands and knees to look under the bed. There was no scrap of paper visible.

He got to his feet and strode to the wastepaper basket, but it was empty, without a liner. He hurried into his room, and that wastepaper basket was empty too.

"I took the trash out to the Dumpster when I left," his sister said. "Save work for Rita."

"If you're sure you—"

"For crying out loud, Scott! I'm sure!"

"Okay." He put down the wastepaper basket and walked back into her room. "But I've got to tell you about your girl Natacha, who you saw get shot, *experienced* getting shot."

Madeline paused by her bed, holding her briefcase; then she shook her head and pulled a sheaf of papers out of the briefcase. "After you see this. I read a lot of Aunt Amity's last-person novel last night—you were asleep by the time I came back up here—and listen, I know what *Oneida Inc* means."

Scott blinked at her. "What it means?"

He stepped to the door and looked up and down the hall, then shut it and twisted the deadbolt knob. He sat down on her bed as she thumbed through the pages, and he saw that she had printed them on the back sides of blank astrological charts.

"Let's keep our voices down," he said. "I heard Claimayne's elevator a little while ago."

"Right. Just a sec, I'll find it. Ah—here." She handed him one of the sheets and pointed at an underlined section in the middle of the page. Scott peered at it—she had printed it out single-spaced and in a 10-point font—and she added, "I couldn't find printing paper, and I didn't have a lot of these sheets."

Scott nodded and began puzzling out the small type.

> *aboard the oneida kosloff let ince see the damn thing and die of it hearst burned it only the taylor film left now we took it running away in adirondack woods natacha or him firing at us travellers now within that valley through the red-litten windows see paul ahead with the film can and me to catch a bullet in my foot and he took the can and left me in hospital rush out forever laugh but smile no more you must get it back charlene*

"I googled *oneida kosloff ince*," said Madeline, "and I got a Wikipedia article about this guy Thomas Ince—he was a movie director in the silent days, and he went on a cruise on William Randolph Hearst's yacht, the *Oneida,* and Theodore Kosloff was on the yacht too, and during the cruise Ince got some kind of sick and died."

"Oneida *Ince,*" Scott said softly. He shivered. "He got sick because he looked at Usabo. We saw him do it. We did it *with* him, twenty-three years ago."

"We didn't die of it," observed Madeline, looking away. "Neither of us."

"It was still no fun. Anyway, we were already in a spider vision when we looked at it with him, so we looked at it through his eyes. He caught the worst of it."

He looked out the window at the late-afternoon sunlight on the tree branches. "I know about the film can," he said. "Yesterday you saw the Kosloff guy get the big spider folder from Natacha after he shot her. Well, sometime after that she and a friend robbed a guy named Taylor, stole a reel of film with the big spider image—they called it the Medusa—on a lot of the frames. It was in a film can."

Madeline was staring at him, so he waved at the page and went on, "And then I guess after that, in the Adirondacks—that's mountains, in New York State—"

"I know."

"—this Charlene and Paul couple stole the film can from Natacha, and Paul ran off with it when Charlene was in a hospital with a bullet in her foot. The 'red-litten windows' business, and the 'laugh but smile no more' are from that same poem in the Poe story."

"Paul and Charlene are the names of Aunt Amity's parents."

Scott nodded. "I remember."

"Natacha stole the film? Where do you get that part of it?"

"In a minute." He pointed at the pages in her hands. "Is there more?"

"Okay. Yes. But don't forget." Madeline flipped through the pages and handed him another. "There at the top, underlined."

retirement check all these years and mister 2by4 stole it
his kids found it gave it back i open it on resurrection day
its gone kids put a squiggle instead wrote a new will made
banners branded in their eyes climb down in her eyes out of
the tomb

"Aunt Amity gave Dad that two-by-four," said Madeline softly, "on that last Christmas, in '91. He's mister two-by-four."

Scott knew he would have to forcefully call her attention to another passage in that section, but for now he just nodded. "And she says here that Dad stole what she calls a retirement check, and you and I gave it back to her, but when she opened it on Resurrection Day, whatever she meant by that, she found that we had switched it with a squiggle."

"The Oneida Ince one. And then she had to write the new will, specifying that we live here for a week."

She waved the typescript. "So how do you know Natacha stole the film from this Taylor guy?"

Scott described to his sister finding the box of spiders behind a drawer in their aunt's office, and the vision he had seen after looking at one of them that afternoon: the intrusion by Natacha and her male companion into Taylor's apartment, what she and Taylor had said to each other, and her shooting him and taking away the can of film.

"Natacha didn't mean to shoot him?" said Madeline.

"No, somebody else had taken control of her body at that point. She was as helpless as I was."

Scott glanced farther down the page and read,

i loved her cyclone I know charlene and alla loved me too
at first then said sick wicked and when she died i bought her
bathtub and when is a door not adore

He tapped the paper. "You saw this? I forgot to mention there's a big old iron bathtub in Aunt Amity's office. Not hooked up to any plumbing."

Madeline shrugged and shook her head. "And she spells *a door* like *worship* there. Spell-check doesn't catch errors if they're actual other words." She took the papers and slid them back into her briefcase. "You feel all right now?"

Scott stretched. "Yeah, I fell asleep for a while, after the vision wore off—" He thought of Louise's visit, and Ariel not waking him up, but pressed on, "and when I woke up I could still sense where the event happened—"

"I know," said Madeline with a visible shiver, "you feel like you can point your finger to it."

"And so I got on my bike and went there—"

Madeline gasped. "You went looking for Usabo?"

"It was decades ago, Maddy! The apartment where the Taylor

guy got shot, the whole building, is gone. It's a Ross Dress for Less parking lot now. But the building across the street was still there, the same as it was in the vision."

"A film that's an exorcism." Madeline giggled nervously and looked around the room. More quietly, she went on, "Of what?"

"Of the big spider, I guess. Maybe of all the spiders. But your Natacha just wanted to cut some frames out of it."

"I wonder if the exorcism would work," said Madeline, "and if it still exists."

"I was sort of hoping to find a clue about that," Scott admitted, "when I rode over there."

"I might need it, if we stay here," Madeline said. Scott looked at her sharply, and she added, "*Might.*" She didn't say anything more.

Scott prompted her: "Oh?"

"I don't think she means any harm, but Scott, last night when I finally went to sleep, Aunt Amity was in my dreams! I mean she was alive, intruding, shaking me and making me look in her eyes, and then I think I was dreaming her memories."

Madeline leaned against the door frame and slid down until she was sitting on the floor with her knees up. "I guess she got into my dreams when I looked at the spider yesterday."

"Maddy, she has got into your *head.*" He finally pointed at the passage on the page that had most caught his attention. "Look what she wrote—*made banners branded in their eyes climb down in her eyes*—if you give her time, she'll get *further* in, and, I don't know, crowd you out. Don't you think that's looking likely? She's begun *possessing* you, through that spider she left for you."

Madeline nodded slightly. "Well, I've been *wondering* about that. I thought I was just, you know, channeling her. We psychics do that."

"You're a psychic? I thought you were an astrologer."

"Well—they're related fields, aren't they?"

"She means to take you over. Already, just when you're talking, some of your word choices—it's like somebody else's vocabulary is mixing in with yours. We *have* to leave here."

"Oh hell." She hugged her knees. "Maybe. Tomorrow. If it happens again, or if it gets worse, or if it gets *scary*."

He stared at her incredulously. "This isn't scary? That a dead old woman has got herself inside your head?"

Madeline looked away and shrugged. "But I'm afraid she'll die if I leave."

"Uh . . ."

"I know, she's dead already. But I think I can help her to, you know, move on."

"Go toward the white light."

"Right, that stuff."

Scott was disconcerted by her evident calmness. "We should leave tonight," he said firmly. "Now."

"No."

"But if she—"

"No, Scott."

He bared his teeth in frustration. "But we *do* leave tomorrow!"

"If it gets too scary." Scott started to say something more, but Madeline waved dismissively. "So what news of the household?"

Scott emptied his lungs in a sigh, then spread his hands. "Well—Claimayne's gone crazy. He shot a gun into the floor not ten minutes ago." Now Madeline was glancing around at the floor, and he added impatiently, "Not here, in the dining room."

"Oh. I saw him downstairs; he said dinner's in half an hour—probably twenty minutes now. He's got a nosebleed."

"Do you want to have dinner with those two again?"

"It's free. I spent your ten dollars on gas."

"There's that. Okay. One last dinner. And remember we—"

A loud explosion from overhead shook the floor and rattled the window.

"Damn!" Scott crossed to the window and saw scraps of yellow lace spinning away down into the garden. "Do you know what Ariel says that noise is?"

"No. I know what it is, though. It's Aunt Amity blowing herself up again. No, not again—still."

Scott had turned to face her. "How do you know that?"

Madeline shrugged. "I don't know. What else *could* it be?"

"What else could—? Maddy—" Scott paused, trying to think of some reply or further question, and for several seconds neither of them spoke.

Then Madeline said in a rush, "I dreamed about what she wrote. I was in a long room, a tent, really, with no roof, and the walls were painted like rooms but they kept wiggling because it was windy outside, and in front of me three guys in D'Artagnan clothes were having a swordfight, and off to one side of them was like a saloon, with cowboys, and on the other side a guy and a girl dressed like for a wedding were sitting on a bench in front of some fake bushes and holding hands, not paying any attention to the sword guys or the cowboys. And behind me guys were yelling at them, like 'Slower, quicker, kiss her hand!'"

"Sounds like they were filming a movie. Several movies. Maddy, what makes you think—"

"Oh!" Madeline's eyes had widened. "Yeah, it does. Silent movies, I guess, what with guys all the time yelling at the actors." She paused, then nodded. "Yes, it was back when I was an actress."

"What?"

"I said it was back when she was an actress."

"What? Who, Aunt Amity?"

Madeline held a faraway stare for a moment, then looked down and shook her head. "Whoever." She stepped to the door and twisted the deadbolt back.

Scott didn't move. "You said, 'when I was an actress.'"

Madeline rolled her eyes. "That was *I* in the *dream*, Scott. *I've* never been an actress."

She started to say something further, then just shook her head. "We better go down to dinner before Salomé feeds it all to the tetrarch."

"You go ahead," he said, "I'll catch up." And when he heard her steps receding in the hall, he pulled the bourbon bottle out of his jacket pocket and hurried into his own room and shoved it under his mattress.

ARIEL WAS NOT SITTING at her place when Scott and Madeline walked in from the hallway, and as Claimayne waved them to their own chairs he said, "Rita isn't here, and so Ariel is cooking dinner tonight."

The tall windows in the dining room were closed this evening, though the long room still smelled faintly of diesel exhaust from down the hill, and lit candles stood in three wax-dribbled wine bottles on the table. Aunt Amity's empty chair still seemed to dominate the room.

Scott glanced toward the swinging kitchen doors—he heard steps and faint clattering, and considered and then instantly dismissed the idea of getting up and going in there to see if Ariel needed any help.

When he looked back to the table, Claimayne was smiling at him, so Scott quickly said, "Is Rita sick?"

"I think she's going to retire, actually," said Claimayne. "Yes, she had something like a stroke today. A window cracked, and she was unwise enough to look directly at it." Claimayne was staring intently at Scott now. "You'd think she'd know better, after working in this house for so many years, wouldn't you?"

Scott sat back in his chair and considered how to answer. Finally, "Yes," he said.

"Is she all right?" asked Madeline.

Still watching Scott, Claimayne said, "I think so. She was very shaky afterward, as you'd expect, but at least it was a fresh . . . set of cracks. Not dirty."

"I hope you broke the glass out of the window," said Scott.

Claimayne pushed at an opened bottle of Mondavi merlot, clearly finding it too heavy to lift. He glanced impatiently toward the kitchen.

"No," he said, "I think it might be rather entertaining to look at it myself one of these days." He slapped the arms of his wheelchair. "Let Rita briefly have seen how the lower half lives."

Scott frowned. "Where is it?"

"God knows! Today's Thursday, her day for vacuuming and dusting everywhere. I found her on the stairs—which is apparently where I'll leave her when our overlap expires."

The kitchen doors swung open, and Ariel, wearing glasses now, stepped into the dining room carrying two plates with wedges of steaming frittata on them; she carefully set them at her place and Claimayne's, then returned to the kitchen.

"I bet I find the window," said Madeline cheerfully, "and I bet I break it. Poor old Rita doesn't deserve to be you, even just for a few minutes. No offense," she added. She looked at the plate in front of Claimayne. "Frittata! With 'sparagus and bacon! Your old favorite, Scott."

"I don't remember that," said Ariel, pushing through the swinging doors again with two more plates. She clanked one down in front of Scott without looking at him, and Madeline took the other from her and set it down gently.

"And you leave Rita alone," said Ariel to Claimayne.

"Your fault," said Claimayne, "for not giving her your glasses. Would you pour the wine?"

Scott looked at Ariel more closely and then smothered a surprised laugh—the lenses of her glasses were rippled in a bull's-eye pattern, making fragmented rings of her eyes.

Madeline had noticed it too. "It's a good thing you were cooking frittata," she said, and when Ariel turned to her, she added, "since it's round. I bet we all look like blowfishes to you."

"I pass on that," said Claimayne. "Salomé, the wine?"

"Leeches is what you look like," said Ariel. She lifted the bottle and splashed wine into her glass and Claimayne's, then pushed it across the table.

Madeline poured a few ounces into her own glass and said, "Is there any more Coke?"

"I don't keep track of such things," said Ariel as she pulled out her chair and sat down.

Madeline started to get up, but Scott waved her back and got to his feet.

"Damn it, Ariel," said Claimayne, "you could fetch him his—"

"It's okay," said Scott, stepping around the table and pushing open the kitchen doors. Behind him Claimayne exhaled in exasperation.

The kitchen had not changed since Scott had moved out thirteen years earlier—the green-and-white tiled counters, the O'Keefe and Merritt double-oven stove—and the old green refrigerator that he had always thought looked like a 1950 Buick stood on end; the refrigerator door looked bare without some of Madeline's crayon drawings held on by souvenir magnets.

He levered open the door and leaned down to peer in at the ranks of yogurt cartons and translucent Tupperware containers half full of unattractive stuff, and by the ice sheet in the back he saw two cans of Coke. He lifted one free and straightened up.

Thinking of Claimayne's irritation that Ariel hadn't fetched the Coke, he looked around at the kitchen, and after a few moments noticed that the lace curtain over the door window was yellowed at the edges but white in the middle, as if it had been fastened aside for a long time and only recently loosed and drawn across the glass.

He crossed the worn linoleum to it and, being careful to stare at the red can in his hand, pulled the fabric to the side. Peripherally he could see cracks in the windowpane, possibly eight of them, radiating from a point in the center. They glowed in the slanting western sunlight.

Scott turned to the sink, unhooked an oven mitt and slipped it onto his free hand, and punched the glass out of the window. The shards clattered on the walkway pavement outside, and the early evening breeze through the empty frame was cold and smelled now of juniper. He beat the mitt over the trash can and hung it up again and then carried the Coke back to the dining room.

"The window was—in the kitchen!" said Madeline to Claimayne around a mouthful of frittata. She swallowed and went on, "You found Rita on the kitchen floor, not on the stairs."

As Scott pulled out his chair and sat down again, Claimayne looked at Scott's hands. "You didn't cut yourself, I hope?"

"Oven mitt," said Scott. He dug his fork into the wedge of thick omelette on his plate.

"Good," said Ariel. To Claimayne, she went on, "And Rita's older than you! You want your blood even more worn out than it already is?"

"It is bitter," said Claimayne with a smile, "but I like it because it is bitter, and because it is my blood." He took a sip of wine and waved his free hand. "Paraphrased from Stephen Crane."

"I was just gonna say," said Scott, who knew nothing about Stephen Crane except that he might have written *The Bridge of San Luis Rey.*

"This is canned 'sparagus," said Madeline, "not fresh. Scott always said canned was better in frittatas." To Ariel she added, "You remember?"

Ariel just frowned and shook her head.

For nearly a minute no one spoke, and the only sounds were chewing and the clink of cutlery. Ariel several times lifted her bare fork to her mouth, then impatiently lowered it and tried again to get some piece of frittata onto it; clearly she couldn't see it through her peculiar glasses.

Finally, "We've all been tense," said Claimayne. "Testy. *Out of sorts.* I think it would relax us all, as a family, to watch a heartwarming movie together."

"A movie?" said Ariel. "No, I'm not going to—"

Madeline shook her head sharply, as if dislodging a fly. "Yes," she said, "I'm afraid it's high time."

Scott thought of the wainscot door in the upstairs hallway. *When is a door not adore?* "It might be worthwhile," he admitted, "at that."

Ariel pulled off her glasses impatiently and glanced from one face to another. "What are you all—oh. The Alla Nazimova movie. *Salomé.*"

"In honor of my mother," agreed Claimayne, "who loved it."

"How do you spell her first name?" asked Madeline. "Nazimova, not your mother. I know how to spell *her* name."

"We won't test you, child. But Nazimova's first name was A-L-L-A. When her estate on Sunset was broken up into rental bungalows, the new owner called the complex 'The Garden of Allah,' with an H at the end, like for the Islamic deity."

"Her real name was Adelaida," said Ariel, rubbing the bridge of her nose. "Back in Siberia or wherever she came from."

Madeline was giving Scott a wide-eyed look, and he frowned and nodded slightly. Yes yes, I remember that passage, he thought—*i loved her cyclone I know charlene and alla loved me too at first*—don't draw attention.

But Ariel had caught the look and nod, and asked, "What?"

"That's the password," said Madeline quickly. "On your computer. Adelaida."

"My mother's computer," corrected Claimayne. Evidently having had enough of the dinner, he pushed his wheelchair back from the table.

Scott glanced at the wall above the hallway door, and noticed for the first time that the long metal retractable-screen case was missing; he could see the patches where the screw holes had been puttied over.

"This room is no longer the home theater," said Claimayne. "Now we've got a TV in the apiary. I've got a VHS version of *Salomé*,

and we've still got the VHS player, so we no longer need the projector and those worn-out reels."

The apiary had been the household name for a ballroom on the
third floor. When they had all been children, it had been stacked
with old furniture.

"Are the bees gone?" asked Madeline worriedly, pushing back
her chair and standing up.

"She got rid of the bees when you were still in grade school," said
Ariel. "You never did grasp that."

"I never did like bugs," said Madeline.

"Bees aren't—"

"I'll meet you all upstairs," said Claimayne.

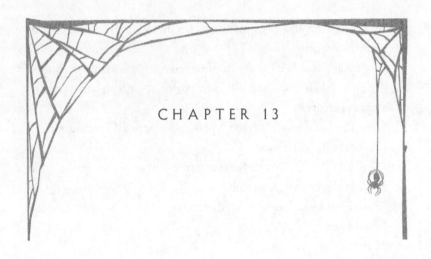

CHAPTER 13

THE LONG, WIDE ROOM had been largely cleared of the Victorian furniture that had once been packed in from wall to wall and nearly to the high ceiling, and now between the legs of neatly stacked tables Scott could see several windows from the inside for the first time. The center of the hardwood floor had been cleared, with a big flat-screen television set on a metal cart at the east end and two dozen mismatched chairs at the western end by the hallway door. A bare lightbulb in an old ceramic socket in the ceiling threw a jaundiced glare over everyone's face.

"You're ready for a lot of guests," Scott remarked to Ariel as he and Madeline walked across the booming floor and took two chairs at one end of the front row.

"Easier than stacking them."

"I don't smell bees," said Madeline cautiously. Scott thought the room smelled of sour dust and, faintly, of anchovy pizza.

The whole house shook then with such a tumultuous clamor that he thought Claimayne's mother must be exploding on the roof again; but a few moments later, after brief further clanging, he heard Claimayne's wheelchair rolling along the hall.

"Ought to just hoist him up and down with a damn pulley," muttered Ariel.

Claimayne appeared in the doorway, pallid and unhealthy look-ing. He wheeled his way across the floor to the television set and began rattling through a stack of VHS cases on a lower shelf of the cart.

"Here it is," he said finally, slipping the black cassette out of its cardboard sleeve and sliding it into the VCR. "Ariel, turn off the lights."

Ariel was still standing by the door. "Tell me again why this is a good idea."

"It's a . . . a shared event," said Claimayne, tapping buttons on the remote control now. "An opportunity for bonding. We all watched it together when we were children." He looked back over his shoulder. "The lights?"

"Bonding!" whispered Madeline.

"We made fun of it," said Ariel. "Only your mother paid attention to it." But she reached to the side and pushed the off button on the old electric switch, then took a seat at one end of the front row of chairs.

The screen lit up.

Scott found that he remembered the movie more than he would have expected—the images were in sepia tones rather than the starkly black-and-white version his aunt had always watched, and there was spooky music now, but the image of a Judean castle on a cliff, behind the opening credits, strongly brought back the smell of his aunt's Pall Mall cigarettes.

The third screen card read, *Sets and Costumes by MISS NATA-CHA RAMBOVA (After Aubrey Beardsley)*, and Madeline leaned over to whisper in Scott's ear, "Natacha! And in the vision, Kosloff called the spider in the folder 'the Beardsley'!"

Claimayne had propelled his wheelchair halfway back across the floor to where the other three sat, and Scott saw the silhouette of his head lift. "Beardsley, you say?"

"Madeline knows I like Beardsley's drawings," said Scott.

"Ah! Very nasty, a lot of his drawings were." Claimayne resumed rolling and parked his chair on the end of the front row, beside Ariel.

"On his deathbed he asked that certain ones be destroyed, though in fact those were . . . abstracts."

"I hate when people do that," put in Madeline. "They should destroy the stuff themselves, if they feel so strongly about it, before they die. Not stick friends with it."

Claimayne shrugged. "Sometimes you have to work posthumously."

The credits ended, and on the screen was a view of the tetrarch Herod's banquet, with black slaves waving fans and smoke curling up from braziers in the background.

Scott found himself remembering each grotesque detail as the movie progressed—the captain of the guard with scale-patterned tights and hair that little Madeline had always said looked like a lot of rum balls stuck to his head, midget white-bearded priests with hugely inflated striped turbans, the fat old tetrarch theatrically ogling young Salomé—and Salomé herself, boyishly slim in a skimpy dark tunic and sporting what might have been dozens of cotton balls suspended on wires in her hair. The action was slow and stylized, the characters frequently pausing to strike poses like figures on an art deco lamp, and Madeline was shifting and twitching in her seat, apparently agonizingly bored.

"We could just go," Scott whispered to her. "We've seen it before."

She shook her head and raised a spread hand.

On the screen, Salomé had eventually made her way from the banquet to a birdcage-like structure on a moonlit terrace, and looked down—a new camera shot revealed that the bars covered a well, and on the floor at the bottom of it stood an emaciated John the Baptist, called Jokanaan in the intertitle cards. The tetrarch Herod sent a slave to summon Salomé back to sit beside him, but she ignored the request and ordered the guards to release the prisoner; and when Jokanaan had ascended the steps and faced Salomé, she begged him to permit her to kiss him.

When Scott and Madeline and Ariel had been children, the teenaged Claimayne had at this point generally provided impromptu

additional dialogue between Salomé and Jokanaan, to much smothered hilarity; but when Scott glanced down the row of chairs now,
Claimayne's smooth face was still, his eyes glittering with tears as he
watched the screen.

It was his mother's favorite movie, Scott reminded himself, and
she committed suicide only a week ago. He looked back at the screen.

Jokanaan, with prolonged eye-rolling and posturing, had rejected
Salomé's advances and returned to the well, and the guards locked
the cage.

The torchlit dimness of the movie's scenes, viewed in the dark
old third-story ballroom of Caveat, made Scott wish he could
race down the stairs and get on his motorcycle and ride it to some
place full of light and cheery music. The awful old movie seemed
to be made of elements from childhood nightmares—stiff figures
moving slowly but ominously, contorted white faces under spiky
headdresses mouthing unintelligible words, screens on which the
stylized ivy patterns seemed to pulse. When they had all watched
the movie in the dining room, years ago, there had been interrup-
tions while Aunt Amity changed reels, but now it was mercilessly
continuous.

At the far end of the row, Ariel was cursing in whispers.

The scene arrived in which Herod's dialogue card read, "Dip
into the wine thy little red lips, that I may drain the cup!" to which
Salomé's reply was, "I am not thirsty, Tetrarch." Scott didn't smile
or glance at the others.

The tetrarch then asked Salomé to take a bite of fruit, so that he
might eat what was left; and Salomé replied that she wasn't hungry.
At last he asked her to dance for him, for which favor "thou may-
est ask of me what thou wilt, even unto the half of my kingdom."
Salomé refused this too and looked through the bars down into
the well; Jokanaan saw her and cried—unwisely, Scott thought, in
retrospect—"Ah, the wanton one! Let the captains of the hosts pierce
her with their swords!" Stepping away from the bars and looking

torn, Salomé asked Herod if he would indeed give her anything she asked, and he swore that he would, "by my life, by my crown, by my gods!" And Salomé consented.

At this point four women wearing black capes as square as boxes came onto the terrace with an oddly halting gait, like huge insects carefully walking upright; they surrounded and hid Salomé, and when they stepped back, their capes swinging now like ponderous bells, Salomé was revealed in a white tunic and with short, straight white hair. She began to dance around the terrace, to music visibly provided by half a dozen dancing dwarves in antlered helmets, and finally she spun rapidly around and collapsed to the floor.

Beside Scott, Madeline was quietly weeping, but when he touched her shoulder, she slapped his hand away.

Now the corpulent figure of the tetrarch Herod, who had appeared to nearly expire of joy during Salomé's dance, straightened up on his throne and asked her "What wouldst thou have?" and, after characteristic delay, she told him, "I ask of you the head of Jokanaan."

"It's coming," whispered Madeline, "it's coming."

What, thought Scott, Jokanaan's execution? As he remembered it, the eventual beheading took place offstage, and even when Salomé would appear ostensibly holding the severed head on a shield, the head was never actually visible at all. It had been a disappointment when he had first watched the film.

The tetrarch Herod, horrified by Salomé's request since he believed Jokanaan was a holy man, again offered her half his kingdom, instead; and she repeated her demand. Then he offered her the largest emerald in the world, and she refused that substitute too.

At this point, and it had always seemed to Scott to be a sharp diminishment in the magnitude of the proposed gifts, Herod said, "Salomé, thou knowest my white peacocks! In the midst of them thou wilt be like unto the moon in the midst of a great white cloud—"

Scott had glanced aside at Madeline then, and so he saw her chair kicked backward as she leaped to her feet; he was peripherally aware that Claimayne had grunted explosively, as if he'd been struck, but Scott's startled concern was with his sister, who was staring at the television screen.

Scott followed her gaze—and cringed back in his chair.

On the screen, against a dark background, was a still image of Salomé's head with dozens of white tendrils curling out from it in all directions across the sky; and it was eerily similar to the moment in a spider vision when the eight limbs broke into many and began to move.

"Claimayne!" shouted Madeline hoarsely. "From the ground, from under the floors and pavements, the blood cries out!"

At the first few words Claimayne had pushed his wheelchair forward and begun rolling down the row in front of the chairs, and now he collided with Madeline's knees and scrabbled at her hands.

"My mother?" he screeched up at her. "Where is it—" he went on, dragging his shaking fingers across Madeline's palms. "You've got a spider of my mother's, how do you dare look at it in front of me—!"

Ariel had stood up and hurried down the row of chairs, and now pulled his wheelchair back. "She didn't look at anything but the screen," she said loudly. "It's just the influence of this damned house!"

"Bullshit she didn't," gasped Claimayne, still flailing toward Madeline. "That was my mother's voice—she must have—"

"I adored her!" shouted Madeline again, still staring at the screen. "But evil things in robes of sorrow . . ."

Then she stopped and raised her hands to her face, and Scott saw scratches in her palms. She held them out and looked around at the taut faces of the others and said, "Did *I* break the window?"

Claimayne exhaled in a long hiss.

Scott was on his feet, and he put an arm around Madeline's shoulders. "Let's go back to our rooms," he said.

Madeline blinked at him, clearly disoriented. "Is the movie over?"

"Oh, it's *over*," said Claimayne, spinning his chair and pushing it out across the floor toward the television.

Ariel stared after him. "What did you hope to do here?" she called.

"To—turn back some pages," said Claimayne, so quietly that Scott barely heard him. Claimayne had turned the television off and was gripping the remote control with both hands. "Not that many."

Ariel turned to Scott and Madeline. "Go," she said.

After a pause, Scott nodded and led Madeline across the dark room to the hallway door.

In the light from the hallway he could see the glint of tears on Madeline's cheeks. "Am I—your sister again?" she whispered to him.

"Yes," Scott told her, "and we'll keep it that way."

MADELINE WAS STANDING BY the window of their parents' room looking out at the dark garden. She seemed to have stopped trembling.

"Blood under the ground?" she said finally.

"That's what you said," Scott replied, shaking a cigarette out of a pack of Camels. "And under pavement, as I recall. 'Crying out.'"

"And I adored her?" Madeline hugged herself and shivered. "I mean *she* adored her? Adored who, that Alla? Nazimova?"

"I guess so." Scott snapped a Bic lighter at his cigarette. "You were looking at the screen."

"*She* was looking at it. Aunt Amity. *I* was asleep or something. How old do you think that Nazimova woman was, in that movie?"

"Oh—thirty?"

"I'll look her up on Google. But she'd have been pretty old by the time Aunt Amity could have met her, if she ever did." She looked at her scratched palms. "You said Claimayne thought I looked at a spider of hers?"

"Well, you did, yesterday," said Scott, exhaling smoke. "This was apparently a continuation of that."

Madeline clenched her fists, wincing, and for a while neither of them spoke.

"You're right," she said finally. "I haven't been channeling her—

she wants to possess me, she *was* possessing me a few minutes ago." She rubbed her jaw. "She used my mouth all wrong, talking."

Scott leaned back against the closed door and said, carefully, "Is it too scary yet?"

She giggled, though there were tears in her eyes. "Me getting kicked out of my own body, and next time maybe never coming back?" She walked quickly to the connecting door and back. "I don't want to inherit this creepy old house anyway." She was pacing back and forth across the bare floor now. "Let's get our stuff packed, and sneak out tonight after Claimayne and Ariel have gone to bed. Should we leave a note?"

Scott thought of what Ariel had said to him at the front door this afternoon—*Could you just not speak? Could you please do me that one favor?*—and he answered, "No."

Madeline sat down on the bare mattress and flexed her hands in her lap, wincing.

"You don't think it's wrong to . . . abandon her here?" she said. "She did love us. Does."

"She loves you the way a drowning person loves somebody they can push down and climb on top of." Madeline was still staring at him, so he clarified, "No, it's not wrong."

She nodded solemnly. "Thank God. Thank God she went too far. It's been no fun after all, being back here."

She leaned to the side and picked up the phone book Scott had brought back from Amity's office. "I hope they don't stay up too late. Whose blood do you think she meant? Crying out?"

"Hard to say."

"Aunt Amity stopped watching that movie when we were kids. Do you remember when she stopped?"

"Some time before we looked at *Oneida Inc,* for sure." Scott took a long draw on the cigarette, then said, exhaling, "Otherwise that scene where Salomé had the tendrils growing out of her head would have had you and me diving right out the window."

Ride down Sunset again, he thought, tonight, with the cold fresh wind in my face, and never ride up Vista Del Mar again.

"I only saw it for a second, before she shoved me," said Madeline, nodding, "but it knocked me for a row of carrots." She had been flipping through the pages of the phone book and paused at one page. "Here's Paul Speas, in L.A. It's old, a four-digit number. That was Aunt Amity's dad, right?"

Scott dropped his cigarette into a coffee cup on the windowsill. "Let me get the envelope." He hurried through Madeline's room to his own and lifted one corner of the mattress. Under it, the unopened pint bottle of Wild Turkey was lying beside the manila envelope on which their mother had written *Backup copies.* He pulled out the envelope and carried it back to their parents' room, where he shook out the papers onto the ruined mattress beside Madeline.

He picked up one of the photocopied pages and peered at it. "Right. Paul David Speas married Charlene Claimayne Cooper in '21." He looked up. "And sometime a Paul and Charlene stole the exorcism film reel from your Natacha, according to your printout. And presumably that's the same Natacha Rambova who made the sets and costumes for that damn movie."

"And here's a Genod Speas, in Culver City."

Scott nodded. "I found a bunch of checks Aunt Amity wrote to him. Claimayne says it's a brother of hers."

"A brother? Who knew?" Madeline was still leafing through the phone book. "And here's Adrian Ostriker. Where did we hear of the name Ostriker?"

"Here." Scott picked up the sheet that was a copy of notes their mother had made. "Mom wrote, *Ten percent finder's fee to Ostriker?* And she put the name Ostriker in quotes, like it's an alias. *If he squawks. And point out that he should be grateful for no exposure of him, i.e., wheelbugs,* and under that she wrote, *And WDT murder?*"

Madeline shivered. "That Taylor guy you saw get shot, I bet his initials were W. D. T. I'm glad we're getting out of here. Do you think she remembered the canned 'sparagus?"

"What?" Scott shook his head. "Who, Mom?"

Madeline giggled. "No—Ariel. Tonight at dinner."

"Oh! I don't know. That'd be nice."

"She said she didn't mean to, but she *would* say that. She wants to make sure she doesn't like you anymore." Madeline put the phone book down on the mattress. "What's the other book?"

"I think she's pretty sure." Scott picked up the Valentino biography and handed it to her. "There's no writing or bookmarks or anything, except for a note on the front flyleaf in Mom's handwriting."

After glancing at the cover picture, Madeline opened the book to the flyleaf and stared at the writing for a moment. "*Keep it, I've got more copies,* Mom wrote. That sounds like, 'Keep this print, I've got the negative.' More and more it looks like blackmail."

"True. Though I don't see how anything to do with Valentino could be relevant."

Madeline flipped through the pages of the book, pausing at the section of photographs in the middle.

"I think—" she began; then she gripped the book tightly, staring at one photograph. "Oh my God, Scott, oh my God!"

Alarmed, Scott sat down beside her on the bed; the pages the book was opened to showed two black-and-white photographs, one of Valentino in sporting clothes in front of a car and a house, the other of Valentino in a sweater standing with Douglas Fairbanks and a young Jackie Coogan.

"What?" Scott asked, a bit shrilly.

"That!" exclaimed Madeline, letting go of one side of the book to tap the picture of Valentino alone. "And there he is too," she added, sliding her finger to Valentino's half-shadowed face on the opposite page. "That's—I swear that's the man I saw in the Usabo vision! When we were kids! He took my hand and led me out of the horrible rush of . . . *avalanche* of other people's experiences, *stinging* experiences. He told me 'My dear, my dear, it is not so dreadful here.'" Scott saw tears actually spurt from Madeline's eyes as she asked, "Is he dead?"

Scott spread his hands helplessly. "No deader than he was when he spoke to you then. He died young, as I recall. Is this really the first time you've ever seen a picture of Rudolph Valentino?"

"No—but like on the cover, he was always made up and wearing a, an Arab curtain-hat, you know? Not like a normal person, like he is here." She exhaled shakily. "I found him. I knew I would, I *always* knew I would."

Scott remembered finding Madeline in the basement yesterday— she had at first mistaken him for someone else, come to save her: *somebody I sort of met in this house once . . .*

He peered over her shoulder at the pictures in the book, and now his chest suddenly felt hollow. "Madeline," he said carefully; he paused to stare again at the face in the two photographs. Certain now, he went on, "Madeline, that's the guy who was with Natacha when she shot the Taylor guy."

"What, are you sure? But—you said he didn't want her to, right?"

"He didn't seem happy to come back inside and see she'd done it. Of course it wasn't *really* her that did it."

Madeline hefted the book. "I finally know who he is!"

Was, thought Scott. He reached past her elbow and flipped through the other photograph pages, and at one he paused. "That's weird," he said.

He leaned over the photocopies on the mattress and palmed the top sheets aside. He found the copy of the nude photograph of their aunt and straightened up with it.

"Oh, put that down, Scott," Madeline said, again looking away from it. "I wasn't—"

"Look at it—not at her, at that couch-thing behind her, and that bolster on the carpet."

Madeline peered at the paper sideways. "I see them."

Scott held it up beside the book Madeline was still holding. "Now look at that picture of Valentino."

Madeline looked from the photocopied page Scott was holding to the picture in the book, which showed Valentino dressed as some sort of rajah in front of the same ornate settee.

"It's the same place," she said.

"Maddy, look at the wrinkles in that bolster on the floor! Look at the angles of the pillows! It's the same *time*!"

Madeline frowned at the two pictures, and nodded. "I thought Valentino was in silent movies. Like in the '20s."

"He was—here, give me the book." Scott opened it to the beginning of a chapter near the end and flipped through several pages. "Uh, it says he was married to Natacha . . ." He saw Madeline frown and quickly turned some more pages. "Ah. He died on August 23, 1926."

Madeline took the photocopy page from Scott and finally looked at it closely; then she looked at the photograph in the book. "But— Aunt Amity was born in 1944."

"That picture of her was taken no later than 1926, unless nobody moved those cushions and stuff for about forty years."

"It looks real. And it's her, unless she was a twin of her mother."

"With the same mole on the throat?"

"Oh. Yeah." Madeline looked away. "Could it have been photoshopped?"

"Why would somebody fake up a photo that's obviously impossible? And anyway, it's been in the wall here since at least 1991. I don't think Photoshop was around yet."

"*This* must be the blackmail thing, somehow," Madeline said, "not her being naked."

Scott took the book from Madeline and flipped to the page before the section of photos, and then he picked up the photocopy sheet with the picture of the two naked women in a passionate embrace.

"Right. Look at the Post-it note on this one—'*IS following 244.*'

The photos in the book follow page 244. And," he went on, closing the book to look at the cover, "the author's name is Irving Schulman. *I.S.* The blackmail . . . thing, issue, is apparently that she's documentably there in the 1920s."

"And all that stuff," said Madeline, waving at the copies of the birth certificates and the marriage license, "must be part of it, right? Or else why would Mom and Dad have included them in the blackmail package?"

"And who could Mom and Dad have been threatening to show it all to?" He waved his free hand. "Whoever Aunt Amity . . . I don't know, stole a time machine from?"

"Maybe she just walked back to 1920 the same way I did yesterday." Madeline yawned. "It looks like she got to stay a lot longer than I did. At least she had time to take off her clothes."

Scott got to his feet and gathered up the papers and slid them back into the envelope. "We should pack up our stuff, and we might as well take this with us." He was more saddened than he would have expected at the prospect of never seeing Ariel again. *She wants to make sure she doesn't like you anymore,* Madeline had said.

He looked at Madeline. She had stood up and was giving him a stricken look.

"What?" he said, suddenly apprehensive.

"Oh, hell," she wailed, "I can't leave now, Scott!"

His heart sank, and he pretended to misunderstand her. "We can wait till morning—I'll stay up with you—"

"*He's* in all this! Him, Valentino! I can get back to him if I stay, I know it. Aunt Amity—I'm scared of her, but it was her Oneida Ince spider that led me to him. That spider's gone now, but . . . Aunt Amity isn't." She crossed to her purse and slid the Valentino biography and the old phone book into it.

Scott forced his voice to stay level. "It's all just ghosts, Maddy. Like watching the people in that old movie. When I saw Valentino at Taylor's apartment, he wasn't aware of *me.*"

"He was aware of me in the Usabo vision," said Madeline. She sniffed and looked around the bare room. "But you don't have to stay; you can leave. I've just got to find *him* again. He'll know what to do."

"Maddy, he's *gone*. That was *me* who found you in the basement yesterday."

"I know. But it was almost him."

Scott wondered bleakly if he could somehow just kidnap his sister and forcibly take her far away from all this.

I need to find the exorcism, he thought.

CLAIMAYNE WAS SWEATING, AND his heart was pounding at an alarming rate; the pains in his chest were like tightening wires. He sat back gingerly in his bed and switched off the intercom when the tinny speaker transmitted the clumping of Scott walking back to his own room. The notes he had scribbled on a legal pad were crabbed and hasty, and he painfully leaned sideways to see them better in the light from the bedside table lamp.

He took a deep breath and let it out. His heartbeat was beginning to subside, the pains lessening. I *knew* they looked at the *Oneida Inc* spider! he thought. Apparently that was the occasion of what Madwoman calls the . . . what was it, the Gustavo vision? The Ysabeau vision? Something like that.

And—Rudolph Valentino spoke to her in it? Poor child, I think *that* was definitely an hallucination! But she may well have walked to 1920, through the same kind of spontaneous gap that let Ariel see that old car in the driveway today.

He shook his head sharply and looked at another of his notes.

They'd discovered an awful lot about his mother. Oh well, can't threaten a dead woman.

Who, he wondered, is Adrian Ostriker? Art and Irina were apparently considering paying him a finder's fee, for the blackmail information. I knew they tried to blackmail my mother, but I never managed to find their evidence. Hidden in a wall and an old biography of Valentino!

And Scott was clearly lying this afternoon, when he said he had not found my cloisonné box.

Claimayne took several deep breaths to let his heart slow down again.

The pad fell to the carpet as he groped for his cell phone on the bedside table; and when he had got it, he had to dig into the pocket of his dressing gown for the business card.

At last he was able to punch in the numbers on the card.

"Hello?" he said after a few seconds. "Mr. Ferdalisi? This is Claimayne Madden. I'm sorry our meeting this afternoon ended in some acrimony." After a few seconds he went on, "But I find I *do* after all have something concrete to bargain with. And I want to keep one-half of it."

PART II

Little Miss Muffet

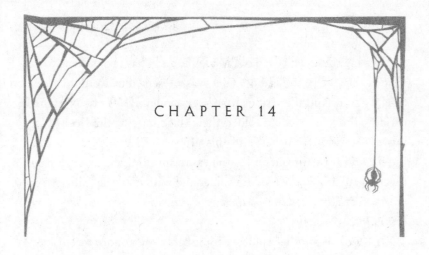

CHAPTER 14

AFTER LYING IN BED in the dark for an hour, Scott swung his feet out from under the covers to the floor. He was oddly tense, and at first he assumed that it was the bottle of Wild Turkey under the mattress that was nagging at him. Like the princess and the pea, he thought. He considered pulling the bottle out, and when he discovered that the idea held no particular attraction, he went on to imagine opening it and taking a fumy mouthful of the bourbon.

But that felt . . . irrelevant. What, he thought cautiously—have I lost the old compulsion?

Then it occurred to him that he had discovered a new one.

He didn't switch on the light, because the connecting door to Madeline's room was open, but he picked up his leather jacket from the floor and carried it to the window, where a shaft of moonlight illuminated the windowsill and a patch of the wooden floor.

I'm thinking of Madeline, he told himself. Now that she's convinced that Rudolph Valentino—for God's sake—is a part of all this, accessible here, she won't ever leave this house and Aunt Amity's predatory presence. But Taylor's exorcism might very well tear the whole web apart.

And I saw it, that film can. I held it—decades ago, through Nata-cha Rambova's hands.

During these last two days, Madeline and I have consistently had visions in which the Usabo spider was present, but we didn't look directly at it. And the visions have been sequential—I saw Natacha's hand holding the Medusa folder, then Madeline saw the Kosloff fel-low get it away from her, and this afternoon I saw Natacha steal the film with the image on it—the exorcism film, which Taylor put together to nullify the Medusa spider and with it all the spiders. *You must know I've tried to stop the havoc this sickness has caused in our community, Natacha!*

If I look at another spider, I'll probably see a more recent loca-tion for that film reel. Possibly I'll see where it is now.

Scott reached into the pocket of his jacket and pulled out one of the three remaining folded spiders that had been in the cloisonné box. It was crumpled, and he straightened it between shaking fin-gers. Squinting, he could just make out the word *Innamorati* pen-ciled on it.

That moment of no identity, he thought, of not being *me* for a blessed measureless interval—

No, he told himself, you're doing it for Madeline.

Quickly, before the ostensible virtue of that thought could fade, he opened the paper and stared at the eight radiating lines.

WHEN THE VERTICAL FIGURES moved aside and he was again aware of who he was, he was staring at a lamplit face a few feet away from him, and it was the face of the young man who had been with Natacha at Taylor's apartment—this was Rudolph Valentino.

Only after a moment did Scott become aware of the long jaw, the unlined forehead under close-cropped brown hair; the heavy-lidded eyes caught and held his attention. One looked straight into his, and the other stared slightly to the side.

The lips parted. "You narrow your eyes in a strange way," said Valentino. "I think you are not Natacha."

Scott was able to interrupt the steady breathing of the body he was occupying. "No," he managed to say. *And this encounter is obviously not much more recent than our previous ones, damn it. Too far back!*

"Can you move your hands?" The voice was faintly accented; Italian, Scott supposed.

Scott concentrated, and then saw Natacha's right hand rise in the lamplight, fingers spread. The chain bracelet slid down the wrist.

"Here." From his pocket Valentino produced a pack of Black Jack gum and pulled out a stick and pressed it into Natacha's palm. His quick smile was sympathetic.

Scott frowned in puzzlement, tensing Natacha's forehead. He opened her mouth and said, "Gum?"

"The tinfoil," said Valentino patiently. "Chew on it. It will hurt, against her fillings in her teeth, but not do any damage to her. It's better than her thumbtacks, which I tell her could give her an infection."

Scott had got Natacha's fingers to close on the stick of gum. "Why," he articulated, "hurt?"

Valentino cocked his head. "Spirit, are you a novice? Pain makes the visitation last longer. Why have you come? Natacha was hoping to hear from herself in the future."

I preempted her, Scott thought, *because the Usabo image must be nearby.* "A film can," he said clearly. "It's here."

But, he thought, *according to Aunt Amity's last-person novel, at least, it will eventually be stolen from Natacha, somewhere in the Adirondacks, by Charlene and Paul. How reliable is her crazy novel, though?*

Valentino sat back in what Scott could now see was a carved and polished wooden chair. Behind him, gold lettering on book spines gleamed in dimness. Scott carefully rotated Natacha's head, and to his right saw a curved wall with five tall arched windows and dark-ness beyond; looking the other way, the room seemed to be all black marble and red curtains. All he could smell was mimosa perfume.

Valentino was frowning now. "Are you the one who killed Bill Taylor?"

Scott made Natacha's long fingers tear the paper from the gum and unfold the thin sheet of foil, and he pushed the foil between her lips and bit down; bright razory pain lanced through her jaw, and he winced, but the pain seemed to settle him more firmly into the host body; and it was slightly preferable to the thumbtack Natacha had had piercing her toe in the earlier vision.

"No," he said, "though I was present then, just as I am now. Someone else overrode her and me, and shot him."

And in fact Scott thought he could sense another presence now, hovering unfamiliarly in Natacha's nervous system; but it didn't assert itself and in any case the sensation was faint.

Valentino shook a cigarette out of a pack on which Scott could read the brand name Abdullah and lit it with a gold lighter. "So you know she was innocent of that. We had hoped that it would be her future self who came now, and she would tell us that Natacha—and I—are never to be connected with that murder."

Scott wished he had at least skimmed the biography before look-ing at the spider. "I never—heard that you were," he said lamely.

Valentino pushed out a puff of smoke and then inhaled it. "I think you are a human being, since you speak easily. Are you a man or a woman?"

Scott looked down at the body he was in, disoriented to see the cleavage of breasts under a white blouse. "A man, in spite of—" He waved his hand.

Valentino laughed softly. "It must be . . . disconcerting!"

Scott nodded Natacha's head.

Valentino leaned forward. "What is your . . . concern, with the film in the can?"

"It's here, isn't it?" Scott inhaled with the foreign lungs. "In this room. Otherwise I wouldn't have ended up here." Remembering how short these visions could be, he bit down on the foil again, and shuddered, wondering if the thumbtack had really been that bad. "I need to know where the film goes, in the future." *And this visit is no help,* he thought, *if Aunt Amity's disjointed typescript is accurate. But maybe it's not.*

Valentino stood up, and Scott saw that he was wearing a gray sweater vest over a white shirt, and tan slacks; it was still odd to see him in anything but Arab garb. Valentino stepped lightly to an arch behind his chair.

"Can you walk?" he asked. "I'd sooner talk outside."

Scott pushed down with the unfamiliar arms, straightened the long legs under a linen skirt, and managed to stand up. Luckily Natacha was wearing slippers. "Yes," he said breathlessly. "But bring the film can. I think it's my . . . tether, here. Now."

Valentino crouched and reached under the chair, and when he straightened, he was holding the flat metal can that Scott had last seen in Natacha's hands outside Taylor's apartment.

Squinting through the curling cigarette smoke, Valentino said, "I'll hold it, if you don't mind."

Scott nodded and followed him out of the room, bare legs clumsy under the skirt. A door in the far wall opened onto three steps that led down to a gravel path in a moonlit garden. The night breeze was cold, and smelled of recent rain and occasional wisps of Arabian tobacco smoke from Valentino's cigarette. Scott wished Natacha had been wearing a blouse with long sleeves.

"I grew up," began Valentino rapidly, then he went on at a more measured pace, "in a town in Taranto, in Italy. Do you know of the tarantella?"

"No. Unless you mean the dance?"

Valentino nodded, and in the moonlight Scott could see the tip of his cigarette glow brightly as he inhaled. "It is," Valentino went on, each syllable riding a puff of smoke, "where the name of the spider, tarantula, comes from. The dance, the old version of the tarantella, was to cure what they call *tarantism*—a kind of spider bite; but not a literal bite of a literal spider." He began striding toward the front of the house. Over his shoulder he called, "You know the kind of spider I mean."

"Yes," said Scott, shuffling and spreading his arms to keep his balance as he followed him.

Valentino said, "I was always a good dancer."

A lawn sloped down to a narrow curving street with the dim bulk of a terraced Spanish-style house on the far side under bending palm-tree silhouettes. Valentino dropped his cigarette onto the gravel and looked up at the half-moon.

"There were many gorges, ravines, near our town," he went on, "and caves, some with old frescoes on the walls, and crazy men living in them. Hermits, *filosofos naturales*. Priests and my mother said not to go into those caves, but—I was a wild boy with no care for my life. When my mother told me the meek would inherit the earth, I told her all I wanted of it was the shovelful that would cover my cold face. My friends and I went into the caves, and in one I saw the very old fresco, in the deep tunnels." He smiled and raised the film can. "It was this one, the mother of them all, the Medusa. The government dynamited that tunnel, later. People said the Vatican ordered it."

Scott hastily bit the foil again, suppressing a whimper and blinking tears out of his left eye. "The dance?" he said. "Saved you?"

"It's not the dance, it's the music." He shook his head. "It's not the music, in fact, it's the *time*. Eighteen eight! Nine beats in a four-four measure; it's too many for you to keep track of the rhythm; you can't tap your foot to it, and dancing to it needs a lot more than just footwork. One of my friends was able to sing and beat out the rhythm with rocks while another ran home to get a drum. I was . . . insane, with the too many visions all at once, but my friends saved my life. It was dark outside by the time the chattering noise drove the spider out of my head, and even so I had nightmares for a year, other people's nightmares, people long dead . . ."

Valentino had the cigarette pack out again and shook one onto his lower lip. As he bent over the flame of the lighter he was squinting at Scott, and Scott suddenly hoped the man wasn't thinking about the body he was wearing.

"It's decidedly odd," Valentino said, "to talk about Natacha with what seems to be Natacha herself!"

"It's not, though," said Scott hastily.

"No. But I still want to say 'you.' But she found a—an incarnation? Should we spell it with a K, like ink?—of the Medusa spider in a portfolio of abstract drawings by an English artist, this Beardsley fellow. You could look at it safely in a mirror, and she believes that Beardsley drew it in a mirror too."

Scott remembered the tilted mirror that had stood over Taylor's film-editing machine.

"Beardsley," Valentino went on, "got it, figured out how it should look, from studying a portfolio of lesser spider drawings his father brought back from India. The studying was bad for Beardsley, I gather—his health was destroyed, and he died very young." He looked at Natacha's eyes. "What do you hope to do"—he waved the film can—"with this? If you find it where you come from?"

Scott hesitated. Natacha had wanted a frame from the film—presumably to use its power somehow. She would not have wanted anything like an exorcism.

"Tell me the truth," said Valentino.

He apparently experienced the Medusa spider in that cave, Scott thought, and directly, not secondhand through somebody else's eyes, the way Madeline and I did. And it came close to killing him.

"I mean to use it to exorcise the Medusa spider. And I hope it will kill all the lesser spiders too."

Valentino laughed softly. "It would do that, yes. The lesser ones are reflections of the Medusa herself. But someone—the way that poor Taylor fellow meant it to work—someone has to *watch* the film, and I think it would kill that person. I think Taylor meant to do it himself, because a woman he loved was addicted to the spiders."

"My sister—is caught in the web." And imagines that she met you there, he thought, and that she might meet you there again.

"Of course you want to save her. Does your sister, too, intrude in our visions?"

Scott remembered Madeline's story about Kosloff shooting Natacha, and the taxi ride to the hospital. "She has."

"Is her name Madeline?"

Startled, Scott nodded Natacha's head. "Yes."

"Natacha was grateful for Madeline's company and comfort, when she was wounded." Valentino took a long draw on the cigarette, dropped it to the gravel and stepped on it, then tapped the film can. "I was going to burn this tonight. Natacha would have hated me for it, but—but instead I believe I will take the . . . *easy way out* and leave it under the chair in the dining room for now. And I'll hide the film in this house, for you to find, in your day. In the attic, behind a board I will paint red, yes?"

Scott spat out the bit of chewed foil. He was still holding the stick of Black Jack gum, and he slid it into the pocket of Natacha's blouse, wondering what she would think when she found it . . . very soon.

Maybe Aunt Amity was wrong, he thought; maybe Paul and Charlene steal a different film can, by mistake, or a decoy—it doesn't seem they ever actually *looked* at it—and maybe the exorcism film stays in this house.

"Thank you," Scott said. "And if you move, leave it there—"

And then he jerked spasmodically, for he had fallen facedown in cold mud; he rolled over, gasping and spitting. Had Valentino knocked him down? All he could see was darkness stippled with meaningless spots of light. His arms and legs and teeth ached, and he wondered dazedly if he had somehow tumbled down the slope in

Valentino's front yard. His bare legs shivered in a chilly wind and his heart was thudding rapidly in his chest.

Scott sat up and raised a hand to his face, then flinched at a branching pale shape that suddenly filled his vision; but when he spasmodically thrust his hand toward it, the thing shrank, and he knew the shape was only his own hand.

He had fallen out of the vision. He still couldn't see clearly, but he slapped at his chest and legs and realized that he was wearing only what he'd worn to bed, a T-shirt and jockey shorts; and when he tried to stand up, his bare toes slid through mud and cold, wet grass.

Gasping with panic, nearly sobbing, Scott rubbed his eyes fiercely. I need to *see,* he thought. Where in hell *am* I? The cold wind seemed to burn his bare arms and legs.

He opened his eyes and forced himself to identify the depthless shapes. A patch of light wiggled as he shook his head; too low to be a streetlight, he thought, it's probably a light on a house. He tilted his head back and saw a glowing half disk—the moon, surely. And when he leaned farther back, the edge of blackness cut off more of the disk. I'm next to a fence or low wall, he thought, and it's partly blocking my view of the moon.

He reached out toward the obstruction, and even as his fingers felt the small flat pieces of stone, he was able to make out the curling dark patterns on the Medusa wall.

I'm still at Caveat—thank God, he thought.

He struggled to his feet, shivering in the wind and wincing at the pains in his legs and back, and he stumbled toward the light that he now recognized as the light over the back door. The knob turned—the door was blessedly unlocked. He hurried inside and exhaled in relief at the slightly warmer, still air of the laundry room.

Scott limped into the dark hall and then painfully made his way up the stairs, stepping on the edges of each tread to keep it from squeaking. He wondered if Natacha, in his body, had bothered to be quiet when she descended these stairs a few minutes ago; at least there was no sound now of anyone awake.

Back in his unlit room at last, and without waking Madeline, he slid his legs under the covers and slowly leaned back, inhaling through clenched teeth at the pain in his back and shoulders. He glanced at the open window and was glad that Natacha had apparently not felt suicidal. Of course the fall probably wouldn't have been fatal—he would simply have come back to find himself sitting in the planter below, freezing in his underwear, probably with a compound fracture or two.

As he lowered his head to the pillow, Scott let his arms relax—and then he was shivering and had to clench his teeth to keep them from chattering. He knew he was in his bed, but the stark, insistent memory of having only moments ago awakened cold and nearly naked in the mud, in the middle of the night, seemed too likely not to be a memory at all—what if he was still out there, and had only shut his eyes and imagined returning to his bed?

He gripped the sheet under him tightly enough to make his abused elbows and shoulders throb. I am in my bed, he thought. His forehead was chilly with relief. But I *cannot* do that again. I *will* not. There's some way to free Madeline without using the exorcism film, even if it still exists—there must be. Natacha said it's full of images of the big spider. *Someone has to* watch *the film*, Valentino had said, *and I think it would kill that person.*

I can't possibly sleep, Scott thought.

The bottle under the mattress, which had held no attraction for him a few minutes ago, now seemed to radiate a warm oblivion; and he subjected his knees and shoulders to more agony as he hunched out of bed and slid a hand under the mattress. He pulled out the bottle, and he was compensated for the pain in his wrist, as he unscrewed the cap, by the first aromatic, warming mouthful.

He climbed back into bed, carefully so as not to spill any, and leaned back against the headboard for another profoundly comforting swallow. It was the taste of the golden past, of books on the shelves and his parents in the farther room, of a dimly heard Harry James and Kitty Kallen song playing on their stereo. He took another sip and, finally, relaxed.

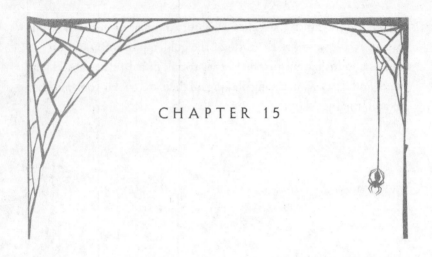

CHAPTER 15

MIDMORNING SUNLIGHT REFLECTING OFF the bare floor shone on the plaster ceiling, and Scott was peering through watering eyes as he rolled out of bed, sure that he was about to vomit; but he paused, leaning against the wall beside the open window, and after a few seconds the chilly air blowing in on his sweaty face emphasized his headache instead. He looked back at the disordered bed and the bottle on the floor, and he felt old and exhausted and corrupt. He had only begun to try to dismiss the memories of last night as dreams, when he saw the dried mud stains on his bare feet.

I will not go to that house where Valentino was, he told himself firmly; I can clearly sense what direction it's in, but I will not go there. He glanced down again at his blackened feet, and shuddered. I am through with spiders.

There must be another way to get Madeline out of the web, out of Aunt Amity's posthumous domination. He sighed from the bottom of his lungs and began wearily pulling on his jeans and a flannel shirt.

The orange couch and the heraldic wet bar, he thought. What *did* Aunt Amity do with all of Mom and Dad's stuff? They had some specific fact-in-context to blackmail Aunt Amity with, and if I can find out what that was, then maybe it's something I can use to banish her ghost, and nobody need ever look behind the red board in the attic of that house out there. To hell with Taylor and Valentino and that whole crowd. That whole dead and buried crowd.

Scott squinted against the brightness at his black plastic bag on the shelf beside his remaining dried-out cigarettes, but dreaded the effort of digging through its contents to try to find clean socks, and he pulled on yesterday's, then slid his feet into his shoes and clumsily tied them. Then he made the effort to pick up the bourbon bottle and shove it back under the mattress next to the manila envelope.

He looked through the open connecting door, but Madeline's bed was empty and neatly made up. God knew what time it was. He stepped softly into the hall and down the stairs.

From the dining room he heard the tinkling of a spoon stirring coffee in a ceramic cup, and someone closed a cupboard in the kitchen beyond, so he stole to the right from the base of the stairs, through the laundry room—scuffing aside bits of dry mud that were too clearly footprints—and lifted a dusty key ring from a hook and sidled out the back door.

He didn't even glance toward the spot by the Medusa wall where he had awakened last night, but hurried past the kitchen windows to the driveway and the long west lawn. Nobody opened the kitchen door to call after him.

The walk out to the road that led up to the old garages stretched his cramped thigh muscles, and the cold, soil-scented breeze in his nostrils made his headache recede.

When he got to the top of the hill, where the narrow road curved to the right just short of the tall eucalyptus trees that marked the north end of the property, he was surprised to see a new white Saturn parked sideways in front of the first of the row of four neglected garages. Morning sunlight glinted on the bumper chrome.

And as he paused, wondering if a neighbor from over on the Gower Street side was using this seldom-visited pavement for extra parking, a woman stood up from behind the Saturn, staring at the door of the garage in front of her. She was tall and slim, in faded jeans and an untucked brown flannel shirt, and a pair of sunglasses was pushed back on her short blond hair. She was holding a hacksaw.

It wasn't until she noticed him standing there and jumped in surprise that he recognized her.

"Louise!" he said hoarsely. The breeze in his face suddenly seemed several degrees colder.

After a stiff pause, "Doctor Scott!" she said. It chilled him further—her reply had turned this moment into a grotesque reenactment of a bit of dialogue from *The Rocky Horror Picture Show,* a movie the two of them had seen together many times, fifteen years or more ago.

Helplessly going along in mimicking the remembered exchange, he repeated, "Louise!"

"Doctor Scott!" she said again, still following the movie's script. It was clear that she was staving off the moment in which she would have to explain why she was evidently breaking into one of the garages.

Suddenly very tired, and careless of his uncombed and unshaven appearance, Scott interjected, "You don't need the saw. I've got a key."

Her shoulders slumped. "Oh. Good. The saw was only *polishing* the bar of your damn padlock." She gave him a crooked grin. "They said you all never come up here. And anyway I figured I'd hear a car. I didn't expect somebody to *walk* up."

"It's hardened steel." He stepped forward across the cracked asphalt, wincing at a reviving pain in his knee. "Who said?"

"I bet you don't look as bad as this all the time, right?"

"Debatable." He lowered himself carefully onto one knee and lifted the padlock. One side of the U-bar was indeed shinier where the hacksaw teeth had skated impotently back and forth over it. He fitted the key into the lock and the bar sprang open.

Still on one knee, he peered up at her. "Who said?"

Her smile was glassy. "Oh—people paying me."

He stood up. "People who pay you want something out of our garages?" His shoulders were nearly twitching with the reflex to take her into his arms, but it certainly didn't sound as if she had come back into his life to reestablish their relationship. He wished he'd brought a pack of cigarettes—and possibly the Wild Turkey bottle too.

"I tried to tell you about it yesterday, Scott. I went to the Ravenna Apartments, and the gentleman there said you were staying here for a week, and when I came here, a woman said you weren't home. But I waited on the street, and after a while I saw you taking off on your bike. That's the same bike as before, isn't it? So I followed you. You went to the Ross for Less on Alvarado. Did you know there was a man in a white Chevy Blazer following you?"

Her hair was shorter than it had been fifteen years ago, backlit now by the sun. He squinted at her, trying to read her expression; all he could conclude was that she was very embarrassed . . . and, behind that, it occurred to him, scared.

"No," he said, "I didn't know about the Chevy Blazer." He wondered if it was true.

"I was—" he paused, then went on, "yesterday I was glad to hear that you were trying to get in touch with me." He bent down and gripped the handle at the bottom of the wooden door and hauled upward; he felt as if he was dislocating his shoulder, but the door rocked up, squeaking, to its overhead horizontal position.

Inside, standing lamps and ornate tables and chairs were stacked to the low ceiling and nearly to the edge of the cement floor. It was furniture that had been stored in the apiary when he had lived at Caveat, stashed here sometime after he had moved out.

He turned to Louise; she had stepped closer, and the sun was on her face. It was thinner now, and there were new lines under her pale blue eyes and in her cheeks, and before she turned hastily away he noticed a spot of red beside the iris of her left eye.

"I'm sorry," she said. "I still wouldn't lie to you. I was going to tell you about it all." She frowned. "You really do look like hell. But so do we all, these days."

"There's nothing in here for me," Scott said, nodding at the furniture in the garage. "Were you after a lamp? A set of chairs?"

"I don't think so. Unlock another one."

He pulled the door back down and knelt to resecure the padlock. "That's the plan."

"How's Madeline?" she asked as they walked to the next garage.

"Oh—same."

"Ah."

Louise had to get her hands under the edge of the door of the next garage and help him lift it; and he noticed an apparently constant tremor in her hands. The old wood groaned loudly, and dust sifted down from the door when they had worked it into the raised position.

Cobwebs were draped in diaphanous gray sheets over a white-painted desk and half a dozen cardboard boxes and, sure enough, the orange couch and the high mirrored cabinet that was the wet bar. The confined air had the rancid-oil smell of mildew, and Scott wondered if this roof leaked too.

He turned to Louise and raised his eyebrows in inquiry. He felt brittle and tense.

She shrugged and gave him a defiant look. "Maybe."

"Me too." He knelt on the asphalt and then just sat down and dragged one of the boxes closer. Louise leaned over him as he brushed dust off it.

She put her hand on his shoulder. "Uh . . . open it slow, Scott."

Black widows? he thought. Rats? But he obediently took several seconds pulling the cardboard flaps up.

The box was packed with old paperback romances, and he pushed it away and slid another box in front of him. "You said you were going to tell me about it all. So tell me."

"Ask me."

Scott sat back. "What are you looking for here?"

At first he thought she wouldn't answer him—she was staring at him with an expression of sadness or pity—but finally she reached up and pulled the sunglasses free of her hair.

He waited, expecting her to put them on, then realized that the sunglasses were somehow related to his question. He rocked his head to get the sunglasses between him and the daylight, and he could see crossed ridges on the lenses. And he remembered Ariel's distorting glasses at dinner last night; and when Ariel had told Claimayne not to take advantage of old Rita's accidental viewing of the spider pattern in the broken window, Claimayne had said, *Your fault for not giving her your glasses.*

Tears stood in Louise's eyes. "I used to think I was better than you, damn it."

Scott's chest felt hollow. "So did I."

She sniffed. "Probably I am anyway. But Scott—*give them the damn spider,* the big one, their Medusa, or tell them where it is!"

"I don't know where it is."

She pursed her lips. "You almost do, though, don't you? And you know what I'm talking about. You've got clues people want. That Ross parking lot is where Taylor's apartment was! And you didn't go into Ross, you just looked around and then left! It changed everything when you went there yesterday. Until you did that, nobody really figured Amity Madden's weird old family had any line on the Medusa spider. They were following you and your sister and what's her name, Ariel, just to see if any of you . . . I don't know . . . were getting ready to leave the country, or consulted the police, or a Catholic priest, or went to see any of the other old-school spider addicts around town. A few days ago they . . . hired me as a consultant, since I knew—I'm one of the few people!—who knew you all. They wanted me to hang around and hear what you all had to say about your dead aunt. They even wanted me to pretend I still loved you. I told them they weren't paying me enough to lie to you."

"I wish you had, actually. I'd have been easy to fool."

"Oh, stop it. I was going to tell you about all that—it would have been kind of funny, and I was curious to see you again. And Madeline. But then you went to Taylor's place, and now there's red lights all over everybody's dashboards. I don't know what they've got other people doing, but they told me to try to find where your crazy aunt might have stored papers, and steal them if I could. They suggested these garages." She spread her hands and smiled ruefully; her hands were still trembling. "And I figured if I got caught, you wouldn't call the cops on an old . . . friend of the family."

"Who are these employers of yours?"

"I've only met one guy, though he says 'we.' He hasn't told me his name. He's met me three times, at a Starbucks, and he pays me cash." She went on defensively, "It's freelance; my real job is part-time teaching at USC."

"How did they get in touch?"

"He called me on Tuesday, and I went to meet him. I think they've been keeping track of—spying on, really—all the longtime covert Hollywood spider addicts, for years, and your family is one of the oldest, and lately they're worried by some other crowd that's apparently been doing the same thing. Your man in the Blazer would be one of them."

Scott shook his head as he brushed cobwebs and drifts of dust off the top of the box. "Why do they *want* the big spider?"

She was peering over his shoulder. "You think I'd *ask*?"

"I think you'd guess."

"Well—yeah." She put on the sunglasses. "What's in the box? Maybe I should look first."

For several seconds Scott stared at the gleaming black ovals that hid her eyes; then, "I'll take my chances," he said. He pried up the cardboard flaps.

At first he thought a reflected gleam of morning sunlight was lighting the litter of cards and papers in the box, but when he looked closer, he saw that they were somehow lit from underneath. Smothering an exclamation, he pushed the cards and folded sheets aside, and saw a metal flashlight lying in the bottom of the box, its bulb glowing brightly behind the glass lens.

Louise snatched off her rippled sunglasses and blinked at it. "Someone's already been," she began in a loud voice—then, evidently remembering the dust and cobwebs that had covered the box, she finished weakly, "here?"

Scott thought of Madeline's view of old Hollywood yesterday. "I think it'll fade, since we moved the box from where it was sitting."

"What? But there were cobwebs on it! Why would someone put a flashlight in it, still lit, and then—it can't have been later than last night, but how could they know—"

Scott interrupted, "If you hadn't seen the flashlight, when would you say this box was last touched?"

"Uh—twenty years ago!"

"Close. Twenty-*three* years ago. 1992. I'm pretty sure that's when this box was last closed. Like I say, the flashlight will fade."

Louise laughed breathlessly, though she was frowning. "You're thinking about the batteries? Twenty-three years?" She laughed again. "Those would be some miracle batteries."

"See if you can touch the flashlight."

Louise crouched and reached into the box with her free hand, and her unsteady fingertips struck the cardboard bottom, for the flashlight had disappeared.

And then she had spun away and stumbled across the driveway and was leaning against the white trunk of one of the eucalyptus trees. Her short blond hair fluttered in the wind.

Scott sighed and stood up, and he stepped out into the sunlight and walked over to stand beside her. She seemed to be calm, though she was panting.

"That was good," she said. "That threw me. What is it, hypnosis?"

"That flashlight—" Scott paused for several seconds, his mouth open, then he went on doggedly, "That flashlight was never here. No, that's not quite right—that flashlight was never here *today*. It was here in 1992, when my cousin Claimayne was stowing my parents' stuff, a month or so after they left." He spread his hands apologetically. "Time is kind of screwy around this house. Who was Taylor?"

"Oh no you don't. *The flashlight was never here, time is screwy*? That's like something I'd expect Madeline to say. Honestly now, Scott, are you kidding or have you gone crazy?"

His headache had not gone away. "There's things Madeline understands better than you do. Who was Taylor?"

"Taylor Taylor Taylor! You don't know who he was, but you went to where he lived?—and died?"

To his surprise, Scott found that he had become very angry. "I know a woman shot him in the back to steal a reel of film from him. I'd *like* to know more than that."

"Ooh, you're in this, all right. I have to tell you, I'm going to tell them what you just said." After looking in his face, she went on hastily, "He was William Desmond Taylor, a movie director in the silent-movie days, he was in love with the actress Mabel Normand, and yes, he was shot in the back, killed, in 1922. But nobody—except you?—knows who shot him."

Scott had heard faint music playing behind Louise's words, and now that she paused he recognized it as the old Kansas song, "Dust in the Wind." He glanced around at the car and the garages, but the music became louder when Louise pulled a cell phone out of her jeans pocket.

She glanced at the phone. "It's them. Be quiet."

"What do they want with the big spider?"

"I get the idea . . . that they imagine they can evade death, with it, somehow. Though you die if you look at it. Go figure. The other group, I think, just wants to destroy it." She swiped a finger across the screen and raised the phone to her ear. "Hello?"

Scott leaned forward. "Talk to me direct," he said loudly. "Don't send ex-girlfriends around."

Louise's lips were a tight line; after a few seconds, she said, "Yes, okay," and handed the phone to him. "It's for you now, asshole."

Scott took the phone. His headache was strongly reasserting itself behind his left eye.

"Mister Madden!" came a man's voice from the little speaker. "We'd like to hire you to help us find something."

"What do you want it for?"

"We want to ascertain its benefits, sir, and use those. We'd be happy to have you participate. And we'd protect you and your family from others who want it. What led you to visit the parking lot at Alvarado and Maryland yesterday?"

Scott held the phone away and touched the red square that ended the call. He handed it to her and limped back to the open garage.

Louise came hurrying after him. "Good work," she said. "I don't know that I'm any use to them now."

Scott sat down and picked up a handful of the papers and cards in the opened box, shaking coffee grounds and ancient eggshell fragments off them. "You said you were going to tell me all about it," he said over his shoulder, "but first you told them that I went to Alvarado and Maryland."

"Damn it, I didn't know what it meant, then, when I told them! They told me after, about Taylor living there." She sat down on the other side of the box. "That guy in the Blazer knew about it, though—he was on his cell, all excited. I wondered why."

But Scott could hardly hear her over a sudden ringing in his ears. "This," he said carefully, holding up a blue plastic rectangle, "is my dad's Visa card." He took a deep, shuddering breath. "It expired in 1993, a year after it was put in this box." He dropped it and looked at another card. "And this is his driver's license.

Expired in 1996. Oh—here's my mom's. Here's their checkbook."

"Why would they—what are you thinking?"

He wiped his hand across his mouth, careless of the coffee grounds that clung to his fingers. "They didn't go away."

He stood up and yanked open a drawer of the white desk; and then another, and a few seconds later he had discovered that all of them were empty. He went to the bar and opened the drawer that had once held corkscrews and jiggers and strainers, and the cabinet door below it where bottles had stood, but everything was gone.

He crouched and ripped open the four remaining cardboard boxes, one after another, and the first three contained nothing but more paperbacks, the bar tools that had not been in the bar drawer, and an electric fan that Scott remembered roaring in the window of his parents' room on hot summer evenings; and the only thing in the fourth box was the beige telephone that had sat on his mother's desk. He looked at the clear-plastic dial and wondered whose finger had last spun it. There was of course no sound at all in the earpiece when he picked up the receiver, but he lifted the telephone out of the box and tucked it in the crook of his arm.

There was nothing else in the garage. If his parents had discovered something that might somehow be used against his now dead but intrusive aunt, it wasn't here. He glanced again at the box that contained the licenses and credit cards, then looked away, dizzy and breathing hard.

Louise was leafing through the paperbacks, but Scott stepped out onto the sunlit asphalt and reached up to take hold of the rope that dangled from the bottom edge of the garage door.

"We're through here," he said.

"But I need to—" she began; then, seeing him tug at the rope, she got to her feet and hurried outside.

The door crashed down in a shower of dust and splinters, and Scott crouched to slip the padlock through the hasp and click it closed. He stood up, still carrying the telephone.

"There's no spiders in there," he said breathlessly. "Claimayne put all that stuff in there, and he'd have looked through it all and taken any."

He straightened up, coughing. "Don't waste your time following me anymore. I'll be watching."

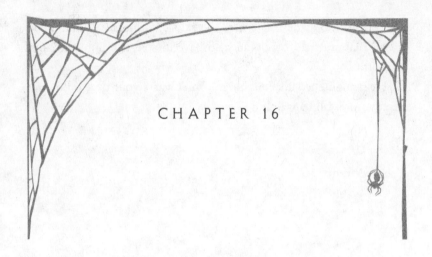

CHAPTER 16

WHEN SCOTT PUSHED OPEN the kitchen door and stepped inside, he was disconcerted to find Ariel and Madeline sitting stiffly at opposite sides of the kitchen table; Madeline, in sweatpants and a Gumby-and-Pokey T-shirt that served as pajamas, had her eyes tightly closed and her fists clenched on the table edge, and Ariel had pulled up the hood of a pink terrycloth bathrobe and was peering out from behind her bull's-eye glasses. Her eyes appeared to be clusters of concentric rings, and her right hand was groping among a dozen shortbread cookies on a plate that sat on the table between them.

"Is that Scott?" said Madeline. "Scott, look at the ceiling!"

He did, and saw nothing remarkable in the expanse of yellowed plaster; and he was already dizzy. He was about to look back at his sister, but she added, "Keep looking at it till I tell you to look down! There's cracks in the plate these cookies are on."

"Cracks," he said impatiently. Then, "Like spider cracks?"

"Right," said Madeline, "like the windows! Ariel's trying to break it up without spilling all the cookies on the floor."

"I can't see worth a damn through these stupid glasses," Ariel said tightly.

"For God's sake. How long have you two been sitting here like this?"

"It *just happened,* Scott," said Ariel in an irritated tone. "We're not *idiots.*"

Scott lowered his head enough to see the plate in his peripheral vision, and then with his free hand he just reached down and swept it off the table. Cookies and plate fragments spun across the floor. He was breathing fast.

"You pig," said Ariel, snatching off the glasses to glare at him.

"Madeline," he said, "you and I need to go out and get breakfast somewhere."

His sister stood up, eyeing him cautiously. "Okay. But you have to pay the check." She hurried out through the door to the dining room.

"And first you'll clean up these cookies!" added Ariel. "And you have to buy more!"

Scott started after Madeline, then swore and pulled open the broom closet. He set the telephone on the table, yanked out a broom, unclipped the plastic dustpan from it and hastily swept up the debris. He dumped it into the Trader Joe's bag standing beside the outside door and clipped the dustpan to the broom again, tossed it back into the closet and retrieved the telephone, then hurried through the dining room and up the wooden stairs.

FORTY MINUTES LATER HE and Madeline had found a parking space for her old Datsun in the lot behind the 101 Coffee Shop on Franklin at the bottom of Vista Del Mar, and now they were sitting in a vinyl-padded booth at the back, between the window and a wall with rocks cemented all over it. Madeline had a glass of iced tea on the Formica table, and Scott, his hair still damp and spiky from a hasty shower, was unenthusiastically sipping a cup of coffee.

"Where did you find the phone?" asked Madeline as she picked up the menu. "I'm glad I'm not a vegetarian," she added as she scanned its columns.

The place smelled wonderfully of bacon and onions, but Scott wasn't sure anything more than coffee would be a good idea yet.

"It was in one of the uphill garages," he said, and he added, "I saw Louise this morning." When Madeline raised her eyebrows, he went on. "She was there, trying to break into the garages. She's working now for people who want . . . Medusa, Usabo. They think I can find it for them." He told her about the conversation he'd had with Louise, and with one of her employers—and, finally, about finding their parents' driver's licenses and credit cards.

"Oh," said Madeline. "Oh."

"I didn't want to tell you about it back at Caveat, with Ariel and Claimayne banging around."

The waitress arrived then, and Madeline distractedly ordered catfish and scrambled eggs, while Scott just pointed at his coffee and handed his menu back.

"They didn't go to the Riviera," Madeline said. "I guess their blackmail project didn't work out." She looked up at him with tears in her eyes. "Do you think they're dead?"

"I don't—well, yeah, Maddie. And I've been *hating* them all these years—for nothing." He sipped his coffee. "If they are dead."

"If they're not, you'll keep hating them?" She blotted her eyes with a napkin. "I never hated them. I figured they knew what was best."

"You did not. Did you? They *abandoned* us!—in that madhouse! What might have become of us—?"

"Besides what did?" She balled up her napkin. "But if they died in '91, they *didn't* abandon us."

"Oh, yeah." Scott nodded reluctantly.

Neither of them spoke, then, and Scott wished restaurants still permitted smoking; and he told himself that he had not started drinking again. One slip didn't mean a relapse. Madeline slowly turned her fork around and around on the table with her finger.

"I wonder how they cook the catfish," she said finally.

Scott thought about it, then shrugged.

Madeline went on, "So Mom and Dad were blackmailing her. I can't believe she'd kill them over that."

"We don't know what *that* is. It must have been Claimayne or Aunt Amity who packed that box, and not long after Mom and Dad disappeared."

"But why would they *save* the stuff, if Aunt Amity killed our parents?"

Scott opened his mouth, then closed it. "Well," he said finally, "that's a good point. If she killed our parents and wanted to make it look as if they'd left town, she'd hardly save all the stuff they would naturally have taken with them." He stared out the window at the sunlit traffic on Franklin, disoriented at having used the phrase *killed our parents*. Madeline was still turning the fork in circles on the table.

"I stayed up late last night," she said, "reading the Valentino book. And this morning I looked him up on Wikipedia—Natacha Rambova doesn't sound like a nice person, though she and I got along." She looked down at her left thumb and flexed it.

Scott considered telling his sister about his conversation with Rudolph Valentino last night, but decided it could wait. For one thing, he didn't feel ready yet to describe his own near-naked awakening in the dark garden.

The waitress returned and set a plate in front of Madeline, and the browned catfish smelled so good that Scott almost wished he had ordered something to eat. She made a sort of sandwich, with scrambled egg and pieces of catfish between slices of toast, and took a big bite of it.

"Do you still have Aunt Amity's phone book in your purse?" Scott asked. "And your phone?"

Her mouth full, Madeline nodded.

"I'm going to try to talk to that Ostriker character, if he's still alive. Mom wrote that they might offer a finder's fee to him, for whatever the blackmail information was, and she wrote that if he squawked, they'd tell him he should be grateful they're not exposing *him*. I'd really like to know what fact they were blackmailing her *with*—what it was that she wouldn't want known, and to whom."

Madeline swallowed. "Call him right now?" When Scott nodded, she opened her purse and began digging through it. "What are you going to say?"

Scott's headache had not receded much, and he considered ordering a beer; but it would upset Madeline.

"I don't know," he said. She had laid the phone book and her pink cell phone on the table, and he opened the book at the O tab and found Adrian Ostriker. He picked up the phone and tapped in the number.

The line buzzed five times, and then he got a recorded message in a gruff male voice: "You've reached who you've reached. Speak."

"Mr. Ostriker," Scott said, "I'm Scott Madden, nephew of Amity Speas, or Madden. You may have heard that she passed away last week. She left me a message to give to you—"

The phone clicked, and a man's voice, more clearly now, said, "She's the one that wrote those detective books. I read she died. A *message*?"

Scott was sweating. Forge on, he thought. "That's right."

"So what's the message?"

"She made me promise to deliver it in person."

"How did you get this number?"

"She gave it to me, sir." Across the table, Madeline rolled her eyes, and Scott shrugged irritably.

"Why should I bother meeting you?"

"Oh—curiosity, I guess. If you don't want to hear it, that's fine; I've done my best to keep my promise."

"I can whup your ass."

It occurred to Scott to wonder if the man was drunk. It was only a little past eleven in the morning, but Scott could understand it.

Before Scott could think of a reply, the man went on, "You got a pencil?"

"Just a sec." Scott made writing motions with his hand, and Madeline quickly pulled a pen and a wrinkled Taco Bell receipt out of her purse.

Scott took them and flattened out the receipt. "Yes."

"What was her favorite movie?"

"*Salomé*," said Scott. "Alla Nazimova."

"Okay. You're in L.A.?" When Scott confirmed it, the man gave him an address. "It's up Laurel Canyon from Hollywood Boulevard. Go left, uphill, at Jorgensen Road." He described a few more turns, and added, "Come alone."

"Right," said Scott, but the line had already gone dead.

He sat back and laid Madeline's phone on the table. Madeline spread her hands.

"He wants me to go over there," Scott said, "to his house, it sounds like."

"Right now?" When Scott nodded, she pushed her plate away and said, "Let's go."

"I have to go alone. He specified it. You could drop me off back at Caveat and I could—"

"I don't care what he specified. I *am* coming with you."

"Maddy, he sounds crazy. He said 'I could whup your ass.' I couldn't let you—"

"Oh, *big brother.* They were my parents too. What, he's going to think I'm threatening?" She quickly slid the phone and the phone book back into her purse. "If you don't let me come along, I'm going to call him back. His number's right on my phone, I just have to touch it."

Scott smiled sourly. "What are you going to say?"

"I'll say . . . your real purpose is to sell him a solar water heater. Anyway, he must be pretty old by now, right? I don't think he could *really* whup your ass."

Scott stood up from the booth and dug out a couple of twenty-dollar bills from his pocket. "Okay. You're probably safer at his place with me than at Caveat anyway."

MADELINE DROVE WEST ON Franklin to avoid the traffic on Hollywood Boulevard two blocks south, and at Wilcox Scott told her to pull into the parking lot of a dry cleaner's so that he could look at the cars that had been behind them; he didn't see Louise's white Saturn, or a white Chevy Blazer, but he told his sister to wait until half a dozen cars had gone by before resuming their route. She fluttered the gas pedal to keep the engine from stalling while they waited.

As she steered the car back into the lanes, Madeline was frowning and hesitantly turning her head back and forth as if her neck was stiff, but when Scott asked her if anything was wrong, she lifted one hand from the wheel and waved dismissively.

Apparently to change the subject, she said, "You've got cigarettes? Go ahead and smoke if you want. And don't forget you've got to buy cookies somewhere. They were Pecan Sandies."

" . . . Okay."

Past Wilcox, Franklin narrowed to one lane each way, and all the buildings beyond the curbside trees seemed to be apartments; after another half a mile the street was interrupted by the broad, curling lanes of Highland Avenue, but Madeline managed to get into the southbound right lane and catch Franklin when it resumed its westward course around the white Gothic bell tower of the United Baptist Church. Then it was apartment buildings again, of more modern architecture, that swept past on either side.

"You'll want to take La Brea down to Hollywood," said Scott. He had lit a cigarette and rolled down the window, and the grass-scented morning breeze ruffled his hair.

"There'll be another street after La Brea," Madeline said.

"Why bother—" began Scott, but she had already pressed the gas pedal, and the old Datsun roared ahead and rocked right across the La Brea intersection.

"Okay," said Scott, "what's wrong with La Brea?"

"This isn't out of our way," said his sister stubbornly. "Just a little farther—it can't be more than a block or two ahead . . ."

"What can't be?"

She didn't answer, but a few seconds later hit the brakes suddenly enough to make Scott grab the dashboard and drop his cigarette.

"There!" she said, pointing to her left.

Scott bumped his head retrieving his cigarette and peered irritably past her at a very new-looking brown-and-tan four-story apartment building with well-trimmed palm trees standing taller than the sidewalk ficus trees.

"There what?"

A car behind them honked, and Madeline let the car roll slowly forward, still looking at the building.

"Eyes front," said Scott. "What about that place?"

Madeline finally looked away from it to the lanes ahead and sped up. "That's where the house was, where Kosloff shot me! Shot Natacha. It must have been La Brea where the taxi driver turned right, on the way to that hospital." She gave him a brief, wide-eyed glance. "It makes it seem more real, to see the actual place where it happened!"

"Well—"

"It's still the actual place, Scott, even if the house is gone."

She finally turned left at Camino Palmiero and drove between still more apartment buildings, these separated from the street by wide lawns and ranks of stately palm trees, and drove down to Hollywood Boulevard, where she turned right.

"Up Laurel Canyon?" she asked.

"That's what he said."

"I wonder what would happen if I was to knock on a door, at that place we just passed."

Scott was nervously puffing on his cigarette again, trying to think of what to say to this Ostriker person, but he mentally replayed what his sister had just said. "You think Natacha would open it? Or Kosloff?"

"Neither of them would know me by sight. I'd ask for sanctuary." She glanced sideways at him. "In her last-person novel, Aunt Amity wrote 'when is a door not adore,' spelled like—"

"I remember." Whatever I say to Ostriker, Scott thought, I have to frame it as a message from our aunt.

"And when Aunt Amity used to knock on it and ask us that, the answer wasn't 'when it's ajar.' It was—"

" 'When it's a wainscot.' Paneling."

"Maybe we misunderstood her. Maybe she was saying, 'when it's a way in, Scott.' "

I've got to *somehow* ask him about Mom and Dad, he thought. "Hm? Well, it's not a way in to anything. There's a solid wall behind it."

At Laurel Canyon Boulevard Madeline followed the slanting lanes north, and now a brush-covered slope was on their left, and Scott glimpsed an occasional house fronting the road or half hidden behind trees to their right. Through his open window he caught the smells of sage and wild anise on the chilly breeze.

After half a mile, Scott tapped the windshield. "Left there."

Madeline swung the little car left, by a dozen blue and green plastic recycling bins at the foot of a grassy slope, and the four-cylinder engine was roaring as she drove up a steep narrow road between stone walls and the trunks of tall oaks and chain-link gates barring private driveways.

After several sharp curves and a tight turn onto a narrower road, Scott said, "I think this must be it on our right. Watch for a driveway or something."

A low stone wall, stepped down every dozen feet because of the incline, partially blocked dense greenery on that side; and then there was a gap, a stone arch with a tall cypress on either side, the one on the left sporting a green branch stuck out sideways like a cowlick.

Madeline steered the Datsun through the arch and then up a curling driveway that was a tunnel through vine-hung tree branches. The pavement leveled out as soon as the road below could no longer be seen, and she braked to a halt on a wide cement apron and clicked the gearshift into park.

They were in front of a two-story adobe house tucked back into the trees. A wooden verandah ran along the entire front, matched by a long balcony hung below the red-tiled roof. A new neon-green Ford pickup truck and a gleamingly maintained black 1970 convertible Camaro stood on the far side of the house.

Madeline switched off the engine, and the depth of the trees and the expanse of the clearing seemed to become bigger in the ensuing silence; Scott could hear birds calling, and the breeze fluttering through high branches.

He clearly heard Madeline whisper, "We don't belong here."

"Tell him he needs a solar water heater," Scott whispered back as he levered open the passenger-side door and stepped out onto the pavement.

Together they walked across the damp cement to the steps and clumped up onto the boards of the verandah, and Scott knocked on the iron-banded door. He heard floorboards creak inside, and he was sure someone was looking out through the iron-ringed peephole.

"You should have shaved," said Madeline, still whispering.

A bolt clunked back, and then the door swung inward, and a burly man with long dark hair and a short gray beard assessed Scott and Madeline with narrowed eyes. He was wearing a baggy olive-green flight suit that seemed to zip from ankle to neck, and his right hand was held out of sight behind him. His unlined face reminded Scott of Claimayne, and even with the beard he looked no older than fifty.

He didn't step back. "You're the kid that called," he said in a gravelly voice. "Do you remember me telling you to come alone?"

"I didn't have a car," said Scott. "This is my sister."

Ostriker stared at Madeline for several moments and then nodded, and Scott briefly wondered if the man somehow recognized her. Then his gaze swept back to Scott. "You're here. What's the message?"

Scott had considered several things he might say. "It was," he said now, "'I want to protect my son, Claimayne. Let Scott'—that's me—'see you burn the originals of the birth certificates and the marriage license and the photographs.'"

Scott was hoping this might get a useful response—as the "finder," Ostriker must at least have known of the items at one time, whether or not he had actually possessed them.

Madeline clearly remembered their mother's note too, for now she piped up, wide-eyed at her own temerity, "She said there was the risk of wheelbugs getting involved."

Ostriker was smiling and frowning. "Birth certificates, marriage license? Photographs? What is this, genealogy?"

Scott shrugged. "She seemed to think you'd know what she meant."

"And that's a threat, isn't it," the man went on, "about wheelbugs? What have you got, somebody holding a letter that they'll open if you don't report back that I . . . gave you what you want? You little shit." Scott could smell brandy on the man's breath.

Ostriker stared out over their heads for a while, as a drop of sweat ran slowly down over Scott's ribs and Madeline shifted her old Reeboks on the porch boards.

Finally Ostriker looked directly at Madeline again and bared his very white teeth in what might have been a grin. "Come into my parlor, my dear." He pulled the door open wider and stepped well back, and beyond him Scott could see a broad, polished expanse of pale hardwood floor and a standing lamp with three round chrome reflectors.

Scott stepped past Ostriker over the threshold and heard Madeline shuffle in behind him. The door closed with a boom that echoed in big empty volumes of air.

"Walk ahead," said Ostriker, "to the kitchen on the left."

Scott took Madeline's elbow and started across the broad living room, the floor creaking under their shoes. A long couch on a zig-zag frame of blond wood stood against the wall on the right, below bookshelves on which the books had been arranged by the colors of their spines in a rainbow pattern. Several issues of *GQ* were fanned out on a coffee table that was a sheet of glass supported by arcs of polished wood.

The open kitchen area was all chrome and glass and white enamel—the only spots of color were the deep amber of a pear-shaped bottle of Hennessy cognac on the marble counter and the interrupted red and green rings on a dartboard on the wall beside the refrigerator.

"You two stand over there by the window," Ostriker said, and when Scott and Madeline had shuffled back to the far side of the kitchen, he shook his head and stared at them.

Finally he swung his right hand out from behind his back and carefully laid a stainless-steel semiautomatic pistol on the counter.

"*Amity,*" he pronounced, shaking his head as he twisted the cap out of the brandy bottle. "I'd offer you a drink," he said, "but all I have is the good stuff." He lifted the bottle and took a sip right from the neck of it, then exhaled sharply and leaned sideways to brace himself against the wall with his free palm against the dartboard. Scott noticed that the twisted-wire numbers on the dartboard were the twelve numbers of a clock face, not the nonsequential twenty numbers of a standard dartboard.

Ostriker inhaled noisily. He had regained his balance and now laughed heartily. "Was she crazy in her old age? She named a kid Claymation? For one thing, there's no such thing as 'the originals' of birth certificates. They issue certified copies."

It occurred to Scott that a forged one would be an original.

"I can only tell you what she told me," Scott said, wishing now that he'd thought of a better opening line. "You *did* know her?"

"What would it matter? She preferred women."

"She got married," said Madeline. "She had a son."

"That settles that, then, doesn't it?" Ostriker picked up the gun again. "What do you two really want? Did she leave some kind of suicide note, mentioning me?"

"No," said Scott, "there was no—"

"How did she kill herself? The paper didn't say."

"She climbed onto the roof," said Madeline, "with a grenade, and blew herself to pieces."

"That doesn't sound like a suicide."

Scott blinked at him. It certainly didn't sound like a murder.

Ostriker went on, "Did her *foot* ever heal?"

"She always limped," said Scott. He shifted his own feet on the tiles, and Ostriker quickly pointed the gun straight at him, with his finger inside the trigger guard.

"Okay," Ostriker said, "you've used up your bullshit allotment."

"Wait," Scott said hastily, "we did come here about birth certificates and the rest of it, but not because Aunt Amity asked us to."

Ostriker kept the gun pointed at him. "Amateurs!" he said, almost spitting. "Is this some kind of dipshit blackmail?"

"No." Scott licked his lips, aching for the man to point the gun somewhere else. "You knew our parents," he said carefully, "Arthur and Irina Madden."

"They talked to you in 1991," spoke up Madeline. "*They* wanted to blackmail *Aunt Amity*. They left notes, and copies of her birth certificate and her mother's, and her mother's marriage license, and some . . . pictures. Your name was in the notes, in quotation marks. Put the gun down, mister, we just want to know what happened to our parents!"

And find a way to force Aunt Amity to rest in peace, thought Scott.

Ostriker exaggeratedly raised his eyebrows. "Art and Irina," he said. "Fat little bald charlie, and a ratty-haired beanpole, right? That them?"

Scott kept his voice level. "They disappeared on New Year's Eve of 1991. They wrote that they spoke to you."

"Yeah, I remember 'em. Couple of fools. Quotation marks is cute." With his free hand Ostriker hoisted the bottle and took another swallow of the brandy. "They, yeah, they wanted some dirt on your *Amity,* and they figured I'd know something because she and I had a . . . history. So she *knew* about me, even knew my phone number! But all these years she never bothered with me. That would have to be because"—he laughed and swayed, and Scott exhaled silently in relief when the gun's muzzle wobbled away—"afterward she found something else, something better."

Scott wondered if he meant a woman or his uncle Edward.

"Did you ever hear from our parents after 1991?" asked Madeline plaintively.

Ostriker stared at her, shaking his head, and Scott wondered again if the man somehow recognized her. "I got no time for losers—or their idiot kids rummaging around. *You,* Little Miss Muffet," he said directly to Madeline, "are a kid poking your hand through the bars at a zoo."

Madeline looked bewildered. "Me?" she asked. "Particularly?"

Ostriker obviously considered saying something and then thought better of it; finally he just muttered, "Both of you, probably."

The interview, such as it was, seemed to be ending. Scott asked quickly, "Do you know what information they were blackmailing her with?"

Ostriker clanked the bottle down. "I don't think you two know anything at all."

"We know about Natacha!" burst out Madeline.

Ostriker cocked his head. "I really don't think you do. I think you found some old notes and stuff in that crazy house, and my name, and figured you could try to stick somebody up for money. How did that work out for your folks?"

"You tell us," said Scott.

"How about I tell you this instead—if you come around here again, I'll kill you both for trespassers." He was grinning broadly. "That sound equitable? That work for you? Now—ankle your sorry little asses out of my house."

Scott started toward the living room, then paused. This had accomplished nothing. Desperately, he asked, "Do you know where William Desmond Taylor's exorcism film went, after Paul and Charlene took it from Natacha Rambova?"

Ostriker stood perfectly still for several heartbeats, staring at the spot by the window where Scott and Madeline had been standing. Then he said, quietly, "Maybe you're the ones who should be worrying about wheelbugs."

He appeared to have nothing more to say. Scott took Madeline's elbow again and led her through the cavernous white living room to the front door. Ostriker was still standing in the kitchen, facing the window, so Scott unlatched the door and pulled it open.

They hurried across the pavement to the car, and when they had slammed the doors and Madeline had started the engine, she said, "What did we learn there?"

"Everybody knows more than we do, that's what." Scott rubbed his face and exhaled shakily as Madeline reversed on the broad expanse of cement, and he whispered, "I hate people pointing guns at me!"

Madeline shook her head. "He had something Aunt Amity wanted, and he hid from her under this fake Ostriker name—Mom had the name in quotes, right?—but after a while it didn't matter anymore because she found something better."

"I thought he meant she found something better like a boyfriend . . . or a girlfriend."

"No. Some thing."

He turned to look at his sister. "Have you *met* him before? Like, was he ever an astrological client of yours? It sure looked like he recognized you."

"It did look like that," she agreed, "and what was that business about me and a zoo? But no, I don't think I've ever seen him before. He didn't look as old as we thought he would, did he?"

Her purse was in the backseat, and Scott hiked around to get his hand in it. Madeline had got the car in drive and begun guiding it down the long driveway when he sat back down in his seat, holding their aunt's old phone book.

"Let's see if Genod Speas still lives at the address she's got here," he said.

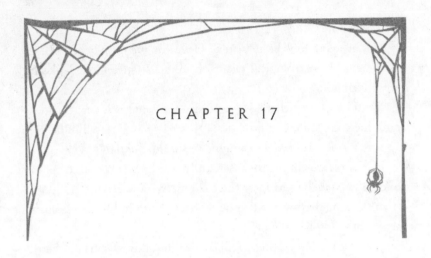

CHAPTER 17

THE ADDRESS IN THEIR aunt's phone book for Genod Speas, east of Fairfax Avenue and just north of the 101 Freeway, proved to be a small pistachio-green stuccoed house with bars over the windows and front door, and a short, patchy front lawn. An adult-sized tricycle was locked with a cable to the post of a mailbox by the front step.

"Her brother," said Madeline as she spun the steering wheel to drive up the two cracked concrete strips that served as a driveway.

"According to Claymation."

They climbed out of the car and trudged up the walkway to the cement steps below the door; Scott stood on the lower one and rapped on the perforated black metal door between the bars.

"It's not my dog!" came a quavering voice from beyond the door, and Scott realized that the solid inner door was open. He tried without success to peer through the rows of tiny holes in the metal sheet.

"I'm not here about a dog," said Scott loudly. He looked back at Madeline and spread his hands.

"Message from Amity," she prompted in a whisper.

"It's about Amity Speas," called Scott. "Or Madden."

He heard creaking and squeaking from inside, and after several seconds the metal door was pulled open, and between the bars Scott saw a sagging, wrinkled face below wispy white hair appear out of the interior shadows.

"You brought my check?" said the old man, blinking up at Scott. "It's more than a week late. They think it's my dog, but it's not. I don't have a dog."

"I'll tell them. Can we come in? I'm Scott Madden, and this is my sister, Madeline. Amity Speas was our aunt. You're Genod Speas?"

"Yes, I—" Speas clenched his eyes shut, then said hollowly, "Was?"

"I'm sorry," said Madeline. "She . . . passed on, last Wednesday."

The face contorted in a hundred new wrinkles, but the old man lifted one spotted hand from the grip of a walker and turned the interior knob on the barred gate. Scott pulled it open.

Speas, in worn purple flannel pajamas and barefoot, tugged his walker back across scattered newspapers that rattled under its wheels. The walker had a seat attached to it, and he sagged down onto it and laid his head on the crossbar between the grips. His scalp was clearly visible under his scanty white hair.

Madeline gave Scott an anxious look.

"You're her older brother?" she said.

Speas raised his head. "I have no older brother," he said brokenly. "How could she die? I'm not—but I need my check."

Scott looked around the room. Age-darkened curtains hung over two windows flanking the door, and the outside bars cast vertical shadows on the fabric. Folded brown paper shopping bags were stacked on a blue vinyl couch against one wall, and an old television set with rabbit-ear antennas stood on a painted table against the opposite wall. It wasn't turned on, and Scott was pretty sure it couldn't work. The air was warm and stale, with a whiff of corn tortillas.

"She's dead?" said Speas. "You're certain?"

Madeline nodded at him, wide-eyed. "I'm sorry," she said.

The old man stared at her and then swiveled his head to peer at Scott. "You live at Caveat?"

"For the moment," said Scott.

"She would never let me live there. She paid me to stay here. I don't even *have* a dog!"

"She was your sister?" asked Madeline.

"No," said the old man, suddenly angry. "Is that the story? She was my *mother*."

Scott looked up and met Madeline's glance and shook his head slightly.

But Speas saw the look. "*I've* got a birth certificate," he said querulously, "a *real* one, if you don't believe me." He blinked around the narrow room as if hoping to see it.

"When were you born?" asked Scott.

"Nineteen twenty-three," said Speas, apparently proud of remembering it, "and she was twenty-four years old."

"We saw a picture of her that was taken before 1926," said Madeline.

"She was an actress," said Speas, his voice catching. "She got work in every scene—because she was too smart to ever let the camera see her face close up! You can't have a, a French peasant girl in a crowd recognizably show up later as a lady in King Louis's court!" He glared at Scott and Madeline as if they had suggested that one could. "Pro—*professional*. She always wore yellow, because that looked white on film. You know what actual white would do?"

Scott shook his head.

"It would flare so bright on the screen that people's faces looked like mud. But she lost her career, changed her name, lost it all, the year before I was born."

"What happened?" asked Madeline.

"Somebody *shot* her, in the foot. With a gun. It never healed straight. I worked in the movie business myself, later." He peered around again at the shabby living room as if wondering what his original topic had been. "Ava Gardner and I . . . meant something to each other, at one time." He looked up at Madeline. "You'll get me my check, won't you?"

"I'll see that they get it to you," she said. "Quick."

"Who was your father?" asked Scott.

Speas covered his face in his wrinkled hands. "She would never say his name. I think he was the devil."

"What was *her* name," Scott went on, "before she changed it?"

"She made me promise never to tell. I never have."

"But now that she's—" began Scott, but Madeline interrupted him with a wave.

"When did you last see her?" she asked.

"I haven't seen her since . . . right after *Night of the Iguana* came out. She never let me go to Caveat. I think she married again and had another son. I never could read her books."

Over the old man's head, Scott mouthed at Madeline, *We need to know her name.*

Madeline shook her head impatiently, and her lips clearly formed the words, *We know it.*

"Ava Gardner was in *Night of the Iguana*," said Speas softly, perhaps talking to himself now. "She and I . . ." He nodded. "I'm sure she remembers."

Scott was pretty sure Ava Gardner was dead.

SCOTT WAS SMOKING ANOTHER cigarette, his right arm out the car window, as Madeline drove up Fairfax past watch-repair shops and vintage clothing stores, and finally Madeline spoke.

"Aunt Amity was a hundred and sixteen years old when she died. Not seventy-one, like everybody thinks."

Scott blew smoke out the window. "Ostriker and Speas, both, made me think of a forged birth certificate." He laughed. "It makes sense, sort of, but I really don't actually *believe* it."

"I do," said Madeline, keeping her eyes on the traffic ahead but nodding emphatically. "Her last-person novel is all *Charlene* talking to that detective from her books. Not *Amity*. Charlene stole the exorcism film from Natacha and got shot in the foot doing it."

"Aunt Amity always did limp," Scott admitted.

"I don't," said Madeline. "I wonder if that's why she wants to possess me."

"I'm sure that's it."

Madeline sighed. "You're making fun of me."

"Sorry."

"The 1899 birth certificate was her real one; her real name is Charlene Cooper. Was. The 1944 one, and the Amity Speas name, were fakes. She got so old that she had to pretend that she was her own made-up daughter."

Scott took a long draw on the cigarette. "When you lay it all out that way, it sounds—insane."

"Think about it."

He caught himself thinking instead of how the sun had lit Louise's hair this morning, and even of what brush he would use to capture it in paint on canvas, and he forced the unwelcome thought away. "We'll want to look at those photocopies again," he said.

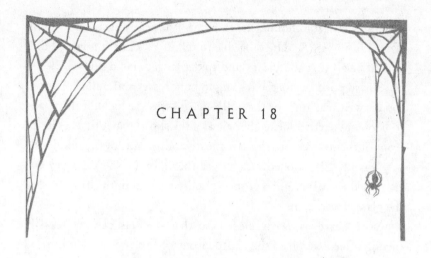

CHAPTER 18

THE BOOM ON THE roof and the grinding crackle in Ariel's bedroom wall were simultaneous, and her first panicky thought was that her aunt's suicide reruns were going to knock the house down. But when she glanced at the wall, she quickly looked away, her heart pounding. She had peripherally glimpsed eight cracks radiating from a central point at about eye level, and for several seconds she just stood in the middle of the floor, trembling, breathlessly wondering if she had seen it clearly enough to be tipped into a spider vision.

After twenty heartbeats, it was clear that she had not. She was simply looking out the window at the sunlit houses on the slope across Vista Del Mar.

But I *could* look at it, she told herself, relaxing. It's clean, it just happened, obviously nobody has looked at it before; and I can . . . afterward I can get a hammer and knock all the plaster off the wall with my eyes closed, so I won't look at it again, it won't have an after for me or anybody else. It's not like I'm relapsing, I can't help it, I didn't go looking for it, the damn thing just appeared in the wall! And the spiders are going to stop working soon anyway!—at least according to that strange little man in front of the spiderbit shop.

She half turned toward the cracked wall, then stopped. Scott is staying away from liquor, she thought. I have at least as much will-power as he has. And he'd be able to tell, if I look at it now—at din-ner I'd be all stiff and bleary and spider lagged. He'd know.

She stepped across the rag rug to her dresser and pulled open the top drawer, reaching for the bull's-eye glasses she had left there; and so her hand partly blocked her view of the slip of paper that lay in the front of the drawer, but she saw the diverging ends of the ink lines.

"Fuck!" She looked straight at the floor as she clutched and crumpled the paper, then groped blindly around in the drawer—but the glasses were gone.

With her eyes nearly closed, so that she was peering blurrily through her eyelashes, she shuffled out of her room, then hurried wide-eyed down the hall to the next bedroom door. She turned the knob and yanked the door open.

Claimayne was sitting up in his ornate bed, hunched over the bedside table, and his pale, surprised face was turned toward her. On the table were a dozen glittering strips of foil and a gun she hadn't seen before—it was a revolver, but it looked bulkier than the one she'd taken from him yesterday and pitched into a bush by the driveway.

She burst out, "On Tuesday night when I asked you for one, you told me not to do a spider, and now you leave one in my drawer? Did you hope to still have enough volition left to let you *walk around* in me?" She took a deep breath. "You miserable shit," she added.

He was blinking at her with his mouth open.

"My God," she said more quietly, "you *did* want to switch with me!"

His mouth snapped shut. "There was—are you saying there was a spider in your drawer?" The lamplight glittered on tiny drops of sweat on his forehead.

She looked at the stainless-steel revolver and shivered. "What were you going to do, in my body, if your trick worked? Or did you just want to rejuvenate your creepy old blood one more time, with mine? And why the gun?" She strode to the bedside table and picked up one of the glittering strips. "What are these, gum wrappers?"

Claimayne visibly pulled himself together. "You found my spider," he said with a fluttering smile. "I was wondering where I left it. I was carrying it around, and snooping, and I must have accidentally left it in your drawer." He frowned and nodded. "I'm sorry—you know I don't approve of you using them."

"Then what's become of my bull's-eye glasses?"

After an expressionless pause, Claimayne said, "I wouldn't know. But you can get more, can't you?—from your . . . *allies*."

Ariel let go of the foil strip and gave him a puzzled frown. "Is it because I went there? To the spiderbit shop?"

Claimayne pulled open the drawer in the bedside table and lifted the revolver and laid it in the drawer, then carefully swept the foil strips in after it.

He slid the drawer shut and folded his hands. "I don't have time to answer all your idiotic questions."

"*Allies?* Do you think the spiderbits asked me to spy on you? Damn it, tell me what you were going to—"

"Please leave my room. Be grateful I don't tell you to leave this house. I'm the owner now."

A line of bright blood abruptly ran down from one nostril to his lips. He licked it away, but made no attempt to block the flow, and a moment later the line ran down his chin and drops of blood were falling metronomically onto his embroidered dressing gown.

"See what you've done," he said.

Ariel opened her mouth to say something further, then just turned and hurried out of the room, slamming the door behind her.

SCOTT HEARD A DOOR slam, and then footsteps hurrying in the hall and knocking away down the stairs. Madeline was with him in their parents' room, so he knew it must have been Ariel.

"I don't think we've brought peace to this house," said Madeline, sitting on the water-stained mattress and holding the Valentino biography. Their parents' telephone sat on a shelf beside the door, yards from the short wires that stuck out of the wall; Scott had said that if it worked at all, it would probably work better unconnected.

"I don't think Aunt Amity meant us to," Scott said. "I'll fetch those papers."

Scott walked through Madeline's room to his own, and he stepped around the bed and lifted the mattress; then his face was suddenly cold and he lifted the mattress higher and peered around at the shadowed surface of the box springs.

The manila envelope was not there, though he could see the pint bottle of Wild Turkey lying faceup, glittering even in the dimness. After a few more seconds of useless scrutiny, he dropped the mattress and got down on his hands and knees to look under the bed and around at the floor. But the envelope was nowhere to be seen.

It had been under the mattress this morning when he had pushed the abused Wild Turkey bottle in beside it.

He walked back through the two doorways to their parents' bare room. "Let's take a walk in the garden," he said.

"Didn't you want to look—"

"I can look for my cigarettes later," he said, winking at her.

"Oh." She stood up uncertainly. "Okay."

The two of them hurried out of the room and down the hall past Ariel's and Claimayne's rooms, and as they passed the wall of doors, Scott was tempted to knock on the one from the Garden of Allah—*when is a door not adore,* he thought; and he remembered Madeline's guess that the answer was, *when it's a way in, Scott*—but Madeline was already clattering down the wooden stairs, and he lengthened his stride to catch up.

On the ground floor they could hear banging from down the hall in the direction of their aunt's library, but Scott shook his head and pointed at the shorter hall that led to the laundry room and a back door.

When they had walked outside, the cold breeze blew the door shut behind them. Scott led his sister along one of the gravel paths up the slope, and he halted a dozen yards short of the Medusa wall.

Madeline said, "You think Claimayne's got microphones in our rooms?"

"The envelope's gone," he said. "It was under my mattress."

Madeline glanced ahead toward the Medusa mosaic and then up at the sky, where clouds were shifting in from the east. "I wouldn't have thought Claimayne could *lift* a mattress. Maybe it was Ariel."

Scott felt his face getting hot at the thought that Ariel might have seen the pint bottle of bourbon under his mattress.

He shook his head, angry at himself. "I don't know why anyone would want those papers—even if they are evidence that Aunt Amity was a hundred-something years old." He rubbed one hand over his face. "What do you remember from them?"

"There were two birth certificates—one for Charlene Claimayne Cooper, born in 1899. That has to be Aunt Amity's real one, and her real name, even though she wrote 'Mother' on it. Then there was another one for Amity Imogene Speas, saying she was born in 1944. I'm sure that's a forgery; you remember Genod insisted that *his* birth certificate was 'a *real* one.' And there was a marriage license, Paul David Speas and Charlene Claimayne Cooper, from 1921." She glanced nervously back at the house. They couldn't be overheard, but she leaned closer to whisper, "And there was a copy of the little envelope the *Oneida Inc* spider was in."

Scott shivered in the wind. "That's right. Somebody might get the idea that we have it."

"Her retirement check. We ripped it up—but maybe somebody else wants to retire with it. The people Louise is working for, or the guy at Ross in the . . . what was it?"

"Chevy Blazer. Unless Louise was making him up for effect."

Scott heard the kitchen door squeak open, and then footsteps on the cement walkway; and a moment later Ariel stepped around the corner into the sunlight and scowled at them. She looked over her shoulder, then came striding toward them past the tall aluminum ladder that still leaned against the roof. Her flat shoes crunched on the gravel of the path, and she halted a few feet short of where Scott and Madeline stood and took a deep breath.

"Did you take an envelope from under Scott's mattress?" asked Madeline before Ariel could speak.

Ariel blinked and exhaled. "What? I was just in my aunt's library! Scott doesn't sleep there! Are you crazy?"

Scott cocked an eyebrow. He was relieved that she apparently didn't know what Madeline was talking about—but Ariel nevertheless sounded defensive, and he guessed that she had in fact taken something from the library. She had certainly been making enough noise in there when he and Madeline had come downstairs.

"And nothing in that library is any of *your* business anyway," Ariel went on, visibly regaining confidence, "and I wouldn't have to do *any* of this if you two hadn't come back here! You two are wrecking Caveat! Cracks in the walls—old cars in the driveway—!"

"What is it you have to do?" asked Scott.

Ariel glanced over her shoulder toward the driveway—anxiously, Scott thought. She started to speak, then shook her head. "Nothing you'd want to know about," she said finally. "If I had any sense, I wouldn't even come back here. I might not anyway."

She turned and stalked back down the path and around the corner; and he heard her car door click open and then clunk shut.

Madeline gave Scott an urgent look, and he nodded. "No time for the car," he said, slapping his jeans to be sure he had his keys. "That sounded almost suicidal, didn't it?"

She nodded rapidly. "Helmet?"

He shook his head and hurried back down the path and along the walkway to the kitchen corner, and he waited until he heard

Ariel's Kia shift from reverse into drive, and move away down the bottom half of the driveway, before he stepped out and sprinted to his motorcycle.

It started at the first kick, and he let it coast down the driveway idling quietly in neutral as he squeezed the front-wheel brake lever to stay well back, because the back-wheel brake squeaked in damp weather.

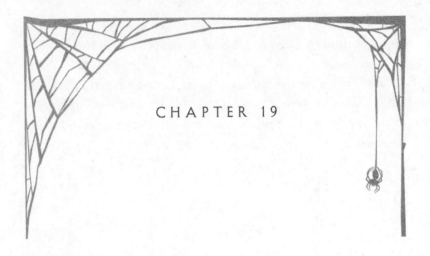

CHAPTER 19

AS SHE BRAKED TO a stop behind the crosswalk just short of the 101 Freeway overpass, the buildings around Ariel all at once seemed too low, or at least too widely spaced—in the crystal winter sunlight the gray strip mall with its furtive pizza parlor to her right, and the red and blue Mobil gas station to her left, were isolated structures on a stepped plain of asphalt, and the taller buildings farther away, behind the power lines hanging slack between their poles, looked abandoned; the windshields of the cars around her were blank reflections of the sky. She looked down and clicked the turn signal left and then right and then off, just to break the stasis of the moment; and then she leaned forward and glanced through the tinted top edge of the windshield at the sky, momentarily fearful that she had made herself conspicuous in this cluster of otherwise lifeless-seeming vehicles.

A flicker on the far side of the intersection caught her eye, and she focused on it and then hastily looked away—for the angle of two streetlight poles, one behind the other, with a traffic-signal pole angling out from the closer one, had seemed for an instant to stand out sharply from the gray concrete background, lacking only a few more lines to make a spider pattern specific to her position and perspective. She took hold of her silver gyroscope pendant and stared at it instead, watching the traffic light out of the corner of her eye.

The light turned green at last, and she gunned the car through the intersection with narrowed eyes. For a moment she was in shadow under the freeway bridge, resolutely not glancing at the jagged graffiti patterns that crazed the plywood barriers on either side, and then she was out in the sunlight again, swerving left with the road as it swept past old apartment buildings, and when she saw a gate open on her right, she steered through it onto a narrow dirt-paved yard and braked to a halt.

Why the new gun? she thought. Why the strips of gum-wrapper foil?

She slid her iPad out from under the seat and pushed the power button, and after a few taps on the on-screen keyboard, she was connected to the deep-web server and had entered the .dark spiderbit web address. The poster for Bergman's *Through a Glass Darkly* appeared, looking a bit grainier than it had yesterday, and she recalled that a character in that 1961 movie claimed to have seen God as a huge spider that tried to rape her before fading into a wall. An effective incentive to find the current location of the spiderbit store! Ariel tapped in her password and zip code and touched the sign-on icon.

The map that appeared was formatted differently from the one she had seen yesterday—and it was black and white now—but the pulsing dot was clearly visible. It was east of where it had been yesterday—on Sixth Street now, apparently right by the L.A. River, just short of the Sixth Street bridge. Drive over the bridge and you were on Whittier Boulevard—it was only a few blocks southeast of the new Catholic cathedral and the government buildings of downtown L.A., but it was definitely on the wrong side of Alameda.

She pulled her phone out of her blouse pocket and checked the time. It's only a few minutes past two, she told herself, and you've got a gun of your own—and you do need something more now than warpy glasses.

She reversed her car in the dirt lot and got back onto Franklin, then turned north on Cahuenga—the buildings still seemed too low and spread out in the cheerless sunlight—and steered onto the south-bound 101 Freeway.

When she saw the huge brown box of the cathedral on her right, and on her left the Arts High School building that looked like a giant chrome robot aiming a ray-gun at the cathedral across the freeway, she slanted into the right lane and got off at Alameda.

She drove south, away from the angular new hotels into a region of sparse trees and For Lease signs and long windowless warehouses and parking lots with concertina wire along the tops of the chain-link fences. At Sixth Street she turned left, and after a few unin-spiring blocks, she saw rising pavement and the stone railings of the bridge on both sides of the street ahead of her, so she turned left and then right onto a narrow street or alley that ran parallel to Sixth Street, in the bridge's shadow. The mutter of her car's exhaust echoed back at her from featureless cinder-block walls close at her left, and to her right the dark arches under the bridge were blocked by webs of chain link.

The new location of the spiderbit store should be very close by.

Several old cars were parked along the narrow pavement, all facing her, and she wondered if this was a one-way street; and sure enough, a pair of dusty pickup trucks swung onto the street ahead and were rocking toward her, side by side.

She braked and reached for the gearshift—and then was rocked sharply back in her seat as a car behind her crunched into her rear bumper.

She swore and clicked the gearshift into park.

Opening her driver's-side door, Ariel stepped out onto the bridge-shadowed pavement, and she had her phone in her hand as she hurried back to take a picture of the damage. It was an old tan Dodge Dart that had hit her, and its driver had opened his own door and was climbing out.

"I hope you're insured!" she called angrily. A motor oil–scented breeze was funneling down the narrow street from the west, and she peered in the shade of the bridge to see the man.

He straightened up, and she saw that he was wearing horn-rimmed glasses and a sport coat over a red T-shirt.

Ariel's hand darted into her purse, but just then her arms were gripped strongly from behind, and even as she inhaled, a rough-skinned palm was slapped over her mouth.

Her hand was on her .32 semiautomatic, and she tugged at the trigger—the slug blew a hole in the leather of her purse and knocked the pavement before hissing away into the sky in ricochet, but the gunshot was just a muffled thump.

She pulled the trigger again, but nothing happened; the slide had apparently been blocked by the purse lining and hadn't cycled a fresh round into the chamber.

Light-headed and breathless, she drove a heel back toward where she thought a shin would be, but the kick missed and she lost her balance. The hands gripping her arms were all that was holding her up. She tried to bite the palm on her face, but could only scrape it with her teeth.

The little man in glasses rapped a knuckle very hard against the point of her elbow; the blow numbed her forearm, and when he yanked her purse away, the gun went with it. With his other hand he held up a sheet of cardboard in front of her face, but she glimpsed the radiating lines inked on it and clenched her eyes shut.

"I've got five or six hundred dollars in that purse," she panted, "and the car's almost new. Take them and I'll walk out of here."

Her arms were yanked behind her, and she fell to her knees on the asphalt and winced as her wrists were pressed together.

Then there was a loud mechanical roar and a thump, and the man in glasses was propelled forward—his belly slammed into her head, and both of them fell sideways onto the street. Lifting her head from the pavement to peer dazedly over the man's legs, she saw the headlight and front tire of a motorcycle topple to the pavement, and Scott Madden was rolling to his feet a yard away.

"Gun in the purse!" she choked.

Boots scuffed on asphalt behind her, but Scott had snatched up the purse and hopped backward as he reached into it, and a moment later he had the gun in his hand. He dropped the purse and pulled the slide back and let it snap forward, chambering a round.

THE TWO MEN WHO had got out of the pickup trucks flailed to a halt. They were in blue jeans and T-shirts and looked to be in their thirties, both wearing glasses but apparently pretty fit; Scott couldn't imagine how he and Ariel were going to get out of this.

She had scrambled to her feet, looking uninjured, though her skirt was ripped. When she had stepped quickly around the man rolling on the street, Scott handed her the gun. She gripped it with her left hand and took a step back and kept the muzzle steady, pointed toward her assailants.

Scott crouched and took hold of the handlebar grips and straightened, heaving the motorcycle upright. The clutch lever now slanted up, but he was able to squeeze it as he straddled the seat, tapped the gearshift pedal down with his left foot, and drove his right heel down on the kick-starter.

The engine roared, and he exhaled, dizzy with relief.

"Keep it pointed at 'em and shoot if they move," he called to Ariel. "Aim at the middle of their stomachs—and get on the back here."

Ariel bent to pick up her purse, then slid her right leg between Scott and the sissy bar, and a moment later her feet were on the passenger footpegs and her left arm was extended over Scott's shoulder.

"I'm gonna pass 'em on the left," Scott said, and she shifted her arm over his head to his right shoulder.

Scott let the clutch out a bit, edging the bike slowly forward, then let it pop out as he twisted the throttle, and the front tire was in the air for a second as the bike leaped forward and accelerated past the trucks.

The left-side mirror had broken off, but in the other one Scott could see the two men scrambling into the pickup trucks, and immediately one of the trucks reversed and spun around in a cloud of dust.

Scott wound the throttle rapidly back and forth as he shifted gears, his eyes narrowed to slits as the strengthening headwind battered his face and the arches of the bridge flashed past taller and taller to his right. He snatched a glance at the mirror and saw one of the trucks now close behind.

His eyes were already stinging and watering from the ride to Sixth Street on the freeway. I can't get into a chase on streets, he thought desperately, on this old bike, with no goggles and a hundred-something pounds of passenger!

The street ended at a crosswise fence ahead of him, but he saw a narrow open gate in the fence and slanted through it, and then he was out of the bridge shadow onto packed, oil-stained dirt, and all that lay ahead were rows and rows of railroad tracks, stretching from left to right as far as Scott could see.

He glanced back. Both trucks had stopped outside the fence, and the driver of one of them was now out of the cab and through the gate and sprinting toward the motorcycle. Scott leaned to the left and gunned the bike north, parallel to the tracks; the man on foot turned and began running back toward his truck, while the other vehicle paced Scott on the far side of the fence. Behind it, the tan Dodge that had hit Ariel's car swung into view, catching up fast.

Scott braked to a skidding halt. He clicked the gearshift into neutral and brushed sweaty hair back from his forehead. Dust swirled away to his right, across the tracks and out over the broad concrete channel at the bottom of which, unseen from where they were, flowed the L.A. River.

"Who *are* they?" Scott asked. The three vehicles were paused now outside the fence, and a white SUV was driving slowly past them. Scott was bleakly sure it was a Chevy Blazer.

"Wheelbugs," said Ariel. "One of them tried to show me a spider."

Scott's first thought was a profound wish that he had ridden away from Caveat and all its concerns yesterday evening; he brushed it aside and said, "You got sunglasses? Normal ones?"

"Yes. You want them?"

"For goggles."

She dug in her purse and pulled out a pair. "Turn around," she said.

Scott hiked himself sideways on the seat to face her, and she unfolded the glasses and slid them over his eyes, hooking them behind his ears and pushing the nosepiece into place.

He gave her a brittle smile and turned back around on the seat. "Three of 'em," he said, "four, probably. They can stay with us whichever way we go and fade back into the streets if cops show up."

He felt Ariel shiver against his back. "I don't think they want to shoot at us," she said.

"Not entirely good news."

One of the pickup trucks moved ahead, picking up speed.

"There *will* be a gate they can get through," said Ariel.

"Without a doubt." He looked the other way, at the tracks, and saw that they were all clear at the moment. "Get off the bike."

Ariel swung off the seat, hopping on the dirt to catch her balance. She gave him a blank look. "Why?"

Scott pushed the motorcycle backward with his heels and pointed the front wheel at the nearest pair of rails. "I can get over the tracks easier without you on the back. Walk alongside—I won't be moving fast."

He shoved forward now with his toes until the front wheel was pressed against the polished steel rail, and then he tapped the gearshift pedal down into first gear and let out the clutch lever.

The motor roared and the bike reared up, and then the back

wheel was on the rail and the front wheel had rolled over the farther rail and thumped into the gravel on the other side; the front shocks clanked shut and Scott managed not to pitch forward over the handlebars, and then his spine shook as the rear wheel crunched down.

He grabbed the clutch and let the motor wind down. "That's one," he said dizzily. "How many more to the river fence?"

Ariel had stepped over the rails and now shaded her eyes to look east. "Seven or eight." She looked over his shoulder. "One guy's reversing back toward that gate we came through. I guess he figures he can catch up to us here on foot."

"Hah. Loser." Scott released the clutch again and went jolting and bouncing over the next pair of rails, and then immediately the pair after that; the bike didn't fall or throw him off, but he had to catch his balance by slamming his foot to the gravel, and pain lanced up through his knee to his hip.

He was sweating and shaking, and his head throbbed with every rapid pulse as he squinted ahead at the remaining tracks.

Ariel had walked alongside his stressful progress and now stood a couple of yards away, looking past him toward the street. "You look sick," she said. "Did you do a spider last night?"

Scott gunned the engine. "Among other things."

He couldn't hear footsteps behind him over the pulse thudding in his ears, but Ariel had her little .32 semiautomatic in her hand, and she said, "I'd hurry."

Scott had got the rhythm of riding over the tracks now, and he was able to guide the bike over three more pairs of rails with only moderate use of the throttle, standing on the footpegs and leaning forward and backward as the bike pitched like a boat in a heavy sea.

He paused to catch his breath after the third set of tracks, and Ariel said, "Did you hear him? No? He shouted at us—says he can shoot to wound us."

Scott nodded and gripped the clutch. "Run ahead of me."

Then Ariel's torn skirt and short brown hair were fluttering ahead of him as he crossed the three remaining tracks quickly enough to make her visibly pick up her pace. He didn't hear any shots from behind.

The rear wheel skidded around as he put his weight on the back brake pedal just short of the river fence, and he didn't have to tell Ariel to get back on. With her arms clamped around his ribs he rode fast south along the fence, under the arch of the Sixth Street bridge and out the other side; when he glanced to the right, he saw the white SUV and one of the pickup trucks keeping up with him on the far side of the tracks and the fence.

A hundred feet farther there was a long gap in the fence to Scott's left, so he steered the bike through, and then they were riding straight down the twenty-five-degree concrete slope toward the fifty-yard expanse of churning green water. Scott was leaning back against Ariel, gripping the front brake lever and standing on the back brake pedal. The back brake squealed.

He leaned to the right and managed to keep the bike upright as it swooped around and then straightened out a few yards above the water, and the rumble of the engine echoed back from the slope on the far side of the river as the motorcycle wobbled along the slanted concrete surface, parallel to the river. Slowly he increased the speed.

After a few tense seconds, "This is a good trick!" said Ariel behind him.

"Don't lean," he called back. "Sit straight up against the bar."

They passed through the shadow under the Seventh Street bridge, and Scott could see the multiple bridges of a big freeway interchange a quarter of a mile ahead. He realized with a chill that although he could maintain this straight-line progress forever, he wasn't sure how he would steer back up the slope. A long, very shallow slant, he decided. But when and if I get to the top, will I see those damned vehicles still pacing us?

"Eighth Street is right under that freeway ahead of us," called Ariel, "and there's an on-ramp pretty quick."

Time to try that slant, he thought, and he leaned his shoulders to the right—he was sweating with the thought of the wheels losing traction on the incline and spilling them down the slope into the river—but the motorcycle gradually angled up the concrete slope, and in a minute the chain-link fence was rippling past only a few yards to his right.

When a gap in the fence appeared—a wheeled gate was pulled back as if to ramp a boat down to the water—he had passed it by the time he was able to gingerly brake the bike to a halt; Ariel got off and stood in the gap while he carefully walked the bike back and then turned it and gunned it up onto level pavement.

"I don't see our guys," she said. "I bet there's no underpass at Seventh Street, and they had to shift a block west. But you've got tracks to cross again."

Scott took a deep breath and let it out. "I'm pretty good at it now."

Several of the tracks had merged, this far south, and he only had to go seesawing over seven pairs of rails, while his arms shook in their sockets and Ariel paced alongside.

When he halted on a wide patch of asphalt under the high shoulder of the freeway bridge, he saw that they were in a long parking lot. A sign between the lot and the street indicated that they were on private property—an AMTRAK maintenance yard—but the street-side gate was open, and when Ariel had climbed back on, he sped through without raising any alarm.

Then it was more low anonymous warehouses with bricked-over windows and Dumpsters on the sidewalks and barred gates across rolled-down segmented metal doors. When they bobbed across Santa Fe Avenue, Ariel glanced north.

Her arms tightened around his ribs. "Here they come," she said loudly in his ear. "Freeway on-ramp should be soon on your left."

Scott downshifted and twisted the throttle, and the motorcycle howled and leaped forward; in the right-side mirror he saw a pickup truck and then the white SUV come leaning into view in the lanes behind them, but looking ahead he could see the green freeway sign, and he leaned left onto the on-ramp, then quickly leaned right as the ramp curved to join the westbound lanes of the 101 Freeway.

As he clicked up through the gears and merged out onto the freeway, he saw signs for exits at Spring Street and Alameda, and he could see the peak of the old city hall jutting above one of the new white government buildings half a mile ahead.

He felt Ariel's arms relax, though he had accelerated to sixty miles an hour and the headwind must have forced her to nearly close her eyes, and his own shoulders lost some of their tension—the lanes of the 101 between the interchange and the Cahuenga exit always felt like home.

He opened the throttle and sped across the lanes to the fast lane. If the pickup trucks and the SUV had followed him onto the freeway it would do them no good—on this uninterrupted thoroughfare any motorcycle could outrun them, and if traffic jammed up he could ride between the lines of stopped cars or on the narrow median shoulder.

But he knew he should get off the freeway before a Highway Patrol car pulled him over because he and Ariel were not wearing helmets.

"Have you had lunch?" he called.

She leaned forward to speak directly into his ear. "No."

"Miceli's?"

"Damn you. All right."

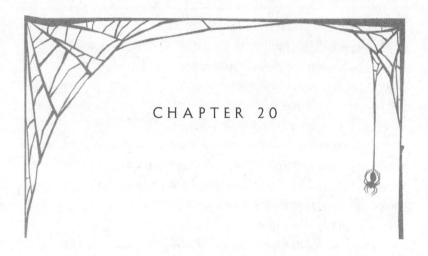

CHAPTER 20

TO STALL FOR TIME, Claimayne spun his wheelchair away from his visitor to face the back of the old garage. Daylight shone on the wooden ladder and the stained cement floor back there, because the rooftop hatch had been left open. And the driveway-side door was broken right off and now lay flat on the pavement outside. This must be the way Scott descended from the roof on Wednesday, Claimayne thought. The three decrepit rubber space aliens beside the aluminum foil spacecraft seemed to peer at him, and he shuddered, remembering how they had frightened him when he was young, and peopled his nightmares recently. Their green arms seemed poised.

Claimayne made himself think instead about the man standing impatiently behind him. Do I trust him? he wondered. Well, no. Do I trust him to see mutual benefit?

He reversed the wheelchair to face the man again.

"There's Taylor's film," Claimayne said at last. "It contained many copies, maybe hundreds, of the Medusa spider, but it was stolen from my mother in 1922 and hasn't been heard of since, and anyway the image was raw, it would kill you—you'd need to extend it through proxy retinas, get some poor devil to look at it in a before, and then use his posthumous after."

He wrinkled his nose at the smell of damp rot, which was hardly at all dispersed by the breeze through the open doorway. "Sorry about the accommodations," he added, "but I couldn't let you be seen in the house, and even wheeling myself around the outside of the house to here has been more tiring than I anticipated. I don't know why I've never got a motorized wheelchair."

Jules Ferdalisi nodded rapidly, still fingering the rip in his trousers that he had apparently suffered in getting through the old ivy-tangled Vista Del Mar gate. His bald head gleamed with sweat, and the beard that ran weirdly around under his jaw had a couple of bougainvillea petals stuck in it.

"This is concrete information," he said, "but of little current use; and your mobility issues—" He raised a hand and let it drop, then peered into the dimness beyond Claimayne, presumably at the awful old aliens beside the spacecraft, and shook his head.

"My mother," Claimayne went on, "loved the two children of her stepbrother-in-law more than she did me. Instead of me, really. I'm getting to it, bear with me."

He cleared his throat. Here we go, he thought. "*They* both looked at the Ince spider in 1992 and survived because of course it was at secondhand, through Ince's eyes—their own retinas weren't the ones called on to fully reciprocate. The actual Ince spider is apparently lost, but it's available in their memories, you see. *They're* not lost— they're both staying right here in this house."

"Ah." Ferdalisi nodded slowly as he visibly relaxed. "Yes. And they visited a couple of interesting people this morning."

"Really. I'll want to hear about that. But you have the resources to take them, force spiders on them, get into their heads—and then reach sideways."

Ferdalisi's brow knit in a fastidious frown. "By the imprecise analogy 'reach sideways' I assume you mean—"

"I mean forcibly strip-mine their psyches, to give you another analogy. Plunder their memories, which include the Medusa, which is the link to a near infinity of hijacked experiences. A hundred years, at least, of retrograde world to live in and control."

"Oh. Yes. We—"

"Listen. You'll need my help. I can arrange for you to take them both at once, quietly, during the party we're hosting here tomorrow afternoon."

"Very good. We can pay you—"

"I'm afraid I have no further use for money."

Ferdalisi raised his eyebrows. "What then?"

"Surely it's obvious? There are two of them, one for each of us. You take the man's mind, and I'll take the girl's."

Ferdalisi glanced at Claimayne's wheelchair. "Immortality in the past."

"A very wide and varied past," agreed Claimayne, touching his gold DNA-coil pendant. "I have no interest in, or likelihood of, see-ing 2016, but there are some fine years behind us to be experienced, in a multitude of lives." He stretched, wincing. "I should tell you that my other cousin, my real, blood cousin, Ariel, has been in touch with the spiderbit people—" He paused when Ferdalisi nodded, then went on, "And I don't know what she may have told them. I tried to take her out of the picture this afternoon, unsuccessfully."

Ferdalisi frowned. "Was she . . . aware of your efforts?"

"I'm afraid I did rouse suspicion in her, yes. She drove away an hour ago—to tell you the truth, she's probably seeing the spiderbit people right now."

"Not if she consulted their website today," said Ferdalisi blandly. "She may be no problem."

"Huh." Then I doubt that she did consult this spiderbit website, thought Claimayne, since she'll apparently be alive and well this eve-ning, to do the reciprocal second viewing of the spider she looked at on Tuesday night. *Come in out of the rain, Scott . . . there's cookies in the kitchen* . . . She seemed entirely cheery and untroubled in that flashback from a few hours in our future.

I'll certainly have to kill her. God knows what she may already have told her spiderbit comrades. But I probably blew my chance to do it through a spider—she'll be alert for any more such tricks now. What a waste—all those secondhand experiences she contains that I could have had!

"In any case," he said, "I doubt she'll survive tomorrow's party."

SCOTT PARKED THE MOTORCYCLE in the lot behind Miceli's, hidden between a couple of vans that he hoped would stay there for a while, and Ariel walked slowly to stay beside him as he limped to the sidewalk and past the green canvas awnings and potted plants to the restaurant's polished wooden front door.

Ariel pulled it open for him.

"I'm not an invalid!" he protested.

"Sorry—I guess I'm too used to Claimayne."

The air in the restaurant was welcomely warm after the breezy shirtsleeves ride up the freeway, and smelled of garlic and fennel, and Scott was abruptly very hungry. Hanging lamps over the tables illuminated the dark, carved wood of the booths, and clusters of hanging wine bottles in straw jackets almost hid the glossy beamed ceiling.

A waiter in a white apron led them down past the row of tall booths to a table up three steps and behind a railing, under a big copy of the *Mona Lisa*.

"We've sat here before," said Ariel as Scott pulled out her chair. He couldn't tell if the look she was giving him was reproachful or ironic. Possibly both.

"I remember," he said, sitting down on the seat opposite, against the brick wall. "It was raining outside, and the out-of-town newsstand across the street was lit up like Van Gogh's *Café Terrace at Night*."

"I need help," she said. "You hurt me, years ago, but that was years ago. I—"

Scott shook his head in incomprehension. "Hurt you? How? Hurting you was the last thing I ever meant to do."

"You completed your list, then. These wheelbugs, and Claimayne—"

"How?"

"Could I have a glass, no, a bottle, of the Gnarly Head zinfandel, please," she said, and Scott noticed that the waiter had returned.

"Two glasses," he said.

After the waiter had nodded and walked back down the steps, Ariel looked at him with something like alarm. "You quit!"

"I started again last night. I'll quit again, probably. Hurt you how?"

"Is it my fault, picking on you and Madeline—"

"No. How?"

She sighed, staring at him. "You're not curious about those wheelbugs who tried to, I don't know, kidnap me?"

"Terribly curious, yes. But let's get the important stuff out of the way first."

"Hah. Well, you don't remember it. God, I need some wine in me first." She sat back and gave him a falsely bright grin and pointed at the woodwork over his head. "Remember when you explained about the pigs?"

He smiled reluctantly. "It was a . . . misunderstanding."

It must have been in about 2000, when he'd have been twenty-one and Ariel would have been eighteen—he had told her that the woodwork here had once been in the Pig and Whistle restaurant around the corner, and had been bought by Miceli's when the Pig and Whistle closed after World War II. While showing her the dancing pig figure that could be seen in many carved panels around the restaurant, he had gestured at one booth and said, *And the pig is here, too*—only to belatedly notice a surprised woman sitting in the booth, across from a burly and suddenly angry male companion. Scott had managed to stammer out a hasty apology and explanation before the man had got all the way to his feet.

"And the pig is here, too," said Ariel now, reminiscently. "I bet my hair is a mess. And what am I going to do about my car?"

Scott shook his head. "Thank you," he said to the waiter, who filled two glasses and set the bottle down on the red-and-white-checkered tablecloth. "We could go back for it," he said when the man had again retreated.

"Too likely that they'd wait there for me."

"For us. I'm pretty sure that white SUV was there because of me."

"For us." Ariel took a deep sip of the wine, then sang, "We're little black sheep who have gone astray," from *The Whiffenpoof Song*. "I wrote you a note," she went on, staring into her glass. "When you were packing up, leaving Caveat to marry that Louise woman. I was twenty, I was a kid—it was a love note, damn it. And you—" She paused to take another sip of the wine; then, still looking down, she went on, "You wrote *idiot teenager* over my signature, and you threw it in the trash." She held up her hand. "It shouldn't have affected me the way it did, the way it has . . ."

Scott leaned forward. "*I—did—not*. I never saw any such note. I'd have—I might have left Louise, if I'd seen it. I always—"

She looked up at him in apparent dismay. "Don't say that! Yes you did, you just don't remember it. I don't blame you—I mean, I do, I always have—oh, my car is going to be stolen, I know it—"

"I could never have forgotten it."

"But obviously you have, and I—no offense, but I hate you for that too."

"Listen to me," he said urgently, though he wasn't sure how he would continue. After a moment's thought, he went on, "I thought our parents abandoned us, Madeline and me—I was *sure* of it—and I've hated them all these years for it, but this morning I found evidence that they didn't." He took a deep breath. "I almost can't let go of it, can't stop hating them, it's been my main . . . but . . . I may have misunderstood the circumstances, like the guy here who thought I called his girlfriend a pig."

After several long seconds, Ariel nodded. "When I was ten, I found their driver's licenses and credit cards in the compost barrel, and I put them in a box and stuck it in the garage where Claimayne had stored all their furniture." She blotted her eyes with her napkin. "You really didn't see my note? Not at all?"

"I really did not. I wish I had."

"Of course you'd *say* that."

"Ariel, if I—"

"Oh hell, I believe you, God help me." She gave a shuddering sigh. "I don't know what to do. I almost don't know who I am if you didn't throw me away. I wish you weren't drinking."

"We're two black sheep who have gone astray," said Scott.

Ariel ran a fingertip around the rim of her glass, but it produced no audible note. "Could I have the chicken Marsala, please," she said, for the waiter had come up the steps again.

"Uh, the lasagna, please," said Scott absently. In his head he was rehearsing what Ariel had said a few moments ago—*I found their driver's licenses and credit cards in the compost barrel, and I put them in a box and stuck it in the garage* . . .

"What—are wheelbugs?" he asked.

"I think I'll report the car as stolen. Then I'll just have to pick it up at an impound yard . . . It was Claimayne. Claimayne must have found the note I left for you, and he wrote on it and threw it in the trash. He was always a mean little shit—why does that only seem obvious now? Did I *want* . . . ?"

Scott spread his hands helplessly.

She leaned back in her chair and stretched. "You used to give me rides on your bike. It didn't cramp me up so much in those days." She paused, then said, "Wheelbugs are spider addicts who prey on other spider addicts. It seems you can tap into, access, another person's spider experiences, if you get him to look at one and then later look at it yourself. Not just occupy him for that brief interval, see, like you'd expect, but—you can learn to sort of dig in, and stay, and occupy all the spider visions he's ever had; even his plain old life experiences, if you're strong enough. It breaks his mind, the victim's mind." She refilled her glass. "The guy in the car that rear-ended me, he tried to show me a spider."

Scott shook his head, horrified. "Why on earth were you down there, by the river?"

"You think I wanted to go there? There's a shop that caters to spiderbits—that's spider users who have quit, and I'm one. It's where I got those glasses yesterday; they sell stuff to help insulate you from spiders. The shop moves around a lot, because wheelbugs love to find spiderbits—people like me, with lots of accumulated spider experiences to hijack. You have to go to a website and enter a password to see where the shop is each day, and today the site said the shop was down there on East Sixth. I wanted to at least get some flash bangs—you know what those are? Ah, *I* didn't. So I stole some money Claimayne had hidden in the library, and went there, but I guess the site got hacked by wheelbugs. Led me into a trap."

Scott was thinking of his parents' threat to expose Claimayne's mother, and possibly that Ostriker fellow too, to wheelbugs. "I'm glad I followed you."

"Me too. Why *did* you follow me?"

"Back at Caveat, you sounded like . . . like you were going to run away and never come back, or even kill yourself."

She shrugged. "We'll never know now. But any longtime spider user, like Claimayne, or his mother, or me, is an unending feast for a wheelbug. He can opt out of reality, live in all our past or future visions—well, apparently they're all past these days. Still. It would be like living forever in a virtual reality game."

"Some of the visions might be a bit unpleasant."

"But forever. That outweighs unpleasant."

Scott signaled the waiter and ordered a club soda. "You can have mine too," he said, pushing his wineglass toward Ariel.

"Back on the wagon?"

"For now. Listen, do you think a wheelbug can pull that trick on somebody even after the wheelbug's dead?"

"Wow. That's a terrible thought. But . . . yeah, I suppose. After all, he's not dead in the strip of time he imposes on the unlucky person who does the after, the person who eventually consummates the quickening of the dirty spider. So yeah, the wheelbug would be alive in the poor sucker's head, even though he'd be dead out in the real world."

"Quickening! What, are the spiders alive?"

"Claimayne says they are. So . . . do you know of some dead wheelbug who's trying to eat a living person's memories?" Suddenly her eyes were wide. "Last night, during the movie! It wasn't just the scrambled house, working on Madeline?"

"No. Aunt Amity left a spider for each of us, and we both looked at them, but she seems to have got into Madeline's mind. And she's dug in there, like you said."

"But Madeline was never any kind of—oh. When you were kids. Claimayne says you both looked at what he calls the big spider. The Medusa."

"Yes. We did."

"That would definitely be a forever feast." Ariel shuddered visibly, then drained her own glass and snatched up Scott's. "It'll destroy Madeline."

"There's got to be a way to . . . yank Aunt Amity out of my sister's head."

"How? You can't kill spiders."

A passing patron grinned up at her from the lower level and audibly stamped his foot on the red linoleum in helpful suggestion.

"Maybe you can," said Scott. He looked at the glass of wine in Ariel's hand, then looked away. "There's, or there was at one time, an exorcism."

"There is? An exorcism for the spiders? Do you know how to do it?"

"Yeah. It's a film. You watch it, and it banishes the Medusa spider, allegedly, and all the other spiders too. But I have it on good authority that the movie probably kills the viewer."

Ariel took a sip of his wine and carefully set the glass down on the tablecloth. "That's no good, then."

"It's certainly not *very* good." God help me, thought Scott. "When we're done here," he said slowly, "there's a stop we've got to make before we head back to Caveat."

I'll hide the film in this house, Valentino had said, *for you to find, in your day.* And Scott had told him, *if you move, leave it there . . .*

She eyed him cautiously. "Where?"

He looked out over the rail, over the booths and lamps and hanging bottles, not seeing them. "I don't know exactly, but—it's north of here, and close by."

AT THE TOP OF Whitley Avenue, north of Franklin, they had to double back downhill and take Whitley Terrace north, but that led them to a narrow street with tall white houses among lush cypresses and pines to the left, and nothing to the right but an ivy-covered brown cinder-block freeway wall beyond a low hedge. Widely spaced cypresses and antique-looking streetlamps stood up along the hedge. The westering sun threw long shadows down the pavement.

Scott braked the motorcycle to a halt at the curb and stared at the wall while the engine chugged in neutral.

"The houses are on the other side of the street," ventured Ariel, sitting behind him.

He turned to look that way and felt the hairs standing up on his arms—behind an iron railing and up a grassy slope was a two- or three-story Spanish-style house that he now recognized. It had been across the street from Valentino's house, in the spider vision he'd had last night.

To his instant shame, the first thing Scott felt was relief. The place where Valentino's house had stood—where the Taylor exorcism film had probably once been hidden behind a red board in the attic—was now a volume of turbulent air over the lanes of the 101 Freeway on the other side of the wall.

"The house was right there," he said, facing the wall again and pointing at it.

"Not lately," said Ariel. "The freeway's been there since . . . before you were born. Before Claimayne was born."

"I know." Scott trod the gear shift into first gear. "This was in the 1920s."

Ariel shivered on the seat behind him. "I'm freezing. We'd better be heading back to C-Caveat. I've got calls to make, and Claimayne will be mad if sinners date." She laughed awkwardly. "Two glasses of wine! I mean *if dinner's late.*"

Scott nodded and let out the bent clutch lever.

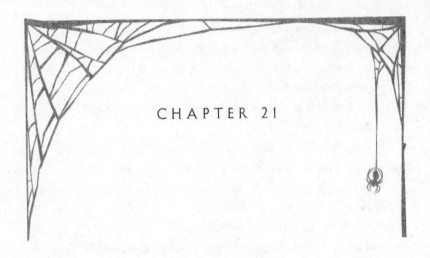

CHAPTER 21

SCOTT PULLED OPEN THE kitchen door, his hand tingling and almost numb from having gripped and twisted the motorcycle's throttle so much that afternoon, and Madeline stood up from the kitchen table and smiled to see Ariel.

"We were worried about you," she said.

Scott noticed that Ariel was blinking back tears. "You poor sweet child," she said, and hurried out of the room.

Madeline watched her until the dining-room door swung closed, then turned to her brother. "What's with her?"

"She's got to call the cops, report her car stolen." Scott ran his fingers through his wind-disordered hair. "It wasn't stolen, but some bad guys tried to grab her down by the Sixth Street bridge and she had to abandon it, and she's scared they might still be there, waiting for her. I guess I'm cooking dinner."

"Did you rescue her? Her skirt was torn. You're wearing her sunglasses."

"Oh. Yes." He took off the sunglasses and laid them on the table. "And she doesn't hate us anymore, or not at the moment."

Scott found bacon and cheddar cheese in the refrigerator, and a loaf of sourdough bread and a net of onions on the counter, and as he cooked he described to his sister the encounter with the pickup trucks and the escape along the river embankment and onto the freeway. Within half an hour he had fried the bacon, browned sliced onions in the bacon grease, laid it all on slices of cheese on the bread, and then fried up four big, somewhat greasy sandwiches. As he lifted them onto plates with a spatula, he heard the booming and squealing of Claimayne's elevator.

"That smells wonderful," said Ariel, stepping into the kitchen from the dining room. She had changed into gray woolen trousers, and her silver pendant hung outside a red checked flannel shirt.

"It must have been scary," said Madeline, "riding along that slanted cement by the river."

Ariel cocked her head. "That was one scary part," she agreed.

"You two wash your hands now," said Madeline, and she stepped away into the dining room.

Scott and Ariel exchanged a puzzled glance. "I just did," said Ariel.

"Me too. I guess I—"

They were interrupted by a shout from Claimayne, and each of them hastily picked up two plates and hurried after Madeline.

The lights weren't on yet in the dining room, and the jacaranda trees glowed in the sunset light outside, beyond the tall open windows. Claimayne's wheelchair was at its customary spot on the south side of the dining table, but Madeline was now sitting at the head of the table. Stepping around Claimayne to set down the plates he was carrying, Scott saw that they were glaring at each other.

"She's . . . *presuming* to sit at my mother's place!"

"Madeline," said Scott, but she ignored him.

Claimayne leaned forward and snarled, "What are you *doing* in my mother's *chair*?"

Madeline twitched, and then blinked in evident bewilderment at her angry cousin. "I . . . don't know," she said wonderingly. She hastily got up and walked around to her usual chair.

Claimayne slumped back as Ariel sat down next to him and Scott took his place on the other side of the table, beside Madeline. Scott noticed that Claimayne had a long brown-paper-wrapped package laid across the arms of his wheelchair.

"What have we here," Claimayne said, finally glancing down at his plate. "Cholesterol sandwiches. You know I have a bad heart." He looked at Madeline and then at Scott, taking a deep breath as he spread his hands on the table. "So who *is* Adrian Ostriker? Some old friend of my mother's? You two didn't stay long."

Scott didn't look at Madeline. Claimayne himself must be in touch with the people who hired Louise to spy on us, he thought. "No," he said. "He wasn't . . . friendly."

"Ah. And how is poor old *Genod* these days?"

"Old," said Scott.

"You're supposed to send him a check," added Madeline. "A thousand dollars. Every month. Your mother did."

"Did he tell you about his relationship with Ava Gardner?" When Madeline nodded, Claimayne went on, "Did he tell you the *extent* of it? Hah? Genod was what they call best boy—that's the assistant gaffer, lighting technician—on a movie called *Ride, Vaquero!* in 1952. One time on the set, Genod yawned, and Ava Gardner saw him do it, and she yawned too."

Madeline cocked her head, clearly expecting more to the story.

"That was the entirety of it," said Claimayne. He shifted to peer at Ariel. "And where did you and Scott get to, once you were on the freeway, with no helmets?"

Ariel smiled at him. "You called that Ferdalisi guy back, didn't you?" When he shrugged, she went on, "You have untrustworthy friends. Be careful. Scott and I had lunch at Miceli's."

"All happy family again, hah?" Claimayne sat back. "And so you're not hungry and you cook me up this *shit*? I won't eat it." He pushed his plate away.

Ariel rolled her eyes. "I could fix you something else."

"I'll keep it from going to waste," said Madeline, reaching for the plate.

"No you won't, *curiosa*," Claimayne said to her, tugging the plate back. He was trembling, and a tight smile twitched at his smooth cheeks. "Maybe somebody *else* might want it, turnabout being *fair play*."

He thrust a hand into the pocket of his dressing gown and pulled out a folded slip of paper; Scott noticed the two words of his own mother's handwriting on it in the moment before Claimayne opened it and stared at it, and he pushed his chair back with a smothered exclamation—but Claimayne's hand had already dropped limply to the table, and his face was expressionless, his lower lip sagging.

Scott froze, half standing up.

Ariel stared uncertainly at Claimayne, then at Scott.

"What?" said Madeline in the silence.

Claimayne abruptly swiveled his head and gaped at the faces around the table. His pale hands rose up in front of his face now, the paper falling away from his pale fingers.

"This isn't me!" The voice that rattled out of his throat was shrill. Claimayne's eyes were wide as he looked from Scott to Madeline to Ariel. "Who are you?" His hands slapped his chest. "Who is *this*?"

"Mom," said Scott hoarsely as sweat broke out on his forehead, "I'm Scott, this is Madeline—we—"

Ariel's teeth were bared, and she was squinting as if against a bright light.

"Scott," came the voice out of Claimayne's mouth, "is it you? You're old, what did we—oh Jesus, am I *dead*?"

"I love you, Mom!" called Madeline. Her napkin was crumpled tightly in her fist.

Ariel was whispering, "Motherfucker, you motherfucker . . ."

Claimayne's bald head had rocked back, his eyes scanning the cobwebby beams far overhead. "Still at Caveat . . . ? It didn't work, and I'm dead?" The head swung down to look at the hall doorway.

"God, is my Arthur dead too?" Scott saw tears spurt from Claimayne's eyes, and more trickled down his twitching cheeks. The gaze swung back to Scott and Madeline. "What did we do, what did we do to you . . ."

"We," said Scott, staring into the face that was Claimayne's and forcing the words out, "love you, Mom." He made himself go further: "I love you."

"Are you . . . please . . . happy?"

Claimayne's head sagged forward then and he seemed to snore.

"Mom!" yelled Scott, getting up and starting around the table, but Claimayne held up a hand.

"Wait," Claimayne whispered. He inhaled deeply and leaned back in his wheelchair, and he stared unseeingly toward the wall. "Wait."

The air seemed to Scott to be ringing like a struck piano. Madeline was sobbing quietly into her napkin.

"It's you again, Claimayne," said Ariel, "isn't it?" When he nodded, she went on, quietly, "You're worse than contemptible. I hope you die, soon, stinking, shitting yourself and choking on your own vomit."

Scott was standing at the hallway end of the table, his fists clenched.

Claimayne waved clumsily across the table in Madeline's direction. "Only fair. Balancing the scales. She looked at one of *my* mother's." He fumbled at the long package on his lap, obviously not able to see clearly yet, and he lifted it and let it clunk onto the table.

"Speaking of my mother," he said in a nearly conversational tone, "she gave this to your father, but he didn't want it. You remember? It's time to clear all old debts." He tore at the brown paper impatiently. "Damn, why did I *tape* it?"

At last he had pulled all the paper away, and Scott saw what it had concealed: a three-foot length of two-by-four, the last foot wrapped in tan carpeting.

"Christmas," said Madeline weakly, "1991."

"That's right, child," said Claimayne, nodding. He picked up his napkin and wiped the tears from his face. "A week after she had the carpeting—*this* carpeting," he said, dropping the napkin in order to lift the piece of wood, "—removed from the stairs." He could see in perspective now, for he was staring directly at Scott. "Do you know where my mother got this thing?"

Scott let out the breath he'd been holding. "No, Claimayne."

"She found it under your parents' bed. Your father was planning to beat my mother to death with it because she had turned his black-mail scheme back on him. And then he was going to push her body down the stairs." Claimayne's hand ran up the wood and slid over the carpeting. "He took this piece of carpet from one of the risers, so that his . . . *murderous blows* would seem to have resulted from impacts with the stairs." He laid the piece of wood down and turned to Ariel. "Actually, if you could fix me a bowl of tomato soup . . ."

"For the sake of your rancid soul, I pray you're insane," she said, pushing her chair back and standing up.

She started toward the hall doorway. Scott caught Madeline's eye and rocked his head that way, and Madeline pushed back her chair and stood up.

As his three cousins left the dining room, Claimayne called, "Have a shot of that Wild Turkey under the mattress, Scott, it'll relax you."

ARIEL DIDN'T STOP AT the second-floor landing. "The apiary," she said, continuing up the stairs. "He won't have put microphones there."

Madeline was hiccuping as she yanked herself up each step by pulling on the banister. "I'm glad you—*hic*—told her you love her, Scott."

"I don't know that I do," Scott said, watching and ready to catch her if she missed her next banister grab. His heart was still pounding. "I suppose I should; and it seemed like the right thing to say."

"Do you think—*hic*—that was true? About our father wanting to kill Aunt—*hic*—Amity? I hate hiccups."

"Yes. I hope Mom didn't know."

Madeline hiked herself up another couple of steps. "Have you really got a—*hic*—bottle of Wild Turkey under your mattress?"

"What's left of one."

At the top of the stairs they clattered along the hallway and into the apiary, and Ariel slid the heavy door shut, though they would certainly hear Claimayne's elevator if he were to come upstairs after them. Scott clicked on the overhead lightbulb.

The big television screen, black now, still faced the two dozen mismatched chairs, and windows visible between the legs of stacked tables along the walls let in the apricot glow of sunset. Scott thought he still caught a whiff of old pizza.

"I think Aunt Amity killed our parents," Scott said to Madeline. "And it looks like it might arguably have been self-defense."

She hiccuped.

"That was twenty-something years ago," said Ariel, sitting down in the same chair she'd occupied to watch the movie last night. "I believe Claimayne tried to kill me today."

She told Scott and Madeline about coming across the spider in her dresser drawer, and confronting Claimayne and finding him with a revolver and the puzzling strips of foil.

"I think he hoped to occupy me and, while he was in my body, use that gun to shoot my head off." Her voice had been strong at first but had wavered by the end of the sentence. She took a deep breath and let it out. "Apparent suicide," she added.

"Why would he want you dead?" asked Madeline. She sat down beside Ariel, then bobbed on her chair as she smothered a hiccup.

"Because he knew, from the crazy glasses I had on at dinner last night, that I went to a shop—I told you about it, Scott—a shop where they sell counterspider things: warpy glasses, plexiglass for windows, tarantella cassettes—"

Scott cocked his head at that, but when Ariel paused and looked at him, he waved at her to go on.

"Anyway," Ariel said, "Claimayne apparently saw it as communicating with the enemy. I think he's worried about what I might have learned, or said; or might learn or say the next time I go there. He thinks I'm a spy, basically." She shook her head. "I do wonder what the foil strips were for."

"He was going to chew them," said Scott, "while he was in your body. You've probably got fillings in your teeth, so it'd hurt—pain prolongs a spider vision." He smiled crookedly at his sister. "Rudolph Valentino told me that last night."

Madeline twisted around on her chair, staring up at him.

He sighed and sat down beside her. "I looked at a spider last night," he began, "after we both went to bed . . ." And he told his sister and cousin about his talk with Valentino, and even about waking up out by the Medusa wall in the middle of the night, in his underwear. "That's whose house I was looking for," he told Ariel, "up Whitley. And the house is gone," he added to Madeline. "The 101 Freeway is there now."

"You didn't tell him about me?" Madeline asked.

"He said to tell you that Natacha was grateful for your company, on that taxi ride to the hospital." Ariel was shaking her head in bewilderment, but Scott held up his hand and went on, "Mainly I told him I wanted to exorcise the spiders and all their works, to free you from Aunt Amity."

"But," said Madeline, "that would . . . *free me* from any chance of finding *him*! Oh, Scott—you love me, but I'm glad the house is gone."

"Why did you sit down in Aunt Amity's chair, at dinner?" he asked.

"I . . . don't remember doing that," she admitted.

Ariel leaned forward. "Foil, fillings? Why would Claimayne want to prolong his occupation of me? It wouldn't take more than a few seconds to have me walk to his room and pick up the gun."

"I imagine," Scott said slowly, "that he wanted enough time to climb you up that ladder onto the roof, before he pulled the trigger."

Ariel gave him a horrified look. "Why?"

Scott shrugged. "Aunt Amity has been pretty active in this house, postmortem, typing a new novel—yeah, we'll tell you about that too—and speaking through Madeline. Maybe Claimayne hoped that your violent death on the same spot where the old lady blew herself up would fragment and dilute her lingering aura, confuse her—"

"Make interference fringes in her waveform," said Madeline.

"Uh, right," agreed Scott.

"And I would have been stuck in Claimayne's body while he did it," said Ariel with a shudder, "probably handcuffed to the bed, and probably—" She suddenly sat back, her face stiff. "If," she began, but her voice was weak; she coughed and went on, "if you wanted to prevent a, a *lingering aura,* or minimize it at least . . . a grenade, outside the confinement of the house and garden, would probably . . ." She leaned forward and looked across Madeline at Scott. "When Aunt Amity was climbing up onto the roof with the grenade last week—surely in pain from climbing with her bad foot!—Claimayne was locked in his room, yelling and crying. And for four days afterward he was totally bedridden. He missed the funeral."

"Wow," whispered Scott after a pause.

Madeline cleared her throat and said, "Could you hear what he was yelling, in his room?"

"No. Why?"

Madeline rocked her head. "I would have liked to know what Aunt Amity's last words were."

"I don't know. She didn't sound happy."

"He must have been *covered* with bruises afterward," said Madeline in an awed tone. "I had a bruise on my leg after Natacha got shot."

"I guess it was worth it, to him," said Ariel.

Scott wondered if Claimayne, in Aunt Amity's body, had taken the Clara Bow umbrella with him up to the roof because it had been promised to Madeline instead of him.

"Um," said Ariel cautiously to Madeline, "what was that about finding Rudolph Valentino?"

Madeline glanced at Scott; after a moment, he shrugged and nodded.

"I guess we *trust* you," said Madeline. "Well—Scott and I found some spiders in an envelope when we were kids—"

"The ones your parents stole from Aunt Amity," interrupted Ariel. "Claimayne told me about this. And you gave them back to her, but you had already looked at one called *Ore-Ida Fries* or something." Scott and Madeline were both looking at her in alarm, and she went on, slowly and almost apologetically, "And he said that's the big spider, the *Medusa,* and somebody's going to look at it again, and that's *crumbling our local chronology*—he made me remember that phrase." She inhaled, then added, "He wants it, pretty bad."

"He knows a lot," said Madeline in an awed tone.

". . . You were going to say, about Valentino?"

"Oh, right," said Madeline. "When Scott and I looked at the big spider—it was like a million lives at once, all jerking us every which way—"

"Total nervous-system seizure," said Ariel.

"Okay. And then in the worst of it—Scott didn't experience this—a young man was there, *outside* of all the exploding scenes, and he came to me and pulled me out too. He led me into a quiet moonlit garden, and he comforted me, told me it wasn't so bad, where he was. And last night Scott and I were looking at a book about Rudolph Valentino, and I recognized him." She looked with mild defiance from one to the other. "And I won't leave this house till I find my way back to him."

"I, uh, think that's death," said Ariel. "Actually."

"If he's there, it won't be so dreadful."

"Gently into that raucous night," muttered Scott. "Some great plan."

Ariel shifted on her chair. "This is the old movie star you're talking about, right? *That* Rudolph Valentino?"

Madeline and Scott both nodded.

"Okay."

For several seconds none of them spoke or looked at one another.

Then Ariel slapped her hands on her thighs and smiled. "How would you two like to get cussed at and insulted?"

Madeline grimaced. "I couldn't bear seeing Claimayne again tonight."

"Not by him," said Ariel cheerfully, "by me."

"I thought you liked us again," said Madeline.

"Oh, I do, sweetie—I *always* liked *you,* really. But this is to balance the books. I'll be back in a minute." She stood up and hurried to the door, pulled it open, and tapped away down the dark hall.

"I think something's wrong with our whole family," said Madeline seriously.

Scott exhaled in a long, diminishing whistle. "Hard to argue." His throat tightened, and he was surprised to find that he was shivering, remembering their mother's tormented voice grating out of Claimayne's mouth. "I hope Claimayne dies like Ariel said."

Madeline glanced at him in evident surprise. "Why? He let us tell Mom we love her."

"I didn't want to tell her that. It was just—like putting an injured animal out of its misery."

"Sometimes you gotta."

Scott shifted in his chair and glanced behind him at the open door, wondering what Ariel was up to. "That box in the garage?—with our parents' credit cards and driver's licenses in it? Ariel put it there when she was ten. She found the stuff in the compost bin."

"Oh," said Madeline, nodding. "Oh."

Then Ariel came hurrying back up the hall and stepped into the apiary and pulled the sliding door closed. She was smiling, but it was a tense smile.

In her hand was a folded slip of paper. "You guys know how the before-and-after effect of spiders works, right?" Then she visibly recalled Claimayne's performance at dinner half an hour ago, and went on quickly, "This is a spider I looked at three days ago, on Tuesday night, just as you two arrived. Remember it? You met a *me* then who was cheerful and welcoming, right? Well, that was me from right now—and when I look at this, you're going to get the *reciprocal* me, the me from that night. I'm afraid she's going to be very rude."

She dragged one of the chairs out of line and spun it to face Scott and Madeline.

"Uh," said Scott, glancing at his sister, "why do it in front of us?"

"Because right here, with you two, is where I found myself when I looked at this spider on Tuesday night. Just like this—me sitting here, you two sitting there. It must have been right now."

Which only means, thought Scott, that tonight you decided to do it in front of us. But he said, "That makes sense."

Ariel nodded. "I apologize in advance, okay? This, what you're about to see, is the old me—three days old."

She flipped open the paper and stared at it almost hungrily; and her eyes unfocused and for several seconds she just stared blankly at the floor. Scott braced himself to catch her if she fell out of her chair.

But she stiffened, and when she looked up, she was scowling. "*You* two! What fucking day is it?" She glared around the room. "Why are you in *here*? It better not be more than the week—"

"It's Friday night," Scott told her.

"Three nights in your future," put in Madeline.

Ariel spat on the floor, and both Scott and Madeline rocked back in surprise. "Four days from, from *this,*" Ariel went on, grimacing as she waved her hand in a circle, "we'll have to fumigate the rooms in the apartments down there, burn the sheets—after a drunk and a bag lady stayed there—a couple of ghouls—grave-worms! And if you imagine you're going to inherit this place—"

"Really, Ariel," Scott interrupted loudly, "this is all unnecessary. We understand—"

"We don't hold this against you," said Madeline, eyeing her seated cousin with something like wonder.

"We're not at odds," added Scott. He was surprised to find that he was sweating.

"Liar! You pathetic—"

Scott stood up quickly, for Ariel's eyes had half shut and she was swaying, and he caught her before she could topple forward. Holding her under her arms, he considered propping her back up in her chair, then just lowered her to the floor.

"I don't think she'd have done it here," said Madeline breathlessly, "with us, if she'd remembered how mean she was."

Scott straightened up. "I wonder." He was glad that the bag-lady remark didn't seem to have upset his sister, though it had angered him for her sake. The drunk accusation hadn't bothered him—*it* hadn't been a prediction, after all, just a statement of presumed present fact.

Ariel had dropped the slip of paper, and he picked it up, glancing at it peripherally through nearly closed eyes just to be sure there really was an eight-limbed figure on it, and that Ariel hadn't improvised her diatribe on the spot, with a blank piece of paper.

Ariel sat up, blinking; she fumbled at her chest until she gripped her silver gyroscope pendant, and she waved it in front of her face; her eyes didn't follow its motion. "It worked," she said hoarsely. "I saw you two on Tuesday night, all soaked in the rain. It *was* enchiladas, that first night, wasn't it?"

Madeline nodded, then said, "Yes."

Ariel let go of the pendant and flexed her hands, and seemed to see them clearly. She peered around, frowning, and saw the paper in Scott's hand. She reached for it and he handed it to her, and she shakily tore it to pieces. "That spider's done, consummated. And I'm never doing another. Was I very horrible? It's been three days, I don't exactly remember."

"Yes," said Scott, a little stiffly.

"Oh, Scott, don't pay any attention to all that! It was me before . . . before I knew what was what."

But you figured we ought to hear it, he thought.

"That's okay," said Madeline. "Do you want help getting up?"

"No, I—" Ariel folded her legs with some evident effort, but remained sitting on the floor. "Well, yes."

Scott reached a hand down to her, and when she grasped his wrist, he pulled her erect; and she gripped his shoulder tightly.

"I'll be all right in a minute," she said. "I hate to leave you right after that . . . version of me, that old version, but I'm . . . I think I'm going to turn in."

"I'll help you down the stairs," said Scott. "And I advise locking your bedroom door."

Ariel nodded, though it made her wince. "And I'll put a chair against it. And I've got my .32 with only one round used up." She started to yawn, but that seemed to hurt too. Scott thought of old Genod Speas, all his life treasuring the memory of a yawn shared with Ava Gardner. Ariel went on, "And Claimayne will probably be busy making phone calls and planning for his party tomorrow night."

"I'm going to retire too," said Madeline, getting up.

Ariel told her, "I'm sorry I said all that awful stuff."

"That's okay. I don't think you meant it, even then."

"Maybe you're right."

Ariel leaned on Scott all the way down the hall, and her arm around his waist reminded him of their hectic ride on the motorcycle this afternoon. Her hair smelled faintly and not unpleasantly of diesel exhaust. In spite of his misgivings about her performance a few minutes ago, he found that he wanted to tip her face up and kiss her. He sighed deeply and resisted it.

It was a love note, damn it, she had said at Miceli's. And he had said, *I might have left Louise, if I'd seen it.*

And I would have, he thought now.

At the stairs, she held on to the banister and put both feet on each step before attempting the next. Scott held her arm and Madeline held his, evidently meaning to belay both of them if Ariel should tumble.

Ariel was more steady in the dark second-floor hall, and trudged to her door without support.

"You two should sleep with the lights on," she whispered. "Or better, don't sleep at all."

"I'm not afraid," said Madeline.

Ariel shook her head and stepped into her room. When the door closed, Scott and Madeline could hear a chair being dragged across the floor inside.

"I'm going to put my blankets on your floor," Scott told his sister as they walked back toward their own rooms, "and sleep there tonight. If you suddenly turn into Aunt Amity, I'll slap you out of it."

"That's no good," she said. "Pain makes it last longer. Sing me a lullaby."

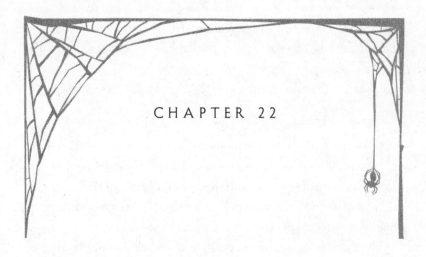

CHAPTER 22

MADELINE WAS BREATHING WITH reassuring evenness in the darkness, but lying on the floor reminded Scott too much of having come to his senses half naked in the garden last night.

He was wearing his jeans and shirt, and he stood up silently and stole through his own room and out into the dark hall. The house creaked in the night wind that rattled the window at the far end of the hall, and the air seemed to be full of ancient whispered questions.

He walked barefoot to the head of the stairs. Claimayne's elevator had not yet banged up through the walls, and he wondered what the man might be up to, alone down in the dining room or the kitchen or his mother's library.

Briefly he thought of tiptoeing down to spy on him—and he was ruefully surprised to discover that the idea scared him. What if Claimayne were sitting down there in the lightless dining room, staring at the entry hall? Scott imagined Claimayne holding the revolver Ariel had seen on his bedside table, but that actually seemed to make the idea more mundane; it was more disturbing to imagine Claimayne just sitting there with empty hands, staring, his bland face perhaps smiling.

Scott hurriedly turned back toward Madeline's room, brushing his hand along the row of fixed doors that lined the south wall, and he automatically knocked at the one that had been salvaged from the Garden of Allah.

"Come in," said a woman's voice.

SCOTT FROZE, HIS HANDS tingling and his scalp suddenly tight.

"Doody?" said the voice. He heard footsteps on the other side of the door—but there was only plaster and brick on the other side of the door!—and then the knob turned and he stepped back as the door swung open, spreading radiance into the hallway.

He squinted against the new light at a short, trim, gray-haired woman in horn-rimmed glasses who was peering up at him, and then past him, in evident surprise. She was wearing tan slacks, and the fuzz of her green sweater was backlit by sunlight in a window behind her.

Scott's breath was caught in his throat, and for a moment he couldn't think at all, and simply stared.

The woman stepped back too, then whispered, apparently to herself, "Thou art a scholar—speak to it, Adelaida." She met Scott's wide-eyed gaze and gave him a forced smile, and waved into the room. "Do come in, O Spirit. And close the door behind you—I want to believe my sundeck and the pool are still out there."

Scott was breathing again, deeply. This is what happened to Madeline two days ago, he told himself; Ariel said something about our local chronology crumbling. This will fade away in a minute or so.

His heart was almost clanking in his chest, and he shifted his weight to his back foot, ready to run down the hall to his own room, no, to Madeline's room—

Madeline, who needs to somehow be saved from Aunt Amity. *When is a door not adore? When it's a way in, Scott.*

Scott nodded several times, then made himself take the long step forward across the threshold; into a small living room with a long violet couch, a black enameled desk by a window on the right, and a potted orchid curling its green leaves and lobed yellow flowers across another window straight ahead. The room glowed with midday sunlight. When he closed the door behind him, he noticed a framed fire evacuation notice screwed to the wood; evidently this was a hotel. He was still squinting and blinking in the bright light.

The woman raised her chin. "This is that old *black geometry*, isn't it?" she said. "We try to avoid having anything to do with that stuff."

"I, uh, suppose it is, more or less." Scott was panting. "Sorry."

She cocked her head, smiling quizzically now. Her eyes were vivid blue behind the glasses, and her gray hair was done in a pageboy cut. "I do believe you're more startled by this . . . impossible intrusion! . . . than I am!" She spoke with an accent, pronouncing "r"s as soft "d"s. Scott caught a whiff of lemon verbena perfume.

"Yes, ma'am," said Scott. "Very likely, I mean." He hoped he had zipped his fly and buttoned his shirt correctly, and wished he'd shaved; at random he said, "Doody?"

"My secretary," said the woman. "She's gone across the street to Schwab's to fill a prescription—do sit down—look at you, not even any shoes!"

With a shaky hand she waved him toward the couch and sat down in an armchair on the other side of a low coffee table, by the near window. On the table was a copy of *Life* magazine with a black-and-white picture of teenaged Shirley Temple on the cover, and the woman reached out to pick nervously at the glued-on address label.

"It's not her real name, of course," she went on distractedly. "In a movie we saw, a man referred to his wife as his sacred duty, and he pronounced it *doody*—not that—" She clenched her fists and let out what was left of her breath, and then looked straight at him. "Where were you a moment ago?"

Scott slowly sat down on the couch and peered around at the

books and framed black-and-white photographs on several shelves. A mandolin hung on one wall. "Uh, Hollywood," he said.

"Hmph." From the coffee table she picked up a flat black box and a matchbook, and when she opened the box, Scott saw a row of black cigarettes with gold filters. She took one out and lit it with a steadier hand, blew smoke toward Scott, and leaned back in her chair.

She waved the cigarette toward her closed front door. "Night-time?"

"Hm? Oh." Scott rubbed his forehead. "It was, yes."

"So you're not a *local,* by at least a few hours. Very well. Why did you knock at my door, since"—she glanced at his bare feet and no doubt disheveled hair—"you clearly didn't expect a response?"

My door. With a sudden cold hollowness in his chest, Scott belatedly realized that this woman must be Alla Nazimova, and that this place was surely the Garden of Allah, some time before it was torn down in 1959. He looked more closely at the woman sitting across from him, and he was able to recognize the actress who had played Salomé—older, but still almost boyishly slim.

"Your door . . ." Scott began; he hesitated, then went on, " . . . is one of a row of doors salvaged from old demolished hotels, lining a hallway in a house, in 2015."

Nazimova stood up lithely, strode to the door, and pushed it open on a view of green tree branches in sunlight. A warm breeze ruffled her gray hair, and Scott could smell roses and chlorine.

"Seventy-three years from now," she said, barely loud enough for him to hear. "Is it a transfigured world?"

"I—guess not."

"The Allies *do* win the war, I trust?"

"Yes. In 1945."

"That long." She shivered. "Do you know who I am?"

"Yes, ma'am. I knew whose door it was. I watched *Salomé* only last night." He reached for the box of cigarettes, then caught himself. "My aunt used to knock on the door every time she went by it."

She had turned around and now waved impatiently at the cigarettes. "Please be my guest. Your aunt wasn't—isn't?—Natacha Rambova . . . ?"

"No."

Nazimova drew on her cigarette and sighed, exhaling smoke. "Good, I hope Natacha keeps her resolve . . . and dies, I hope—happy, I hope!—before the now you come from. *Claim* to come from."

"My aunt's name was Amity Madden." Nazimova shrugged and started to say something, but Scott remembered the conclusion he and Madeline had come to, and added, "Or Charlene Cooper."

Nazimova straightened up, and her face tightened. "Was?"

"She died. A week ago. Killed herself."

"In *2015*? That little *vampire!*" Nazimova seemed poised by the open door, as if considering running out. "You didn't . . . work for her?"

"No, ma'am. I haven't seen her in thirteen years. Hadn't." Except in a mirror in a vision, he thought. *Welcome home, Scott.*

Nazimova was watching him closely. "How old are you?"

"Thirty-six."

She cocked her head. "That seems right. If anything, you look a bit older than that. You don't have the characteristic puffy smoothness of the predators." She scrutinized him for several more seconds, staring into his eyes, then nodded with apparent reluctance. "I believe what you say. How well did you know her?"

Scott smiled bitterly. "Not very well at all, it seems. She raised my sister and me, after—" He shook his head and went on, "After, perhaps, killing our parents." He waved away any interruption, though Nazimova had not moved. "We thought she was born in 1944, but in the last couple of days we've found evidence that she was actually born in 1899. She, uh, never looked her age."

"I imagine not." Nazimova closed the door and resumed her seat by the window. She crushed out her cigarette in a glass ashtray on the table. "Are you *sure* she's dead? *Really* gone, in every respect?"

Scott met her gaze and said, "No. She's trying to take possession of my sister."

"Your sister? Why? What has your sister got?"

"She—and I—both looked at—do you know what spiders are?— the patterns on paper?"

"Yes. Go on."

"We both looked at one, when we were children. 'The big one,' I'm told. The Medusa. It belonged to my aunt."

"That would have to be the Ince version of it, or *another* once-removed one, since it didn't kill you." Scott nodded, and she went on, "But if Charlene had that, why does she need your sister's experience of it now?" She pursed her lips. "In *2015*, I mean?"

"We tore it up, after we looked at it. And I drew a squiggly asterisk and put it in the envelope the real one was in. I was thirteen years old. She never found out."

"Oh, she found out, or she wouldn't be trying to mine your sister's experience. *Seventy-three years* from now! Wait a moment." She stood up and hurried into the little adjoining kitchen; Scott heard her open a drawer and rattle around in its contents, and then she had hurried back into the living room and dropped a handful of rubber bands onto the table.

"Stretch a tight one around your wrist," she said. "Both wrists. And your head, like a circlet. Uncomfortably tight." When he hesitated, she reached down and pinched his cheek, hard. "Hurry!"

Scott had flinched, but now he quickly pulled a rubber band around each wrist, and another around his head over his eyebrows.

"Every few seconds," said Nazimova, "you must pull one out and let it snap back. It must hurt, or you're liable to disappear from here."

"I get it." Better than chewing on foil, Scott thought, or poking a thumbtack into my toe.

He pulled the rubber band a couple of inches away from his forehead and let it snap back; it stung enough to make his eyes water.

The doorknob rattled then, and Scott looked over in alarm as it swung open, but it was still sunlight and blue sky that shone out there, behind a short flaxen-haired woman who stood now at the threshold staring at him in surprise. She was holding a white paper bag.

"Doody," said Nazimova, standing up, "this is—well, actually I don't know his name." She turned to Scott with raised eyebrows.

Scott belatedly stood up too. "Scott Madden, ma'am." He snapped his forehead rubber band as if tipping a hat.

"He's leaving, I assume," said the woman in the doorway. She looked to be in her thirties, wearing high-waisted tan slacks and a long-sleeved white blouse.

"Mr. Madden," said Nazimova, "this is Glesca Marshall, my secretary." To Glesca, she added, "No, let's hope he's not leaving."

Scott nodded. "Pleased to meet you, Ms. Marshall."

"Miss," she corrected, "not Mrs." She was frowning. "I'm not married."

Scott didn't try to explain *Ms.* "I'm sorry," he said. "My hearing isn't great."

Glesca turned to Nazimova. "He looks like a hobo!"

"It wasn't a planned visit," said Nazimova. "He wants help saving his sister from the—webs?—of Charlene Cooper; and making Charlene stay dead."

"Well, that's good." Glesca took two steps inside and closed the door, keeping a wary eye on Scott. "He lives here at the Garden?"

"No, child, I'm afraid this is black geometry. I'm sorry. He lives in the year 2015, seventy-three years in the future, by which time the Garden has apparently been torn down." She glanced at Scott, who shrugged and nodded apologetically. "Charlene died only a week before," Nazimova went on, waving toward Scott, "the evening he came from." She shrugged. "You know this is possible—I believe it's all true."

Glesca glanced at the rubber band stretched across Scott's forehead and didn't seem at all incredulous. "That serpent lives till 2015?" she exclaimed, tossing the paper bag onto the table. "Shouldn't she . . . die much sooner?"

"Spider rejuvenations," said Nazimova, "dilutions with young blood and bone, you know the story. Snap!" she added to Scott.

He hastily snapped his forehead rubber band and then the ones on his wrists. "I shouldn't stay away long, though," he said. "My sister is alone back there."

"Why do you imagine clocks here would have a connection with clocks there?" said Nazimova, sitting down again. "This isn't an *exchange,* such as you get with a spider. You came in here through a crack in time, and you'll go back through that crack."

Glesca stepped wide around the couch where Scott sat and leaned against the wall on the far side of the window. She was still staring mistrustfully at him—evidently this talk of stepping from one century into another didn't strike her as unprecedented, but he was surprised that she didn't seem curious about the future. Maybe she just didn't want to know any of it.

Nazimova leaned forward, her hands clasped, and looked piercingly into Scott's eyes. "Tell me it all; there are no secrets between Doody and I. You want to save your sister? Of course you do. And I would like to help you banish *Charlene.*"

Scott took a deep breath and began speaking, haltingly at first and then, after a few sentences, in a compulsive rush. His wrists and forehead were stinging like burns by the time he had told the women about the Usabo spider and his parents' blackmail attempt, and the exorcism film and the murder of William Desmond Taylor, and his aunt's possible murder of his parents, his peculiar cousins, and Madeline's supposed relationship with Valentino.

He sat back finally, and was surprised to realize that his face was wet with tears; he blotted them on his shirtsleeve.

"It's a painful story to tell, isn't it?" said Nazimova. She waved at his hands and his face. "And not just because of the circumstances."

Her Russian accent became more pronounced as she went on, "When I was seventeen, a student of Vladimir Namirovich-Danchenko at the Philharmonic School in Moscow, he had a copy of the first version of Henrik Ibsen's *A Doll's House*. Do you know that play?"

Scott shook his head. "Heard of it."

"Ibsen's agent had made him rewrite the second and third acts, but in the original manuscript the heroine, Nora Helmer, intercepts a letter addressed to her husband from an enemy—it contains a 'symbol,' and after she has looked at it, she has to dance the tarantella, so fast that it alarms her ignorant husband; and when she has recovered, she leaves her husband and her children because she has no longer any sense of being the person she has been until then. The revised version of the play omits the symbol and her literally broken identity, but Ibsen insisted on retaining the frenzied tarantella dance.

"When I came to Hollywood, I discovered that the symbol Ibsen referred to was real. I never looked at a spider—my own identity, shabby as it is, has always nevertheless been too precious to me—but I knew people who did." She paused to light another of her black cigarettes.

She sat back in her chair, glancing up and to the side at Glesca. "Charlene Cooper was an extra," she told Scott, "a girl in a café crowd scene in the film *Eye for Eye*, when I met her in 1918. She was quite a pretty little thing, and I took a fancy to her. I told her I believed I could get her a more visible part in my next picture, *Out of the Fog*. But she was soon involved in the spiders, through the man who married her in 1921, Paul Speas. She wanted the experience of being a famous actress, but not directly—she wanted it through me. She loved me, worshipped me—so much that she wanted to *be* me. She wanted to move past mere adoration and find a way into my actual identity. I had to wear distorting glasses everywhere until I had her banned from the studio."

"Serpent!" whispered Glesca.

Scott snapped his wrist rubber bands.

Nazimova puffed on her cigarette and went on. "The spiders are apparently two-dimensional creatures who have no conception of time or spatial volume. Sometimes they are summoned into our continuum, and they experience every event here as the same event—and they impose that discontinuous experience on anyone foolish enough to participate in their perspective! I gather," she said with evident distaste, "it's exciting to occasionally lose one's identity through them. They were like a new drug in Hollywood, thirty years ago; and they were supposed to prolong one's youth, and everyone wanted that. You said you watched *Salomé* last night—Natacha did the set designs for that picture, and, unknown to me, she even inserted an image that spider users would recognize, as a sort of wink to the *cognoscenti*."

"More like a punch in the nose," murmured Scott.

Nazimova drew deeply on her black cigarette, frowning. "But," she went on, exhaling smoke, "predators soon sprang up who enjoyed planting dirty spiders where they'd be seen by someone, and then doing terrible things in that other person's body, even committing suicide, so that they could experience death without quite dying themselves. Your cousin seems to be one of these."

"Yes," Scott agreed grimly. "He is."

"Bill Taylor wanted to find a way to eliminate all the spiders," Nazimova went on, "because a woman he loved had begun experimenting with them, and it was ruining her health. I suggested to him how he might use the extreme tarantella rhythms to banish the big spider. Spiders spin—" She smiled. "Well, everybody knows that, don't they? But in their own universe they're evidently spinning like tops, and I told Bill that if he could make a film in which the image of the Medusa spider was kept on the screen, interspersed with black frames timed to the period of the spin, it might in effect make the spin appear to—definitively appear to—stop. Like a phonograph record spinning on a turntable in a dark room, illuminated by a light flashing seventy-eight times a minute; the record would appear to be stationary. And the spider, this is the *master* spider, remember, would effectively lose its spin—become stationary. It would thus find here an impossibility of itself, and be excluded in future from this universe. The patterns on paper would still exist, but they would no longer have a connection to that other universe or anything in it."

She ground out her cigarette and lit another.

"And so Bill made his banishing film, but before he could use it, Natacha, with poor Rudolph along, unknowingly led some monster to his bungalow down there on Alvarado, and you saw what happened. And then, yes, Charlene and Paul Speas stole Taylor's exorcism film from Natacha, and disappeared. Natacha and Rudolph have been doing penance ever since."

"Penance?" asked Scott.

"In Purgatory, for Rudolph. Did you know it took two priests to hear his last confession and administer the sacrament of Extreme Unction? Too many lives in one body, too many conflicting sins! And after he died, he was evidently there to pull your sister out of the psychic maelstrom when you were children; because she was a child, and afraid, and helpless in Medusa." She fixed Scott with something like a glare. "And *before* he died, he told you how to kill the spiders."

"Yes, but I have to find another way—"

"There is no other way."

"But damn it, I *tried* to find the film!" Scott protested, reaching up to stretch the rubber band and sting his damp forehead. "Even though *my* identity, shabby though it is, is . . . ! But Paul Speas took it away while my aunt was in a hospital, and I haven't found any trace of him. He's probably dead by now, by 2015. It's an ice-cold trail."

"Ah, but you have a terrible gift," said Nazimova, speaking almost gently now, "don't you? You know how to see places where it is in time. If you look at enough places, you might find where it is, in your 2015. And then, I think you know, you must use it—as Taylor intended to use it himself, to save someone he loved."

"Charlene will destroy your sister," said Glesca.

Scott recalled what Ariel had said: *It breaks the victim's mind.*

Nazimova reached across the table and touched his hand. "What is your sister's name?" she asked, though he had mentioned it in his account.

"Madeline," he said, and in saying her name again he realized that he had no choice but to do as Nazimova said.

"I think you can take off the rubber bands," said Nazimova.

Scott pulled them off, no doubt messing up his hair even more. He stood up and turned to the door.

"I should probably step outside," he said dully. "I don't want to materialize inside the wall, in 2015." He finally picked up one of Nazimova's black cigarettes and lit it.

He pushed open the door and stepped outside. Beyond a narrow sunlit porch, tiled stairs led down between red-stippled pyracantha bushes to a cement deck and a glittering turquoise pool, and beyond it he could see the tile roof and streaked white walls of a long three-story building. The warm breeze whispered among pepper trees and bird-of-paradise bushes, and Scott could hear Frank Sinatra's unmistakable voice echoing from a nearby apartment.

The door at his back opened and Nazimova joined him, squinting through cigarette smoke at the taller building on the far side of the pool.

"This whole block of Sunset Boulevard was my estate until 1928," she said. "I lost it through admiration of the wrong person, and now I rent this apartment and only go to the main house over there to pick up my mail." She smiled up at him and touched his arm. "But I can still admire people."

The Sinatra song paused in midphrase with a cough, and then the voice started again from the beginning. Nazimova listened for a few seconds, then nodded. "I think he's got it now," she said, and Scott realized that it was Sinatra himself, in one of the nearby apartments, practicing. How old would he have been, Scott wondered, in 1942?

The landscape flickered.

He heard her say, faintly, "Go with God, Scott Madden," and then the light vanished and his bare feet were on the wooden floor of the Caveat hallway. The coal of his cigarette was all he could see in the sudden darkness, and he inhaled deeply on it, tasting 1942, as he padded back to Madeline's room.

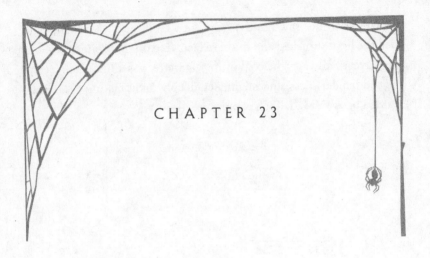

CHAPTER 23

SCOTT AWOKE TO THE sound of banging and men's voices below the window. He rolled over stiffly on the floor and was surprised to see Ariel lying beside him, blinking and frowning in the gray morning light.

Madeline had sat up in her bed. "Hullo, Ariel," she said; then, "What's going on outside?"

"Claimayne's cleaning crew," said Ariel hoarsely, sitting up and rubbing her eyes. "It sounds like they're throwing out all our pots and pans." Scott saw her .32 semiautomatic lying on the floor on the other side of her. "You're some guard," she said to him. "I snuck in here and neither of you woke up."

Scott could think of nothing to say to that. He watched her warily.

"Neither of *you* woke up," said Madeline cheerfully, "when I went downstairs at five. I printed—" She visibly caught herself, then finished, "some cat pictures off the Internet."

You printed some more of Aunt Amity's demented monologue, thought Scott sourly, and with some embarrassment he remembered that *he* had been scared by the mere *thought* of going downstairs last night.

"You shouldn't wander around here by yourself," he said.

And all at once he remembered his visit with Alla Nazimova, in her apartment at the Garden of Allah. For a moment he tried to imagine that it had been a dream—but he could still taste the cigarette he had lit there.

"Scott's right," said Ariel, "this house is dangerous for you." She looked from Madeline to Scott and put her finger to her lips and looked meaningfully around the room.

Madeline rocked her head, clearly indicating, *I remember.*

Scott threw off his blanket and stood up and crossed to the window. Under an overcast sky he could see the Medusa wall out there in the garden, and then he looked down at his bare feet, with no mud on them this morning.

Nazimova is long dead by now, he told himself, carefully tasting the thought. I didn't even promise anything. And, and—there might be a clue to *another way,* in whatever Madeline printed out at dawn. There might be. I should have asked Nazimova what can be done if the Taylor film simply can't be found.

Ariel stood up too; she had at some point changed to flannel pajamas, and she slid her feet into a pair of slippers that lay near her gun.

"I could use some coffee," Scott said.

"Yes, let's talk in the kitchen," said Ariel, crouching to pick up her gun.

Madeline rolled over and pulled on a pair of khaki cargo pants and put a sweater on over her T-shirt, and they stepped into the next room.

And then the telephone rang; or, more accurately, a ringing started up near the wall. The telephone was on the other side of the room, on a shelf.

Madeline's eyes were wide, and even Ariel was glancing in obvious bafflement from the sourceless sound in the corner to the inert telephone several feet away.

Scott stared at the thing, wishing it had waited until he had got coffee and was more awake.

"Um," said Ariel, "answer it, maybe?"

What if it's our mother, thought Scott, from somewhere in the past? But would she call her own phone?

He held his breath and picked up the receiver. ". . . Hello?"

"Dad?" came a young girl's voice out of the earpiece. He recognized it as Madeline's. "I know it's a school night, but is it okay if I go see *Beauty and the Beast* with Darlene and her mom and dad?"

Scott's face was cold. I'm not our dad! he thought. Does my voice *sound* like his?

But he cleared his throat. "Sure, Maddy," he said; then, remembering that this call didn't actually get through, he added, "I mean, can you call back on the downstairs phone, to confirm it? I'm—distracted right now—I won't remember."

He heard her sigh. "Okay, Dad. I love you."

"I love you, Maddy," he said, hoping their father had said it to her a lot. The line clicked, and then the phone was silent.

Madeline stared at him. "*Me?*"

Scott shakily replaced the receiver. "Yes." His hand was sweaty, and he wiped it on his jeans. "It sounded like you were about seven. You thought I was Dad, and you were asking if you could go see *Beauty and the Beast* with Darlene."

Her mouth was open. "I remember he said yes, and when I called back he said no."

Scott waved at the phone. "It was me who said yes."

"I wish you'd let me talk to me."

"Wow," said Ariel softly. She shook herself, then waved around the room and rolled her eyes.

Right, thought Scott, Claimayne probably heard all that.

"Coffee," he said; but when Madeline had snatched up a sheaf of papers and she and Ariel had stepped into the hall, he said, "You two go ahead, I—have to put some shoes on."

When they had descended the stairs, Scott hurried down the hall to the wall of decorative doors, found Nazimova's, and knocked on it.

He waited for several long seconds, but there was no answer. He turned the knob, and when he tugged on it, the door once again swung open.

The room that impossibly lay beyond was empty now, except for a worn tweedy gray couch that had not been there on his earlier visit, and hot sunlight through the uncurtained window on his right that lit streaks of dust on the bare floorboards.

Still barefoot, he stepped hesitantly into the room and closed the door behind him; it echoed in the vacated room, and his gaze darted to the empty spaces once occupied by Nazimova's desk, and the table, and the orchids.

He heard steps ascending the stairs outside, and he realized there was no place to hide, so he just crossed his arms and looked out the window. The cement deck around the pool was crowded with people in shorts and straw hats and sunglasses, and a ladder stood in front of the arches of the main house on the far side.

He heard the door open and looked around with the best imitation of relaxed confidence that he could muster.

A middle-aged man in Bermuda shorts and a polo shirt was holding the door open, and a moment later a blond young woman in a gray pantsuit and a brimless velvet hat walked into the room. The knock of her low shoes echoed in the empty space.

They both gave him a cursory glance, and the man nodded, and then they walked past him to peer in through an open door beside the bare little kitchen.

And as she limped past him, Scott recognized her—more from the author photos on the dust jackets of her novels than from his own later acquaintance with her.

"I want to buy the front door, and the bathtub," said the woman who by now was probably calling herself Amity Imogene Speas, not Charlene Claimayne Speas anymore.

"The bathtub?" said the man beside her. "Not just the faucets, you mean the whole tub? How do you figure to get it out?"

"You can arrange it, I'm sure," she said. "Cleveland Wrecking is tearing the whole place down after you've sold all the furniture and fixtures, right? And hauling all the rubble away? So save me the tub. And the door. I can pay you for your trouble."

Tearing it down? Scott thought. He shivered. Then this must be 1959.

The woman turned and looked down at Scott's bare feet, frowning. "I'm not interested in the couch, if that's what you were after," she told him. She stepped back then, and he realized he must have been staring at her face, which was jarringly smooth and unlined. He shook his head and looked away from her, toward the window and the wall where Glesca had been leaning, seventeen years earlier.

"No," he said. "I think I came too late for what I wanted."

For a moment the urge to say something more to her made the breath quiver in his throat. *Don't write a last-minute will for me and Madeline. Don't leave spiders for us. Please don't kill our parents.* But Amity Speas wouldn't even meet his parents for another decade, and he and Madeline wouldn't be born till years after that—and in any case he was sure that whatever he might say here, now, would have been said in the same 1959 that had inevitably led to his opening the door this morning . . . or, locally, evident afternoon.

Finally all he could think of was to take this disorienting opportunity to say the two syllables of "Good-bye" to the woman who had raised Madeline and him, and he did, a bit huskily.

She gave him an uncertain nod, and when she turned back toward the bathroom, he opened the front door and stepped quietly and directly into the dim Caveat hallway and closed the door behind him.

You have a terrible gift, Nazimova had told him last night or seventy-three years ago. And, *Go with God, Scott Madden.*

He glanced apprehensively down the hall toward his own room, where waited his leather jacket with Claimayne's two remaining spiders in the pocket. Losing his identity, even just for a timeless moment, was still not an altogether repellent prospect, no matter what calamities might follow.

"Coffee first," he whispered, and hurried down the stairs.

Before he reached the bottom he heard men's voices in the dining room, and when he stepped through from the hall, he saw that the long table had been turned on its side against the north wall; two young men in overalls were hard at work, one of them washing the windows and the other running a big steel vacuum cleaner over the carpet. Scott nodded as he strode past them.

Only Madeline and Ariel were in the kitchen, though a couple of wheeled yellow plastic buckets and a big clipboard on the counter indicated the recent presence and imminent return of Claimayne's cleaning crew. Ariel handed Scott a steaming cup and said, "I thought you were going to put on some shoes."

He saw a jar of Taster's Choice coffee beside the microwave oven and knew that she and Madeline had decided on instant coffee under the circumstances. "I forgot," he said. "Let's take this outside."

His sister nodded, and he followed her and Ariel out onto the driveway and around the north corner to the sidewalk facing the wilderness of the garden. A couple of strangers at the far end of the house were wheeling more buckets along, but they were moving in the other direction.

Ariel's dark hair was blowing around her face in the chilly breeze. "There's no place to sit," she said crossly. "And it's cold."

"We can go back inside when we've said everything we don't want Claimayne to hear," said Scott. He waved at the papers Madeline was holding in her free hand. "Did Aunt Amity have anything worthwhile to say?"

"Did I sound happy?" asked Madeline. When Scott gave her a blank look, she added, "On the phone, twenty-four years ago?"

Scott shivered in the morning wind, reflecting that every moment he spent with Madeline was making his quest, his surely useless and damaging quest, more impossible to avoid.

"Yes," he said.

After a pause, Madeline shrugged and then just blew across the top of her coffee cup.

"What would you have said?" Ariel asked her.

"Be patient."

Scott pointed at the papers. The pavement was cold and damp under his bare feet.

Madeline nodded and crouched to set her coffee cup on the cement, then straightened and held the papers up in front of her. "It repeats, the way she always does, but I thought I ought to bring all the pages along. The gist of it is . . ." She paused and fixed her eyes on the top sheet. "I'm guessing at punctuation . . . '*The freeway ends, Cyclone, I've got to take the wheel and swerve to the exit*' . . . uh, I think she meant to put in '*and*' or '*even though I,*' . . . '*risk rolling the glory that blushed and bloomed, a dim-remembered story of the old time entombed—You've got to take that exit before the freeway ends, Charlene, and I think it ends very soon.*'"

Madeline's voice had taken on a singsong cadence, and when she had spoken the last few words, she had not been looking at the paper.

"Make her stop," said Ariel suddenly, but Scott had already tossed his coffee cup into a rosemary bush and stepped forward to take hold of Madeline's shoulders.

She went on, "'*I wasn't supposed to be like this—hampered, confused—*'" and then her fingers sprang out straight, and the papers flew away across the weeds; but she stared straight ahead and kept speaking: "'*Steer Madeline off at the Ince exit, Charlene, and then find Alla in the infinity of surface streets.*'"

"Watch her," said Ariel quickly, stepping away. "I'll get the papers."

Madeline's head swiveled to face Scott, and he was sure it was not his sister behind the pinched mouth and narrowed eyes.

"It will destroy her," he said levelly to his aunt, "and you love her."

"But you all *meddled*," came a strained voice from Madeline's throat, "your whole family is terrible nosy parkers, interferers, busy-bodies! I needed my retirement check, but it was gone, you put a foolish asterisk in the envelope, and my son has obviously killed me, same as he did your *curiosi* parents." She nodded jerkily. "From the ground, from under the floors, under an iron cross in the darkness, their blood too cries out."

Scott rocked back on his heels, his face suddenly cold and tight; his hands had fallen away from her shoulders.

The scare-bat in the basement, he thought, the gold-painted lug wrench—their headstone? The writing in the cement, *Hic iacent curiosi*—their epitaph? Does it mean something like *Here lie the interferers?*

I always did feel safe beside the scare-bat, Madeline said when I found her down there three days ago. Was that as close as she could get to her long-lost mother and father?

"You can't keep her," he managed to say.

"I can. I will. The living image is in her memory, and I'll salvage it and go back—to when Alla loved me. And then I'll do much more than simply adore her from afar. I'll find the way in to *be* her."

Then Madeline sagged, and Scott caught her and held her against his chest to keep her from falling down. He could feel her rapid heartbeat. His foot was in a puddle of warm coffee—at some point Madeline had kicked over her cup.

After a few seconds she shook herself, twisted her head around, and grinned sheepishly at him. "What," she said, straightening and stepping back, "did I faint? Thank you for catching me."

"You were Aunt Amity again," Scott said breathlessly, "and it was possession again, not a spider vision—and she's not *gone*, even now, just . . . resubmerged. She said she was going to steer Madeline off the freeway at the Ince exit, and find Alla, in the past." He took a deep breath and added, "And she doesn't care if it destroys you."

Madeline nodded, but she was staring up into the branches of a big mesquite tree. Following her gaze, Scott saw nothing but a scrap of yellow lace caught in the high branches.

Ariel stepped up beside him, having lost her own coffee cup somewhere, and she waved two fistfuls of the printout pages. "Is this by any chance the novel you said she's been typing?"

Scott caught his sister's shoulder. "You are Madeline, right?"

She nodded, then looked down and smiled at him. "I'm Madeline, all right, as long as I concentrate on it."

Scott turned to Ariel. "Yes," he said, and he briefly told her about the discovery of the active keyboard and how Madeline had been following the disjointed and nearly incoherent narrative.

When he had finished the story, assisted by interjections from Madeline, he said, "I've got to go get something from my bike. Does Claimayne have his crew messing around in the apiary?"

"No," said Ariel. "The party's entirely on the ground floor, in the dining room and the music room."

"Meet me in the apiary then."

"I'll bring up coffee," said Madeline, stooping to pick up her cup.

Ariel gave Scott a mistrustful look and then followed Madeline.

SCOTT FETCHED THE SECURITY chain and padlock from the sissy bar of his motorcycle, and he sidled past Ariel and Madeline and the buckets in the kitchen on his way to the stairs. He stopped on the second floor to finally put on shoes and socks and pick up his leather jacket—and consider and then regretfully dismiss the idea of sneaking a gulp or two of the bourbon. When he walked into the apiary on the third floor, Madeline and Ariel had already arrived and were sitting down and blowing on fresh cups of coffee; Ariel had even found time to shed her pajamas and pull on a sweater and jeans. A third cup had been filled and was sitting on a chair next to Madeline. Scott draped the chain down beside it and slowly slid his arms into the sleeves of the jacket.

He dug a pack of Camels out of his left jacket pocket and shook a cigarette onto his lip, and as he struck a match to it he looked around the long room. The gray daylight in the windows cast no clear shadows, and the room was nearly as cold as the sidewalk outside had been.

A two-inch-wide pipe stood in the corner on the far side of the door, rising from a mound of ancient putty on the floor to disappear through a square hole in the ceiling, and Scott crossed to it and gripped it; it didn't shift when he tugged at it. He sighed and walked back to where the women sat, his footsteps echoing.

"I'm going to finish this cigarette and drink that coffee," he said, "and then I'm going to chain myself to that pipe." He reached into the right jacket pocket and pulled out one of the two remaining crumpled, folded slips of paper; he flattened it out and saw that Claimayne had lettered *Scaramuccia* on it.

"Like Odysseus tied to the mast," said Ariel, nervously touching her silver gyroscope pendant.

Madeline too had guessed what sort of paper Scott held. "Why?" she asked plaintively.

"If he's going to do without his drink," said Ariel, "he needs to get his precious oblivion somewhere."

Scott took a drag on the cigarette and exhaled a pale stream of smoke before he looked up from the folded paper to squint at Ariel.

She shook her head sharply. "I'm sorry. I've read that amputees still feel pains and itches in their missing limbs. The place in my head that hates you has been cut off, but—there's still a twitch there sometimes."

Like when you chose to do the after of your three-day-old spider in front of us last night, Scott thought; and he thought of the box of credit cards in the uphill garage and the scare-bat in the basement, which ought to be negations of his years of hating his parents.

He smiled at her. "I know how that works." He turned to Madeline. "The spider visions always show us a place, a time, where the big spider image is—and after Hearst burned Natacha's original, that leaves just the images in the Taylor film. So far it's always been a time in the 1920s, but I think they've been chronological, each one a bit more recent than the last. I've got to . . . hope to . . . see a place where the film might still be now."

"Chain *me* to the pipe, then," Madeline said. "You did *two* spiders, day before yesterday. It's bad for you to do a lot of them—look at Claimayne."

Scott knew she wasn't craving the moment of selflessness—and he insisted to himself that he wasn't either—but that she hoped to see Valentino again, as Scott had on Thursday night.

To Madeline, Ariel said, with evident skepticism, "I thought you didn't want the film to be found."

"But I think it'll be okay if I can be the one to *watch* the film," Madeline said. "That would block Aunt Amity out of me, and at the same time spill me into the hurricane."

From which, thought Scott, you imagine the spirit of Valentino will again rescue you and take you back to that moonlit garden.

"We can watch it together," he said, though he was resolved not to let her do it. "We looked at the Oneida Ince spider together."

"No, Scott," Madeline said. "I know you don't mean to let me watch it at all—because you love me!—but Rudolph Valentino might not save *you*. He told you that whoever watched it would die of it."

Scott suspected that she used Valentino's whole name because just the first name would have seemed presumptuously familiar, while just the last name would have seemed too remote.

"I don't think you have any hope of finding it *at all*," said Ariel, standing up. She waved toward the pipe. "So go ahead."

"Right." Scott picked up his cup and drained it in four big swallows, then had a last deep inhalation on the cigarette and dropped the butt into the cup and set it down. "Pay attention to whoever occupies me while I'm gone," he said, picking up the chain. "But don't let him know we're after the film."

"Or her," said Madeline.

"Or, as it might be, her." Scott tossed his keys to his sister, then walked to the pipe and flipped the chain around it and drew the two ends together over his belt buckle. It was a comfortably snug fit. He clicked the padlock shut through the two end links.

He felt jumpy and sick and wondered if his imminent occupier would vomit. "Geronimo," he said and flipped open the *Scaramuccia* paper.

For a breathless and vertiginous moment the spider expanded to fill his vision, its lines bristling and spinning, and then he was nobody; after a measureless time, he found himself moving through the deceptively vertical-seeming things—

Then he was standing on a thin carpet and looking out through an open door at a sunlit wooden balcony. He took a careful step forward, out onto the balcony, and saw that he was two or three floors above a street that sloped steeply downhill to his left; hotels or apartment buildings with pillars and ornate turrets lined the street, their first-floor windows level with the second- or even third-floor windows of buildings farther down the incline. He gripped the balcony rail and looked down. The bonging sound he'd been hearing was coordinated with Stop and Go signs that swiveled out of traffic signal boxes on the street corner, and the cars moving up and down the lanes looked like models from the 1940s. San Francisco, he thought. He stepped back and looked down at himself and saw that he was in a male body, dressed in gray slacks and a short-sleeved white shirt.

He turned to face the room, and he could feel the presence of the Usabo image like static electricity in the hairs on his arms. The room was narrow but high ceilinged, with a transom window over the door; an iron-frame bed with a battered leather trunk beside it, a dresser with a lamp, and a couple of metal-tubing chairs at a Formica-top table were the only furniture, aside from a big chrome clock and an age-darkened framed print on the yellowed plaster wall.

He glanced around nervously, but his impression that someone else was present seemed to be wrong.

With his hands out in front of himself he shuffled across the carpet toward the door, trying to feel where the faint vibration in the air and the sensed-but-not-quite-heard roar were most detectable; and he found himself facing the wall with the bed and dresser against it.

On the dresser were only a ring of keys and a scattering of coins and a clean tin ashtray. Scott pulled open the drawers, but they contained nothing but socks and shirts and boxer shorts and a bottle of Korbel brandy. He patted the bed and lifted the mattress, but found nothing. The latches on the trunk weren't locked, and when he pulled the lid up, he discovered a collection of small tins and glass jars and brushes, and several wigs and false beards—blond, brown, and black. Was the person whose body he was in an actor?

He got awkwardly down on his knees and peered under the dresser—and saw only some old cigarette butts—and then under the bed; a stainless steel .45 semiautomatic lay where a person in the bed could easily reach down and grab it, but there was nothing like a film can.

How long will I stay here? he thought worriedly. He glanced up at the clock, which was made from a flat hubcap with wire numerals around the rim; its triangular chrome hands showed ten minutes to ten. I should be okay for several minutes in any case, he thought, but I should find something I can hurt myself with, to prolong this. As hard as he could, he pinched the wrist of the body he was in, but it didn't seem like enough.

There was no bathroom or kitchen. A narrow closet proved to contain a wide-lapeled striped seersucker suit and a pair of polished wingtip shoes; Scott felt through the pockets of the suit but found nothing besides a silver-certificate five-dollar bill and a matchbook from the Trocadero. On the shelf above the hangers was a hatbox that proved to contain only a man's fedora hat.

He turned back to the room. *It's* here, he thought, somewhere—

and then he noticed that the hands of the clock were still at ten minutes to ten.

How long have I been here? he thought.

He hastily dug out the matchbook again and flipped it open, intending to strike a match and burn his finger—but his vision lost all depth and the colors changed, and he knew that the sudden pain across his abdomen must be the chain holding him to the pipe in the apiary. He got his feet under himself and stood up straight, easing the chain, and concentrated on breathing deeply. He was alarmed to taste blood in his mouth.

Shapes changed in front of him, and he tried to recognize human figures. Madeline's voice said, "Scott? Are you with us?," and he recognized the brown of her sweater.

"Maddy," he said, keeping his voice level, "am I bleeding?"

"Here," she said, and he felt her hand press a wad of paper tissues into his palm and then raise his hand to his nose. "You've got a nosebleed. Press on it."

"Oh," he said hoarsely. "Thanks." He held the tissues to his nose and cleared his throat. "Have I been shouting?" He narrowed his eyes, and he was able to pick out the figures of Madeline and Ariel among the shifting fields of muted colors.

"Not shouting," said Madeline, "but your voice was grittier."

"Did you see your film can?" came Ariel's voice.

"No. I felt it, it was there—maybe taped to the back side of the dresser—but I didn't see it." He could feel blood on his chin, and he wondered what his shirt must look like. "It was in San Francisco, I'm pretty sure—1940s, from the cars." He held out his free hand. "Can I have my keys?"

He saw Madeline's hand come closer, and then he was able to see the whole room in perspective—the two women standing a yard away, the TV screen behind them, and the stacked tables farther away against the wall.

Scott took the keys from Madeline, found the padlock key and freed himself from the chain, and immediately stumbled to the nearest chair and sat down, still pressing the tissues to his nose.

"It's a nice drive, to San Francisco," said Madeline.

"You wanted to know—" began Ariel. "I mean, the guy in your body wanted to know who we were, and who you were, and what year it is."

"He seemed scared," put in Madeline, "by us, as much as by the chain around him. He said you ambushed him—he meant to be in his own body, someplace he was familiar with."

Scott gingerly prodded his stomach. "He was straining pretty hard against the chain. What did you tell him?"

"I told him it was 2015," said Madeline, "and he looked at the window and said I was lying."

"He thought you were telling him what time it was," said Ariel. Madeline raised her eyebrows and nodded.

"Did he say who he was?" asked Scott.

"I asked him," said Ariel. "He sort of laughed and said he was between names."

Scott held the red-blotted tissues away, and his nose seemed to have stopped bleeding. Looking down, he saw that his shirt was streaked with blood.

"I couldn't get close enough to give him tissues while he wasn't you," said Madeline apologetically.

"No," Scott agreed. He started to stand up, then sat back down, peering left and right. He pointed at the hallway door. "That's north, isn't it?"

Ariel rolled her eyes. "You lived here how long? Yes, that's north."

"San Francisco is north of us," he said.

Ariel visibly smothered a sarcastic rejoinder and just nodded.

"The place I was at was that way," he said, pointing away from the door at the windows, "south, and not far from here." He dabbed at his lips and chin with the tissue. "I sure didn't recognize the neighborhood, but I want to go check it anyway."

"You're probably a bit wobbly to be riding your bike," said Ariel. "And I still haven't heard back from the cops about my car. Maddy, you up for a drive?"

"Sure. Won't your guys from yesterday follow us?"

"I bet they don't know about the back driveway. Nobody's used it in forever." She smiled brightly. "We can have lunch somewhere—no use trying to do anything today in the kitchen here. Let's meet in your room in half an hour."

CHAPTER 24

WHEN THEY STEPPED OUTSIDE, Ariel glanced at Scott in the gray daylight, and she pointed at a rosemary bush beside the driveway. "There's a gun in that bush," she said. "Grab it, would you?"

He gave her an uncertain smile, but shuffled across the asphalt and bent over. The revolver she had taken away from Claimayne two days ago was suspended in the aromatic branches, and he tugged it free and carefully tucked it into the right-hand pocket of his jacket. He straightened up with an effort.

"Would you rather do this later?" Ariel asked. "How long do you think you'll be able to sense where the thing is? Or was?"

"Hours, at least," he said, starting forward toward Madeline's car. "But let's do it now."

"Hello, Louise," said Madeline, and Scott wheeled around.

He could make out the figure of Louise Odell leaning against the wall beside the kitchen door, dressed in woolen trousers and a dark blue quilted jacket. Her short blond hair looked as if she'd just run her fingers through it, and sunglasses hid her eyes.

"Hi, Maddy," Louise said. Then she faced Scott. "I need to get to the bank and pull all my money out," she said, her voice quavering. "I drove here, and I'm parked by those trucks in your driveway—

but they're *following* me. They may even have some kind of tracker attached to my car!"

"Who's following you?" asked Ariel.

Louise shook her head. "Damn it, it's Scott's fault, he *talked* to them on Thursday, on my phone, so they can't use me as a, a *spy* anymore. I've got a friend in—well, never mind where, but I can hide out at her place till they're done with all this—if I can *get away from them*." She snatched off her sunglasses and blinked at Scott. "You've got guys doing work on the place? Pay one of them to sneak me into their truck, rolled up in a carpet or something."

"Is one of your *them* a guy named Ferdalisi?" asked Ariel.

"I don't know any of their names. Scott, you owe me—"

Ariel went on, "Bald, with a beard but no mustache, so his face looks upside-down? He seems to be their field man."

Louise looked dismayed. "That's the one I've met."

"The workmen here were hired by our cousin," said Ariel, "and they might want to get his okay on your girl-in-a-carpet stunt, and I'm pretty sure he's in touch with Ferdalisi. It might be Ferdalisi that'd unroll the carpet."

Louise moaned faintly and stamped her foot.

Ariel went on, "Do your friends know about the back easement down to Gower?" When Louise gave her an uncomprehending look, she clarified, "A driveway from the uphill garages that leads down to the next street east."

"I guess not. I didn't know about it. Yesterday I came right up the main driveway from Vista Del Mar. And they're not my—"

"Let's go," said Scott. "Everybody in Madeline's car. Close the doors quietly."

"I'm abandoning my car here," said Louise. "Sorry." She pulled her phone out of her pocket. "And I don't dare keep this either," she added, dropping it onto the cement.

Madeline tossed some papers and clothing from the backseat of her car into the trunk, and then opened the driver's-side door and slid behind the wheel. Scott got in on the passenger side, and Ariel and Louise folded themselves into the backseat.

"I figure north and then west," Madeline said. "Basically up Gower and then out through the bendy streets like Primrose to Cahuenga, and get on the 101 from there."

"And south on that," agreed Scott as she started the car and clicked the console gearshift into reverse. He pulled the seat belt across himself and clicked the tongue into the buckle; Claimayne's gun was pressing against his ribs.

"Uh," said Ariel, "don't back down the driveway to where the garage road branches off. You'd be visible from the street. Drive straight across the lawn and catch the garage road up here."

"There's logs bordering the road," said Madeline.

"Scott can roll one of the logs out of the way."

"No problem," said Scott, privately dreading the effort of using his aching muscles.

Madeline clicked the gearshift down to drive, steered the car off the cement onto the grass, and set out slowly across the west lawn. Scott peered nervously past her profile in the direction of Vista Del Mar, but all he saw from this high up the slope were the rooftops of buildings on the other side of the street; Madeline's Datsun wouldn't be visible from pavement level.

Scott hiked around in his seat when Ariel said to Louise, "What can you tell us about the people you were spying for?"

Louise looked down at her hands. "The guy with the beard started talking to me at a Starbucks and said I could make some money by getting back in touch with Scott and you all—find out what you know about your dead aunt and the spiders. I owe a fortune in student loans, and after I got my degree in education and tried to apply it, I caught on that the emperor had no clothes—"

"Who?" interrupted Madeline. The logs bordering the garage road were visible now between the widely spaced palm trees, and she was slowing down.

"Who what?" said Louise.

"Who had no clothes? When was this?"

"The emperor," said Louise impatiently. "Like in the kids' story."

"That's in a kids' story? What did he do? The naked guy, this emperor."

The car had come to a stop on the grass, and Scott had his hand on the door lever.

Louise whispered, "For God's sake."

"You were going to tell us," said Ariel, "about the people you took money from, to spy on us."

"The emperor just went home," Scott told Madeline, "after everybody laughed at him."

"Some story."

"Wait till I get back in," Scott said then, opening the door and swinging his legs out. When he straightened up, wincing, he saw that Ariel had got out too. The two of them walked across the damp grass to the log, and with one of them at each end of it, it rolled easily back from the garage-road pavement, and then they both pushed at one end until it had rolled aside.

"Thanks," said Scott quietly, wiping his hands on his shirt as they walked back to the car.

"I know how it is."

When they had got back in, Madeline drove over the groove in the dirt where the log had been and steered right, up the hill.

"The bald guy is the only one I met," said Louise, "and I've only met him three times. Each time he gave me money. He wanted—"

"How much?" asked Madeline.

"I don't think that's relevant."

"Back down the hill, Madeline," said Ariel. "All the way to the street."

"A thousand dollars each time," Louise said quickly.

Madeline had taken her foot off the accelerator, but now pressed it again, and the old Datsun surged on up the hill. Scott turned his head to see Louise.

She went on, "He wanted me to . . . renew my relationship with Scott, but I told him I wouldn't do that, I'm not—" She sighed shakily. "He wanted me to find spiders. There's one he's very interested in, that belonged to your aunt, and he was going to give me a ten-thousand-dollar bonus if I could lead him to that." She glared at Scott. "But after you told him *don't send old girlfriends around,* he told me he's got a better informant and doesn't need me, and now he won't answer his phone when I call, and I think—I think they don't like it that I know so much about what they want."

Ariel turned away and smiled out the window. "Do they strike you as the sort of people who would commit murder to keep their secrets?"

"I'm not sure they're not, and I can't risk—"

"But you'd help such people get at our family."

Madeline had crested the rise; the treetops up here were bending in the breeze. The row of garages where Scott had found Louise yesterday morning was on the right as Madeline angled left and kept driving, downhill now.

"I was *protecting* Scott, and all of you," Louise said flatly. "I was going to tell you all about it. His new informant won't."

"Would you like us to drop you off somewhere?" asked Scott as Madeline carefully nosed the car down the narrow, curving strip of asphalt between walls overhung with bougainvillea and glossy banana leaves.

"Where are you all going?"

"On an errand," Scott said.

"Can I come along?" When Scott gave her a puzzled frown, Louise went on, "I might be able to help. I heard Ariel ask you how long you'll be able to sense where *the thing* is. That's what led you to that parking lot on Alvarado on Thursday, isn't it? Where Taylor was killed in 1922?"

"You're still hoping for that ten-thousand-dollar bonus," said Ariel.

"No! But I do know about the man with the beard, and what his group wants, how they work." She was speaking rapidly. "He told me a lot of things, like about the other group, the guy in the Chevy Blazer. This thing goes way back in L.A. history—for instance, did you know your aunt's office on Sunset is right where an old actress named Nazimova lived? Upstairs and everything, the exact same spot."

"We know about Nazimova," said Scott. "And other people too."

"Did you know that this spider they're after killed a famous movie director on William Randolph Hearst's yacht, in 1924? A whole lot of famous people were on the yacht when it happened, Charlie Chaplin and everybody, but afterward none of them even admitted they'd been aboard."

"The director's name was Thomas Ince," said Scott. "Yes."

Louise exhaled through clenched teeth. "Do you know how to avoid drawing the attention of wheelbugs?"

"The beardy guy told you how to avoid that?" asked Madeline, her eyes on the pavement ahead.

"Yes, he . . ." Her voice trailed off.

The engine roared steadily along in low gear, the mutter of the exhaust sounding loud between the close walls. Low-hanging branches bumped along the roof of the car.

"You said he first approached you on Tuesday," he said, without turning around. "Was that the first time you looked at a spider?"

Madeline steered around one last curve and turned left on the scarcely wider pavement of Gower Street.

"Yes," said Louise dully. "He showed me one, out in his car. I didn't know what it was. It was a clean one, and he tore it up afterward, but—"

"How many have you done since?" asked Ariel.

"I don't know, half a dozen. He gave me a pad of them, but I only have a few left—obviously I can't get any more, from him—I tried reusing one, and afterward I felt like I got beat up—"

"Take a picture of one with your phone, and e-mail it to yourself," said Ariel, "and then print it out. It'll be clean; the continuity of the image is broken when it's converted to digital. You can use the same spider forever, that way. Don't try photocopiers, though; they don't break the continuity."

Scott heard Louise shift around on the seat. "E-mail? Are you sure?"

"*Oh* yeah," said Ariel.

Scott thought of the tremor in Louise's hands, and the new lines in her face, and the broken vein in her eye, and he remembered her radiant health all those years ago, when they had hiked in the canyons and body-surfed at Laguna Beach and made love in his apartment, until she had left him in 2004. "So now you don't need to come with us," he said, more flatly than he had meant to.

"He showed me the spider before we talked about anything," said Louise, "okay? And I want to get my money out of the bank and get away from them, but—I do want to help you, too."

"So how do you avoid wheelbugs' attention?" asked Ariel. "Hang a left there, sweetie," she told Madeline.

"I know," said Madeline.

"Well, for one thing," said Louise, "you shouldn't be wearing that gyroscope pendant, Ariel. The guy said spider users sometimes spontaneously lose their depth perception, their view goes flat, and then they like to have some very three-dimensional thing handy that they can feel the shape of while they look at it. It snaps them back to seeing volume quicker. Sometimes it's a little ball in a cage, or a miniature Rubik's Cube, or a chain bracelet. They're all likely to catch the attention of wheelbugs."

Scott and his sister exchanged a brief glance. And Claimayne's gold DNA coil, too, Scott thought. I could have used something like that myself, on Alvarado yesterday.

After a pause, Louise went on, "Act like somebody who's *not* afraid of losing depth perception at any moment—jaywalk in traffic, weave around any pillars or trees or parking meters, go up or down stairs fast. Go over and under things—step over curbs, duck under branches. As much of that stuff as you can manage. Wheelbugs pay attention to young-looking people who seem to move too carefully.

"Another reason to act agile is because people who use dirty spiders get bad joints, bad backs, loose teeth, from their body being so often combined with other bodies. They get blue stains on their skin from overlapping with people who had tattoos. And they lose their hair—if that happens, wear a wig. Scott, it's good you haven't shaved in a couple of days."

Scott thought of the contents of the trunk he'd seen in the spider vision this morning. "Noted," he said. "Is Ferdalisi's beard real? He's bald on top."

Louise shook her head. "How would I know."

"Was there anything else?" Scott asked her.

Louise was sitting lower in the backseat now, peering out the side window at the tops of phone poles and palm trees. "Well, there's websites," she said, "and shops that sell stuff to keep you from accidentally seeing spiders, like crazy glasses with big ripples in the lenses. You don't have anything to do with any of that stuff, of course."

"Of course," said Ariel.

"If you want glasses that disrupt an accidental view of a spider," Louise said, "just make a cross on the inside surface of each lens with thin strips of Scotch tape, three or four layers. Just as good as the ripply glasses, and you can still see."

"Shit," said Ariel.

"Ferdalisi told you a lot," said Scott.

"He thought I'd be working for him for a while," snapped Louise. "Nobody knew you were going to wreck it all."

Wreck it all, Scott thought. Well—ideally, I guess.

Madeline had steered onto the southbound 101. "Straight on?" she asked Scott.

Scott sat back and closed his eyes. "For now. But I think it'll be south of the freeway." He hiked around in the seat and looked at Louise.

"So who's the other group?" he asked. "The guy in the white Chevy Blazer?"

"They're local, L.A. area," Louise said, "maybe covertly funded by something bigger, like the government or even the Vatican. I think your Ferdalisi guy is Spanish. Ferdalisi's group is real panicked that spiders will stop working sometime soon, and they want to prevent that, or at least get maximum use out of them now. They've been recruiting newcomers to look at spiders and go read future newspapers, and then report back on stuff like stock and gold prices, though I gather they've been drawing duds—lately if somebody looks at a spider, meaning to look at it again in a week, it's clean, there's no after at all."

Scott thought she sounded wistful.

She waved her hands. "Anyway, the other crowd, the L.A. crowd—Ferdalisi says they're vandals, vigilantes. What they want is to just banish all the spiders from our reality, not let anybody have a chance to study them properly."

For several minutes they drove south in the slow lane without speaking. Scott looked out at ivied slopes and brown cinder-block walls like the one he and Ariel had stopped on the other side of, yesterday; and he wondered what other long-gone houses had occupied space in the air the Datsun was rushing through.

Louise spoke up, "Right now I'm pretty sure you're not being followed—but don't go anywhere you've been to during the last week. You've been followed every time, and ever since Scott stopped at Alvarado and Maryland they'll be watching whatever places you went to."

Three big green freeway signs loomed over the lanes ahead, and Madeline asked, "South on the 110?"

"Uh," said Scott, "no, stay on the 101 but get off, going south, as soon as you can."

When they had driven over the 110 overpass, she said, "Off on Temple?"

"Uh, yeah. Damn, it feels like it's close, but there's no hills like I saw, around here. Maybe it's not as close as it seems, maybe it's all the way down by San Pedro or somewhere."

Madeline followed the Temple Street exit off the freeway, between low, tire-marked cement walls, and then they had crossed the lanes of Temple and were driving past the high, pillared white portico of the Ahmanson Theatre on the left.

"Whoa," said Scott, "it's shifting—"

The Ahmanson's high roof extended south of the theater building, and now they were passing the big white hatbox of the Mark Taper Forum, with the winged glass front of the Dorothy Chandler Pavilion coming up fast.

"Now it's over there," he said, pointing out at the black statue that stood on the broad square between the Mark Taper and the Chandler. "Maddy, pull over and let me out here, then go around the block and pick me up."

Madeline swung the car to the curb by the stacked protruding floors of the Water and Power building, and Scott hastily climbed out; and a rear door opened and Louise got out onto the sidewalk too, frowning as if daring him to object.

He shrugged. "Okay," he said, and they both closed their doors and Madeline drove on, signaling for a left turn.

"Here's our chance to deflect wheelbugs," said Scott, glancing up and down the street.

The wind out of the gray sky seemed damp with imminent rain, and Louise's hair was blowing around her pinched face.

"What?" she said, looking around in alarm.

"We jaywalk," Scott said, and he had to resist the impulse to take her hand as he sprinted across the lanes to the far sidewalk.

They walked out across the open square, both of them peering mistrustfully at the few tourists hurrying from one end of the square to the other. In the center of the square the tall black statue, which looked to Scott like a couple of muscular people holding up a giant split fig, stood at the center of a cross pattern in the pavement, and now fountains shot up from nozzles set flush in the cross, and Scott stepped back to stay out of the drifting spray.

He turned in a slow circle, eyeing the monolithic modern architecture at each end of the square.

"It was here?" gasped Louise, who had been slow to move away from the pavement cross. Locks of wet hair now clung to her forehead. "Damn it, is this the place where you saw . . . *it*?"

"Where I sensed it," said Scott, peering up past the top of the statue. He laughed helplessly and pointed. "It was *up there*, a couple of hundred feet in the air."

"Shit," she said. "Is this all you can come up with? The Ross parking lot and . . . the *moon*?"

Scott finally lowered his head and stared at her. "You care?"

She shook her head. "We drove all the way down here, for nothing. And now I'm all wet."

The fountains subsided, then sprang up again. "Let's jaywalk back," Scott said tiredly, "and see if we can catch Madeline on her first trip around the block."

THE OLD GREEN DATSUN pulled to the curb just as Scott and Louise had ducked their way through traffic to that side of the street, but when Scott pulled open the passenger-side door, he saw that Ariel was behind the wheel now, and Madeline was sitting in the backseat, looking embarrassed.

Ariel accelerated out into the lane as soon as the front and back doors had closed.

"Madeline had a," she said, looking ahead at traffic, "an episode."

"I blacked out," said Madeline meekly.

"She was—" began Ariel; then she looked at Louise in the rear-view mirror and snapped, "Where's your goddamn bank?"

"I don't know where the nearest Wells Fargo is," said Louise, "and I don't have my phone. Scott could google it."

"I left my phone at the Ravenna Apartments," Scott said, and he added defensively, "It's the one the tenants call, with problems."

"I turned into Aunt Amity again!" burst out Madeline. Her face was pale.

Ariel sighed and nodded. "Our aunt apparently just figured out that Claimayne not only killed her, but did it by taking her up on the roof with the grenade. She said it tore up her aura."

"Stands to reason," said Madeline, who had taken her phone out of her purse and was tapping at the screen.

"She can't drive," Ariel went on. "Aunt Amity, I mean, not Madeline. I had to grab the wheel and put my foot across and stand on the brake, and pull over . . . well, up the curb. Lucky we didn't blow a tire. Lucky a cop didn't come by. And in a minute it was Madeline again, but—"

"Like people who have seizures," Madeline said. "I shouldn't drive."

"And I probably shouldn't get rid of my gyroscope yet," said Ariel. She looked sideways at Scott. "Obviously you didn't find a street that looked like San Francisco."

"No," said Scott, turned around in his seat to peer worriedly at his sister. "And now I'm wondering if my . . . *tracking sense* has broken down. The impression I got was that the room in the vision was there, had been there, but it was like a couple of hundred feet straight overhead!"

"Ah," said Ariel, "and you said the cars outside looked like 1940s models? It was on Bunker Hill."

Scott knew that Bunker Hill had been a neighborhood in Los Angeles full of big old Victorian houses that had been torn down to make way for anonymous office towers. "I knew they got rid of the houses," he said uncertainly.

"They got rid of the whole hill," said Ariel, "in the '60s. Dumped all the dirt and rocks in the ocean off Long Beach or somewhere."

"Well," said Madeline, "once again, maybe the film was destroyed." Her tone was wistful.

"What film?" asked Louise.

"A lost Bugs Bunny cartoon," said Ariel.

"Uh-huh." Louise leaned forward from the backseat and said to Scott, "Yesterday morning you said something about a woman who stole a reel of film from William Desmond Taylor. And Monalisa told me Taylor at one time had a copy of the big spider. Was the copy on this film?"

"Ferdalisi," said Scott. "Not Monalisa."

"There's a Wells Fargo bank just a couple of blocks from here," said Madeline, peering down at her phone. "Loop back up to First Street. It's open till four on Saturdays."

"But when do they open?" asked Louise. "It's not ten o'clock yet." Clearly she didn't want to be put out of the car.

"This is about when the clock was stopped," said Scott absently, watching his sister for any signs of their aunt reasserting herself, "in the room I saw on Bunker Hill."

Madeline looked up from her phone. "The bank opens at nine." To Scott she said, "I'd like to have a clock that would *stay* stopped."

"You'd have liked this one," Scott told her, "it was made out of a hubcap, with little wire numbers."

"Wire numbers," said Madeline slowly. "Like twisted wire?"

Scott drew a 2 in the air with his finger. "Right. Like—"

His face was suddenly cold, his gaze locked on Madeline's.

For several seconds neither of them spoke.

"It wasn't a working clock," said Madeline. "Maybe it had no machinery inside it at all." She took a deep breath and exhaled, shuddering, still staring into Scott's eyes. "Was it the same size?"

Scott compared his memories of the two wall-hung disks. "Yes."

Ariel was able to make a left turn on Fourth Street, after having cursed at two previous streets for being the wrong one-way.

"The wire numbers must have suggested the dartboard disguise for it," said Madeline.

"But neither of us *sensed* it," said Scott. "And we were right there in his kitchen with it."

Madeline rolled her eyes. "We were there in actual *real life,* Scott; we weren't in a spider vision! It's the spiders that sense it. You gotta be riding a spider to share that."

Louise was looking intently from Scott to Madeline and back. "This is important, isn't it?" she said. "A clock the size of a hubcap, with no machinery in it? A dartboard disguise? The film can—it's disguised as a dartboard now? Where?"

When Scott and Madeline ignored her question, Louise went on, "You need me as a consultant. I know more about this stuff than you do." After another pause while Ariel inched forward through traffic on Fourth, Louise said, "I'm on your side now—I was never *against* your side."

"You don't want to come," said Madeline, still staring at her brother. "It's in a place we went to yesterday."

Ariel sighed. "I think we have to let her come along now."

"Oh," said Madeline. She shook her head as if trying to clear it. "Yeah. Sorry."

"He still has it," said Scott. "And you remember how he seemed to recognize you? Little Miss Muffet, sticking your hand between the bars at a zoo?—like teasing a restrained animal, right? He *had* seen you before—sometime in the 1940s, when he did a spider and found himself chained to a pipe in the apiary, staring at you and Ariel through my eyes. And when you told him it was 2015, he thought you meant what time it was."

"Oh!" exclaimed Madeline. "Yes—you must be right. And when

Ariel and I asked him who he was, he laughed and said he was between names."

Scott turned to stare ahead, for his face was numb and he had no idea what his expression was. He was, at least at this moment, certain that he knew what the man's previous and subsequent names were.

So was Madeline. "Paul Speas, and Adrian Ostriker," she said hollowly. "*His* beard must *really* be fake."

"Even in the '40s he had a trunk full of wigs and beards," Scott said.

"Genod's father," said Madeline. "Genod said he was the devil. He sure looks younger than Genod."

"Spider rejuvenations, dilutions with young blood and bone," said Scott, quoting Nazimova.

Louise had clearly been mentally reciting the Little Miss Muffet nursery rhyme, for now she said out loud, "Along came a spider who sat down beside her and frightened Miss Muffet away." She looked at Scott. "The guy's name is Paul Speas?—or Adrian Ostrich? And you found an old spider of his and looked at it?"

"Sat down beside her," echoed Madeline, talking to herself.

Scott looked around at his sister and saw tiny beads of sweat along her hairline. "Are you okay?"

Madeline gave him a brief, frail smile and nodded. "I just have to concentrate on staying me. I feel her pushing up like a burp."

"We've got to steal his dartboard," said Scott, "and quick." The bulk of Claimayne's gun in his jacket made him dizzy. "Ariel, never mind the bank. Get back on the 101 north."

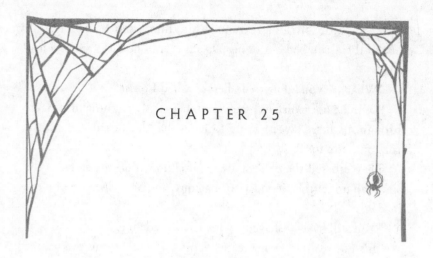

CHAPTER 25

TWENTY MINUTES LATER ARIEL steered the Datsun off Laurel Canyon Boulevard onto Jorgensen Road, past the blue and green recycling bins, and she switched down to low gear to drive up the narrow road between stone walls and twisted oak trees. Scott and Madeline remembered the route they had followed yesterday well enough to guide her through the sharp turns.

"Turn right by that wooden fence," said Scott finally, "and then it'll be on your right, a stone arch between two cypress trees."

Ariel made the turn and bumped cautiously along the narrow road, then braked and spun the steering wheel to make the sharp right turn through the arch. Now they were grinding up the curling driveway under overhanging vines, and finally they emerged in gray daylight on the wide cement apron in front of the two-story adobe house set back among the pines.

The neon-green Ford pickup truck and the black Camaro convertible sat where they had been yesterday morning, but now a gleamingly restored yellow Chevrolet station wagon was parked next to the Camaro. Scott judged it to be roughly a 1957 model.

"A hundred-something years old," said Scott nervously, "and all he cares about is old cars."

"They probably look real modern to him," said Madeline as all four of them climbed out of her Datsun. "And he cares about whiskey."

"What are you going to do here?" asked Louise.

"Brandy, not whiskey," said Scott, nervously running his fingers through his hair. "We're going to fetch that dartboard—he stole it from our aunt in 1922."

They crossed the cement area and clumped up the steps to the verandah under the second-floor balcony, and Scott knocked on the door.

"You still haven't shaved," whispered Madeline.

"It's not really a formal call," Scott told her, trying to imagine what he would do here.

The door swung inward, this time without the preliminary snap of the bolt being drawn back, and Adrian Ostriker was staring at them with an expression of tense appraisal. He was wearing another one-piece flight suit, or possibly the same one as yesterday, and the fabric was dark with sweat under the arms; but he wasn't holding one hand behind his back now. Scott paid attention to the man's long hair and beard, wondering if they were among the specimens he'd seen in the trunk in the Bunker Hill hotel.

"More of your sisters?" Ostriker said to Scott.

"Couple of friends."

And before Scott had decided among several ways to try to get invited inside again, Ostriker took a step back.

"Why waste time," Ostriker said, waving toward the living room.

Scott stepped over the threshold onto the pale hardwood floor, noting the zigzag framed couch and the spectrum of books on the shelves above it. As he slowly walked across the room he let himself glance at the open kitchen area, peripherally noting the dartboard on the wall beside the refrigerator. He heard Ariel and Madeline and Louise shuffle in behind him, and Ostriker closed the door and audibly shot the bolt.

Ostriker moved a few yards away, and both his hands were still visible and empty. Dazedly Scott realized that within moments he meant to pull out Claimayne's revolver and point it at Ostriker—and he reminded himself that Ostriker was the man who had gone by the name of Paul Speas, at least until 1922, and that he had taken the contents of the dartboard from Aunt Amity while she'd been in a hospital. I'm just going to take back what was hers, he told himself. Sweat was cold on his forehead, and he swallowed against nausea.

"Let's talk in the living room today," said Ostriker. His voice was pitched higher than it had been yesterday.

Scott took a deep breath and put his hand in his pocket—

And two men stepped out from the hallway behind Ostriker, and they had big-caliber semiautomatic pistols in their hands. Ostriker showed no surprise, just stared wrathfully at Scott.

"You blundering little *fools*," he muttered.

Louise sat down on the couch. "I *told* you not to go back to places you've been to before!"

Scott blinked at the newcomers. Both were tanned and wore dark windbreakers and slacks, and both had close-cropped gray hair; clearly not wigs.

One held a cell phone to his ear. "No, they're not," he was saying. "They're *here,* at the Ostriker place. And they arrived in the green Datsun. You tell me. Yeah, till you send somebody over." He brushed a thumb over the screen and put the phone in his pocket and looked at his partner. "Asleep at his post?"

The other man shook his head. "Doesn't matter now." Speaking loudly, he said, "You can call me Polydectes, and my buddy here Perseus. Everybody sit down. You too," he added, waving his gun toward Ostriker.

Ostriker and Ariel sat down on the couch beside Louise, and Scott and Madeline sat on the floor.

The man who was calling himself Polydectes dragged up a wooden Danish Modern chair and sat down facing the couch from several yards away. "You've all got the stink of spiders on you, and if we have to kill every one of you and burn this place to the ground, we won't lose any sleep over it. But we'd rather find Taylor's exorcism and let you all go your ways."

"Why would you kill us?" asked Madeline, sounding only curious.

Polydectes shrugged. "You're all users, infected—possibly even by the big spider itself, through proxy retinas. And," he added with a chilly smile, "we'd be saving you from the strenuous attentions of wheelbugs. But if you tell us what we want to know, all those issues evaporate."

It occurred to Scott that these two represented the group that Louise had said was in opposition to Ferdalisi's group—these were the "vandals" and "vigilantes" who wanted to banish the spiders.

"You guys drive a white Chevy Blazer," he said.

The man looked at Scott. "Sometimes. I was ready to try rescuing you two from those wheelbugs yesterday. We've got a camouflage station wagon today." He sighed. "We think *you* know where the exorcism film is, Scott Madden, or at least you know how to find it. Two days ago you went to where Taylor's apartment was. So where's the film now?"

Scott chewed his lip. "What do you want with it?"

"Not your concern. Where is it?"

"If you're going to *use* it, banish the spiders, then we're on your side. I—"

"But *I* need to use it," said Madeline anxiously.

Polydectes grimaced. "Shut up. You're not on our side. Ferdalisi has been to your house twice; you've got his girl with you."

"Twice?" murmured Ariel.

"When would you use it?" said Scott desperately. "When would you watch the film? It's got to be right now, today."

"I don't know these people," interjected Ostriker, starting to stand up and then sitting down again when Perseus raised his pistol. "I use spiders, sure, but I don't know anything about a *big* spider—"

"How old are you?" interrupted Polydectes. "You appeared out of nowhere with a fake birth certificate in 1960, looking about like you look now. Who were you before that?"

Ostriker opened his mouth, then closed it without saying anything.

Before that he was between names, thought Scott; and before *that,* his name was Paul David Speas.

"I'll make you a deal," said Scott, "if you can assure me—"

"No deals," said Polydectes. "This is your sister, right?" He pointed his semiautomatic at Madeline's knee. "A .45 Hydra-Shok round there won't kill her, but it'll probably take her leg right off. Where is it?"

Even as Scott opened his mouth to say *In the dartboard in the kitchen!,* the couch shook as Madeline sprang up from the floor and threw herself onto Ostriker.

Ostriker neighed in alarm as he blocked her with a hastily raised forearm, trying to keep her fingers from getting at his eyes. She caught the edge of his beard and pulled it half off.

"I need it now!" Madeline was screaming in something like Aunt Amity's voice. "You're my *husband,* and you stole it for yourself while I was in the hospital! I'm hanging on by my fingernails; I'm in shreds!"

Perseus tried to grab her shoulder with his free hand, but she was clinging to Ostriker; Perseus tucked his pistol into his belt and took hold of her with both hands.

Polydectes took a step back, his own pistol raised.

And then a jarring explosion shook the house; the entire pane of a window at the back of the room fell out of its frame and shattered on the floor.

Polydectes turned his head toward the noise, and Scott yanked Claimayne's revolver out of his pocket and stood up.

"Drop it!" he yelled, pointing the revolver at the man's chest. His pulse made the barrel jerk rhythmically, but he kept it effectively aimed.

Peripherally he saw that Ariel was now standing on his right, pointing her old .32 Seecamp at Perseus. "Let go of her," Ariel said. "Hook your gun out with your left hand and let it drop."

Beyond Perseus, Scott saw yellow scraps spinning down outside the window.

Polydectes stared speculatively at Scott, then let go of his gun. It clattered on the floor.

Perseus had stepped back, and now he pulled his gun free and it too fell to the floor.

Ostriker had got hold of Madeline's wrists and was keeping his face well back from her teeth. He managed to stand up and throw her onto the couch where he had been sitting, and he darted one hand to a pocket on his thigh, and then he was holding a short, gleaming knife and drawing it back for a thrust at Madeline.

Without thinking, Scott swung the revolver toward him and pulled the trigger. The deafening bang seemed to momentarily compress the air, and confetti flew around Ostriker's startled upturned face.

Ariel had moved back to cover Polydectes as well as Perseus.

"Drop the knife," gasped Scott, speaking loudly over the ringing in his ears, and he was horrified to realize that only luck had kept him from hitting Madeline with his unaimed shot. One of the books in the yellow section of the bookcase now had a ragged hole in its spine.

Ostriker tossed the knife toward Scott and hurried to stand behind Perseus. The knife rattled across the floor. Scott swung the revolver back to cover the three men.

Madeline glowered at Ostriker but didn't get up. "Never morrow shall dawn upon him, desolate!" she said. It was another line of the poem in Poe's "The Fall of the House of Usher."

"Kill them," Louise said, getting to her feet. "They were going to kill us."

"No," said Scott, panting, "those two are on our side, though they don't know it. We—"

Polydectes was looking from the broken window to the front

door and back. "That bomb," he said quickly, "that's the Spanish group, they'll be in here in a moment—"

"That's just our aunt," interrupted Scott, "blowing up again." The man started to say something else, but Scott said loudly, "Walk backward toward the broken window, slowly, all three of you. You saw I'm willing to shoot somebody—next time I'll aim better."

"You stole it," said Madeline from the couch, glaring at Ostriker, "you abandoned me pregnant, with a shattered foot, and you abandoned our son; you left us with nothing. I need it now."

Ostriker was shuffling backward with Polydectes and Perseus, who were eyeing him as cautiously as they were Scott and Ariel.

"You bitch!" Ostriker shouted. His face gleamed with sweat and the left side of his jaw was bare, that half of the beard hanging now from his chin. "You think I didn't know you were planning to show me a spider, and then in the after look at the Medusa? Through my eyes! I'd have died like Ince, and you'd have had a safe passage!"

Keeping all three of the men in view over the muzzle of the revolver, Scott stepped toward the kitchen and called, "Ariel, get their guns and the knife."

Crouching but not lowering her own gun, Ariel tucked one of the dropped guns into the back of her waistband and gripped the other; the knife she kicked toward the front door.

"*Yes,* like Ince," yelled Madeline in their aunt's voice, "and you need to do it now; you owe me. I have nothing."

Scott crossed to the refrigerator, and with his free hand lifted the dartboard from a hook on the wall.

He looked at Ariel. "Get Madeline and Louise outside. We can shoot out their tires and go."

"That's it," called Polydectes urgently, "in the dartboard, isn't it? We can make your deal, I can guarantee—"

"You were going to shoot my sister's leg off!" shouted Scott. The grip of the revolver in his right hand was slick with sweat, and he held it more tightly.

Ariel and Louise had taken hold of Madeline's arms and lifted her to her feet and marched her toward the front door. Louise reached out and turned the knob, and Scott followed them out onto the verandah, still facing the room as he held the dartboard to his chest and kept the gun trained on the three men standing by the empty window frame on the far side of the room.

"I'm gonna close the door," he called to them, "and if it opens, she and I will both shoot at whoever's peeking out."

He slammed the door, then spun in alarm when he heard two close gunshots from behind him—but it had been Ariel shooting at the tires of the station wagon. One tire had gone flat.

"The second one bounced off!" she said.

"One'll do. Cover the door, but watch the sides of the house too." Scott hurried down the steps and across the cement apron to the pickup truck and the Camaro, where he quickly fired a shot into a back tire of each; the sound of the shots echoed away among the pines, and both vehicles abruptly sagged as the bursts of compressed air blew dust across the cement.

"Your turn!" Ariel called. Scott raised his right arm and pointed his gun at Ostriker's door, keeping a wide focus on the whole house. *We're nearly away*, he thought, still clasping the dartboard to his chest; *we're nearly away*. Madeline and Louise were already in the backseat of the Datsun, and now Ariel got in on the driver's side, started the engine, and backed toward the verandah. She leaned across and pushed the door open, and after Scott had hurried to the car and slid in, she accelerated down the steep driveway until the house was out of sight. Scott shoved the revolver back in his pocket and slumped down in the passenger seat, and he let the fingers of his left hand unclamp from the dartboard.

"Curl around west and find a way down to Sunset," gasped Louise as the car swayed around the curves of the driveway. "Cops will arrive by way of Laurel Canyon." She reached a shaky hand between the front seats and touched the rough surface of the dartboard on Scott's lap.

Madeline was blinking around as Ariel got to the bottom of the driveway and made a bouncy right turn. "I was Aunt Amity again, wasn't I? He shouldn't have pointed a gun at her foot."

"It was a lucky break this time," said Scott. "She tried to poke Ostriker's eyes out and then blew up on the roof."

"Couldn't beat it as a distraction," agreed Ariel, her eyes fixed on the road swooping past under the tires.

Madeline was pale and massaging her throat. "It feels like she did a lot of yelling too."

After Ariel had made a number of tight, random turns, and hurriedly backed out of several narrow cul-de-sacs, with the clear intent of consistently aiming downhill, Scott peered out through the windshield and read a street sign. "This is Sunset Plaza Drive. I'd stay on it."

Louise had been silent for several minutes, and now said, "What are you going to do with it?"

Scott looked at Ariel. "Do you know where Aunt Amity's old projector is, at Caveat? And the screen?"

"In the apiary," she said.

He sighed in something like surrender. "We've got to get it set up." *And then by God I* will *do what Valentino and Nazimova wanted me to do, and Madeline will be free. Maybe it won't kill me, maybe my childhood exposure to the big spider—to Usabo, to the Medusa—will give me some degree of immunity.*

He felt ready to vomit.

Madeline touched his shoulder. "It has to be me that watches it, Scott."

"At Caveat?" said Ariel doubtfully. "Won't those guys come there, after it?"

"They're not following us right now," said Scott, leaning back in the seat and breathing deeply, "and they think we somehow snuck past their watchers on Vista Del Mar—go back by way of the easement, from Gower, and with luck they'll think we're still out driving around the city somewhere. And anyway, it'll be eleven by the time we get there; the house will be full of Claimayne's cleaners and caterers. Practically a public place."

"And where else are we going to find a 35-millimeter projector instantly available?" asked Madeline. Scott could only see Louise in the rearview mirror, but he knew that if he could see Madeline, she'd be giving him a defiant look.

ARIEL DROVE SLOWLY UP Gower past Franklin from Hollywood Boulevard, and when she could see no cars in the uphill or downhill lanes she swerved to the left into the narrow driveway that curved up between stone walls and overhanging greenery to the level area by the garages above the broad slope of the Caveat garden. She coasted down the main driveway, and at the gap where she and Scott had rolled one of the bordering logs aside she turned off the pavement and drove across the grass to the driveway by the kitchen door. A red Ford sedan that Scott didn't recognize was parked beside his motorcycle.

He handed the dartboard across to Ariel as he climbed out. "Let me go in first," he said.

Louise had got out and was looking around at the landscape uneasily. "I'll wait outside," she said.

Scott nodded as he crossed the cement and opened the kitchen door. "Fine."

Foil-covered platters now covered every inch of counter space in the kitchen, and the warm air smelled of lemon and blue cheese; but there was no one in sight, and he pushed open the swinging doors to the long dining room. All the French windows were open to the cold breeze, and this room too was empty. He could hear voices and the clatter of collapsible chairs down the hall in the direction of the music room.

"I'll grab the old 220-volt extension cord," called Ariel from the kitchen.

" 'Kay."

Madeline stepped into the dining room, and Scott nodded to her and led the way through the room to the hall and the stairs. He was relieved not to have come across Claimayne. As he tapped up the uncarpeted stairs, hearing Madeline's sneakers scuffing behind him, he was trying to remember how his aunt had threaded film through the projector and turned it on—feed roller, film gate, sprocket . . .

He had nearly reached the third-floor landing when he realized that he didn't hear Madeline's feet on the stairs now.

"Maddy?" He paused, then hurried back down the two flights of stairs.

She wasn't in the hall at the bottom of the stairs, nor down the laundry room hall, and his heart was pounding as he rushed through the dining room and pushed open the kitchen doors.

Madeline was crouched by the sink, gripping the counter and straightening up. Blood gleamed bright red on her mouth and chin and had stained the front of her blouse.

She saw Scott and waved toward the kitchen door. "Claimayne and that guy," she gasped, "grabbed Ariel."

Scott ran to the door and pulled it open—the red Ford was gone; Claimayne's empty wheelchair stood near Scott's motorcycle. He hurried out across the driveway, but the only vehicles he could see down the slope were cleaning and catering trucks and Louise's white Saturn. He looked across the lawn, but there was no car on the garage road. He didn't see Louise either.

He rushed back inside. Madeline was standing now, leaning over the sink and running water on a dish towel.

"Are you all right?" he asked.

She pinched the bridge of her nose. "Not broken," she said, "just bloody. Ariel was in the dining room, behind me, and when I was on the stairs, I heard a scuffle and went back. Claimayne was walking! And that Ferdalisi guy was with him. He punched me."

"Did she have the dartboard?"

"I couldn't see. She didn't have the extension cord." She pressed the wet dish towel to her nose. In a muffled voice, she added, "Louise was with them. Voluntarily. She must have seen them in the garden, was why she hung back."

"Terrific." Scott was snapping his fingers rapidly. "Why would they take *Ariel*, if they had their damn dartboard?" Then he remembered something Ariel had said at Miceli's yesterday: *wheelbugs love to find people like me.* He waved a hand. "Talking to myself. How the hell are we going to find her?"

"Call 911."

"And tell them she's in a red Ford somewhere. We need to find her *now*." He strode to the door and looked uselessly out through the shard-edged window frame at the driveway and the lawn. He took a deep breath and let it out through clenched teeth—

—then reached into his pocket past the bulky revolver and pulled out the fourth of the spiders that had been in Claimayne's cloisonné box, the one labeled *Il Dottore.* It was crumpled, but he knew the lines on it would still be clear.

"Oh, don't even bother, Scott," said Madeline, stepping forward and catching his arm. "It'll just show you where the dartboard was in 1950 or 1960. Not where it is *this minute*."

"I'm not going to look at it dirty." He turned around and held the folded slip of paper toward her. "Take a picture of it with your phone, and e-mail it to yourself, to break the dirty continuity. Quick! We can open it and print it out in the library."

"So it'll be clean—so what?"

"*Eventually* I'll learn where they're taking her, right? So I'll look at it now, but I won't look at it again, I won't do the after, until I know where they've taken her." Madeline stared at him blankly. "Listen," he went on quickly, "when Ariel looked at a spider Tuesday night when we first got here, she was suddenly the Ariel from last night, who knew we weren't enemies, right? So she was friendly then, on Tuesday night, till that after wore off."

Madeline's eyes widened and she nodded. "So when you look at it right now, you'll be the Scott who looks at it later, after you've found out where she is."

He nodded. "Hurry. But don't look at it yourself."

"It doesn't make sense. You'll find out where she *is* now because you'll eventually know where she *was* now?"

"Spiders see it all at once, not divvied up into *then* and *now* and *later*. Hurry!"

Madeline found her purse under the table and pulled her phone out of it.

"Focus on the edge of the sink first," Scott told her, "so you know how high to hold it."

Madeline nodded and moved the phone up and down over the sink, peering at the screen; then she held it steady. "Okay."

"Don't move your hand, but close your eyes." Scott unfolded the piece of paper, looking away, and by touch laid it on the Formica. "Now."

The phone clicked, and he hastily folded the paper and shoved it into his pocket.

Madeline was stepping toward the door even as she tapped the screen. "There," she said, pushing through the doors to the dining room, "let's go open up AOL."

They hurried down the hall, past several impatient strangers in white coats with a caterer's logo stitched on the breast pockets, to their aunt's office, and Scott closed the door behind them while Madeline turned on the computer.

As the Windows screen appeared, Madeline asked, "So where will *you* be, when you look at this?"

"God knows *where* I'll be, but I'll have found out where she was now."

"But even then, you won't know what happened, where they took her."

Scott frowned. "That's true. Yeah, I'll have *traded places* with the Scott who found that out. Just like the Ariel who cussed us out last night—*she* didn't know anything that had happened since the moment she looked at a spider three nights earlier." He shrugged. "But at that point I won't need to know; it'll already have happened, and presumably I'll have . . ."

"Saved Ariel. Again."

"Ideally. I hope so. Get into AOL, and don't look at your e-mail."

Madeline tapped the keys on the white keyboard, then looked away, and a few seconds later the printer started humming. When it stopped, Scott peered sideways through slitted eyes at the piece of paper lying in the tray and saw the lines of a spider. He looked at the ceiling as he lifted the paper out of the tray and folded it twice.

As they hurried back down the hall toward the kitchen, he pulled out of his pocket the old crumpled spider that Madeline had photographed and tore it to pieces in the palm of his hand.

A couple of men in aprons were in the kitchen now, and they watched in mute disapproval as Scott took a clean wineglass from a box and broke it in the sink. He snatched up a solid piece of the stem with a wing of glass still attached, and then he and Madeline pushed past the caterers and out the door. Scott tucked the piece of glass into his pocket, not looking forward to gripping it tightly in his fist.

"Helmet?" said Madeline as he swung onto the motorcycle and bent to fit the key into the ignition. "Goggles?"

"Damn. No time. They might be killing her right now."

He drove his foot down on the kick-starter and the motor roared.

Madeline was wringing her hands. "I should have cast a chart for you!" she called.

"It'd just tell me what I should have done last month," he said. He looked at his watch—it was exactly 11:10. He took a deep breath, then unfolded the sheet of freshly printed paper and looked squarely at the spider.

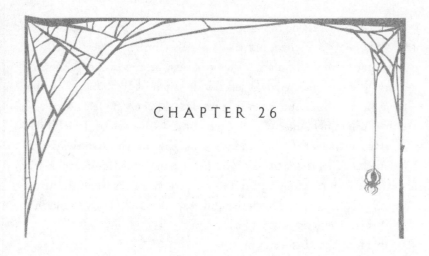

CHAPTER 26

THE HOUSE AND THE gray sky and his anxious sister were all blotted out as the spider's limbs expanded and split and split again and again and began to spin; or else it and Scott held still while the universe spun around them. And for a precious, measureless period he was nobody at all.

Then he was among the vertical-seeming shapes, and it came to him that *they* were spiders, viewed from the two-dimensional spider perspective, end-on; and that their apparent infinite height was a compensatory illusion provided by his mind, in an attempt to normalize the perception of figures with breadth but no height at all.

They moved aside, and he fell through them.

And his motorcycle was gone, and he sagged to his knees in damp grass, and pain shot up his left arm when he leaned forward and his weight came onto his palms. He rolled jarringly onto his left shoulder and looked at his left hand; fresh blood was smeared across his palm, almost hiding an inch-long gash at the base of the thumb, and his fingers were sticky with it and the black cuff of his jacket was gleaming.

He sat up and found himself facing the south wall of Caveat, just to the right of the front porch, under an overcast sky. He got his legs under himself and managed to stand up.

What day is it? he thought.

His joints all ached, but that was the familiar spider-lag effect; he didn't seem to have any other wounds, or any broken bones. A moment later he cringed to see a wide patch of fresh blood on the front of his shirt, but when he prodded his chest he felt no cuts— either he had held his cut hand there, or it was someone else's blood.

He shifted stiffly around to look toward the driveway and exhaled in relief to see the roofs of the catering and cleaning vans. It's the same day, he thought; I didn't have to wait days to do the after, didn't have to get a call from the police about Ariel's body found in a culvert somewhere. *But did I save her?*

He looked at his watch: 11:29.

Only nineteen minutes since I started the motorcycle in the driveway and looked at the spider and exchanged places with me in this vision right now. What did I learn a few seconds ago—standing right here!—that led me to look at the spider again, do the after? What made me believe I knew where she was?

He peered around at the long grass and the descending over-grown slope down to Vista Del Mar. Whatever the encounter was, he told himself, it must have been close by, for it all to be over in only nineteen minutes. If in fact it is all over. I wonder where my bike is.

The piece of glass that had presumably cut his palm was gone; and when he patted his right jacket pocket, he realized that the revolver was gone too.

If I did rescue her from Claimayne—Claimayne was up and walking?—and Ferdalisi, where is she now? In an ambulance? In Madeline's car, racing out of Los Angeles? Waiting for me in the api-ary? And if I didn't succeed in rescuing her . . . is she injured, dead, somewhere? Still with Claimayne and Ferdalisi? Did I run into trou-ble and then abandon her? What did I do with the damn *gun?*

Suddenly the aches in his head and spine doubled, and he real-ized that he had sat down again, involuntarily. Sweat ran down his forehead into his eyes, and he was shivering violently in the cold; he took several deep breaths to quell a surge of nausea. *My body has taken the shocks of two spider viewings within the space of nineteen minutes*, he thought dazedly; *I'm lucky I'm not dead.*

Unless I failed her, in which case I'm not lucky at all.

It was harder to stand up this time, and he took two lurching steps and held himself up by leaning against the rough stucco wall of the house.

He dragged himself along the wall and then worked his way around the porch, leaning on the outside of the marble rail. The two steps up to the porch were dizzying enough to make him sit down on the bench where he had set his bundle and Madeline's bag in the rain on their first night at Caveat.

When his head had cleared, Scott lifted his wrist and made himself focus on his watch: 11:44 now. He stood up and walked fairly steadily to the front door. He touched the knob, and the vision faded.

HE FELL TO HIS hands and knees again, and instantly lifted his left hand as it flared with pain.

"God!" he croaked. He could feel that he was on damp grass again, but all he could see was a mottled gray and green surface with red streaks across it. He gingerly stretched the fingers of his left hand and saw the red streaks change their shapes. *It's my hand*, he thought—*see it as three-dimensional.*

He rotated his hand and watched the red patches merge and separate—wishing he had Ariel's gyroscope instead—and after several seconds, he was able to perceive that the gray and green shapes were grass and, several yards away, the marble railing and pavement of the Caveat front porch; the red shapes were clearly his own blood-wet fingers only inches in front of his face.

Scott lowered his hand and scowled across the grass at the Caveat porch and the front door and the doorknob he seemed to have touched only a minute ago. That vision had ended, and he was back in real time.

He sat down in the grass and focused on his watch. Squinting hard, was able to see that the hands stood at 11:26. And the vision he'd just recovered from had started at 11:29!

Three minutes from now, he thought bewilderedly, I'm due to look at the spider again. In these next three minutes I'll apparently, somehow, satisfy myself that I know where Claimayne and Ferdolisi took Ariel.

He got to his feet once again—though the two times in his immediate memory wouldn't actually occur for several minutes yet—and just stood there panting. Had he been running? He turned and looked behind him, toward the east. Is that the direction I came from, he wondered, after whatever happened happened? Where the hell *is* everybody?

There was something lumpy against his stomach, under the jacket, and it didn't feel like the revolver. Whatever it was, it hadn't been there . . . wouldn't be there, a couple of minutes from now, when he would look at the spider again. He took hold of the zipper tab with his left hand and pulled it down.

At that moment he heard the front door open, and he shifted his feet around on the grass to be able to look toward it.

Louise was standing on the porch, staring at him in horror. She was holding Madeline's purse. The left side of her face and her hair on that side were bright neon orange, and streaks of the same color slanted vividly across her dark blue quilted jacket.

"I'm sorry!" she wailed. "Is Ariel dead?"

"Where are they?" he called hoarsely.

And then she just shook her head and ran away from him, toward the driveway. He started after her but slid to a gasping halt after only a couple of paces.

Louise had left the front door open, and from inside Scott now heard the clanging and booming of Claimayne's elevator starting up.

Where is Claimayne coming from? thought Scott in alarm. Where is he going?

His instinctive impulse was to go inside—find Claimayne, confront him. But he looked again at his watch and saw that it was now 11:28. He couldn't go after Claimayne now, he was due to look at the spider again in less than *one minute*—and experience the moments directly after he had first looked at it, sitting on his idling motorcycle while Madeline said she wished she'd made an astrological chart for him.

But I won't know where to go! And I've only got seconds left!

Impatiently he pulled the lumpy object out of his jacket.

It was a green rubber hand with long pointed rubber fingernails.

I know what that is, he thought; I've seen that before. Where?

The rubber space aliens in the east garage.

Claimayne and Ferdolisi hadn't taken Ariel far at all.

He tossed the rubber hand aside, pulled the spider from his pocket, and unfolded it and stared at it.

FOR THE SECOND TIME the thing expanded to fill his vision, dividing and fissipating and spinning, and in this impossible-seeming perspective his consciousness had no place in which to exist, and so it did not.

Eventually the view of the spider rotated ninety degrees, and Scott was again able to comprehend the spiders from their own perspective, horizontally, though his mind imposed an arbitrary verticality on their infinite flatness. They parted, and he moved forward between them—

And he was in the reciprocal vision, experiencing his body nineteen minutes earlier. He was astride the idling motorcycle on the driveway outside the kitchen door, and he folded the freshly printed spider paper and shoved it into his pocket, then clicked the bike into first gear.

Madeline was standing in the kitchen doorway, staring at him anxiously. He knew she hoped he would call out and let her know what he believed he had learned, but he didn't want her to participate in whatever it was that had made him lose the gun and perhaps get someone else's blood on his shirt.

And so he just nodded quickly to his sister and then let out the bent clutch lever and twisted the throttle grip, and he gunned the bike out across the grass. Now he could see that there were more tire tracks flattening the grass than just those that had been left by Madeline's Datsun.

To his own surprise he felt optimistic and almost eager, and he realized that it was because his aches and nausea were gone, and his left hand was still strong and undamaged, and he could again feel the weight of Claimayne's revolver in his right jacket pocket. It's temporary well-being, he told himself as he steered the motorcycle through the gap where he and Ariel had rolled the bordering log aside this morning, but use it while you've got it. He inhaled the cold eucalyptus-scented air and raced up the driveway toward the ridge garages.

Scott clicked the gearshift down into neutral when the road leveled out in front of the garages, and when he had sped past them, and past the easement down to Gower, the driveway curved to the right and began to descend toward the old east-end garage.

The red Ford sedan was parked down there on the wider section of pavement. Scott reached under the gas tank and switched the engine off.

As the motorcycle coasted down the curving driveway back toward the east end of the house, it was silent except for the faint whir of the chain; Louise's question—*Is Ariel dead?*—echoed in his head, and he was not even tempted to let his right foot touch the rear brake pedal.

Where the driveway broadened in front of the garage, Scott slanted the bike to the right and gripped the front brake lever; the front end nosed down sharply, and the bike came to a silent halt beside the big mesquite tree that shaded half the garage roof. He swung the kick-stand down and got off the motorcycle, pulling Claimayne's revolver from his jacket pocket. He knew he still had two unfired rounds in it, and he resisted the temptation to swing the cylinder out and check them. He was sweating and trembling, and as he stepped around the corner of the garage he reminded himself to breathe. With his left hand he dug the piece of broken wineglass out of his pocket, and he gritted his teeth and made himself squeeze it—the edge cut into the base of his thumb, and he gasped at the bright heat of the pain.

The doorway of the garage was open, the door he had knocked out of its frame on Wednesday still lying on the asphalt in front of the red Ford. Scott sidled up to the door in time to hear Claimayne say, "Where the hell is your *backup*?"

Ferdalisi's Spanish-accented voice said, "The party isn't to start until two; this preemptive capture was serendipitous. Now, girl, tell me where you put the—dartboard?—or I'll cut out your eyes. A misfortune for a spider addict."

Scott whispered a brief prayer, then raised the gun and stepped through the doorway, swinging the barrel back and forth in the dimness.

Claimayne was instantly visible, sitting down on the cement floor and massaging his left leg; he blinked in surprise at Scott's sudden appearance. Ariel was sitting on the floor to the right, her head lowered and her arms awkwardly bent behind her, and beside her crouched Ferdalisi, who, Scott was now able to see, was holding a pistol, its barrel pressed against Ariel's temple.

"Drop it," Ferdalisi said calmly. When Scott hesitated, he went on, "She had only moments to hide the dartboard after she saw us coming, and Louise has gone to look for it. She will almost certainly find it very quickly. I really don't need this woman to tell me where it is."

"She'd only tell you someplace wrong anyway," said Claimayne, straightening his leg and wincing. "She's perverse."

When Scott still didn't let go of the revolver, Ferdalisi shrugged and lifted the grip of his pistol so that the barrel was aimed more directly at Ariel's temple, and Scott hastily opened his right hand. The revolver clanked on the cement floor.

Ferdalisi let his arm relax, but he kept the muzzle pressed against Ariel's hair, and it didn't waver when running footsteps approached from outside. Scott looked to his left and saw Louise step into the doorway, panting and holding the dartboard in both hands.

She gave him an incongruously apologetic grimace as she edged past him into the garage. "It was on top of a cabinet in the dining room," she told Ferdalisi.

"Step away from her," Ferdalisi said sharply to Scott. And when Scott shuffled aside, furiously squeezing the broken glass in his left hand, Ferdalisi told Louise, "Open it. There must be a way to open it."

Louise sat down cross-legged on the cement near Claimayne and pried at the rim. "It shakes like there's something in it," she said helpfully. After a few more seconds, she said, "Aha." Scott heard a click, and then she had lifted away the top surface of the dartboard. Inside the shallow round tray lay the film can Scott had last seen in William Desmond Taylor's apartment in 1922.

"The exorcism," said Ferdalisi with evident satisfaction. "Now it will never be viewed."

"You'll destroy it?" asked Claimayne.

"After saving some frames of the Medusa."

Claimayne's smooth face was twitching as he shifted on the floor and massaged his left arm now, but he looked up at Scott with a tight smile. "So near and yet so far, eh, old boy? *You* were the one watching when I killed Taylor and took it from him, weren't you? And at Valentino's house where the freeway runs now, and Speas's hotel room on Bunker Hill. That was *you*, riding along on *my* spiders." He nodded toward the film reel in Louise's lap. "And now you lose it, and everything."

Ferdalisi pushed Ariel away and got to his feet. "Put the lid back on," he told Louise, "and give it to me."

Louise bent over the dartboard to reattach the lid, and only Scott was facing the back end of the garage as she handed Ferdalisi the dartboard; the trapdoor in the roof was still open, and the shaft of drab daylight back there dimmed for several seconds and he thought he heard faint scuffling. Scott made himself squeeze the broken glass edge harder into the flesh of his palm; sweat broke out on his forehead and he breathed deeply to keep from fainting.

Ferdalisi stepped back and waved the barrel of his pistol from Scott to Louise. "You two lie facedown now, with your hands behind you."

"Are you going to kill us?" gasped Louise.

"Just bind you, for now. Lie down."

A wild yell and loud clattering suddenly erupted from the back of the garage, and even Scott gasped in astonishment at what came wobbling out of the shadows.

One of the rubber space aliens had been propped up on a bicycle with training wheels and propelled toward the fan of daylight by the open doorway. Its knees pumped up and down and its long arms waved loosely over the handlebars and its big-eyed head wobbled in all directions.

Claimayne inhaled a scream and flopped onto his back, twitching and clutching at his chest.

Ferdalisi had spun to face the oncoming thing, and now he fired two fast loud shots at it, to no evident effect.

Scott dove for the dropped revolver.

Ariel rolled over and kicked upward, driving her shoe into Ferdalisi's groin. He hunched forward with a shrill grunt and spasmodically slammed the butt of his pistol against her head, and as she tumbled away from him he aimed the pistol at her.

Crouched on the floor, Scott pointed the revolver up at the middle of him and pulled the trigger; the noise of the gunshot echoed in the garage. Ferdalisi lowered the pistol and slowly turned around to stare at Scott with wide eyes; Scott wasn't sure where his shot had hit the man, if it had hit him at all, and he gritted his teeth and centered the muzzle on Ferdalisi's chest—

But at that moment Madeline came rushing out of the darkness at the back of the garage with a spray-paint can in each hand, and she sprayed bright neon-orange paint into Ferdalisi's face and eyes; the man exhaled sharply and then fell to his knees, and the gun tumbled out of his hand.

Louise had snatched up the dartboard, but she dropped it when Madeline swept the spray in a zigzag pattern across her face and chest.

Ferdalisi pitched forward across Ariel's legs.

The floor of the garage shifted, and streaks of dust fell from the ceiling. The cobwebby flying saucers swung back and forth over the plywood Los Angeles skyline against the wall.

Madeline threw the spray cans at Louise and kicked the dartboard aside, and then crouched to roll Ferdalisi off Ariel. Louise moaned and ran out empty-handed through the doorway.

Scott glanced at Claimayne, but he was just gasping and pressing both hands to his chest, his eyes tightly shut. Scott hiked himself across the floor to where Ariel lay.

Madeline had rolled Ferdalisi's heavy body off Ariel's legs— Scott looked away from the man's slack orange face and open orange eyes—and Ariel had sat up, her arms still bent around behind her. Blood ran down from her scalp and streaked her face.

"Gimme a lighter," said Madeline. "They've got a cable tie around her wrists."

Scott dropped the revolver and dug a Bic lighter out of his pants pocket and handed it to Madeline; a moment later he smelled melting plastic, and then Ariel's arms were free and she tilted forward. Scott caught her; her head was against his chest and he could feel her hot blood through his shirt.

"Your hand," she muttered. "All bloody."

Scott remembered to squeeze the wineglass fragment again, and now he let himself wince and let out a harsh *"Ah!"* at the pain. "I'll live," he gasped.

"He's in a spider vision," said Madeline. Ferdalisi was lying on the floor with his bright orange face and beard tilted back, and she prodded him and then felt his throat. "I think my spray paint killed him!" she whispered. Her nose was bleeding again, and she absently swiped a hand across her red-streaked chin.

"Scott shot him," said Ariel. She lifted her head from Scott's chest and peered around. "Claimayne."

A couple of yards away across the cement, Claimayne opened his eyes and looked across at her. His teeth were bared, and his face was sweaty and white as chalk. He waved one hand weakly.

"Salomé," he gasped, "hand me my gun, so that I may have shot our guest!"

Ariel reached to the side and picked up the revolver Scott had dropped, and she walked on her knees to where Claimayne lay.

"But he—" began Madeline.

"My cousin," said Ariel, "has no reason to hurt us now. We need him to fire it."

Madeline threw a wild glance at Scott, who shook his head helplessly and then nodded.

Ariel took hold of Claimayne's right hand, and she gently laid the grip of the gun in his palm and guided his forefinger into the trigger guard. She lifted the hand so that the barrel was pointed at the ceiling.

"Thank you, Tetrarch," she said softly and squeezed his hand. The gunshot seemed louder than the previous ones had been, and the gun had jerked out of Claimayne's hand in recoil and now spun on the floor.

"Nobody touch it now," said Ariel. She stood up; both Scott and Madeline got to their feet to help her, but she waved them off. "I can walk," she said. "Slowly."

"But I'm not sorry," whispered Claimayne, lying on the floor behind her, "Ariel. For anything." The exhalation that followed was shaky and seemed never to end. Ariel peered down at him, frowning.

Scott tried to comprehend the evident fact that Claimayne was dead.

And he glanced at Ferdalisi's sprawled body and flexed his right hand; it wasn't the hand that was bleeding, but he had actually killed that man with it.

He forced the thought away, took a deep breath and let it out, and crossed to the space alien, which was now leaning backward on the still-upright bicycle. He took hold of one of its hands and twisted it; it resisted for a moment, and then a glued seam gave way and he was able to pull the hand off a rusty wire support. He tucked the thing inside his jacket and tugged the zipper up.

Madeline had picked up the dartboard with one hand, pinching her nose with the other.

"I—might still be able to stop Louise from stealing your car," Scott said to her. "You two meet me in the apiary. I'll surely be a while getting there, so wait for me." He looked with concern at Ariel, who was now pressing one bloody hand to her scalp. "You two take Claimayne's elevator rather than the stairs." Madeline nodded. It's Ariel and Madeline, Scott realized, who were using—will shortly be using, that is—the elevator; it wasn't—won't be—Claimayne after all.

"What about Claimayne?" asked Madeline.

"He's dead too," Ariel told her flatly. She looked at Scott. "See you in the apiary."

He nodded and opened his left hand, and then he had to shake his hand to dislodge the glass fragment. He hurried out of the garage and around the corner of the house and started across the grass. He was still several yards short of the Caveat front porch when he fell out of the spider vision.

ALL SCOTT COULD SEE was a field of brown. He could feel that his right hand was holding a metal knob, and he sagged and gripped it tightly as the weight of having just done two spiders fell on him again. He was back in real time again.

Where am I? he thought dizzily. Well, where was I in the last moments of the after vision? In it I found myself on the grass out in front of Caveat, and I dragged myself along the wall and the railing to the front porch, and I had just touched the doorknob when I fell out of that vision. So that's where I am—I'm holding on to the doorknob and this brown expanse must be the front door.

He looked away from it at a broad gray shape that mingled along one edge with mottled, shifting green, and he knew he must be seeing the gray sky and the jungly front slope.

Scott looked back at the door, and it seemed to move away from in front of his face to a distance of about a foot. He looked down and saw his left hand on the knob, and he could see that his hand and the knob were not part of the plane of the door. His depth perception had returned.

He glanced behind him at the bench where he had sat to catch his breath, only a minute ago in real time. Smears of blood streaked the marble seat where he had touched it with his left hand.

Lowering his head, Scott allowed himself a brief smile. And when I was sitting there, he thought, I wondered where the gun had got to, and whether or not I had managed to find and save Ariel. I wondered if she were dead, or in an ambulance. Well, I did save her—with the help of Madeline and the rubber alien.

He patted the front of his jacket and of course didn't feel the rubber alien's hand. He looked at his watch: 11:45. I walked out of the garage with the rubber hand in my jacket—leaving Claimayne and Ferdalisi dead on the floor nineteen minutes ago!

He glanced to his left, toward the driveway, then shook his head wearily. Let Louise take Madeline's car, he thought. She's surely gone by now, and I'm in no shape to struggle with her if she's not—and anyway, I've got to save *Madeline* now.

Twisting the doorknob, Scott pushed the door open. He stepped wearily into the entry hall; for a moment he considered climbing the two flights of stairs, then shook his head and started for Claimayne's elevator. He won't mind now, he told himself.

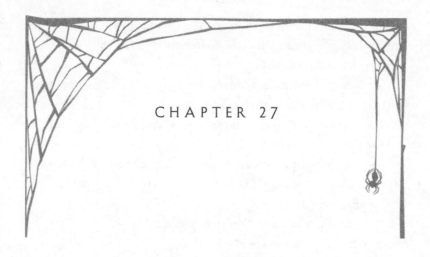

CHAPTER 27

"WE'RE ALL A MESS, aren't we?" said Ariel when Scott finally limped into the apiary. She was frowning critically, but there was relief in her voice.

And it was certainly true. Madeline and Ariel had wiped most of the blood off their faces, but Madeline's right eyelid was swollen and taking on a silvery blue color, and Ariel's hair was darkly matted on top. Scott hadn't yet washed his hand, and he could smell his own sweat.

"Thank you," Ariel said to him. "That was clever and brave."

Everything Scott could think of in reply sounded flippant or shallow, so he just nodded and waved it away.

Madeline had the dartboard under her arm, and Ariel was unspooling the 220-volt extension cord as she walked toward the window. One of them had already wheeled out Aunt Amity's tall old 35-millimeter projector and opened the round film magazine on top of it.

A square metal can hung below the projection mechanism where the take-up reel would ordinarily be; Scott recalled that Aunt Amity had always called it the molasses can, and said that a take-up reel was the part of a projector that generally caused problems and interrupted the film, since it steadily got heavier and slower, whereas just letting the exiting film fall and coil loosely into the can avoided all such mechanical difficulties.

I wonder if her damned old machine still works, Scott thought. Would I really be unhappy if it didn't?

"You're going to have a real black eye there, Maddy," he said.

She shrugged and looked away. "You should see the other guy."

Scott suppressed a shudder as he recalled the revolver's recoil in the palm of his hand, and his last view of Ferdalisi. *Orange beard, dead orange eyes . . .*

He forced the intolerable memory aside. "You're all right?" he asked Ariel. "No concussion?"

"Fine except for a headache." She sat on the windowsill and gave him a tired smile. "Madeline tells me my pupils are the same size."

"You've done two spiders in less than an hour," Madeline said to Scott. "You're in no shape to watch this film."

"I'm fit enough," Scott said. And I don't think it matters, he told himself bleakly. Say good-bye to Hollywood. He took the dartboard from Madeline and turned it around, looking for the switch or latch that Louise had found. "How did you know where we were?"

"You went up the hill and on past the ridge garages," Madeline said, "but I heard the bike's engine stop, instead of fade away down the easement on the far side. I figured you'd want to coast silently, and so you were either heading for the apartment building or the old east garage. I ran over and saw your bike by the garage, so I climbed the tree and came in through the roof. Luckily the trapdoor was already open."

"I'm glad you did," Scott said. He had found a lever on the rim, and when he pushed it to one side, the top of the dartboard was loose. "And the alien on the bicycle was genius."

"I had to pull the seat off the bike and then . . . *impale* him on the post. Anally, as it were. God knows what somebody will think happened, if they go in there."

"My blood's on the floor," he said, taking the film can out of the round case. "So is Ariel's, and yours too, probably. Talk to a lawyer before you say anything to the police." He opened the film can and carefully lifted out the reel of film.

"It'll stand up that Claimayne shot Ferdalisi," said Ariel.

"At least neither of you did." Scott lifted the tail end of the film. It was clear, and the word *LEADER* was printed in grease pencil on the last inch of it. "I'm glad Natacha wound it back to front," he said. "Rewinding it here would have been a chore. Madeline, could you get me some blankets—and nails and a hammer—to cover the windows?"

"Right," she said, and hurried out of the room.

"She is *determined* to be the one to watch it," said Ariel when Madeline's footsteps had receded down the hall.

"I know." Scott unspooled three feet of film from the reel and then fitted the reel onto the central bobbin in the magazine. "This is a short film—a full reel's only about fifteen minutes, and look, this is less than half filled." He fitted the film through the slot at the bottom of the magazine and closed the cover, and then he turned and looked at Ariel. "You've got to get me a clean spider."

Ariel's eyes widened, and after a few seconds, she said, "I guess that's kinder than tying her up or knocking her out."

"I'm going to throw the extension cord out the window, so you can plug it into the old 220 socket in the dining room. You can get the spider while you're doing that."

"Scott, I don't think anybody should watch the damn film. It's sure to be dangerous—maybe fatal!—and not at *all* sure to accomplish anything."

"Damn it, do you think I—I'm looking *forward* to this? Sorry, sorry—but it's the only way, if there's any way, to exorcise the spiders, cut them right out of this universe. Taylor thought it would. And with the spider vector . . . conduit, opening, live wire . . . severed, Aunt Amity will have lost her link with Madeline." His hands were shaking. "I truly don't want to do it. I don't. It's only minutes away now."

"Let *me* do it. No, I mean it, listen—you both looked at the Medusa spider when you were kids, maybe a fresh—"

"I think that's what's going to save me, if anything does. It'll be my second time touring special. Ariel, I have to do it." He heard Madeline's footsteps in the hall, and he realized that he had only seconds in which to tell Ariel something important.

"Ariel," he said quickly, "I love you."

She stared at him.

Scott stared back, helplessly. "By the way," he added.

Madeline came shuffling in with a pile of blankets in her arms. Her voice was muffled as she said, "Hammer and nails in my pockets."

Ariel cocked her head at Scott and gave him a wry smile. "Well—likewise. Sincerely. Since I was a . . . an idiot teenager."

Scott's breath caught in his throat, and now more than ever he didn't want to watch the film. But he opened the side panel on the projector and unlocked the lens holder and opened the film gate.

"Ariel will swear Claimayne shot Ferdalisi," said Madeline. "Won't you, Ariel?"

Ariel nodded, glancing at Scott.

Madeline's statement, of course, presumed that Scott would be alive when the police investigated, and therefore that Scott would not be the one to watch the film.

He didn't argue. "You talk to a lawyer before you say anything to anybody," he told her.

He snapped the pressure rollers away from the sprocket wheel and the take-up sprocket, and he twisted the frame-line setting knob until the cross on the sprocket wheel had rotated a few degrees to vertical. As far as he could recall from having watched his aunt do it many times when he was a boy, the machine was now ready to have the film threaded through it. He knew it took oil, and he remembered his aunt cleaning out the oil system with gasoline, but she had done that much more seldom and he didn't remember the procedure. The old oil should keep it running for the few minutes required, he thought.

He sighed deeply.

"Ariel," he said, picking up the socket end of the extension cord, "maybe you could throw the other end of this out the window and go downstairs and plug it in."

She brushed damp strands of dark hair back from her forehead and stared at him for several seconds. "Okay." She unlatched the window and hauled it up, and she gathered up several loops of slack cord and then threw it out the window. "It might take me a few minutes."

"You want help?" asked Madeline.

"I've got it, sweetie. You help your brother." Ariel hurried out of the room without looking at Madeline or Scott.

Madeline shivered in the cold wind blowing in now through the window. "She doesn't want you to watch the film."

"No," Scott agreed.

"She loves you, and you love her."

"Yes."

"We've both found somebody."

Scott knew that Valentino was who Madeline believed she had found.

He nodded and walked to the window. He bent down and rested his right palm on the windowsill and looked out over the waving green trees and vines of the slope to the arched windows and red tile roofs of the houses across Vista Del Mar, and for a moment he thought the sudden yearning that seized him was the desire to go downstairs to his room and finish the Wild Turkey bottle; then he recognized it as a response to the volume and shapes and colors of the view—he very much wanted to capture all the light in dabs of paint on canvas. Reproduce it flat, he thought, in two dimensions!

"Scott," began Madeline, "I hope you—"

He straightened up. "I've got to thread the film," he said, walking back to the projector. "Do you remember how it used to go?"

She pursed her lips. "Oh, I can watch. I bet I'll know if you do it wrong."

He fitted the yard-long strip of film around several rollers and wheels and laid it in the open film gate. He touched the film gate knob, but Madeline caught his hand.

"Slack."

"Oh, right. And below the gate too." He pulled a loop in the film between the feed sprocket and the film gate and did it again between the bottom of the film gate and the sprocket wheel, and then he closed the gate.

Below that, he pushed the film into place around various wheels and rollers to the take-up sprocket and let the end hang down into Aunt Amity's molasses can.

"Look right?" When she nodded, Scott locked the lens turret and then clicked all the pad rollers back into their closed positions, fixing the film into place. "Did you find the screen?"

Madeline nodded. "We can nail its case to the wall, same height she used to have it in the dining room." She carefully took hold of his left hand and looked at the cut in his palm. "You should get Neosporin on that and bandage it. Scott, I may not come back. I may stay in the past, with Mr. Valentino."

"I don't think we can predict what will happen." And will you hate me, he wondered, for supposedly keeping you from Mr. Valentino? Will you ever understand that Aunt Amity would simply have swallowed and digested you, if I had not done this?

Ariel came hurrying down the hall and stepped into the apiary.

"It's plugged in," she said. "Let's get those windows covered." She clasped Scott's right hand as she walked past him, and when she released it and moved on toward the windows, he had a folded slip of paper in his hand.

A FEW MINUTES LATER the bare overhead lightbulb cast the only light in the long room, and Scott held up one end of the screen case against the wall while Ariel stood on a chair to nail the thing to the wall. When she stepped down, he took hold of the ring on the bottom edge of the screen and pulled it down, and the glittering white sheet stayed down and the case didn't fall off the wall.

Scott returned to the projector and made sure the changeover switch was still set on sixteen frames per second, then faced Madeline. She stared back at him defiantly.

"I'll flip you for it," he said.

The spider Ariel had passed to him was now trimmed of all margin and pressed into the palm of his right hand, with the spider lines against his skin.

Madeline laughed in surprise. "Will you abide by it? Will I? Let me see the coin."

He dropped a quarter into her extended palm, and she looked at both sides of it and flipped it in the air several times, catching it and slapping it onto the back of her other hand and peering at the result.

"Does a coin count as two-dimensional or three?" she asked. "I guess three—it's got bumps, and two sides." She held it out, and he carefully took hold of it between his thumb and forefinger. "I guess that's as fair as we can hope for," she said. "Sure, okay, toss. I pick heads."

Good-bye, Madeline, he thought. *Try to remember me with love.*

He tossed the coin spinning into the air, caught it, and slapped it onto the back of his left hand; and he flexed his right palm to free the spider. Luckily the back of his left hand was sticky with blood.

He held his overlapped hands out in front of her, and she pulled his right hand away, bending over to see the result. She gasped and hastily covered the spider with her own hand, but her pupils had already sprung wide open, and Ariel caught her when she sagged.

"Both of you out in the hall," Scott said, and as Ariel walked Madeline to the door, he quickly switched on the projector's xenon lightbulb. "And get the light!"

Ariel reached out to the side and turned off the overhead light as she and Madeline stumbled out of the room. "God be with you," she called over her shoulder.

Scott had never felt so alone as when he pressed the motor start button and the protector-flap open button and sat down on a chair four yards from the screen. He noticed that the spider Ariel had given him was no longer stuck to the back of his left hand, but there was no time to see if it was lying on the floor.

The screen was bright white as the clear leader strip passed through the projector, and then with no preamble he was facing a four-foot-tall image of the Medusa spider.

SCOTT RECOGNIZED IT IMMEDIATELY and intimately, even after a gap of twenty-three years, and in fact he knew there was no meaningful gap at all. He could almost feel eight-year-old Madeline beside him, and see Thomas Ince's hands on either side of the image.

The image was flickering rapidly, visible only in momentary flashes between split-second black frames; and since each new frame was a fresh projection of the spider on Scott's retinas, none had time to split and grow bristly before the next replaced it; and because the flashes were in the tarantella frequency, the spider was always caught in the same segment of its rotation, so that its inherent spin appeared to be stopped.

Scott didn't lose consciousness, and this time he didn't see the illusory vertical shapes of spiders viewed end-on—Madeline's Skyscraper People, the horizontally viewed spiders whose perfect flatness was interpreted by his visual cortex as infinite height.

Instead he toppled into the stuttering Medusa image.

And from moment to jigging moment he strode in a procession between thick pillars that spread like flower petals at their distant capitals, and he cowered in rooms carved into the solid rock of volcanic stone towers, and he glimpsed balconied structures rising to the clouds from the tops of ornate domes, and he chased men through narrow cobblestone streets between overhanging half-timbered buildings in the rain; and he was bleeding, falling, choking, thrusting bladed weapons and firing clockwork rifles, straining to breathe deep under water, straining to give birth to a child, sweating among laboring bodies in harsh sunlight and painfully flexing frostbitten fingers on glacial plains in blinding snow; and his mind reeled helplessly in an onslaught of momentarily urgent emotions: bowel-loosening terror, rage, hilarity, tunnel-vision lust. His ears rang with screams, clanging, roaring, and orchestral music.

But because the spider's rotation was negated by the strobe effect of the fast black frames, each vision was interrupted before Scott had fully fallen into it—and so he was able to remember that he was sitting in a chair upstairs at Caveat—and remember too that he had seen the Medusa spider before, in a very different situation.

He exerted his will over the hampered power of the stilled Medusa, and he imposed on the tumultuous cascade the remembered view of Ince's hands—and the hands appeared, holding the opened brown-paper folder, with the wood paneling and the porthole beyond; all sounds had ceased, and the view was now static, as motionless as a still photograph. Scott projected his consciousness down through the eight unmoving ink lines in the folder—and he found himself staring at a sallow, bony face in a mirror.

It was a young man with red hair cut in neat center-parted bangs. He wore a black bow tie and a high white collar.

A pale, long-fingered left hand reached out and tilted the mirror downward, and in the reflection Scott saw the Medusa inked on a piece of paper on a blotter, the curl of its limbs reversed in the mirror. The ink at the end of one limb glistened for a moment before going matte.

"Who are you?" came a voice from what felt like his own throat.

Scott was able only to exhale in reply, but he felt the head nod in response.

"You arrive unsummoned!" the voice went on in a now evident British accent. "Through her." Scott felt the face smile, though the facial muscles felt stiff. A right hand holding a steel-nibbed pen waved over the paper. "I synthesized her, deduced her lineaments from those of her weaker sisters. She is harmless viewed through a mirror, as Perseus knew. But can we be satisfied knowing her only through her reflections?"

Scott recalled what Valentino had said to him, in his house that had stood in the fated path of the 101 Freeway: *Beardsley got it, figured out how it should look, from studying a portfolio of lesser spider drawings his father brought back from India. The studying was bad for Beardsley, I gather—his health was destroyed, and he died very young.*

"On your deathbed," Scott managed to pronounce through the young man's throat and mouth, "you will—ask that it be destroyed."

The left hand swung the mirror back up, and Aubrey Beardsley was staring straight into his own eyes again—straight into Scott's. The brown eyes narrowed, but then Beardsley shrugged. " 'Indeed, indeed, repentance oft before / I swore,' " he said softly, " 'but was I sober when I swore?' "

Scott recognized the line; it was from Omar Khayyam's *Rubaiyat.* He recalled the last two lines: *And then and then came Spring, and Rose-in-hand / My thread-bare Penitence apieces tore.*

Beardsley was still smiling. "You know the verse, I'm sure. A *deathbed* repentance, though, would surely be a definitive one! That is reassuring to hear, and I thank you for it. But it would seem that this *last instruction* of mine is not to be followed, hm?" He swiveled the mirror down, so that he and Scott together were looking again at the reversed Medusa. "Else you wouldn't have been able to pay me this visit."

Beardsley was fading, and Scott moved his consciousness in a different direction.

Now he stood at the top of a neatly terraced garden slope, and when he turned, he was facing Caveat. For a moment the structure was wood sided, and the inscription on the stone lintel over the front door was complete: CAVEAT PROGENIES; then it was the newer stuccoed walls and the broken lintel that he saw, and he projected his viewpoint inside and up the still-carpeted stairs.

All the wainscot doors in the hallway were open, and daylight or lamplight streaked the floor of the hall in front of several. Voices and laughter and the clink of bottles on glasses echoed up and down the hall. Scott moved forward, and as he was passing one dark doorway, he saw his shadow beneath his feet; he looked up, and for a moment the house was gone, and the full moon shone on low broken walls under a starry night sky. The cold breeze carried the acid reek of doused campfires.

"Scott!"

He turned, and he was in the hallway again, and in daylight streaming from one doorway he saw that Madeline was standing by the stairs, with a man he recognized as Rudolph Valentino.

"Scott," cried Madeline again, hurrying to him and grabbing his arm, "come with us! It's too late for you to get back, you're *in* the Medusa, and the future here is very short."

"Maddy," said Scott, nearly choking, "how are you here? I meant to save you—"

"You are saving me, the Medusa is blocked by repetition, about to go away, and Aunt Amity will be plain dead without its living tentacles to reach in my head with. Oh, I took your coin-toss spider and looked at it again, right away—I didn't really *stop* looking at it—I'm in a spider vision right now, and the Medusa will be gone before the vision would have had an ending. I'm not going back."

"But it was a *clean* spider!"

She held up the crumpled, blood-spotted piece of paper. "He and I will give it a thousand afters."

Scott could feel tears welling up in his eyes. "Where, Maddy? When?"

"In the past. I've been patient."

"Maddy. I've got to go back, to Ariel. I can find the way. Come with me."

Valentino stepped forward and took Madeline's elbow. To Scott he said, "You found the film I hid, my friend. I'm glad. Do not worry about your sister—I will be to her all the things no one else has been."

And he turned and led Madeline down the stairs; she looked back pleadingly, but Scott just waved. "I love you, Maddy!" he called hoarsely.

Then they had disappeared in the entry hall on the first floor. Scott looked into the sunlit room beyond the open door beside him; an old woman holding a violin smiled at him as he crossed to the window and looked out. Behind him the old woman softly began a passage from Rimsky-Korsakov's *Scheherazade*.

Hollywood was a scattering of bungalows and Victorian houses on the descending green hills in bright morning sunlight, and there were no skyscrapers or freeway. He saw Madeline and Valentino emerge from under the hooded porch light below, and as they crossed the short lawn toward the descending steps, Madeline looked back.

"I love you, Scott!" she called. A cat bounded across the grass to her, and Scott was sure it was Bridget, the one they'd seen from her bedroom window Tuesday night. Madeline picked up the cat and then she and Valentino were hurrying away down the steps. Scott turned away.

The room he stood in was empty, the walls bare and spotted with mold. He didn't look out the window again but walked through the doorway into the hall and up the sagging wooden stairs, through sweeps of darkness and flickers of colored light, as voices rose and fell in brief snatches around him.

The apiary was lit only by a stormy gray radiance through the windows, and a crowd of shadowy figures filled all the chairs. Scott could dimly make out bowlers and feathered hats on the indistinct heads, and the cold air was tainted with the smells of cigars and perfume and damp clay.

His own chair was out in front of the others, and he didn't look at the smoky figure there as he disrupted it by sitting down.

Abruptly the room was dark behind him and the screen was again, or still, flashing white like the muzzle of a machine gun. Scott's heart sped up as if trying to match the staccato pace of the flashes, and he was once again in the torrent of vivid but momentary stressful experiences; and his battered consciousness was aware that he was not breathing.

The spider intermittently visible on the screen still seemed to be static, not rotating at all. Alla Nazimova had said, *Like a phonograph record spinning on a turntable in a dark room, illuminated by a light flashing seventy-eight times a minute; the record would appear to be stationary. And the spider, this is the master spider, remember, would effectively lose its spin—become stationary. It would thus find here an impossibility of itself and be excluded in future from this universe.*

But as Madeline had said, Scott's consciousness was *in* the Medusa now. Would he be banished with it? He still wasn't breathing.

He tried to project a thought to the alien entity that was the spider: *Can you hear me, recognize me, perceive me?*

For a moment he was back among Madeline's Skyscraper People, the illusively vertical shapes, and then they parted and he was surprised to find himself experiencing someone's memory of a canvas beach chair rotating as it moved slowly through the air against a blue sky; it sank toward a glittering swimming pool, and then Scott's perspective was from the surface of the water, where the beach chair only existed as several expanding, unconnected intrusions into the plane of the water's surface. Immediately the vision switched to a lit cigarette on a newspaper—Scott could see that the headline was about the repeal of Prohibition—and a ring of glowing red spread out from it across the paper as the circumference of an irregular black disk. Then that was gone, and he saw a column of tan skin that he recognized as a human throat, and the flat blade of a knife moving toward it.

Dazedly he wondered why had he been shown these particular memories: a couple of intrusions of a third dimension into a two-dimensional plane, and then a two-dimensional plane approaching a three-dimensional volume.

He forced himself to concentrate again on altering the visions, in the same way that he used to revise his clear mental image of an intended painting. The newspaper was back in his view, and it was flaming now, but he visualized the flames dying and the bright ring on the page shrinking, and the cigarette rising away to leave the paper unscorched; and when the turbulent swimming pool appeared next, he imagined the chair rising back out of the water and flying away out of view, leaving the surface of the water unbroken.

Then it was the blade and the throat that he saw, and he struggled against mental resistance to impose a view of the blade retreating—and he at least managed to halt it.

The visions faded, and all he could see now was the flickering Medusa image on the screen in front of him.

He had forcibly reversed the sequence of events in the trio of hurled memories, reversed the definitive instances of collision between two dimensions and three dimensions.

And he was able to breathe again. His sense of balance was gone, but he tried to stand up, and then his left hand flared in immediate personal pain. After a moment he realized that he had fallen out of his chair; and the pain was like a long extension cord connecting him to his own cubic universe.

Forcing himself to occupy his own body, he saw that he was now lying on the floor, on his back, with his head toward the screen, help-lessly staring up at the repeating projected image.

And, viewed from this angle, the strobing Medusa on his retinas was narrowed, foreshortened. It was tilted away from him, and he sensed that he had in some way separated himself from it.

He pushed himself forward with his heels and both hands, and as the gash in his left hand dragged agonizingly over the rough floorboards, the Medusa appeared narrower still. He could barely see the gaps between its tensely motionless limbs now.

Another thrust with his feet pushed his head against the wall. Above him, the Medusa had rotated a full ninety degrees and was now a flat line over him—

And then on his retinas it compressed to infinite flatness, and his affronted visual cortex interpreted that impossible state as a shift to infinite vertical height; the Medusa was just another one of Madeline's Skyscraper People now, and as always they parted to let his viewpoint pass between them.

The universe seemed to roll over, and reality seemed to spring back to reoccupy vacated space. For the first time in twenty-three years, Scott was completely alone in his own mind. He could hear himself panting in the chilly air.

Patches of varying color in his vision slowly separated from one another, out of flat uniformity. He was staring up at the metal ring on the bottom dowel of the screen, and at the cracked old plaster ceiling, and the lightbulb in the ceramic socket.

He sat up in flickering yellow light. The projector had caught fire. The round magazine on top was smoking, and flame quickly snaked down the acetate film strip into the mechanism behind the housing door and out into the can of ejected film. Now flames were shooting out of the rim of the magazine and licking at the ceiling.

I should have oiled it, he thought.

He managed to sit up and then struggle to his feet by leaning heavily on the wall and the screen, and the screen case came loose from its nails and fell on his head. He thrashed it aside with his right arm and staggered to the door; and when he opened it, Ariel was standing right outside, and she crouched to get her shoulder under his arm.

"Do we have any fire extinguishers?" she asked, looking past him.

"You live here."

"We don't have any fire extinguishers. Madeline ran to the stairs, but she was gone by the time I—I was right behind her. She disappeared."

"I know, I saw her. Call 911—about the fire."

They shuffled down the hall to the stairs, and Scott gripped the banister and Ariel's arm as he got both feet on one step before reaching for the next. Ariel had her phone in her free hand and was describing the situation to the 911 dispatcher.

"I've got to go," she said finally, evidently interrupting the dispatcher, and she thrust the phone into her pocket. When they reached the second-floor landing, she asked Scott, "Did it work? Is there anything you need from your rooms?"

"It worked," he gasped, "and no, nothing." Certainly not the Wild Turkey, he thought.

Halfway down the last flight of stairs they saw a man in a white jacket pause in the entry hall to stare up at them.

"The house is on fire," said Scott distinctly. "Get everyone out now."

The man ran away toward the kitchen.

"Valentino said it would kill whoever watched it," said Ariel, still supporting most of Scott's weight.

Scott took a deep breath and said, "It would have killed me—the Medusa fell out of this reality like . . . a letter through a mail slot—but I managed to separate myself and rotate out of it, away from it, before it went, so I was . . . flat against the mail slot, as it were." He had run out of breath, but when they reached the floor of the entry hall he inhaled again and added, "Madeline—before the Medusa spider disappeared—escaped into the past with Rudolph Valentino."

Ariel shook her head and sighed. "Might have guessed."

Men and women in uniforms and overalls were hurrying up and asking questions, and Ariel shouted, "The house is on fire! Get everyone out!" In a more normal voice she added, "The party's *totally* canceled."

"I can walk," said Scott. He hobbled to the front door and pulled it open. Already the breeze was spicy with wood smoke. Ariel held his arm as they made their way down the steps and across the patch of lawn to the top of the leaf-strewn and vine-hung stairs. How many years ago, Scott wondered, did Madeline and Valentino and Bridget hurry away down these stairs?—if it happened in actual linear time at all.

Scott could see a crowd of the cleaners and caterers out on the driveway beyond the kitchen now, and when a couple of young men in the catering uniform hurried out the front door, Scott yelled, "Is everybody out?"

"The last of them," one of them answered irritably. "Both crews. Are you sure?"

"Get over here."

The men hurried across the grass, and Scott pointed behind them.

They turned and looked back. Flames danced behind the windows of the gables, and smoke sifted in quickly dispelling streamers from under the roof tiles. As they watched, a gray rectangle spun away into the sky and a jet of flame burst up from the far side of the roof.

"That's the rooftop heater," said Scott.

"Right." Both the caterers hurried toward the driveway, away from Scott and Ariel.

Ariel was holding Scott's right hand. "I'm not sure any copies of Claimayne's books of poetry exist outside of the house," she remarked.

"Firemen might save the library."

In a low but suddenly fierce voice, Ariel said, "I hope nothing is saved."

Scott heard trucks start up and move down the driveway toward Vista Del Mar.

The breeze was chilly in Scott's sweaty hair and shirt, and he wished he had paused on the second floor to grab his jacket.

A moment later he was glad he hadn't. A crack appeared between two windows on the second floor, and the crack leaped up to the roof and down to the foundation and became a widening, roof-splitting fissure, with falling beams dimly visible through it and clay tiles tumbling out in the gray daylight, and then very slowly the entire east side of the house leaned away and separated into uneven segments as it folded and fell in a rushing burst of dust. The noise was like unending close thunder.

Coughing in the dust and sudden heat, Scott and Ariel hurried down the steps as bits of masonry clattered in the leaves overhead.

"All the way to the parking lot," Scott gasped.

"Screw jacks!" said Ariel, scuffing through drifts of dead leaves ahead of him.

"Lousy handyman," Scott agreed.

Each of them stumbled on the cement steps at some point and was helped up by the other, but within two minutes they both stood at the street edge of the parking lot, panting.

Scott was bent forward with his hands gingerly gripping his knees, but he looked up in time to see the western half of the house sink unevenly into the dust cloud. This time the rolling rumble of the collapse was matched by thunder from the sky, and drops of rain tapped at his hands.

Flames flickered into sight above the treetops, apparently along the whole length of Caveat.

"Everything," said Ariel beside him. Then, "The east half of the house fell onto the garage, and it's all burning. They'll find Claimayne and Ferdalisi, and the gun, but I doubt they'll find our blood."

Scott nodded, occupied with breathing and keeping his balance.

Behind him he heard an idling engine and tires slowly turning on asphalt, and when he looked over his shoulder, he saw the gleaming yellow Chevrolet station wagon halt a few yards away. The door opened and the gray-haired man who this morning had called himself Polydectes got out. He was still wearing the dark windbreaker, and his right hand was in the pocket.

"We put on the spare," he said to Scott. He looked up the hill then, and after a moment he added, "Your house appears to be burning up."

"I watched the film," Scott said.

He peered over the man's shoulder but didn't see anyone else in the car. But there were probably other cars.

The man nodded thoughtfully. "You're alive, though," he pointed out.

"I rotated myself out of it," Scott said. "But it did work." He straightened up, against sharp aches in his back.

The fire up the hill boomed and cracked.

"Maybe you watched it, maybe you stashed it."

Ariel reached into the pocket of her blouse and pulled out a folded piece of paper. To Scott she said, "I printed two copies, in case . . . I don't know. Doesn't matter now." She faced Polydectes and held the paper out toward him. "This is a live spider, or it was, before Scott did the exorcism. Go ahead, look at it."

The man cocked his head at her and smiled. "I doubt you'd have a decoy ready—but *you* look at it."

Ariel nodded and slowly unfolded the paper, and her expression was unreadable. She took a deep breath and then stared at the printed spider pattern.

And she exhaled and looked away. "Nothing," she whispered.

She flipped the paper around to show them. Polydectes flinched, then glanced from Scott to Ariel and looked directly at the spider pattern himself.

His shoulders sagged in evident relief. "Nothing," he agreed. He pulled his hand out of his pocket and wiped his face. "We had volunteers—but it's fitting that a Madden finished poor Taylor's project. Our volunteers might not have been able to . . . rotate? . . . out of it." He squinted at Scott and Ariel. "Are you two okay?"

Ariel gave him a bright, strained smile. "What does it look like?"

"Right." To Scott he said, "What you said, at Ostriker's, that was true—we were on the same side." He held out his right hand.

Scott stepped back unsteadily and shook his head. "You were going to shoot my sister's leg off."

The man closed his hand and shrugged. "Did your sister get out all right?"

"She got out."

After another few seconds, the man returned to the station wagon and backed out of the parking lot. Scott heard him sound the horn twice and then once as he drove slowly away down Vista Del Mar. Two acknowledging honks sounded from up and down the street.

The rain was falling steadily now, and Scott looked at the empty parking lot and thought of the night he and Madeline had arrived here.

She got out.

Tears mingled with the rainwater on his face. When she was eight years old, Valentino had told her, *My dear, my dear, it is not so dreadful here.* And all her life since then, apparently, she had wanted to return to wherever that *here* was, and to him. And today, or at least in Scott's recent memory, Valentino had said, *I will be to her all the things no one else has been.*

But—where? thought Scott. When? Madeline, I hope I was sometimes what a brother should be.

When she had told him about briefly stepping into the past on Wednesday, she'd said, *I didn't hurt anymore, and I walked around to the front of the house and—and Hollywood was like a village, beautiful . . . and I started down the steps like I was walking into Narnia . . .*

He sank to his knees on the asphalt as the rain came down harder and blurred his view of the hill, though flashes of flame glared through the swaying veils.

In the distance, over the close clatter of the rain, he could hear the rising wail of sirens.

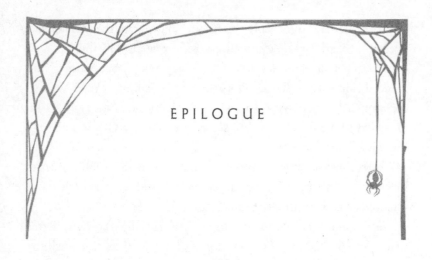

EPILOGUE

THE BLACK KIA OPTIMA made a right turn off Sunset onto Fairfax by the Rite Aid drugstore, and the early evening sunlight slanting across the parking lot on the right lit the film of dust on the windshield, obscuring the view.

Ariel slowed the car and switched on the windshield wipers, which didn't help, but in a few moments the car had moved into the shadows of another apartment building, and she could see out again.

"For two thousand dollars they could have run it through a car wash," she said.

"True," said Scott. "But it's lucky it was just impounded, for being parked in the middle of the street—if it had been stolen, you probably wouldn't have a windshield at all." The interior of the car smelled of nothing now but the submarine sandwiches in the bag on Scott's lap.

"I bet they could have got in touch sooner, though. And the escrow company could have told me they were somehow getting all our mail. And God knows where Madeline's Datsun is. We should have reported it stolen."

"The picture didn't need complicating."

Ariel turned right onto Fountain, and again the windshield became a nearly opaque glowing screen. She slowed the car to a crawl, peering ahead. "At least we can stop taking buses now." She glanced sideways at Scott. "Do you miss your motorcycle? We can certainly afford to get you a new one, if you like. Not right away, after that first month's rent and security deposit on Genod's place—but when escrow closes."

Scott's motorcycle had been found under the rubble by the Caveat east garage, not far from where the bodies of Ferdalisi and Claimayne had eventually been discovered.

Scott shook his head, recalling their ride up the L.A. River embankment. "I think I've used up my luck on bikes. I'll wash the windshield first thing tomorrow."

"The whole car could use it."

"The whole car," he agreed.

Claimayne's gun had been found too, and an autopsy had revealed a .38 caliber bullet in Ferdalisi's abdominal aorta; Scott had been questioned because of the location of his motorcycle, but his explanation that he had parked it by the garage on the previous day in order to work on it over the weekend appeared to have stood up.

"*If* escrow closes," Ariel went on. "They could have put a better name on the parcel than Caveat."

Scott nodded—every prospective buyer had seemed to flinch at the implicit *Emptor* after *Caveat*. "The actual full inscription wouldn't have been much more attractive."

"Scarier, really."

Scott had told Ariel that the words on the stone lintel above the Caveat front door had originally been *Caveat Progenies*, and she had looked it up and found that the Latin phrase meant *Let future generations beware*.

She steered left on Hayworth, and in the lengthening shadows they could see through the windshield again, and soon she steered the car up the driveway of the Ravenna Apartments parking lot and braked to a halt in the space marked *Reserved*.

Scott hefted the bag from Greenblatt's Deli as he climbed out. "The sandwiches smell great," he admitted. He had suggested the Cactus Taqueria on Vine.

"They're the best submarine sandwiches in the world," Ariel said. "Aunt Amity used to bring them home. Her office was just a couple of blocks west of Greenblatt's."

Scott waved at Ellis in the lighted office as he led the way to the stairs. "I remember," he said as they started up. "Right across the street was where I bought my bottle of bourbon."

Tapping up the steps beside him, she asked, "Do you miss it? Drink?"

"It's been nearly a month since my . . . brief relapse," he said, "and I hadn't touched any for more than a year before that. No, I still have dreams about it, but I don't miss it." He looked at her and raised his eyebrows.

Ariel shrugged and shook her head. "I had four years clean before *my* relapse—and *my* vice doesn't even *exist* anymore."

As he stepped up onto the green-painted cement second-floor walkway, Scott said, "Where do you want to eat?"

"Your place," she said. "I want to see that obit."

"If you subscribed, you'd have seen it this morning."

"Why should I subscribe when my next-door neighbor does?"

Scott walked past her door to the door of his own apartment, digging in his pocket for his keys. He unlocked the door and swung it open for her, and as he walked in after her and closed it and switched on the lights, he said, "To drink?"

He had assured her that it didn't bother him when people around him drank alcohol, and he had even bought a couple of bottles of Ravenswood zinfandel to have on hand for her, but she said, "Coffee will be fine," as she crossed the carpeted living room to the kitchen and sat down at the little table.

"Coming up." Scott followed her and got a can of ground coffee out of the refrigerator and began measuring spoonfuls into the coffeemaker on the counter.

He opened the refrigerator again to get a carton of milk, and he set it and a bowl of sugar cubes on the table. Ariel had already picked up the LATEXTRA section of the *Los Angeles Times*.

Scott took it from her, folded it to the obituary page, and handed it back. He tapped one of the names.

" '*Adrian Ostriker, 83,*' " Ariel read, " '*passed away in early January at his Laurel Canyon home. Ostriker had been an actor, most recently in* Empire of the Ants *(1977), though he was best known for his role in* Paradise Alley *(1962). He also appeared in many television series, such as* The Legend of Jesse James *and* The Guns of Will Sonnett. *Ostriker was cremated.*' "

Ariel looked up. "Same guy?"

"Laurel Canyon. Unusual name."

"I remember talking to him when he was between names." She sat back. "I've got to say he looked real good for eighty-three."

"God knows how old he really was. He married our aunt in 1921. I think it caught up to him when the spiders stopped working. Like Dorian Gray when his picture got burned up."

He glanced at the canvas propped on an easel in the living room below a glowing track light, but the coffeemaker started bubbling and hissing, and he turned to open the cabinet and take down the two coffee cups and set them on the table.

Ariel took hold of a lot of the sugar cubes in her fist, then opened her hand and let them fall back into the bowl. She picked up one to drop into her coffee and gave him a wistful smile. "Gotta let go or be trapped."

Scott nodded, mystified. "I suppose so."

He poured coffee into the cups and sat down across from her.

"Claimayne's gone now," she said. "I lived at Caveat with him ever since my parents both died when I was seven, and he was fifteen." She stirred her coffee. "I always wondered . . ." she went on hesitantly, then shook her head. "But my parents *were* amateur mycologists, and they *were* careless in a lot of things—and he really *didn't* like mushrooms. Luckily for me I didn't either."

After a pause, "Good God," Scott whispered. "You think he—?"

"Maybe not." She shrugged. "Everybody's dead, we'll never know."

Scott tried to recall the event, but he had only been ten years old and had never met Ariel's parents. All he remembered of them, and that vaguely, was the funeral. Fifteen-year-old Claimayne had worn a tie, he recalled. Afterward, adults had reminded young Scott not to eat mushrooms he found in the yard.

Now Ariel had turned to look at the canvas, and she got up and crossed the living room to stand in front of it. Scott followed and stood next to her.

It was a painting of Madeline and Valentino descending the stairs at Caveat; Valentino was an anonymous figure looking away, but Madeline's face was turned back toward the viewer, lit by the antique sun that had been shining through the impossible open door to the side. Her expression was wistful, but Scott's brush had also caught the glow of glad anticipation in her eyes.

Like I was walking into Narnia . . .

"You caught her perfectly," said Ariel after a moment. "She's happy."

Scott shrugged. "I hope so. I hope they don't find her under the rubble." Beside the scare-bat, he thought, clinging to the grave marker of her foolish parents.

Ariel gripped his arm. "I was there, in real time. She got out. You know she did."

He exhaled and gave her a smile. "I do know it."

If there is a frail spirit buried down there, he thought, *huddled in mingled love and resentment next to their makeshift grave, may it be the cast-off, always backward-looking ghost of my old self.*

Scott stepped past Ariel to the window and pulled back the curtain.

Outside under the sunset glow the lights would be coming on in Beverly Hills and Westwood and way out along the coast in Malibu, and he thought of all the lights in Los Angeles, from the hills of Griffith Park to the docks in San Pedro, from LAX airport east to the 605 Freeway, and he wondered if every single one of those million lights could be reached from now—if there might not be one where Madeline stood looking out over a very different Los Angeles, thinking of him.

But the sky was dimming behind the palm trees, and the coffee was steaming in the cups on the table. He took Ariel's arm and led her back to the kitchen.

About the author

About the book

Read on

Insights,
Interviews
& More . . .

Meet Tim Powers

Serena Powers

TIM POWERS is the author of numerous novels including *Hide Me Among the Graves, Last Call, Declare, Three Days to Never,* and *On Stranger Tides,* which inspired the feature film *Pirates of the Caribbean: On Stranger Tides,* starring Johnny Depp and Penelope Cruz. Powers has won the Philip K. Dick Memorial Award twice, and the World Fantasy Award three times. He lives in San Bernardino, California. ∽

Reading Group Guide

1. The Madden family is notably dysfunctional. To what extent do relations among them improve or deteriorate throughout the story? Which characters particularly change the situation?

2. Scott and Madeline have a conflicted relationship with Aunt Amity—simultaneously grateful and fearful. How do they feel about her at the end of the story, and why?

3. Alla Nazimova's door has been in the Caveat hallway for decades, and Aunt Amity's knocking never made her react. Why did Scott's late-night knock draw a response?

4. The way Scott rescues Ariel at the end is logically impossible. How did the nature of the spiders get around that?

5. How does the spider addiction affect Louise? At what point do you think she ignores her own principles, and why?

6. While watching the stolen film reel, Scott establishes contact with the Medusa spider. Can you deduce anything about the spider's nature from that brief exchange?

7. What meaning might the full inscription over the Caveat lintel have had for the original builder? What meaning did it come to have?

8. The characters have varying motivations for using the spiders. To what extent were these motivations selfish? Admirable?

9. Do you think Claimayne was redeemed, or not, by his actions at the end?

10. Madeline's life has been dominated, and crippled, by her childhood fixation on the ghost of Rudolph Valentino. Does her ultimate escape with him validate unrealistic fantasies? ❧

Excerpt from *Three Days to Never*

Chapter One

It doesn't look burned."

"No," said her father, squinting and shading his eyes with his hand. They had paused halfway across the weedy backyard.

"Are you sure she said 'shed'?"

"Yes—'I've burned down the Kaleidoscope Shed,' she told me."

Daphne Marrity sat down on a patch of grass and straightened her skirt, peering at the crooked old gray structure that was visible now under the shadow of the shaggy avocado tree. It would probably burn up pretty fast, if anybody was to try to burn it.

The shingled roof was patchy, sagging in the middle, and the two dusty wood-framed windows on either side of the closed door seemed to be falling out of the clapboard wall; it probably leaked badly in the rain.

Daphne had heard that her father and aunt had sometimes sneaked out here to play in the shed when they were children, though they weren't allowed to. The door was so low that Daphne herself might have to stoop to get through, and she was not a particularly tall twelve-year-old.

It was probably when they were too young to go to school, she thought. Or else it's because I was born in 1975, and kids are taller now than they were back then.

"The tree would have burned up too," she noted.

"You're going to get red ants all over you. She might have dreamed it. I don't think it was a, a joke." Her father glanced around, frowning, clearly irritated. He was sweating, even with his jacket folded over his arm.

"Gold under the bricks," Daphne reminded him.

"And she dreamed that too. I wonder where she is." There had been no answer to his knock on the front door of the house, but when they had walked around the corner and pushed open the backyard gate they had seen that the old green Rambler station wagon was in the carport, in the yellow shade of the corrugated fiberglass roof.

Daphne crossed her legs on the grass and squinted up at him against the sun's glare. "Why did she call it the Kaleidosope Shed?"

"It—" He laughed. "We all called it that. I don't know."

He had stepped on what he'd been about to say. She sighed and looked toward the shed again. "Let's go in it and pull up some bricks. I can watch out for spiders," she added.

Her father shook his head. "I can see from here that it's padlocked. We shouldn't even be hanging around back here when Grammar's not home." Grammar was the family name for the old lady, and it had not made Daphne like her any better.

"We had to, to see if she really did burn it down like she said. Now we should see if"—she thought quickly—"if she passed out in there from gasoline fumes. Maybe she meant, 'I'm *about* to burn it down.'"

"How could she have padlocked it from the outside?"

"Maybe she's passed out behind the shed. She *did* call you about the shed, and she doesn't answer the door, and her car *is* here."

"Oh . . ." He squinted and began to shake his head, so she went on quickly.

"'Screw your courage to the sticking place,'" she said. "Maybe there really is gold under the bricks. Didn't she have a lot of money?"

He smiled distractedly. "'And we'll not fail.' She did get some money in '55, I've heard."

"How old was she then?" Daphne got to her feet, brushing down the back of her skirt.

"About fifty-five, I guess. She's probably about eighty-seven now. Any money she's got is in the bank."

"Not in the bank—she's a hippie, isn't she?" Even now, at twelve, Daphne was still somewhat afraid of her chain-smoking great-grandmother, with her white hair, her grinding German accent, and her wrinkly old cheeks always wet with the artificial tears she bought in little bottles at Thrifty. Daphne had never been allowed in the old ▶

Excerpt from _Three Days to Never_ (continued)

woman's backyard, and this was the first time she'd ever been farther out than the back porch. "Or a witch," she added.

Daphne took her father's hand as a tentative prelude to starting toward the shed.

"She isn't a witch," he said, laughing. "And she isn't a hippie either. She's too old to have been a hippie."

"She went to Woodstock. You never went to Woodstock."

"She probably just went to sell her necklaces."

"As weapons, I bet," Daphne said, recalling the clunky talismans. The old woman had given Daphne one on her seventh birthday, a stone thing on a necklace chain, and before the day was out, Daphne had nearly given herself a concussion with it, swinging it around; when her favorite cat had died six months later, she had buried the object with the cat.

She tried to project the thought to him: _Let's check out the shed._

"Hippies didn't have weapons. Okay, I'll look around in back of the shed."

He began walking forward, leading the way and holding her hand, stepping carefully through the dry grass and high green weeds. His brown leather Top-Siders ground creosote smells out of the bristly green stalks.

"Watch where you put your feet," he said over his shoulder, "she's got all kinds of old crap out here."

"Old crap," Daphne echoed.

"Car-engine parts, broken air conditioners, suits of medieval armor I wouldn't be surprised. I should carry you, your legs are going to get all scratched."

"Even skinny I'm too heavy now. You'd get apoplexy."

"I could carry two girls your size, one under each arm."

They had stepped in under the shade of the tree limbs, and her father handed her his brown corduroy jacket.

He shook his head as if at the silliness of all this, then waded through the rank greenery to the corner of the shed and disappeared around it. She could hear him brushing against the shed's far wall, and cussing, and knocking boards over.

Daphne had folded his jacket and tucked it under her left arm, and now she walked up to the shed door and reached out with her right hand, took hold of the brown padlock, and pulled. The whole rusted hasp and lock came away from the wood in one stiff piece.

A few moments later her father appeared from around the far corner, red faced and sweating. His white shirt was streaked with dust and cobwebs.

"Well, she's not back there," he said, brushing dead leaves out of his hair. "I don't think she's been out here in months. Years. Let's get out of here."

Daphne held out the rusted hasp and padlock for him to see, then dropped it and brushed her fingers on her pink blouse.

"I didn't tear the wood," she said. "The screws were just sitting in the holes."

"Good lord, Daph," said her father, "nobody's going to mind."

"I know, but I mean the thing was just hung there, in the holes— somebody else pulled it out, and then hung it back up." She wrinkled her nose. "And I smell gasoline."

"You do not."

"Honest, I do." They both knew her sense of smell was better than his.

"You just want to look in there for gold."

But he sighed and tugged on the purple glass doorknob, and the door creaked open, sliding easily over the dead grass.

"Probably she keeps whisky out here," Daphne said, a little nervously. "Sneaks out at night to drink it." Her father said her uncle Bennett kept a bottle of whisky in his garage, and that's why he kept all his business files out there.

"She doesn't drink whisky," her father said absently, crouching to peer inside. "I wish we had a flashlight—somebody's pulled up half the floor." He leaned back and exhaled. "And I smell gasoline too."

Daphne bent down and looked past her father's elbow into the dimness. A roughly four-foot-square cement slab was leaned up against the shelves on the left-side wall, and seemed to be responsible for that wall's outward tilt; and a square patch of bare black dirt at the foot of the slab seemed to indicate where it had been pried up. The rest of the floor was pale bricks.

The floor was clear except for a scattering of cigarette butts and a pair of tire-soled sandals lying on the bricks.

The gasoline reek was strong enough to mask whatever moldy smells the place might ordinarily have; and Daphne could see a red-and-yellow metal gasoline can on a wooden shelf against the back wall.

Her father ducked inside and took hold of the handle on top of the can and lifted it. She could hear swishing inside the can as he stepped past her, and it seemed to be heavy as he carried it outside. She noticed that there was no cap on it. No wonder the place reeks, she thought.

There was a nearly opaque window in the back wall, and Daphne stepped in across the bricks and stood on tiptoe to twist the latch on its frame; the latch snapped off, but when she pushed on the window the entire thing fell outside, frame and all, thumping in the thick weeds. Dry summer air puffed in through the ragged square hole, fluttering her brown bangs. She inhaled it gratefully.

"I've got ventilation," she called over her shoulder. "And some light too."

A television sat on a metal cart to the left of the door, with a VCR on top of it. The VCR was flashing 12:00, though it must be past one by now.

"The time's wrong," she said to her father, pointing at the VCR as he ducked his head to step inside again.

"What?"

"On her VCR. Weird to have electricity out here."

"Oh! It's always had electrical outlets. God knows why. This is the first time I've seen anything plugged in, out here. Lucky there was no spark." He glanced past her and smiled. "I'm glad you got that window open."

Daphne thought he was relieved to learn that her "time's wrong" remark had been about the VCR. But before she could think of a way to ask him about it, he had stepped to the shelf and picked up a green metal box that had been hidden behind the gasoline can.

"What's that?" she asked.

"An ammunition box. I don't think she's ever had a gun, though." He swung the lid up, then tipped it sideways so Daphne could see that it was full of old yellowed papers. He righted it and began flipping through them.

Daphne glanced at the nearly upright cement slab—and then looked at it more closely. It was lumpy with damp mud, but somebody had cleaned four patches of it—two handprints and two shoe prints, clearly pressed into the cement when it had still been wet. And behind the undisturbed clumps of mud she could see looping grooves in the face of the block; somebody had scrawled something in it too.

She put her father's jacket on the shelf beside the ammunition box and then stepped down onto the patch of sunken dirt next to the block.

She pressed her open right hand into the right-hand print in the block—and then quickly pulled her hand away. The cement there was as smooth and warm as flesh, and damp.

With the side of her shoe, she scuffed mud off the bottom of the slab, and then stepped back. *Jan 12—1928*, she read. The writing seemed to have been done with a stick.

"Bunch of old letters," her father said behind her. "New Jersey postmarks, 1933, '39, '55 . . ."

"To her?"

Daphne pried off some more mud with her fingers. There was a long, smooth groove next to the shoe prints, as if a rod too had been pressed into the wet cement. She noticed that the shoe prints were awfully long and narrow, and set at a duck-foot angle.

"Lisa Marrity, yup," said her father.

Above the rod indentation was a crude caricature of a man with a bowler hat and a Hitler mustache.

"The letters are all in German," her father said. She could hear him rifling through the stack. "Well, no, some in English. Ugh, they're sticky, the envelopes! Was she *licking* them?"

Daphne could puzzle out the words at the top of the block, since the grooves of the writing were neatly filled in with black mud. *To Sid—Best of Luck.* And the last clump of dirt fell off all at once when she tugged at it. Exposed now was the carefully incised name, *Charlie Chaplin.*

Daphne looked over her shoulder at her father, who was holding the metal box and peering into it. "Hey," she said.

"Hmm?"

"Check this out."

Marrity looked at her, then past her at the cement slab; his face went blank. He put the box down on the shelf. "Is that *real?*" he said softly.

She tried to think of a funny answer, then just shrugged. "I don't know."

He was staring at the slab. "I mean, isn't the real one at the Chinese Theater?"

"I don't know."

He glanced at her and smiled. "Sorry. But this *might* be real. Maybe they made two. She says she knew Chaplin. She flew to Switzerland after he died."

"Where did he die?"

"In Switzerland, goof. I wonder if these letters—" He paused, for

Excerpt from *Three Days to Never* (continued)

Daphne had got down on her hands and knees and begun prying up the bricks along the edge of the exposed patch of wet dirt. "What?" he said. "Gold?"

"She *almost* burned up the shed," Daphne said without looking up. "Got the cap off the gas can, at least."

"Well—true." Her father knelt beside her, on the bricks instead of the mud—which Daphne was pleased to see, as she didn't want to wash a fresh pair of pants for him to wear to work tomorrow—and pulled up a couple of bricks himself. His dark hair was falling into his eyes, and he streaked a big smudge of grime onto his forehead when he pushed it back. Great, Daphne thought; he looks—probably we both look—as if we just tunneled out of a jail.

Daphne saw a glint of brightness in the flat mud where one brick had been, and she rubbed at it; it was a piece of wire about as thick as a pencil. It was looped, and she hooked a finger through it to pull it up, but the rest of the loop was stuck fast under the other bricks.

"Is this gold?" she asked her father.

He grunted and rubbed more dirt off the wire. "I can't say it's not," he said. "Right color, at least, and it's pliable."

"She said you should get the gold up from under the bricks, right? So let's—"

From outside, on the street, a car horn honked three times, and then a man's voice called, "Frank?"

"It's your uncle Bennett," said her father, quickly slamming back into place the bricks he had moved. Daphne fit hers back in too, suppressing a giggle at the idea of hiding the treasure from her dumb uncle.

The bricks replaced, her father leaped up and grabbed all the papers in the ammunition box into one fist and shoved them deep into an inside pocket of his jacket on the shelf. He wiped his hand on his shirt, and Daphne remembered that he had said the envelopes were sticky.

"Stand back," he said, and Daphne stepped back beside the television set.

Then he cautiously put one foot on the square of black dirt and gripped the cement slab by the top edges and pulled it toward himself. It swayed forward, and then he hopped backward out of the way as it overbalanced and thudded heavily to the floor, breaking one row of bricks. The whole shed shook, and black dust sifted down onto the two of them from the rotted ceiling.

The block's near edge was visibly canted up, resting on the row of broken bricks.

"Both of us," said Daphne, sitting down on the bricks to set her heels against the raised edge. Her father knelt on the bricks and braced his hands on the slab.

"On three," he said. "One, two, *three.*"

Daphne and her father both pushed, and then pushed harder, and at last the slab shifted, slid to its original position and thumped down flush with the bricks. Its top face was dry and blank.

Daphne heard the click of the backyard gate, and she scrambled up and ran two steps to the VCR and hit the eject button. The machine whirred as her uncle's footsteps thrashed through the weeds, and then the tape had popped out and Daphne snatched it and dropped it into her purse as her father hastily grabbed his jacket from the shelf, slid his arms into the sleeves and shrugged it onto his shoulders.

"Frank!" came Bennett's shout again, this time from just outside the open door. "I saw your car! Where are you?"

"In here, Bennett!" Daphne's father called.

Her uncle's red face peered in under the sagging door lintel, and for once his expression was simply wide-eyed dismay. His mustache was already spiky with sweat, though he would have had the air conditioner on in his car.

"What the fuck's going on?" he yelled shrilly. "Why the—bloody hell does it smell like gasoline in here?" Daphne guessed that he was embarrassed at having said *fuck,* and so hurried to cover it with his habitual *bloody*—though he wasn't British. "You've got Daphne with you!"

"Grammar left the top off a gas can," her father said. "We were trying to get some ventilation in here."

"What was that almighty crash?"

Her father jerked his thumb over his shoulder. "The window fell out when I tried to open it."

"Sash weights," put in Daphne.

"Why are you even here?" Bennett demanded. He ducked in under the lintel and stood up inside; the shed was very crowded with three people in it.

"My grandmother called me this morning," said Marrity evenly, "and asked me to come over and look at the shed. She said she was afraid it was going to burn down, and with that uncapped gasoline can in here, it might have."

Excerpt from *Three Days to Never* (continued)

Daphne noted the details of her father's half lie; and she noted his emphasis on *my grandmother*—Bennett had only married into the family.

"It's a little academic at this point," snapped Bennett, "and there's nothing valuable out here." He looked more closely at Daphne and her father, presumably only now noticing the dust in their hair and the mud on their hands, and suddenly his eyes widened. "Or *is* there?"

His hand darted out and pulled the videocassette from Daphne's purse. "What's this?"

Daphne could read the label on it: *Pee-wee's Big Adventure*. It was a movie she'd seen in a theater two years ago. "That's mine," she said. "It's about bad people stealing Pee-wee's bicycle."

"My daughter's not a thief, Bennett," her father said mildly. Daphne reflected that right now she *was* a thief, actually.

"I know, sorry." Bennett tossed the cassette, and Daphne caught it. "But you shouldn't be here," he said to her father as he bent down to step out of the shed, "now that she's dead." From outside he called, "Not unless Moira and I are here too."

Marrity followed him outside, and Daphne was right behind him.

"Who's dead?" asked her father.

Bennett frowned. "Your grandmother. You don't know this? She died an hour and a half ago, at Mount Shasta. The hospital just called me—Moira and I are to fly up this afternoon and take care of the funeral arrangements." He peered at his brother-in-law. "You really didn't know?"

"Mount Shasta, at like"—Marrity glanced at his watch—"noon? That's not possible. Why would she be at Mount Shasta?"

"She was communing with angels or something—well, that turned out to be right. She was there for the Harmonic Convergence."

Behind the grime and the tangles of dark hair, Frank Marrity's face was pale. "Where's Moira?"

"She's at home, packing. Now if we want to avoid things like restraining orders, I think we should all agree—"

"I'm going to call her." He started toward the house, and Daphne trotted along behind him, clutching her Pee-wee videocassette.

"It'll be locked," Bennett called after him.

Daphne's father didn't answer, but pulled his key ring out of his pants pocket.

"You've got a key? You shouldn't have a key!"

Grammar's house was a white Spanish adobe with a red-tile roof, and the back patio had a trellis shading it, tangled with roses and grapevines. Over the back door was a wooden sign, with hand-carved letters: *Everyone Who Dwells Here Is Safe*. Daphne had wondered about it ever since she had been able to read, and only last summer she had found the sentence in a Grimm Brothers fairy tale, "The Maiden Without Hands." The sentence had been on a sign in front of the house of a good fairy who had taken in a fugitive queen and her baby son.

The air was cooler under the trellis, and Daphne could smell roses on the breeze. She wondered how her father was taking the news of his grandmother's death. He and his sister had been toddlers when they lost their parents—their father ran away and their mother died in a car crash soon after—and they had been raised here, by Grammar.

Her father stopped on the step up to the back door, and Daphne saw that one of the vertical windows beside the door was broken; and when her father walked to the door and twisted the knob, the door swung inward. None of the locks here are any good, she thought.

"You've erased fingerprints!" panted Bennett, who was right behind Daphne now. "It was probably a burglar that broke the window."

"A burglar would have reached through and turned the knob inside," Daphne told him. "My dad isn't going to touch that one."

"Daph," said her father. "Wait out here with Bennett."

Her father stepped into the kitchen, and her uncle at least waited with her.

"Probably broke it herself," muttered Bennett. *"Marritys."*

"'Divil a man can say a word agin them,'" said Daphne. She and her father had recently watched *Yankee Doodle Dandy*, and her head was full of George M. Cohan lyrics.

Bennett glanced away from the door to give her an irritable look. "All that Shakespeare won't help you get a job. Except—" He shook his head and resumed staring at the kitchen door.

"It'll help me get a job as a literature professor," she said blandly, knowing that that was what his *except* had referred to. Her father was a literature professor at the University of Redlands. "Best job there is." Her uncle Bennett was a location manager for TV commercials, and apparently made way more money than her father did.

Her uncle opened his mouth and then after a second snapped it shut again, clearly not wanting to get into an argument with a girl. "You absolutely *reek* of gasoline," he said instead.

Excerpt from *Three Days to Never* (continued)

She heard footsteps on linoleum in the house, and then her father pulled the kitchen door wide open. "If there was a thief, he's gone," he said. "Let's see if she has any beers in her 'frigerator."

"We shouldn't touch anything," said Bennett, but he stepped in ahead of Daphne. The house was cool, and the kitchen smelled faintly of bacon and onions and cigarettes, as usual.

Daphne couldn't see that anything in the room was different from the way it had looked at Easter—the spotless sink and counter, the garlic-and-dried-rosemary centerpiece on the kitchen table; the broom was upside down in the corner, but the old lady always kept it that way—to scare off nightmares, according to her father.

Bennett picked up a business card from the kitchen counter. "See?" he said. "Bell Cabs. She must have taken a taxi to the airport." He set it back down again.

Her father had lifted the receiver from the yellow telephone on the wall and was using the forefinger of the same hand to spin the dial. With his other hand he pointed at the refrigerator. "Daph, could you see if there's a beer in there?"

Daphne pulled open the door of the big green refrigerator—it was older than her father, who had once said that it looked like a 1950 Buick stood on its nose—and found two cans of Budweiser among the jars of nasty black concoctions.

She put one into her father's hand and waved the other at her uncle.

"Not *Budweiser,* thank you," he said stiffly.

Daphne put the other can on the counter by her father, and looked at the cork bulletin board on the wall. "Her keys are gone," she noted.

"Probably in her purse," her father said. "Moira?" he said into the telephone. "Did Grammar die? What? This is a lousy connection. Bennett told me—we're at her house. What? *At her house,* I said." He popped open the beer one-handed. "I don't know. Listen, are you sure?" He took a long sip of the beer. "I mean, could it have been a prank call?" For several seconds he just listened, and he put the beer can down on the tile counter to touch Grammar's electric coffee grinder; he flipped the switch on it, and the little upright cylinder chattered as it ground up some beans that must still have been in it. He switched it off again. "When did the hospital call you? Talk slower. Uh-huh. And when you called them back, what was the number?"

He lifted a pencil from a vase full of pens and pencils and wrote the number on the back of the Bell Cabs card.

"What were the last two numbers? Okay, got it." He put the card in his shirt pocket. "Yeah, me too kid. Okay, thanks." He held the receiver out to Bennett. "She wants to talk to you. Bad connection—it keeps getting screechy or silent."

Bennett nodded impatiently and took the phone, and he was saying, "I just wanted to see if—are you there?—if there was anything here we'd need to bring along, birth certificate . . ." as Frank Marrity led Daphne into the dark living room.

Grammar's violin and bow were hanging in their usual place between two framed parchments with Jewish writing on them, and in spite of having been scared of the old woman, Daphne suddenly felt like crying at the thought that Grammar would never play it anymore. Daphne remembered her bow skating over the strings in the first four notes of one of her favorite Mozart violin concertos.

A moment later her father softly whistled the next six notes.

Daphne blinked. "And!" she whispered, "you're sad about Grammar, and mad at her too—and you're very freaked about her coffee grinder! I . . . can't see why."

After a pause, he nodded. "That's right." He looked at her with one eyebrow raised. "This is the first time you and I have both had it at the same time."

"Like turn blinkers on a couple of cars," she said quietly. "It was bound to match up eventually." She looked up at him. "What's so weird about her coffee grinder?"

"I'll tell you later." In a normal tone he said, over her shoulder, "I don't think my grandmother ever had a birth certificate."

Daphne turned and saw that Bennett had entered the living room and was frowning at the drawn curtains.

"I suppose they don't give birth certificates in Oz," he said. "We should fix that window."

"I can use her Makita to screw a piece of plywood over it from the inside. You think we should call the police?" Her father waved at the violin on the wall. "If there was a thief, he didn't take her Stradivarius."

Bennett blinked and started forward. "Is that a Stradivarius?"

"I was kidding. No. I don't think anything's been taken."

"Very funny. I don't think we need to call the police. But fix the window now—we should all leave together, and only come here all together." He rubbed his mustache. "I wonder if she left a will."

Excerpt from *Three Days to Never*
(*continued*)

"Moira and I are on the deed already. I can't imagine there's much besides the house."

"Her car, her books. Some of this . . . artwork might be valuable to some people."

To some weirdos, you mean, thought Daphne. She was suddenly defensive about the old woman's crystals and copper bells and paintings of unicorns and eyes in pyramids and sleepy-looking bearded guys wearing robes.

"We'll want to inventory it all, get an appraiser," Bennett went on. "She was a collector, and she might have happened to pick up some valuable items, amid all the crap. Even a broken clock is right twice a day."

Daphne could feel that the mention of broken clocks, in this house, jarred her father. There were a lot of things she wanted to remember to ask him about, once they were in their truck again.